WHEN A SCOT LOVES A LADY

"Lushly intense romance . . . radiant prose."
Library Journal (★ starred review ★)

"Sensationally intelligent writing, and a
true, weak-in-the-knees love story."
Barnes & Noble "Heart to Heart" *Recommended Read!*

IN THE ARMS OF A MARQUESS

"Every woman who ever dreamed of having a
titled lord at her feet will love this novel."
Eloisa James, *New York Times* bestselling author

"Immersive and lush. . . . Ashe is that rare author
who chooses to risk unexpected elements within
an established genre, and whose skill and magic
with the pen lift her tales above the rest."
Fresh Fiction

CAPTURED BY A ROGUE LORD
"Best Historical Romantic Adventure"
Reviewers' Choice Award winner 2011

SWEPT AWAY BY A KISS
"Best First Historical Romance"
Reviewers' Choice Award nominee 2010

"A breathtaking romance filled with sensuality
and driven by a brisk and thrilling plot."
Lisa Kleypas, *New York Times* #1 bestselling author

"A master storyteller."
Sandra Hill, *New York Times* bestselling author

I ADORED A LORD

The Prince Catchers

KATHARINE ASHE

AVON

An Imprint of HarperCollinsPublishers

AVON BOOKS
An Imprint of HarperCollins*Publishers*
195 Broadway
New York, New York 10007

Copyright © 2014 by Katharine Brophy Dubois
ISBN 978-0-06-222983-0
www.avonromance.com

First Avon Books mass market printing: August 2014

Avon Trademark Reg. U.S. Pat. Off. and in Other Countries, Marca Registrada, Hecho en U.S.A.
HarperCollins® is a registered trademark of HarperCollins Publishers.

Printed in the U.S.A.

10 9 8 7 6 5 4 3 2 1

For Darlin

"The [ailments] of . . . animals are few and simple, and easily cured . . . for the remedy then consists in little more than putting the animal upon a direct contrary course to that which brought on the disorder."

— JOHN HINDS,
The Veterinary Surgeon (1836)

"With thyself my spirit fill."

— THOMAS KEN,
Hymn from the monastic Divine Office (1692)

Dearest Reader

My first love in fiction is a beautifully written romance. If that romance includes a bit of high adventure, then I am in alt. I also happen to adore mysteries set in country mansions and remote castles, especially murder mysteries. So when Ravenna Caulfield, the free-spirited youngest sister among my Prince Catchers, suggested to me that she was eager for that sort of harrowing fun, I welcomed the opportunity to write it. Packing up my fuzzy sweaters and woolen socks, I headed off to the mountains of France.

France, you say? *Why France?* Well, I supposed that if Agatha Christie's Hercule Poirot, a Belgian, could solve mysteries in England, then my English heroine could solve a mystery in France. *N'est-ce pas?* And I had a hunch that where I was heading I would find the ideal inspiration.

Quel success! Traveling southeast from Paris, I stopped just short of Switzerland in one of the most poetically beautiful regions of a beautiful country: the Franche-Comté. Here the ancient Jura Mountains descend into valleys bathed in sunshine and blanketed with vineyards. In this paradise I sampled morsels of Comte, a delectably mellow hard cheese, washed down with the famous yellow wine of the region. I dipped crusts of crunchy bread into bubbling, steaming fondue pots and savored mouthwatering plum tarts while looking out upon medieval churches and eighteenth-century chateaux. I studied the stairwells, furnishings, bedchambers, parlors, stables, carriage houses, even the plumbing of glorious mansions where princes and princesses once dwelt, and I wandered the manicured parks of these estates in a state of euphoria. In short, I fell in love. It seemed the perfect place for my heroine and hero to fall in love too.

I give you now *I Adored a Lord*, a house party whodunit wrapped in a tender, passionate romance and set in a sublimely gracious place. I hope you enjoy reading it as much as I enjoyed writing it.

Warmest wishes,
Katharine

The Suspects

(In order of appearance)

Sir Beverley Clark—Our heroine's former employer
Mr. Francis Pettigrew—Sir Beverley's friend

Prince Sebastiao—Portuguese prince, host of the party, and younger half brother of our hero

Lord & Lady Whitebarrow—Wealthy English earl and his wife
Ladies Penelope & Grace—Their nasty twin daughters

Sir Henry & Lady Margaret Feathers—Thoroughbred breeders and social upstarts
Miss Ann Feathers—Their unfortunately mousy daughter

General Dijon—Former Napoleonic war hero (on the French side)
Mademoiselle Arielle Dijon—His lovely daughter

Duchess McCall—Highlander widow
Lady Iona—Her stunning and vivacious daughter

Wesley Courtenay, Earl of Case—Heir to Marquess Airedale and elder half brother of our hero

Lord Prunesly—A renowned biologist and baron
Miss Cecilia Anders—His daughter
Mr. Martin Anders—His poetical son

Bishop Abraccia—An ancient Italian archbishop
Miss Juliana Abraccia—His orphaned niece

I
Adored
a
Lord

Chapter 1

The Fugitive

*R*avenna Caulfield's ruination began with a bird, continued with a pitchfork, and culminated with a corpse wearing a suit of armor. The bird came first, indeed, years before the pitchfork incident and Ravenna's untimely discovery of the poor soul in steel—though perhaps that discovery was remarkably timely, depending upon one's opinion of grand matters like Destiny and Love.

Orphaned as an infant and living in a foundling home with her two elder sisters, Ravenna learned steadfast fortitude from Eleanor and indomitable defiance from Arabella. Unfortunately, she never mastered either. So it was that on the day she stole a carrot for the old cart horse, Mr. Bones, and for it earned six hours locked in the attic, when she found the wounded bird tucked in a crevice between two chipped bricks near the window, she did not know to turn her face from it. Its forlorn *cheep cheep* was more than a softhearted girl could ignore. She went to it, discovered its torn wing, stared into dark eyes just like hers, and vowed in an earnest whisper that she would save it.

For four weeks she scrubbed the sticky refectory floor quicker than all the other girls, poking her fingers with splinters to earn ten precious minutes of liberty as reward. For four weeks her heart beat like a spoon upon a kettle as she snuck away to the attic where she chewed the stale remnants of bread from breakfast and fed them to the bird. For four weeks she collected rainwater from the windowsill in a leaf and watched the tiny creature drink until its *cheep*s were no longer despondent but gay. For four weeks she coaxed it into her palm and stroked its torn wing until finally it stretched both feathered limbs and made tentative leaps toward the window.

Then one day it was gone. Ravenna stood amidst broken furniture and old storage trunks, and wept.

A short, joyful *cheep* sounded outside the window. She shoved it open and stared into the eyes of the bird perched on a branch hanging close. It flew into her outstretched palm.

That spring she watched it industriously build a nest in that branch. When it laid eggs she knelt on her small, calloused knees at chapel every morning and prayed for the health of its young that would soon come. To celebrate their hatching she brought the little mother a worm she'd dug up in the cook's garden, and watched her feed the four chicks. Lost in happiness that day, Ravenna was late to evening prayers. With livid cheeks, the headmistress reprimanded her before the other girls, then she made them all peel turnips until their hands were raw and sent them to bed without supper.

The next morning when Ravenna snuck out of the attic, three of the foundling home's meanest girls stood at the base of the stairs waiting for her. With arms crossed and lower lips curled, they said only what they always said to her: "Gypsy." But the following day when Ravenna went into the yard for their half hour of brisk walking, the three girls stood directly beneath the attic window. Before them on the ground were a great big stone and the remnants of a nest of twigs and leaves.

The little bird never returned.

Arabella fought the girls with nails and fists—and won, of course. That night in the cold dormitory, while Eleanor tended to Arabella's bruises and cuts, she spoke soft words of comfort to Ravenna. But despite her sisters' help, Ravenna came to the conclusion that some girls were heartless.

After the bird, the battle lines were clearly drawn. The mean girls did all in their power to trip up the sisters before the headmistress, and most of the time they met with success. Eleanor endured their cruelties. Arabella confronted them.

Ravenna escaped. Losing herself on the modest grounds of the foundling home, whether in the cocooning warmth of summertime, the crisp chill of autumn, the peace of winter, or the soft, damp gray of spring, she fashioned a world in which she could not feel the tugs on her braids or the whispers of "Egyptian" which she did not understand. Outside the white-washed walls of her prison she sang with blackbirds, scouted out fox, nibbled on berries in the briar patch and raw nuts fallen from friendly trees. Mr. Bones was excellent company; he never spit or pinched, and since her skin was quite like the color of his shaggy coat he never commented on it.

When the Reverend Martin Caulfield took her and her sisters away from the foundling home Eleanor said, "He is a good man, Venna. A scholar." *Whatever that was.* "It will be different now."

A man of dust-colored hair and dust-colored garments but a kind face and a quiet voice, Reverend Caulfield brought them to his cottage tucked behind the church in a corner of the small village. Never beating them or making them scrub floors (Taliesin the Gypsy boy did the latter in exchange for lessons), the Reverend taught them to pray, to read, to write, and to listen carefully to his sermons. These lessons proved challenging for Ravenna, especially the last. The cat that the church ladies kept to eat up all the mice would curl into Ravenna's lap during the service and purr so loudly that they always told her to take it outside. Once freed, she never returned. The cathedral of Nature seemed a more fitting place to worship the Great Creator than inside stone walls anyway.

On her eighth birthday the Reverend took her to the blacksmith's shop and opened the door of a horse stall, revealing a sleeping dog and, at her belly, a wiggling cluster of furry bodies. All of them save one were liver spotted. The one, black and shaggy as though he had been deposited in the straw by the hand of Methuselah, tilted his head away from his mother's teat toward her, cracked open his golden eyes, and Ravenna was so filled up that she could not utter even a sigh.

She called him Beast and they were never apart. He attended her to lessons and on Sundays sat beneath the elm in the churchyard and waited for her. But most days they spent in the woods and the fields, running and swimming and laughing. They were deliriously happy, and always Ravenna knew he was too strong, too large, and too fierce to ever be hurt by anybody, and too loyal to ever leave her.

On rainy days, the stable, smelling of straw and animals and damp warmth, became their home. Ravenna watched the old groom treat a sore hoof with a poultice of milk, wax, and wool. The next time he allowed her to do it. Then he told her how to recognize colic and how in the winter good foraging and warm water were better at preventing it than bran mash. In the winter when the Gypsies camped by the squire's wood, Taliesin—whom she always wished the Reverend would adopt too so that he could be her brother—would take her to the horse corrals and teach her even more about hooves and colic and whatnot.

Then Eleanor fell ill. While Papa fretted and Arabella cooked and sewed and did all the tasks about the house that must be done, Ravenna learned from the doctor how to pour a dose of laudanum, how to prepare a steaming linen to set across Ellie's chest, and how to boil licorice root and distill it into tea. In time Eleanor improved, and Ravenna began to follow the doctor on his other calls. At dinner each night she would tell Papa all that she had learned, and he would pat her on the head and call her a good-hearted puss.

When Arabella was seventeen she left to teach the children at the squire's house, but returned only eight months later. After that, Papa told Ravenna she must not wander about the countryside alone.

"Young ladies must behave modestly," he said with a worried glance at Beast sprawled out before the hearth.

"But Papa—"

"Obey me, Ravenna. I have allowed you too much freedom and you have had no mother to teach you the modesty your sister Eleanor has through her own nature and Arabella has learned at school. If you do not alter your habits, I will send you to school too."

Ravenna had no intention of returning to the world of locked doors and switches. "Do not send me away, Papa. I will obey." Confining her escapes to the stable, she strayed no farther. She showed her father that she could be as tame as her eldest sister while inside she suffocated.

Upon her sixteenth birthday she walked to the village and posted a letter to an employment agency in London. A month later she received a reply, and six months later an offer.

"I am going, Papa," she said, hand clutched around the handle of a small traveling case. With relief, it seemed, he gave her his blessing. She went to the stable and fed an extra biscuit to the horse, scrubbed her knuckles over the barn cat's brow, and then with Beast at her side set off on foot.

Eleanor ran after her and wrapped her in a tight embrace. "You cannot escape me, sister. No matter where you hide, I will find you." Eleanor had never regained the bloom in her cheek or softness of form that had made her pretty before she'd fallen ill. But her arms were strong and her hazel eyes resolute.

Ravenna pulled away. "That suits me, for I would never wish to escape you. And at Shelton Grange I will be closer to Bella in London."

"But what do you know of these men?"

"What the employment agency and their own letter told me." That their house was large, their park vast, and their collection of twelve dogs, two exotic birds, and one house pig too much for them to manage without the assistance of a person of youth and vigor.

"Write to me often."

Ravenna did not promise; her penmanship was poor. Instead she bussed her sister on the cheek and left her standing in the middle of the road, silhouetted by the gray stone of their father's church.

Her employers were not pleased to discover that the "R. Caulfield" of her letters was not a young man.

"Impossible," Sir Beverley Clark said with an implacably sanguine regard. Within moments of standing in his drawing room furnished with masculine comfort, Ravenna saw that although his friend, Mr. Pettigrew, was considerably more gregarious, in this house Sir Beverley was master. Resting a well-manicured hand on the top of the head of the wolfhound standing beside him, he told her, "I will not allow a young lady to reside at Shelton Grange."

"I haven't any designs upon you," she said, looking up from the cluster of pugs licking her fingers and chewing her hem to his handsome face, then to Mr. Pettigrew's round, rosy cheeks. "While you are clearly quite wealthy, you are both much older than my father, and anyway I don't ever intend to marry so that puts period to that concern. I merely want to care for your animals, as agreed upon in our letters."

A twinkle lit Mr. Pettigrew's cloverleaf eyes. "Well, that is a relief, to be sure." His voice was as merry as his smile, his hair probably yellow once but now creamy white. "But, m'dear, what Sir Beverley is saying is that it is unsuitable for you to live with two gentlemen who are unrelated to you."

"Then you must adopt me." She set down her traveling bag beside Beast who sat quite properly by her side, as though he understood the gravity of the moment. "I give you leave. My father is not my real father anyway, and I don't think he would mind it as long as you do not beat me or otherwise mistreat me."

Sir Beverley's eyes like clear rain studied her. "From what are you running, Miss Caulfield?"

"Prison."

Mr. Pettigrew's brows shot up. "We've a fugitive in the house, Bev. Whatever shall we do with her?"

For the first time, the hint of tolerant compassion that Ravenna would grow to love ticked up the corner of Sir Beverley's mouth. "Hide her from the law, I daresay."

She spent her days brushing out the shaggy coats of three wolfhounds, clipping the nails of nine pugs, and laboring over letters to experts asking for advice on macaws and parrots. She made friends with Sir Beverley's coachman, a one-legged veteran of the war who marveled at her ease with four-legged creatures and took up her instruction where Taliesin had left off.

Though he enjoyed the comforts of Shelton Grange above all, Sir Beverley liked to travel to entertainments, and to live in grand style upon those journeys. Mr. Pettigrew, whose house was only five miles distant but who liked Shelton Grange better, always accompanied him. While they were gone, Ravenna remained at home with Beast and their menagerie, enjoying the solitude of the lake and woods and fields and the house.

When they were in residence at Shelton Grange, Sir Beverley and Mr. Pettigrew liked to coddle her, like the first time she assisted Sir Beverley's tenant farmers during the lambing and afterward walked about in a daze with purple circles beneath her eyes. Mr. Pettigrew mixed up a batch of his special recipe for recovering from excessive debauchery, and Sir Beverley read to her aloud from *A Treatise on Veterinary Medicine*. Privately Ravenna took this solicitude to heart, while to their faces she teased them, telling them they were treating her as though she were an infant and they her nurses. They seemed to like that. She called them "the nannies" and they called her their "young miss."

For six years Ravenna was deeply happy.

Then Arabella married a duke and Sir Beverley told Ravenna that she must begin to make plans to depart Shelton Grange, for he could not employ a duchess's sister, no matter how fond they all were of her. One morning not long after that, Beast did not wake up, and Ravenna understood that Paradise was only a dream invented by pious men to fool everyone.

Chapter 2

The Kiss

10 February 1818
Combe Park

Dear Sir Beverley,

I have received a letter from Mr. Pettigrew that gives me great sorrow. He writes that Beast is gone and my sister stricken. While I have begged her to come to Combe, she does not respond. I know you will agree that a change would be best. And so I have a proposition for you. I have learned through my husband's dear friend, Reiner of Sensaire, that Prince Sebastiao of Portugal will gather a party in France next month. Will you escort Ravenna to this party? There will be a castle and a great many horses and other creatures, I have no doubt, which might give her some measure

of consolation. I have already secured invitations to
the party for you, her, and Mr. Pettigrew. I beg you
to accept.

With my fondest wishes &c.,
Arabella Lycombe

From behind the mullioned window of a turret
above the forecourt of Chateau Chevriot, Ravenna
peered down onto the drive, pebbled and crisply gray
as a drive in the midst of winter would inevitably be.
A man garbed in a coat of military style with tasseled
gold epaulets and plentiful medals of honor stood
directly beneath her. A young man, Prince Sebastiao
possessed a long nose, reddened eyes, and an aspect
of begrudging dissipation. He had been educated in
England during the war and spoke English as well as
any spoiled young wealthy Englishman, and apparently behaved as poorly as any of them as well. That
a member of the Portuguese royal family—albeit a
lesser branch—considered a medieval fortress situ-
ated in a mountain crevice an appropriate venue for a
party in a season far too early to comfortably be called
spring caused Ravenna no little wonder.

"Despicably wealthy people do anything they like at
any season they like, my dear," Petti said. "Delightful
to be friends with them, I say."

Prince Sebastiao's other delighted friends had been
arriving all day in carriages marked with mud and
dust from long travel yet still fantastically elegant. The
parade of mobile wealth had Ravenna's nose pressed
to the window in the sort of horrified fascination one
has for one's own execution.

"Who is that?" She poked a finger against the
window. Sir Beverley stood beside her. No one below
had yet noticed them spying, and she thought that her

former employers must know everyone in Europe.

"The Earl of Whitebarrow," he said. "Ancient title, and the family is very wealthy."

"Hm." Beyond the guests and past the forecourt, the prospect of the mountain ascended sublimely. As she had walked along the river that morning, winter birds fluttered about bushes, a pair of hawks circled above, and two dozen deer ambled up into the spruce and pines that climbed to the mountain's peak. This collection of fashionable people being disgorged from carriages seemed entirely out of place here.

"Are those his daughters?"

"Ladies Grace and Penelope."

"Twins." Dressed in pristine velvet cloaks, their hands encased in white fur muffs, the two sylphlike blondes turned porcelain faces toward another guest: a young lady who stood alone by a traveling carriage as though she'd been forgotten there. Mousy and trussed to her neck in a long pelisse with not one or two but three rows of furbelows, she stared at the drive with round eyes. Nearby, a pear-shaped matron with similarly ruffled garments chatted gaily with another lady.

Studying the mouse, one of the Whitebarrow blondes lifted her brow. She and her sister shared words, and their lips curled.

Ravenna's throat prickled. She should not have come. But when the invitation to the prince's party had arrived weeks ago, Petti insisted he always wanted to visit the French mountains. As he simply must bring Caesar, Georgiana, and Mrs. Keen on the journey (the other pugs preferring to remain at home), she must allow them a few more months of her company before she left them entirely for her sister's ducal home. When she objected to the distance, he had patted her on the hand and said he understood that it was difficult for her to even come indoors some evenings and leave

Beast in the dark by himself beneath that old oak tree. Her old friend, Petti said, would be as well in her absence in France as when she removed to Combe; he was beyond hurt now.

But that was not the truth of it. Beast had loved the shade of that oak and the field around it bursting with wildflowers. It was she who could not bear being indoors without him.

Now she studied the mouse alone and forgotten on the drive. "Who is that girl?"

"Miss Ann Feathers. Her father, Sir Henry, has made a fortune in breeding Thoroughbreds. Prince Sebastiao's father, Raynaldo, breeds Andalusians. He won't be attending the party, but the prince is to negotiate a joint venture in his stead."

"And that lady?" A girl of exquisitely delicate ivory-and-ebony beauty walked upon the arm of a young gentleman toward the front door.

"Mademoiselle Arielle Dijon. She is daughter of the famed French general Dijon, who saved his troops from utter decimation in 1812 when the Cossacks scorched the earth. He was disenchanted with Napoleon after that fiasco—"

"Understandably," Petti interjected. An hour earlier he had ensconced himself in a cushioned chair and commenced snoring. Three soft, chubby pugs at his feet snored as well.

"After the treaty he left the army," Sir Beverley continued. "He took his family to America. Philadelphia, I believe."

A tiny white dog peeked out from Mademoiselle Dijon's cloak, and she stroked its brow with great tenderness.

"I like her already," Ravenna said.

Another girl, tall, with fiery locks neatly contained by her bonnet, descended from the last carriage. She was astoundingly beautiful, with an air of barely contained energy and bright, seeking eyes. A gentleman dismounting nearby moved to her side, drawing off his hat and offering her a deep bow.

"That is Lady Iona, who has come with her widowed mother, Duchess McCall," Sir Beverley murmured. "She's come a long way to woo a prince."

"To woo a prince?"

Petti chuckled.

Ravenna swung around to peer at him. "To woo a prince?" she repeated.

"You didn't tell her, Bev?" His cloverleaf eyes twinkled.

"Tell me what?"

"This party, my dear," Petti said cheerily, "is not an idle holiday in the mountains."

She looked between them. "Then what is it?"

"Prince Sebastiao seeks a bride," Sir Beverley replied.

"A bride-hunting party, my dear!" Petti concurred. "Isn't it marvelous?"

It required few moments for Ravenna to understand.

"You know about the fortune-teller?" she uttered with dark disapproval.

"What fortune-teller?" Petti stroked a pug's rippled neck.

"The Gypsy fortune-teller who told Arabella that one of us must marry a prince or we would never know who our real parents are. She did tell you, didn't she?"

"You told us yourself," Sir Beverley said. "Years ago."

"Then I must have told you in the hopes of making you split your seams with laughter. And now you have both betrayed me."

"Perhaps you are overstating it," Sir Beverley said with a hint of a smile.

"Your sister wished to put you in the way of a prince, dear girl. We merely agreed to help."

Ravenna could say nothing. Arabella had married

a duke but remained determined to find the parents they had lost decades ago.

Her gaze darted to the door, then to the window, to the drive and the trees and mountain beyond.

"Oh!" she said, snapping her attention to Sir Beverley. "I'm afraid all your matchmaking plans are for naught. You see, in order to wed a prince I need—"

"This?" Sir Beverley produced from his pocket a thick man's ring of gold and ruby.

Ravenna stepped back. "She gave that to you?"

"To give to you." Sir Beverley cupped her hand in his and pressed the ring into her palm. It was heavy and warm as it always had been, even on that day Arabella took it to a fortune-teller and heard the prophecy— that one of them would wed a prince and upon that day discover the mystery of their past. This ring was the key to it all.

But Ravenna didn't care about the mystery of their past. An infant when her mother abandoned them, she had never cared. Finding the prince had been Arabella's dream. But now Arabella was wife to a duke. Ravenna had no doubt as to why Arabella had not bestowed the dubious honor of prince catching upon their elder sister, Eleanor. They never spoke of it, but they both knew the true reason Eleanor had not yet married, and it was not her devotion to Papa.

"Do cease fretting, my dear," Petti said comfortably. "A lady in your sister's delicate condition must be humored."

"I am not fretting." Ravenna dropped the ring into her pocket. It made a hard bump against her thigh. "I gather that all these girls—ladies of enormous beauty, wealth, and status, and every one of them years younger than me—they are all to be my *competition* for the prince's favor?"

"It does seem a shame any of them bothered making the journey here." Petti winked.

"Lady Iona McCall is one-and-twenty," Sir Beverley said. "Only two years your junior."

"You are both batty as belfries. And my sister too." She turned to the window and stared down at the beautiful, wealthy people below. "I do not wish to marry a prince, of course." Or anybody. "Who is that very handsome man taking Lady Iona's arm?"

"Lord Case, heir to Marquess Airedale," Sir Beverley said. "I've no idea why he is here. He hasn't a sister, only a brother no one has seen in years."

"Perhaps Lord Case is looking for a bride too and has heard this is the place to come for one," she said. "No wonder his brother plays least-in-sight, with a sibling of such wise forethought."

"You are still an impertinent girl." Sir Beverley said with a crinkle of his eyes, then returned his attention to the drive below. "Very handsome, you say?"

"Fancy yourself a noblesse, my dear?" Petti said.

"About as much as I fancy myself a princess." She went toward the door. "Now that all the potential brides are here, when does this party begin in earnest? And do you think there is yet time for me to have the carriage readied for an escape before the snow?"

THAT NIGHT IN a bed made with the softest linens and brocaded silk the likes of which she had only ever touched in Arabella's new ducal home, Ravenna lay on her back, aching inside. In two months she had not yet become accustomed to the empty place by her side. No hard spine pressed against her hip, forcing her to the edge of the mattress. No harrumphing half yawns woke her from dreams. No warm breath stirred her to wake in the morning and set off across the park while the sun rose over the hills. Beast would love the softness of this bed. The ropes were so well tied it didn't squeak when mounted.

She squeezed her eyes shut and wanted warmth and a body beside hers to hold.

The stables beckoned. Buttoning herself into an old gown that wouldn't shame Petti too much if anybody else saw her now, she made her way from her bedchamber.

On the exterior, Chevriot imposed, an elegant mass of gray-brown limestone surrounded by an uncompromising wall, with heavy towers and unadorned roofs. But inside the chateau, luxury reigned. Thick rugs running the length of the corridors swallowed the patter of Ravenna's footsteps. Her lamplight danced over a footman sitting on a chair at the head of the grand staircase, who nodded as she passed.

Slipping into the servants' stair through a door hidden in the wall, she descended to the kitchen and followed a thread of frozen air to the door to the kitchen yard. The night smelled of snow, clean and sharp. Throughout the afternoon she had watched the clouds gather in gray-white folds upon the nearest peak. It would come by morning, then she would be good and well trapped.

She let herself out of the yard through the gate and followed the cemetery wall along the edge of the forecourt to the carriage house, then to the stable.

Within the stable, all was cold and still. A single lantern lit the central corridor and her feet padded silently along the clean-swept floor. Blooded beasts slumbered in stalls to either side, like in Sir Beverley's stables, like at home, Shelton Grange, where she and Beast had played and worked. Where he would remain forever. Where she did not belong now because her beautiful, courageous sister had married a duke.

A tear dashed upon her cheek like a tiny scalding slap. Another followed. A third caught on the corner of her mouth. A lone brown cat stared at her from a shadow, condemnation in its glowing eyes. Ravenna shoved the back of her hand across her jaw.

A noise arose from a stall ahead—soft, squeaky, sharp then long, desperate then miserable and weary. The cat slunk away. Ravenna smiled. Nothing else in the world sounded like puppies.

She followed the sound to a room not meant for horses but equipment. Upon the near wall hung a pitchfork, an axe, and a shovel, with a bucket and brushes arranged neatly on a bench. Straw layered the floor thickly, with the pups in the corner. Someone had made a temporary home for them.

She went to her knees. Four little black and white bodies tangled together in the deep shadows, two sleeping, one nodding, the last crawling over its siblings and whimpering. The bitch was nowhere to be seen—perhaps out foraging for food, or perhaps they were weaned already and she was gone. They were old enough, nine or ten weeks probably.

From under a thatch of straw to the side, a black nose poked out. Its tiny nostrils sniffed the chill air.

Setting down her lamp on the bench, Ravenna crouched by the concealed pup, brushed aside the straw, and peered at the runt—for the runt it clearly was, separated from its siblings and smaller by far. Just like Beast.

She scooped it up and her fingers threaded through its chilled fur. Without his mother and not strong enough to contend with his siblings, he would not last long in this cold. Yet in desperate straits he had dug himself a hole in the straw. Resourceful little fellow. She cuddled him to her breast. With boneless gracelessness he tumbled over her chest, his new claws like miniature razors, snatching at the edge of her cloak with a hungry mouth. She laughed and burrowed her nose against its brow.

"I'm sorry," she whispered. "I cannot help you. I didn't think to bring a biscuit."

Holding the runt against her neck, she warmed it until her toes and the tip of her nose grew numb. She placed the puppy beside its sleeping siblings and tucked the straw around it, and its cries of complaint rose pitifully.

A heavy footfall sounded on the other side of the door. A man's tread. Then another. He paused out of sight beyond the opening she'd left.

Silence.

She'd thought the stables empty. Now a man stood on the other side of the door without speaking. If he had come to see the pups, he would enter. If he had followed her inside with ill intent, he might be silent. It would not be the first time a man had assumed she was fair game for a tumble in the hay. But this time her protector did not stand by her side, growling and baring his sharp teeth. This time she was alone.

The pup whimpered more desperately it seemed. No other sound stirred the stillness, no breath, no movement. But the man remained. Every prickling hair on Ravenna's arms felt him.

She slammed the door outward. It jarred and sprang back. His body fell heavily to the floor and a short, deep moan sounded in the hush.

Then . . . nothing.

The pup whined.

Ravenna counted to thirty. Stepping forward, she pushed the door open.

In the dim light she barely made out the man's profile against the floor: cap fallen askew off dark hair that curled around his collar, longish nose, and a jaw shadowed by whisker growth. He wore plain clothing, a loose brown coat, dark breeches, and boots. His hands spread upon the floor were large. A scar ran across the top of his right hand from the V between his forefinger and middle finger into his sleeve, the memento of a sharp-edged tool going astray. She'd seen plenty of scars like that on farmers and stable hands.

This man must be a stable hand—a stable hand who should not have alarmed her. When he regained consciousness he would have a welt on his head the size of Devonshire.

His body blocked the door. To fetch help she would have to step over him. But her narrow skirts would not allow her to traverse him in one step. So much for attempting to dress like a lady to please Petti.

He did not move. He could not possibly be dead. But he remained so still. In the dimness it seemed he did not draw breaths. Ravenna's fingertips itched, habit overcoming fear. She should probe his skull. If the door had cracked it, she knew what must be done. But first she must examine him.

Tentatively she shifted a toe forward and nudged his shoulder.

He groaned. She nudged harder.

His hand gripped her ankle so swiftly her fingers wrenched from the door. Twisting to avoid the pups, she went down fast, her shoulder striking the floor buffered by the thick straw. But he did not release her. Struggling back, she scrabbled for the wall and a weapon. Her hand snagged a handle. She wrenched it forward and it slipped through her numb fingers. The pitchfork crashed down on his leg.

"Good God!" he howled. "Damn it!"

Instead of doubling over, he lurched forward and grabbed her knee, and his other hand cinched around her wrist. Then he was upon her, his weight atop her, his knees and hips and chest pinning her to the straw and his hand clamping over her mouth as a scream jolted from her throat. She thrashed. His ankles twisted around hers, holding her legs immobile. He gripped her arm, the other trapped beneath her.

"Be *still*," he growled like an animal.

She went still.

"What are you doing, attacking an innocent man?" His tongue slurred. "Damn it, my head hurts. And my leg."

Her heartbeats battered against his chest pressed to hers. His face was inches away, satiny hair falling over eyes that were dark sockets of outrage. The icy air between them did not reek of spirits. He was not foxed. The slur must be from the injury. The door had hit him hard.

"I will release your mouth," he said, and squinted as though he were trying to focus. *Long lashes.* Long for a man. "But if you scream, you won't like the consequences. If you understand, blink once."

She blinked. His hand slid away from her mouth. She gulped in air.

"I still can't breathe," she rasped.

The pup mewled.

"Why are you here?" His gaze swept the neckline of her gown, then her hair. "Are you a maid?"

"I came outside—needed air. You're crushing—my lungs. Get—off me or—I'll scream and—bear the consequences."

"No scream will come without air to carry it." He sounded less slurred now. And too rational. "Tell me who you are and I will release you."

"Regina Slate. Daughter—Duke of Marylebone— guest. He'll have you—strung up by your neck when—he learns you've—touched me."

"Marylebone is a neighborhood, not a duke. And

threatening a man with hanging in the uncertain future when he's got you in his power at present is idiocy." Now she heard a round, broken tone in his words. He was a foreigner. But not French, she thought, and he spoke English perfectly. Also, he knew Marylebone was a neighborhood in London. Her poor luck. "And if your father is a duke," he said, "I am the Emperor of China."

"Pleasure—" She gasped. "To make your acquaintance—your imperial majesty."

His hand tightened about her wrist. "What is your name and why are you in this stable?"

"Ravenna—Caulfield. Truly. You were right. I'm—nobody." With no one of her own to wrap her arms around at the end of the day and breathe in deeply, and no one to protect her from men who would throw themselves upon her because she was nobody. "Now get—off me."

"Caulfield." His brow bent. The pressure on her chest relaxed slightly and she tried to fill her lungs. But his grip remained tight around her arm. "You are in Sir Beverley Clark's party?"

As stable hands went, this one seemed unusually well informed. "I work for him." Not really now that she was a duchess's sister, of course. But how much could he know about Sir Beverley's household?

"What work do you do?" His eyes scanned her face with particular interest now, and an odd little eddy of awareness scampered through her. "Are you his mistress?"

Apparently he didn't know much about Sir Beverley after all. "I care for his pet dogs and exotic birds."

Abruptly, his brow relaxed. A crease dented his scruffy cheek.

Ravenna's heart did a peculiar sideways leap.

"You care for his—"

"Dogs and exotic birds. Twelve dogs. Two birds. And one house pig." A strange agitation was rushing into her numb limbs. It must be terror. It could not be caused by the dent in his cheek above his hard jaw. He was a dangerous stranger attacking her. But attackers did not grin like they were curiously pleased. Did they?

A shimmer of red peeked from the fall of hair over his brow, the welt forming. A biscuit poultice would soothe that quick enough. Perhaps in the kitchen she could find milk and some—

"Animals?" he said, his gaze trailing over her face again, the dent deepening.

"I care for them and doctor them. I do the same for everybody's animals in the county when they get sick, without compensation because I am not a man and nobody thinks they need to pay me except with a basket of fresh eggs or a cream or a cake of soap, which I usually take to mean they think a woman should smell better than I do. This struggling in straw soaked with puppy urine isn't helping that problem, by the way. So now *get off me*."

But he wasn't going to release her. She saw the change in his eyes and felt it in his body the instant it happened. She hadn't much experience with men beyond the occasional brush of hands when she was holding on to one end of a lambing ewe and a farmer was hanging on to the other end. But she knew enough about rutting animals to recognize the signs of arousal in the male of the species, even her own.

The pupils of her attacker's eyes were wide in the darkness. Then his gaze dipped to her mouth. He might not have initially followed her into the stall with rapine intent. But it certainly seemed to be on his mind now.

"You smell good to me," he said, his voice deeper

than before, like a warm autumn night, the vowels especially round. Not French. Italian? Spanish? He must have come with one of the other guests—one of the other guests who had wretched judgment when hiring stable hands.

"I—"

"And, *por Deus*," he said upon a catch in his throat, his eyes hard upon her mouth, "you are lovely."

The rutting urge must have overcome him. The only male creature that had ever considered her lovely was Beast, and that was because she sometimes smelled like bacon.

She must distract him.

"I can help with that bruise on your brow," she said, struggling against panic.

"Can you?" He seemed bemused. Jars to the head could scramble the brain.

"It's starting to swell. It will leave a painful wound that could fester. Let me up and I'll ask the housekeeper for—"

His mouth came down upon hers without further warning. Not hard or violently or forcefully. But fully, with complete contact.

Ravenna pinned her lips together. Breathing through her nose, she smelled horses and straw and something else foreign and male and . . . *good*. Like whiskey without the bite. Or well-loved leather. He released her wrist and with his big hand cupped her cheek.

She did not push him away. *She must.* But his scent, the heat of his skin, the sensation of his lips upon hers—teasing, encouraging, urging—paralyzed her. The pad of his thumb stroked gently along her throat. His touch was so warm. Intimate. *Tender.* Tingling pleasure mingled with the panic in her belly. She could kiss him back. She could discover what it was like to really kiss a man.

She couldn't.

He had one thing in mind after kissing, and she wasn't prepared to oblige him.

She did what Beast would have done to an attacker.

"*Colhões!*" He jerked away and rolled off her and to his feet.

She scuttled back, skirts tangling in her boots as she jumped up, leaping to avoid puppies. The man's shadowed eyes swung to her, anger sparking in them in the dim light. Blood dripped between his fingers clamped over his mouth.

"I hope I bit it off," she said, unwisely.

He dropped his hand and his lower lip was still intact, though bleeding down his chin. "Damn it, woman. I only kissed you."

"While you had me trapped beneath you."

"Yes, well, obviously that was a mistake." He dabbed gingerly at the blood with the back of his sleeve. He was tall, his shoulders broad, the sinews in his neck pronounced. He did not sound like a stable hand, rather more like a gentleman, but those sinews were like a farmer's. This man knew physical labor and he had trapped her with little effort. He could have easily done anything to her he wished. He still could. The pitchfork lay close to his booted feet. He blocked the door. She was still trapped.

"Get out of my way," she said, "or I'll kick you in the *colhões* even harder than I bit you."

Without speech he stepped out of arm's range of the door, and she darted past him and ran across the forecourt. Inside, she locked her bedchamber door, wrapped a blanket around her, and sat before the dying embers of the fire, shaking a little. She had never imagined what her first kiss would be like. She had never imagined she would have a first kiss at all.

Now she knew.

Chapter 3

The Monk

*F*lakes of cold crystal fluttered between the trees as Lord Vitor Courtenay tied his horse to a branch and stepped into the church built of gray stone at the mountain's peak. Closing the door behind him, he walked down the nave bare of adornment, his boot steps echoing in the vaulting. Upon the limestone steps to the chancel he went to his knees, pulled off his cap, and touched his fingertips to his brow, his breastbone, and each shoulder in turn.

In years past he had come to this mountaintop hermitage for food, shelter, and safety. On this occasion he needed none of those. The wealth he had earned during the war through labor for both England and Portugal now collected dust in his London bank, and the luxuries of Chateau Chevriot were presently at his command.

This morning he sought another sort of aid altogether.

The church smelled of incense and tallow wax and ancient, sacred aromas: the scents of his blood-father's land. Fourteen years ago, after learning of his true parentage, Vitor had first traveled to that land, only to depart from it when the Portuguese royal family fled the threat of Napoleon all the way to Brazil. But Vitor had not crossed the Atlantic with the rest of the court. Instead, his father, Raynaldo, cousin to the Prince Regent, retreated into the mountains. From hiding he had sent his English son—young and eager to prove himself—into Spain, then France, to learn what could be learned to make Lisbon safe for the restoration of the queen's court. Vitor had not disappointed him.

He probed his sore lip with his tongue. Apparently not everyone respected a war hero.

A door creaked behind the wooden choir boxes. He bent his head and waited. Sandaled footsteps shuffled toward him and paused at his side. The hermit knelt on the cold steps, the clacking beads of his rosary muffled in the wool of his habit.

"*In nomine Patris, et Filii, et Spiritus Sancti.*" No whiff of wine accompanied the murmured words. Yet.

"Amen."

"What sin have you committed for which you seek absolution, *mon fils*?" the priest said, then added, "This time."

"Father . . ."

"Did you act in anger?" The hermit asked this according to ancient tradition, urging a confession from the sinner through questioning. During the two years Vitor had lived in a hilltop monastery in the Serra dal Estrela, he'd read everything in the library of the Benedictine brothers, including confessor manuals. This hermit now did not fix upon the sin of anger at whim. He knew Vitor's special interest in it.

"No," he replied, his throat dry. "Not anger." *Not this time.*

"Greed?"

"No."

"Pride?"

"No."

"Envy."

"No."

"It could not have been sloth." The hermit's voice gentled. "You've never slept a full night in your life, young vagabond."

"No." *Get to the relevant sin.*

"Did you lie?"

"No."

"Did you steal?"

A case could be made for it. "Not quite."

"Did you covet your neighbor's goods?"

Momentarily, though "goods" didn't quite express it, really. "No."

"Son—"

"Father . . ." Vitor pressed his brow into his knuckles.

The priest paused for a moment that stretched in the chill air. "Did you commit murder again?"

"No."

The Frenchman's breath of relief whispered across the chancel. He sat back on his heels and folded his arms within voluminous sleeves. "Then what did you do that brings you from the gathering at the house where your half brother needs you now?"

"I kissed a girl."

Silence.

"Father?"

"Vitor, you are bound for the madhouse."

"Or hell." He raked his hand through his hair and turned to the priest. Patient tolerance lined the old

Frenchman's face. Vitor shook his head. "I shouldn't have done it, Denis."

"You might be taking those monastic vows too seriously, *mon fils*, especially since you left them behind six months ago." He lifted shaggy brows. "Or so you told me then."

After the war, the monastery had made an excellent retreat. But Vitor's fathers, the Marquess of Airedale and Prince Raynaldo of Portugal, complained. Where was the man loyal to both families, the man they had depended upon to do dangerous tasks, to loyally serve both England and Portugal at once? Where was the man hungering for adventure?

Bound to a chair, beaten and cut.

The monastery had suited him. For a time. But once he had put away his anger he'd been eager to move on.

"It isn't about the vows." He turned his face to the bare altar fashioned of granite hewn from this mountain. "She was not exactly a girl."

A choking sound came from beside him. "Perhaps it's time we have a chat about that monastery after all."

Vitor cut him a scowl. "Oh, good God, Denis. She was *female*."

"Ah. *Bon*." The old priest again sighed in relief. "Are you confessing the sin of fornication, then?"

"No." Vitor turned to sit on the step, relieving the ache in his leg that she'd struck with the hardest pitchfork in Christendom. He rubbed a palm over his face. "I only kissed her."

The hermit chuckled. "If she took money for only that, she should be the one confessing." Denis reached into a fold of his habit and drew out a flask.

"She was not a *puta*. She was a lady." Albeit wearing a gown fit for a servant and lurking in a stable at midnight. "I frightened her." Anger and indignation and fear had all swum in her eyes. Beautiful black eyes. He hadn't been that close to a woman's face in years. She'd seemed an angel in the lamplight. A dark, alluring angel. "It was as if a demon drove me. She was there"—beneath him, her curves cushioning him, her small body lush and entirely feminine, her eyes flashing—"and I wanted to kiss her more than I've ever wanted anything in my life. I couldn't stop myself."

He should have stopped himself even before he'd followed her into the stable. She'd walked across the forecourt in the dark like she was accustomed to walking about alone, her stride comfortable, pulling the fabric of her skirts around her behind and thighs and warming Vitor as he stood in the frigid shadows and watched her. No gently bred female walked like that. In the light of her lamp, her hair had shone black and shining and tumbling about her face, begging to be set entirely free from its haphazard confines. He'd followed her as much because he'd wanted to see more of her as because he was suspicious of her intentions.

His younger half brother Sebastiao enjoyed making assignations with serving girls in the stables. Laughingly he said it made him feel like the sportsman he was not. At this gathering, that amusing little pastime would not go over well with the prince's guests.

But Sebastiao had not been in the stable with the girl, only a handful of mongrel pups and a damnably hard pitchfork. Then when Vitor subdued her in the straw and she looked at his mouth . . .

He'd gone a little insane.

Two years of silent contemplation did not necessarily a willing monastic make.

Denis nodded. "The devil is fond of taking the female form."

"No. I mistook the situation." She hadn't been a servant hoping for a quick tup from a groom, but one of Sebastiao's potential brides, apparently. Odd choice: a former servant of a lesser English baronet. But Vitor's duty at Chevriot was not to question his blood-father's intentions, only to make certain his half brother fulfilled them.

Denis glanced at his swollen lip. "Did you beg her pardon afterward?"

"No." He would do so today. Then he would stay as far away from her as possible.

"There are plenty of girls in that castle," the Frenchman said, knowing his thoughts. "Sebastiao will not be wanting for choices if you take an interest in one of them."

No. He'd already once caused trouble coming between one of his brothers and a woman. He would not do so again. "I have no interest in her," he mumbled.

"You are still under the seal of the confessional, Vitor."

He snapped his head around. "How do you do that?"

"Recognize lies upon a man's tongue? It is my gift. As yours is to serve your family. Both of your families. Sebastiao must be corralled. After all the instances in which you have saved him from disaster, you know that better than anyone."

"Forcing a wife upon him may calm him for a time, but it will not alter his character." As falling into the hands of torturers had not altered his. Perhaps his elder brother Wesley had got all the steadiness of the Courtenay blood. Perhaps he, lacking a drop of that Courtenay blood, had got only his mother's inconstancy.

Vagabond, indeed.

"Sebastiao is unstable and prone to excess," Denis said. "But this snow will hold him here until the deed can be done," the hermit said. "And Prince Raynaldo knows you will not deny his wishes."

He never had before. But this mission was beneath him.

"When this is through, Denis, I will return to England."

"To do what, *mon fils*? Spend your gold on drink and game and loose women?"

"Why not? I've nothing else to do with it." During the long, silent nights at the monastery, belly empty and hands raw, he had considered indulging in the life he'd been born into, the life he could well afford. But even then he knew that would not satisfy. Soon he would hear of an opportunity abroad, or smell the freshness of spring wind, and be off anew.

Absently he rubbed at the scar between his thumb and finger through his gloves. It ached.

"*Bon.*" The priest set the flask down on the step and folded his hands. "For the sin of lust you have confessed, *mon fils*," he said in an easy tone, "you are contrite, *n'est-ce pas*?"

Vitor closed his eyes and saw hers before him, sparkling like stars. "Yes."

"For your penance I give you a novena to our Blessed Mother and the task of seeing your brother well matched to a woman who will bring him to heel."

"Only that?" Vitor lifted a brow. "Father, you are too lenient."

The priest drew a cross in the air above his brow. "*Ego te absolvo a peccatis tuis in nomine Patris, et Filii, et Spiritus Sancti.*"

"Amen."

"Now, go find an actual *puta* and work some of that fire out of your blood." He took up the flask.

The path down the mountainside was dusted with snow that tumbled faster now through the canopy of spruce and pine. A horseman appeared as a shadow through the white curtain. Shirt points high, buttons gold, breeches pristine and riding crop affected, he struck a pose even on horseback.

"Up to your papish ways again, brother?" Wesley

Courtenay, the Earl of Case, drawled. Snowflakes caught in his chestnut hair and shrouded the dark blue eyes that they both shared with their mother.

"Up to your lordly ways as always, brother?" They stopped close and clasped hands.

Wesley grinned. "It is good to see you again after so long, Vitor," he uttered low, warmth now in his voice that could at times sound as cold as steel in winter. "But what on earth did you do to your lip?" He waved a hand. "Never mind. It mars those irritatingly good looks, so I am almost in charity with you."

"My valet must have cut it while shaving me."

"I daresay he might have if you had a valet," his elder half brother replied. "Or perhaps you do now. It has been such an age since you were in England last, I barely know how you go along. I was thrilled to receive your invitation to this gathering," he said conversationally, the snowfall muffling sounds beneath the treetops.

"Were you?"

"A whole castle full of damsels intent upon securing a husband?" Wesley mimicked surprise. "Why, of course. What reasonable man would not be thrilled with such a prospect?"

Vitor laughed. "I know the ladies are probably too innocent for your liking, Wes. But their fathers are all deep in the pockets. Late-night play should be good."

"Ah, deep play. Of course. Why did you invite me, Vitor?"

"I didn't. Father did and told you I had. I received his letter only the day before I departed Lisbon."

Wesley drew up his mount.

Vitor continued, allowing Ashdod full rein. "I hear Mother is eager for grandchildren. Perhaps she hopes that, trapped in proximity with eligible maidens, you will find a bride."

"Father wishes to force a reconciliation between us," Wesley said behind him.

Vitor drew the gray to a halt and looked over his shoulder. "For what it's worth to you, I am glad Father did it. I am pleased to see you, Wes."

"After seven years, I should hope you would be."

But it had not been seven years since Vitor had last heard his brother's voice, only four. Wesley, the arrogant fool, did not know he knew that.

"Ah well, I could not possibly resist the invitation." Wesley glanced about the woods so far from his fashionable world of London society. "Town is a dull bore these days, and Mother pesters." His eyes glimmered. "Why you couldn't have been born first instead of me . . ."

"Fate is a comfortable mistress, Wes, if you accept her demands." Fate, the mistress that four years ago had put him the hands of mercenaries who turned him over to the British to be tortured.

"Listen to the monk teaching me about mistresses." Wesley chuckled. "Speaking of . . . The prince seems unreconciled to his matrimonial prospects. Was this party forced upon him?"

"Ask him yourself." Never had Wesley acknowledged aloud Vitor's relationship to Portuguese royalty. But he knew that their mother had slept in another man's bed and bore a son from it. The Marquess of Airedale, an indulgent father to both his sons, had not balked when Vitor had left England at the age of fifteen to live in the house of the man who had cuckolded him. On the single occasion that Vitor had returned to England as a man, the marquess had welcomed him.

Vitor understood his elder brother. However much Wesley cared for him, he resented him because of their father's love. But he hated him too, for a seven-year-old grievance that he could not apparently forget or forgive. Vitor knew this because, during the war when he had been a prisoner of his own country, accused of treason, he had heard it in his elder brother's wintry voice when Wesley tortured him.

RAVENNA TRAILED HER toes along the rug as she neared the drawing room door, digging furrows in the pattern. With the world outside the castle a swirling mass of snow and wind, she could not avoid the humans within unless she wished to remain trapped in her bedchamber. And Petti and Sir Beverley would scold. But she delayed as well as she reasonably could.

She smiled at the footman stationed at the drawing room door and peeked around his shoulder.

"To our host!" Sir Henry, the Thoroughbred breeder, exclaimed. "May he prosper!"

"Hear hear!"

Guests raised their glasses toward the prince. He stood resplendent in the center of the room, wearing collars to his chin and enormous lapels. Eyes red and wandering, and grin sloppy, he bowed with drunken excess.

The Earl of Whitebarrow, a tall, golden-haired man of arrogant eye and patrician nose, cast Ravenna a swift, assessing glance. Young Mr. Martin Anders stared intensely at her from beneath an unkempt forelock. The skin around his right eye was red and shadowed, as though he'd been struck with a fist. His father, the Baron of Prunesly and a renowned biologist, peered at her above his spectacles, then frowned.

Ravenna looked for the delicately dark Mademoiselle Dijon and found her beside her father, the general. Her tiny white dog huddled in her lap, decorated with ribbons that matched her mistress's gown. At least one person in the party kept good company.

Luncheon had been a purgatory of idle conversations, sly, silent assessments from the women, and peculiar perusals by the men. Dinner would surely be the same. And still dozens more of both must be endured before Sir Beverley released her from this prison. She must find some other activity swiftly.

Activity away from the stables, preferably.

Sir Beverley had spoken with the prince's head groom. No stable hand, coachman, or other servant accompanying any of the guests resembled the man that had pinned Ravenna to the ground the night before. A tiny village flanked the fortress, but the groom said that the villagers were few and he knew them all well. Chevriot had been the property of Prince Sebastiao's family for a century through marriage to a French heiress. The villagers here were loyal to their absentee overlords and wary of strangers.

Nevertheless, when the sun rose Ravenna had waded through falling snow to the village and into every craftsman's shop, searching. If she confronted her attacker in the daylight, publicly, the prince would be obliged to take some action against him. There were some advantages to being considered a lady, after all.

But she found no man with broad shoulders, indigo eyes, and a laughing crease in his left cheek that made her stomach tingle. With snow clinging to her stockings and her hems encased in ice, she returned to the chateau out of sorts.

This party did not aid matters any.

Across the drawing room, the blond Whitebarrow twins were moving toward mousy Ann Feathers as though casually strolling. But ill intent lurked in their pale blue eyes. The hair on the back of Ravenna's neck stood up.

Miss Ann Feathers lifted her round gaze from the ground and managed a curtsy for the twins. Then the torture began, like nasty little girls plucking the wings off a butterfly. Ravenna did not need to hear them speak to know the gist of their conversation. Miss Feathers's round cheeks turned red as beets, her eyes rounder yet, and the champagne began to dance in her glass as her hand trembled. She passed a palm self-consciously over the ruffles at her throat and Lady Penelope's smile hardened.

A little growl rumbled at the back of Ravenna's throat. Pushing away from the wall, she moved toward the trio.

A hand touched her elbow and she turned to meet Lady Iona McCall's regard, as blue as the breast of a damselfly in summer.

"Miss Caulfield," she said quietly, a musical lilt in her clear voice. "I admire yer courage." She cast a swift glance at the Whitebarrow sisters torturing Miss Feathers. "But I'd be takin' care no' to cross anybody this early in the game."

Ravenna laughed. "Well, it's refreshing to know that someone else realizes this is a game."

"Aye. 'Tis a competition, for certain." Lady Iona's flaming upswept hair sparkled with diamonds in the candlelight. Daughter to a widowed duchess, the Highland beauty was an heiress and had a better chance of winning the prince's admiration than any other maiden present. "But there be prizes a clever leddy might consider beside his royal highness," she added. Ravenna followed her amused gaze across the room in the other direction.

Lord Prunesly and his daughter Cecilia stood by the hearth with two men, the Earl of Case and another with his back to her.

"Lord Case is handsome, it's true," Ravenna stated the obvious.

"Aye. But his brither's handsomer still," Iona said upon a purr of delight. "We've only spoken once, yet I think I may be in luve wi' him already."

"Is that him?" He certainly made a fine figure from the back, with long legs set in a confident stance and a coat that stretched perfectly across his wide shoulders. "Has he only just arrived?"

"No. He arrived yesterday but no one's seen him till nou. Lord Case said he's passed the day at the hermitage up the hill." She chuckled. "Can ye imagine it, Miss Caulfield? An English laird preferrin' prayer to play?"

He turned his head to Cecilia Anders and an odd little jitter of moths fluttered through Ravenna. His jaw was smooth and strong, his hair almost as dark as hers and falling just short of his collar. Miss Anders laughed at something he said and he smiled. From across the room, Ravenna saw his clean-shaven cheek crease.

Her entire body went hot. Then cold. Then hot again. *Impossible.*

As though he sensed her alarm, he looked over his shoulder and his attention alighted upon her. With that slight smile still shaping his violently bruised lip, he inclined his head to her.

"Why, Miss Caulfield," Lady Iona said, "ye've already got an admirer. Well done, lass!"

It could not be. Yet there he stood, purple lip as evidence.

He was a lord? The son of a marquess? The brother of an earl? Wasn't that just her poor luck? She might have had some success at chastising a stable hand. Now her attacker far outclassed her. No justice would come to her now.

But she could see justice done elsewhere. Nodding to Lady Iona, she continued toward mousy Ann Feathers and the Whitebarrow twins. As she approached, Ladies Penelope and Grace seemed to be studying Miss Feathers's reticule.

"Well, isn't this clever, Grace?" Lady Penelope said.

"Oh, yes, Pen. So many beads," Lady Grace said with a thin smile.

"Beads on reticules and fans were delightfully au courant . . ." Penelope fluttered her fan before her mouth and added in an audible whisper to her sister, "Last year."

Miss Feathers fingered the sparkling beads sewn in a clever little swirl pattern on her reticule. "Papa bought this for me on Bond Street in January."

Lady Penelope offered her a moue of pity. "Well, that explains it. All the best shops in town close up after Christmas."

"Do they?" Like everything about her, Miss Feathers's eyes were round as carriage wheels.

"I doubt it." Ravenna stepped into the little circle that crackled with cruelty and misery. "She said that to make you feel poorly, Miss Feathers. Your beads are quite nice. Nicer than anything I've got, certainly."

"Oh, that is an enviable recommendation, isn't it?" Lady Penelope's half-lidded eyes gleamed.

"Dear Miss Caulfield," Lady Grace purred. "Wherever did you find that gown? In the housekeeper's chamber?"

"In fact, yes," she said, her neck burning. It wasn't true. But when Petti had tut-tutted the gowns she'd had made up for the trip, she'd told him that delicate muslins and silks weren't for her, that she would only ruin such finery and she felt much more comfortable in sturdy woolens anyway. More herself.

"Oh, dear," Lady Penelope said. She was subtler than Grace, and her gaze slipped from Ravenna back to Miss Feathers. "Wasn't your mother a housekeeper once, Miss Feathers?"

"She was cook to an earl when my father and she became acquainted," Miss Feathers whispered.

"A cook? Ah. That explains it," Lady Grace said, glancing at Lady Feathers's rotund form. "But dear Miss Caulfield." She turned back to Ravenna. "You must have spent the entire summer season last year at the sea."

"I did not."

"Then however did your skin acquire that delightful . . . glow?"

"Perhaps she is fond of walking, Gracie," Lady Penelope said. "Do you remember last season when you strolled every day for a week on Viscount Crowley's arm in the park? Even a bonnet and parasol did not entirely protect you from the sun."

"But surely strolling on a viscount's arm has not been Miss Caulfield's trouble, Pen," Lady Grace demurred. "Has it, Miss Caulfield?"

"Oh, I suppose you're right, Grace," her sister said. "But perhaps she is an avid rider. Sometimes that can give a girl a dreadful tan. Do you ride, Miss Caulfield?"

A footman appeared beside Ravenna with a silver tray of glasses filled with sparkling white wine. She didn't usually drink wine. *She must get out of this place.* With all her might she mentally willed the sun to shine and the snow to melt and reached for a glass.

"Allow me." The voice from the shadows the night before, deep and wonderfully autumnal and decidedly not-a-stable-hand's voice, sounded at her shoulder. With his scarred hand he removed Miss Feathers's half-empty glass from her fingers and replaced it with a fresh glass, then offered another to Ravenna. She was obliged to accept it, no matter that he had not looked at her, though he must recognize her.

"Good evening, my lord," Lady Penelope said upon a curtsy. Lady Grace and Miss Feathers followed suit. All three of them stared at him as though he were a god. Ravenna stood immobile. She would curtsy to a man that had attacked her in the dark when Sir Beverley's pet pig flew.

"Miss Feathers, as you are my sole acquaintance among this lovely quartet," he said with a smile that said he was thoroughly aware he was making every female in the room breathless, "would you be so kind as to make introductions?"

Miss Feathers obliged. The twins curtsied again, deeper this time. Lord Vitor Courtenay, second son of the Marquess of Airedale, bowed.

"What happened to your lip?" Ravenna said to him. "It looks sore."

Miss Feathers's fingers darted to her mouth.

"Thank you for your kind concern, Miss Caulfield." His eyes were very dark blue and still rimmed with the longest lashes Ravenna had ever seen on a man. Beauty and virility and confidence and sheer privileged arrogance combined to remarkable effect. No wonder these silly girls stared. "It was bitten," he said.

"Oh, dear." Lady Penelope pouted sweetly. "That must have been alarming."

"Not terribly. I have been bitten by cats before." The corner of his mouth twitched. "This one," he said, turning his dark, laughing gaze upon Ravenna, "was otherwise charming."

"What about the bruise on your brow?" Ravenna said. "Did the cat do that too?"

"I fell off my horse," he said with a slow smile, his gaze dipping to her mouth. "I injured my leg in the moment too."

He was entirely unrepentant, and vastly handsome, one of those overindulged noblemen she'd heard plenty about from Petti, the sort who behaved in any irresponsible manner he wished yet was never obligated to answer for it. Just like the prince, she supposed.

"Oh, that is a shame," she said. "To be abused by both a cat and a horse in succession doesn't say much for your rapport with animals, does it? Perhaps you shouldn't have anything to do with them."

"Actually, it rather strengthens my resolve to pursue the opposite. What sort of a man is he who shrinks from challenges, after all?"

A shiver of panic mingled with the odd heat slipped through her. Something about his smile . . . How did his mouth look so familiar?

Because when he had been pressing her body into the straw, she had stared at that mouth.

She hadn't.

She had. In fear, of course.

Fear or not, his mouth was perfect, both at rest and grinning and marked with a purple wound. And he knew it.

"My lord," Lady Grace said sweetly. "You mustn't fault Miss Caulfield for misunderstanding the ways of gentlemen. Her father is a country vicar. It is not to be wondered at that he could know nothing of noble resolve." The very breath that issued from her lips condescended.

"Ah, but the church is the noblest of professions, my lady," Lord Vitor replied, and reached for two more glasses on the waiting footman's tray. He extended one to Lady Penelope. "Miss Caulfield, what admirable moral guidance you must have enjoyed in your impressionable youth—"

The footman pitched forward abruptly, the tray jerked, and the remaining glass of champagne splattered over Lady Grace.

She gasped. The footman grabbed the glass. Lord Vitor took the tilted tray from his grip and set it down. Ravenna stared, but not at Lady Grace. The dent in his cheek had deepened.

Fury lit Lady Grace's eyes upon the footman. "You—"

"I fear, my lady," Lord Vitor said, "that the fault is not this poor fellow's, but mine."

"*Mais*— monseigneur—" the footman sputtered.

"No, no, my good man. I won't have you taking the blame for it. This dratted injury to my leg caused it to spasm momentarily. I kicked you and I am terribly sorry to have made you trip." He turned to Lady Grace and bowed. "I am devastated, my lady. Can you ever forgive me?"

She opened her lips and after a moment's silence said, "Of course I shall, my lord."

Lady Whitebarrow appeared between Ravenna and Miss Feathers. "My dear Grace, whatever has happened?" she said coolly. "Come. They will hold dinner while you change. Do not fret. We will demand that his highness remove that footman from service immediately."

Lady Penelope set her hand atop her mother's. "That will not be necessary, Mama. Grace will be all right as soon as she changes her gown." Her gaze slid to Ravenna, and the blue of her pale eyes grew diamond hard. "No one is at fault."

Ravenna returned her stare. While innocent Ann Feathers would not understand what had just occurred, Lady Penelope most certainly did. It might have been the nobleman who enacted the insult, but Ravenna would pay for it.

This time, however, there was no bird, no chicks, nothing with which they could hurt her. There was only she, alone yet capable of defending herself even from an attacker in the dark. She could manage two spiteful girls well enough. She could even wrest justice from an arrogant lord too.

Chapter 4

The Knight

$\mathcal{V}$itor had already reached the base of the stairs to the upper quarters when he heard her footsteps, light and far too quick for a lady, coming after him. He lengthened his pace, and she hastened hers.

"Wait, would you!" she shouted up to him.

It could not be avoided. Hand on the rail, he paused on the uppermost step and turned, squelching a grimace from the pain in his leg. Like a dark, homespun fury, she ascended.

"Miss Caulfield," he could only think to say. As in the stable, then again in the drawing room, he felt the most insistent urge to grab her about the waist and kiss her. It was instinctual and animal and thoroughly ignoble and certainly a product of two years of enforced celibacy. It left him tongue-tied.

She came to a halt on the step beside him. "Well?" Cheeks flushed lightly pink and eyes sparkling like stars at midnight, she looked directly at him. There was no coquettishness about this girl, no maidenly reticence or superficial niceness, rather, all justified indignation that made her astoundingly pretty. "Well?" she repeated.

With some effort he unwound his tongue. "I am emboldened by your eloquence, Miss Caulfield, to suggest that you are perhaps as weary as I at the end of this long day—after a rather uncomfortable night, although perhaps not quite as uncomfortable for you as it was for me." He allowed himself the slightest smile. "I advise you to continue on to your quarters for a good sleep as I intend to do."

"Oh!" she said brightly. "Such a wit! I am transported." With a swift perusal of his coat, waistcoat, trousers, and boots—first down, then up—that rendered the tension in his abdomen into an aggressive pressure, she took the final step to the landing above. Her starlight eyes came to his level. *Not good.*

"You tackled me, then you kissed me," she said.

"And you hit me with a door and then a pitchfork and bit me. It seems we are both outrageously *outrés*."

"Perhaps," she conceded with a twist of soft, full lips the color of summer dusk over the Mediterranean. "But you actually deserved it."

"I don't know what came over me." Celibacy. Two long years of celibacy. And ripe lips. Dusky, tempting lips an inch beneath his. And a soft, curved body, also beneath him. Tonight her curves were concealed by yet another gown of plain fabric and serviceable shape, and yet still he could not look away. He didn't know what sins he had done to deserve this torment, but whatever it was he was willing to do a thousand novenas to escape speaking with her in private ever again.

She set her hands on her hips, emphasizing their decadent curve. Never mind her homespun gown and unkempt hair, she made his breaths short.

"You kissed me because you thought I was a servant, which is despicable."

"I kissed you because you were soft and shapely and at the time under me, which is in fact quite reasonable."

"I did not exactly put myself there."

"And I did not exactly plan on being attacked by a feral cat in the dark. It was a mistake. Good night, Miss Caulfield." He continued onto the landing and swiftly down the long, high gallery that his blood-grandfather had constructed to display the family's vast collection of medieval armor. To either side, his forebears had arranged suits of steel, some of plain, pounded metal, others elaborately painted and embossed.

"Is that all I am to have?" She followed him. "I suppose you consider an apology beneath you."

Rather, he was considering her beneath him, how good she'd felt there, and how he would like that again. He halted. "Madam, I offer my profoundest apology. It shan't happen again." As though his feet moved of their own will, he found himself stepping toward her. "Unless you wish it to."

She backed up. "Not in this life." But her eyes were wary.

Good. He did not wish to frighten her. But keeping her wary could work. And yet the most powerful need to be near her would not leave him. *Of course it wouldn't.* After two long years he wanted a woman. Among his brother's potential brides was not, however, the place to go searching for one.

"That must be to my advantage, then," he said.

She screwed up her brow. "Must it?"

"You wield an impressive pitchfork."

"I know how to use the tines too." A smile played about her lips, a reluctant smile that begged a man to set his lips to it and tease it into fullness.

Oh, *no*.

"I do not doubt it," he said, backing away. "And I will hold you to that should I decide I need assistance in hastening my end." Turning away from the temptress, he started along the corridor again. But . . . he had to know. He looked over his shoulder. "How did you know what *colhões* meant?"

"I guessed."

"You guessed?"

"I spend a lot of time with stable hands and farmers. Now, what about the other apology you owe me?"

Looking into her upturned face, he wished he had a list of sins for which he must apologize. Last night, if he'd had his wits about him, he might not have returned her attack. Instead he might have seduced slowly, carefully, and succeeded. He might have enticed her to him, tempting her to touch him voluntarily. Then, in the dark he might have allowed his hands to explore those hips and that waist, to smooth up to her breasts, round and young and the perfect size for a man's hands, to press her knees apart and—

No.

He shook his head. "I did nothing else to you." *Deeply regrettable.*

"Not *that*. What about Lady Grace in the drawing room?"

Ah. The champagne rescue. Cats like Whitebarrow's daughters needed to be served occasional doses of humility. It was good for their souls. "Don't thank me." He waved it off. "I did nothing."

"You made it worse."

"What?"

"They are furious with me for having witnessed Lady Grace's embarrassment."

"But they ceased insulting you, didn't they?"

A mulish frown marred her brow. "I can defend myself."

"You were clearly doing a spectacular job of it."

Ravenna stared into eyes the color of midnight and did not like it that laughter and warmth lurked there. This handsome, virile nobleman could know nothing of her daily struggle not to tell girls like Penelope and Grace exactly what she thought of them. Standing here with a sapphire nestled in his snowy, starched cravat and aristocratic blood stamped all over his face, he couldn't understand anything worthwhile. But nothing came to her tongue. The crease teasing at his left cheek muddled her head, just as his lips upon hers had.

"Mm hm," he murmured, his midnight eyes intent. "I thought so. Good night, Miss Caulfield. Pleasant dreams plotting your revenge." He bowed. His gait as he walked away was not entirely even. He favored his left leg, the leg she'd hit with the pitchfork.

Guilt and some confusion tangled in her belly. "I absolutely will not dream of you, even to plan revenge," she said to his back.

Over his shoulder he turned a smile upon her that sent her breath into her toes. For a moment, almost, his smile seemed regretful. "I was referring to your revenge upon Ladies Penelope and Grace, of course," he said.

An alien sensation swept into her face. She touched her cheek. It was hot. *Hot?*

At a slow pace he returned to her. His smile had vanished. He halted before her and bowed again, this time soberly.

"Miss Caulfield, I beg your forgiveness." His voice was low and his gaze seemed to seek hers quite closely. "I intended you no harm, in truth. Still, I was unpardonably dishonorable to assail you and then tease you and then rescue you and then tease you yet again. Can you forgive me, or will those eyes like stars stare with accusation at me throughout the remaining weeks of this fete?"

Eyes like stars? It was a very good thing she didn't regularly consort with lords. Their rote flatteries were positively inane. "You are still teasing. And you ask my forgiveness in the same words you asked Lady Grace's."

"But in this instance I am most sincere."

"I am not in the habit of forgiving."

"Perhaps you might make an exception this time."

"I don't know why I should."

"Consider my injuries." The dent deepened anew. "Perhaps I am already sufficiently punished."

She tried not to smile. "I won't apologize for that."

"I never expected you to. Now may we put this unfortunate episode behind us and instead pretend to be two people who happened to become acquainted over spilled champagne?"

"Why should we pretend that?"

"It's either that or the pitchfork." His dark eyes glimmered.

"All right. But don't do it again."

"Kiss you in a stable or defend you from tabbies?"

The heat was back in her face. "Either."

"I believe I can promise that." He bowed again. "Good night, madam." He walked away.

Ravenna stared at his back but her cheeks still burned. She dragged her attention to the floor. Nothing there could make her feel peculiarly hot or unsteady as his shoulders and dark hair and the muscular lengths of his legs did.

Where her gaze alit, a blot of dark liquid pooled about the pointed toe of a suit of armor. She crouched and studied the leak. It was not black but dark crimson and congealed. Blood. Undeniably, blood. Far too much blood for a mouse that might have gotten trapped in the armored foot, or even a cat. She sniffed. The scent that came to her was ripe like animal death yet unfamiliar, an odd oniony morbidity. The hairs on the back of her neck prickled.

She stood and peered at the suit's visor. The steel looked impenetrable, with a tiny slit over the eyes that was lost in shadow now, one of those old helmets from which she could not imagine how a knight would be able to see. She reached up and pried open the visor.

She jolted back. The visor clanked shut. But she'd seen enough to make her hot skin turn clammy.

"A student of medieval arms, are you, Miss Caulfield?" Lord Vitor's voice echoed from the opposite end of the gallery. "And here I'd thought you preferred farm tools."

"There is a dead man inside this suit."

He moved to her quite swiftly, no evidence of the injury she'd dealt him now in his gait.

"I saw the blood on the floor from the foot," she said as he came beside her. He lifted the visor, then lowered it and looked down at her. His sapphire eyes were no longer warm and laughing.

"I pray you, go now, Miss Caulfield," he said.

"No."

"Go now."

"Why?"

"Go. A lady should not see this."

"I'm not a lady. And I have seen dead bodies before." That made her stomach tight. Beast's grave was the freshest. She had laid him atop his favorite old blanket and wrapped the wool about him, then she had watered the dirt with her tears.

"Go."

"I wonder who he is. That gold tooth wasn't come by cheaply, so he's certainly not a servant."

"He was a man of more vanity than means."

She looked away from the corpse to the nobleman beside her and her stomach did a little jerk. He was so alive. It struck her as odd that she would think this, that she would notice a man's aliveness. She had never done so before, even when confronted by death. But there was a depth of warm vitality to Lord Vitor Courtenay that shone in his eyes and the manner in which he stood with easy confidence.

"How do you know that?" she said.

"His name is Oliver Walsh. I have known him many years but I did not know he was to be a guest here."

"Oh. I'm sorry." She looked at the suit of armor again. "I suppose he became trapped in there and suffocated, though of course that wouldn't explain the blood. We must—"

Lord Vitor grasped her arm. "Miss Caulfield, will you retire now? I will send the housekeeper to see to your comfort."

She pulled free. "I don't need comforting. I told you—"

"Woman, do as I say," he growled.

"Ah, we've returned to the stable, have we?"

A muscle in his jaw flexed. "Miss Caulfield—"

"You don't think he suffocated. You think someone murdered him, then stuffed him in this suit."

He shook his head. "You are the most peculiar lady I have ever encountered."

"I have already told you, I am not a lady. Let me help."

"Help?"

"Help you remove this suit and examine him."

"No."

"I am quite good at this sort of thing."

"No."

"I have considerable experience caring for both animals and humans."

"Live humans, presumably?"

"Usually, but not exclusively. Three months ago I

solved the mysterious death of the butcher in the local village."

He blinked. Twice. "Did you?"

"It was lye poisoning. The meat he'd eaten was tainted with it."

He rubbed a hand over his jaw and shook his head. "Miss Caulfield, this is not—"

"I am sorry. I realize that Mr. Walsh was your friend, but—"

"He was not my friend."

"You don't know why he is here at the prince's party, but I can see that you harbor a suspicion. What is it?"

"You will not relent until you have had your will in this, will you?"

"No."

"Then go, if you will, and find the *majordome*. Bid him bring two sturdy footmen. Tell no one else."

Ravenna's belly tingled. "You will not disappear with him while I am gone and then pretend you don't know what I'm talking about when I ask you about it later?"

His handsome brow screwed up. "Why would I do such a thing?"

"You have a secretive air about you."

"I am nothing but what you see, Miss Caulfield."

She did not believe him. The quiet distance in his eyes now told a different story.

"I will go find him," she said, and, the tingling in her belly alive, she went.

THEY HAD DIVESTED Mr. Walsh of armor in the gallery while footmen blocked either end of the passage. Now the clock atop the mantel of the chateau's least used parlor chimed two as Lord Vitor dismissed the butler and footmen, and closed the door. The servants had provided lamps. Ravenna watched him place them around the body stretched out on the table.

"Aren't you a guest at this party?"

Lord Vitor untied Mr. Walsh's cravat. "Just as you."

"Not really. You are a member of this society while I am here accidentally."

"Accidentally?"

"Until recently my sister was a governess. Now, however, she is a duchess and she intends for me to wed a prince. Sir Beverley and Mr. Pettigrew know everybody in Europe and England, and they thought it would be great fun to throw me before one and see what happened."

He looked up briefly beneath the fall of dark hair over his eyes, then returned his attention to the corpse.

"If you are a guest," she said when he did not speak, "why did the butler do everything you asked?"

"I am well known to the royal family's servants. I have visited Chevriot before."

"Why doesn't the prince travel with a physician?"

"He did. When we disembarked in Bordeaux, he put his physician and two most trusted counselors in a carriage and sent them to Nantes for a holiday."

She laughed. "Why?"

"I suspect it was because his father insisted upon them attending him here."

"They are at loggerheads over the prince's dissipated lifestyle?"

"Occasionally." He reached into the breast of his coat and drew forth a flat metal object. She watched as he opened it into a blade and, with quick efficiency, cut the coat from Mr. Walsh's body. Then he removed the dead man's boots.

Clearly a blade had done the grisly deed. Blood stained the shirt at his waist and the length of his breeches to his feet, heavily concentrated in the groin area.

Lord Vitor tugged the bloodied shirt from the trousers. "Do turn away now, Miss Caulfield."

"I have seen it before."

The crease appeared in his cheek. "Bulls and rams, perhaps?"

She could not lie, however curious she was to finally see a human man's instrument and ballocks. She had given medical treatment to most animals' male parts, and had assisted at plenty of geldings. But the people whose ailments she had begun treating in the past few years drew the line at allowing intimate care of human men. Mostly she saw women patients and only when Dr. Snow could not be summoned swiftly enough or when the ailment was minor—a simple wound or broken bone or fever. "Yes," she said. "But I am entirely comfortable with this." She gestured to the nether regions of the body. "For both of us to examine the wound will be more thorough."

"You might be comfortable with such an examination," he said, cutting her a slanted glance, "but I don't believe that I am prepared to witness your comfort with it."

"Coming from the man I encountered in the stable last night, I don't believe that for a moment."

It was not chagrin that crossed his face then, or amusement, but clear discomfort.

She turned to searching Mr. Walsh's clothing. Of the finest quality, it suited his young, reasonably fine figure. A high brow and good nose completed the portrait of knightly dash. Ravenna's own nose had long since gone numb, and her toes and fingers too. But Lord Vitor had bid the footmen to carry the dead man to this unheated chamber to preserve the state of the body for as long as possible.

There was little of interest to study among the dead man's outer garments, nothing at least to suggest that Mr. Walsh's gold tooth represented a general state of wealth. His possessions included a snuffbox from which the insignia had rubbed off from wear, a threadbare kerchief, an aged knife scabbard, and a clip for holding bills containing a single pound note.

"If the murderer had intended to rob him," she said, "he might have taken the tooth. It's the most valuable thing about him."

"Perhaps his traveling bags will prove otherwise."

She studied the empty scabbard. "The blade meant for this is at least six inches long. Long enough to do great damage."

Her companion did not respond.

Mr. Walsh's waistcoat pocket offered up a piece of paper. Ravenna unfolded it, then paused.

"May I turn around now?"

"Yes."

Mr. Walsh's breeches were rolled into a ball on the table beside the body, the groin now covered with the bloodied shirt. His legs stretched pale and hairy to his bared feet.

"Shall I read it aloud?" she said.

Lord Vitor extended his hand. She gave it over and watched him read, trying not to think about how the hand holding the paper had been on her face. She could not recall the last time a man had touched her, except Petti, of course, whose displays of affection tended toward fond pats. On her sister's wedding day Ravenna had bussed the duke on his cheek and felt his scar against her lips, and she did the same with Papa when she occasionally saw him.

"What does it say?"

He passed it to her.

"*Come to my chamber at ten o'clock*," she read aloud. "No signature. I suppose murderers don't like to sign their names."

"Not typically," he agreed.

"Really? Do you know much about murderers?"

He wiped his hands on a rag and drew a bed linen over Mr. Walsh's body, covering the face set in its grimace of horror. "I know that there is a murderer nearby now."

"The blood caught in the clothing is wet on the inside but drying on the edges. The blood on the floor was barely dry when I discovered him, and his body was not yet the temperature of the air. I believe he died within an hour of the time we discovered him, which was at twenty minutes past eleven or thereabouts. With the snow, no one from too great a distance could have done it. I wonder if he went to his ten o'clock assignation. Are you convinced it is murder?"

"I am fairly certain," he replied grimly. "Most men do not choose to emasculate themselves."

She could not contain her surprise.

He nodded.

She gathered her composure. "Done in the midst of a snowstorm without ease of escape . . . Stabbing in the groin . . ." Her pulse jiggled. "It was a crime of passion."

"Perhaps. Though the difficulty and thoroughness of the procedure suggest he might have been dead before it was performed."

"I will not ask how you can make that statement with such assurance," she murmured. "I guess it is logical, unless there were multiple killers and someone held him down."

"Multiple killers are unlikely in crimes of passion," he said. "And something else about this wound gives me pause."

"The great quantity of blood."

He looked quite carefully at her. "Yes."

"Castration, even the removal of the male member, does not cause such a loss of blood."

"I should imagine so," he said. "The killer might have intentionally thrust the weapon deeper."

"Through the iliac artery, undoubtedly. Then our question becomes how might he have subdued Mr. Walsh in order to do such a thing? Poison? Or suffocation, as I first thought?" She moved toward him at the head of the table, bent toward the waxy face of the dead man and sniffed. "His tongue is not distended nor his face blue, as the curate's wife's was when she choked on a piece of dried fruit in her pudding last Christmas and expired within moments."

He cast her a curious glance. "Pudding?"

"I don't care for it myself, which is clearly to my benefit. Also, I don't recognize a putrid odor in his mouth."

"Nor do I." He nodded. "Now, Miss Caulfield, I hope your curiosity on this matter is satisfied."

"On the contrary. It has only just peaked."

"I was afraid of that." He moved toward the door. "Allow me to escort you to your quarters."

She went to him. He was nearly a head taller than she and certainly the most handsome man she had ever stood so close to, with his shirt of close-woven linen and waistcoat of brocaded silk. The whisker shadow of the night before that had scratched her chin had gone; his cheeks were smooth and high-boned, his jaw firm. "You seem remarkably comfortable with all of this."

"I was at war, Miss Caulfield. There is little that can discomfit me now."

But that was not the entire truth. He was not at ease as he seemed to study her features now.

"As you can see, I have knowledge that can help you find the murderer," she said.

"What suggested to you that I have any intention of pursuing such a course?"

"Of course you have, or you would not have brought

him here and bribed the servants to keep it a secret from everybody else."

"I did not bribe them."

"You must have. I would have. After you tell the prince, I suppose he will summon the local law to investigate. When it arrives, let me help."

"I cannot in good conscience allow that."

"Then allow it in bad conscience."

"Miss Caulfield—"

"You must allow me to help."

"And yet I will not, despite my wish to please you."

"You don't wish to please me. You wish to thwart me."

"You are correct. In this at least." His gaze slipped to her shoulder, then her arms she was hugging to her waist, passing over her breasts as though they were not there. "Your lips are blue. You must retire to the warmth of your bedchamber. I will instruct Monsieur Brazil to send up a maid to build your fire again."

"Aren't you concerned that the murderer might realize we have discovered the body and will know that I know about it, and will come after me?"

That muscle twitched in his jaw again, but she did not know if humor or pique inspired it. "Yes."

"If you keep me close, he won't be able to get to me easily."

"Interesting choice of words from the woman who vowed not two hours ago that she would not in this life come close to me again."

"To solve the mystery of the murderer," she said, her tongue abruptly dry, "of course."

"Ah." A smile caught at the corner of his mouth, the dent peeking out. "Of course."

"What do you know of Mr. Walsh?" she asked. "In truth?"

"At one time he served as secretary to a man of considerable status and wealth. After that he fought in Spain against Napoleon's army. He was approximately five-and-thirty. And he was fond of dice."

"Based upon that you are suspicious about his presence here at the prince's party?"

"I may have other reasons."

"I suppose a man like him has no more right to be in a prince's castle than I do. But no matter. I have plenty to recommend me to this investigation that the local police will appreciate."

"An expertise in deaths involving medieval armor, perhaps?"

"A female body."

That stalled him. Again his gaze dropped but this time it more than grazed over her breasts; it lingered. "I will admit I am not seeing how that makes you an expert investigator to murder." He lifted his eyes to hers. They were decidedly dark and not entirely focused. The night before, his eyes had looked like this when his body atop hers had become aroused.

"I can speak to the women at this party in a manner in which I suspect you cannot. In regular conversation that seems like gossip I can encourage them to reveal information that could be valuable to discovering why this man was murdered and stuffed into a suit of armor."

The butler of Chevriot appeared in the doorway. She moved toward him.

"Monsieur Brazil, do you have a wife or a grown daughter?"

"A daughter, mademoiselle."

"What is her name?"

"Clarice, mademoiselle."

"If I were to speak to Clarice concerning a private matter, would she reveal more information to me than she would to a man?"

"Eh, mademoiselle, I cannot—"

"Of course she would." She turned to Lord Vitor. "What's more, I can at this moment subtract nearly two dozen people from the list of suspects."

"Can you?"

"You don't believe me. Monsieur Brazil, where were the household and guests' servants before, during, and immediately after dinner?"

"Excepting the cook, kitchen maids, and the footmen serving dinner, they were in the servants' hall taking dinner and reviewing procedures in the chateau."

Lord Vitor turned his attention upon the butler. "Could you provide an accurate accounting of which individuals left the servants' hall at any moment during those hours?"

"*Oui*, monseigneur."

"Do so now, written, as well as a list of the servants who remained in the servants' hall the entire time, with the names of the guests beside their servants' names. Bring it to me as soon as you have finished it."

"*Oui*, monseigneur." The butler snapped a bow and hurried away, the light from his candle sparkling on the silver piping of his smart coat as it bobbed around the corner.

"How did you know to ask him that?" Lord Vitor said.

"For six years I have been a servant in a grand house whose master enjoys entertaining."

"And now you are a lady in a castle seeking a princely groom."

She was not, no matter what her sister wished. "I will investigate this murder whether you or the local police wish me to or not."

There was a stillness about his contemplation of her that at once made her breathe more deeply and unnerved her.

"You have me against the wall, it seems," he finally said.

"I do."

"The moment I have cause for concern over your safety, I will remove you to the village."

"You will do no such thing. You haven't the right. I may not actually be a lady, but I am a guest of the prince—"

"Who will do as I advise." He seemed entirely confident of this.

Suspicion prickled at Ravenna. "Who is to say you are not the murderer, and now that you know I have useful information you won't dispatch me too?"

"None but me."

She glanced into the darkness where the butler had disappeared, then back at the tall, dark man who had subdued her quite effectively in a stable the previous night. "This is the part where you pull out the blood-stained dagger, isn't it?"

"Why wouldn't I have done it earlier, before Monsieur Brazil knew of your involvement?"

"No doubt you only thought of it at this moment."

"It seems I am carelessly shortsighted."

"It does."

"Miss Caulfield?"

"You are not the murderer?"

"Go to bed." He grasped her fingers and tucked them around the lamp handle. For a moment he lingered, his large, strong hand encompassing hers, and she thought that no man who murdered another could possibly have such a marvelously warm, gentle touch. Then he released her. "The prince will call the party together after breakfast. If you truly intend to assist in this—"

"I do."

"You must have your wits about you."

"I always have my wits about me."

"I think I am coming to see that."

"You haven't dispatched me because you know you need my help."

"Do I?" He took a half step closer. "Or perhaps I have not yet dispatched you because, as depraved as I am, when I look at your lips I can feel your body beneath mine in the straw. If I were to do away with you now, that scenario could never be repeated."

Her breaths were no longer deep but tight and quick. "Dream well tonight, sir. It is all you are going to get from me again."

He smiled.

She ducked around him and escaped.

Chapter 5

The Suspects

Snow fell again, casting the drawing room in a pale white light broken by spots of gold from lamps and the hearths on either side of the chamber. Prince Sebastiao's guests sat in anxious little clusters about gilded tables. Above them, paintings of long-dead kings and queens wearing enormous ruffed collars and wigs glittered in gold frames. The prince stood at the doorway surveying his guests, Lord Vitor at his side.

"Why do ye think he's called us all together like this?" Lady Iona leaned into Ravenna's shoulder. "Do ye suppose he's already chosen a bride?"

"I don't think he could have chosen her so soon." This awkward gathering had nothing to do with brides.

"I wish he'd choose brides for his friends. Better yet, why dinna we? I'll let ye choose whichever ye wish— Lord Case or Lord Vitor—an' I'll have the thither. Is it a deal?"

Lord Whitebarrow and his pinch-nosed wife entered the drawing room. Lady Iona hummed low in her throat. "Nou, there's a laird I wouldna mind tossin' dice for," she whispered. "For all that he's five-an'-forty, he's a fine man. I do like guinea hair. 'Tis a shame the Ice Shrew's already got him. She probably won him over wi' that pretty face afore she revealed her heart o' stone."

Ladies Penelope and Grace, both cut in Lady White-barrow's cool image, followed their parents into the drawing room. Penelope paused beside Lord Vitor and the prince to modestly bat her golden lashes.

"I'd like to pinch that one," Lady Iona whispered. "The one wi' the simper she leart from her mither."

Ravenna laughed. Lord Vitor's attention turned to her and something hot and unwelcome wiggled through her belly.

The footmen closed the doors.

"I am devastated to dampen spirits so early in the festivities," Prince Sebastiao said upon a slur that might have been affected lisp or overindulgence. At eleven o'clock in the morning, Ravenna hoped it was affectation. But he had the most wonderful accent when he spoke in English, soft over some words and uncomfortably broken over others. "Yet I fear I must announce a terrible tragedy: a death in the house."

The room fell quiet. A few murmurs of displeasure sounded and guests cast covert glances around the place.

"Who was it, your highness?" Mr. Martin Anders finally asked, a dramatic gleam in his single visible eye; a curtain of dark hair entirely concealed the other.

"An Englishman by the name of Oliver Walsh. The trouble is," the prince continued with a flip of a hand cuffed in military gold cording, "it seems he's been murdered."

Lady Margaret gasped and the jewels hanging from

her ears, wrists, and neck jangled. Mademoiselle Arielle Dijon's slender hands covered her mouth. Dressed
all in purple gown and cape, an ancient Italian bishop
who had arrived just before the snow the previous day,
crossed himself with weary holiness. His taking little
niece, Miss Juliana Abraccia, followed suit, bowing her
dark head piously and folding her gloved hands. Miss
Ann Feathers's round cheeks paled to Shetland white.
Lady Iona's bright eyes stared at the prince rather
blankly.

"Given the snow that has entrapped us, and the
fellow not a full day cold," the prince said with remarkably theatrical panache, "we have concluded that
the murderer must be one of us."

"Good God!"

"*Mater Dei.*"

"Your highness!"

"There's nothing to be done for it, I'm afraid," the
prince said with a sorry shake of his head. "The local
police will arrive shortly to interrogate each of you."

"Your highness." The Earl of Whitebarrow stepped
forward, thrusting out his square jaw. "This is an
insult."

"To us all," Lord Case agreed, a gleam lighting his
eyes as he looked at his brother.

"I assume you will not question the noble families
present," Lord Whitebarrow said.

"A servant must have done it, of course," Lady Whitebarrow said, turning up her nose pointedly toward
Lady Margaret and Sir Henry with their mousy daughter. "The servile class is never to be entirely trusted."

"My Merton would not have done it," Lord Prunesly
commented abstractly, squinting through his spectacles. "Been with me for years."

"Most of your servants were together in the servants' hall when the murder occurred," Lord Vitor

said. "As such they are largely accounted for and are now en route to the village. They will lodge there until the identity of the murderer is discovered."

"Our servants have gone?" Lady Penelope's golden lashes popped wide. "Mama, you cannot allow this."

"Such a pity," Duchess McCall said, "for a lass to be beholden to servants for her beauty." She cast a proud glance at her daughter. "If ye like, child, Iona can try to help ye."

"Will she iron my gowns and clean my shoes as well?" the crystal-eyed blonde shot smoothly back.

"Penelope, hush," Lady Whitebarrow hissed. She turned to the duchess. "Duchess, living in London as she always has, my daughter is unaccustomed to the common ways I am sure your household practices so far in the north. We shall make do nonetheless. Thank you."

Miss Cecilia Anders chuckled. Lady Penelope cast her an icy glare.

"The servants unaccounted for during the entire time the others were together," Lord Vitor said, "include the kitchen maid, the cook, three footmen, and Lady Iona's personal servant. They will remain in the castle until the mystery of Mr. Walsh's death is solved. His highness's guards will also remain."

Lord Whitebarrow scowled. "This is an outrage."

"Ach," the duchess said. "If ye didna do it, whit's got ye worried?"

"I beg your pardon?"

The duchess's eyes twinkled with the same devilish light in her daughter's. "Mebbe 'tis no' my pardon ye should be beggin', but the dead man's."

"Well, I—"

"Now, now," Prince Sebastiao said with an expansive swing of one arm. "Who knows but an intruder did not arrive while we were all drinking champagne and stumbled upon the man by accident?"

"In the name of Zeus, who was this unfortunate fellow Walsh?" Sir Henry said. Beside him, his timid daughter ducked her head.

"A distant friend of the family," the prince replied with a swift glance at Lord Case, then tipped his drink to his lips. "Why, Sir Henry? Did you know him? Perhaps well enough to wish him dead?"

Sir Henry's heavy brow cut down. "Now, see here, your high—"

"Papa," Ann Feathers whispered. "Please."

Her mother rose to her feet with a creaking of stays. "Well, I've never heard of such alarming goings-on. But if your highness requires an interview from us all, I'll be the first to agree to it. I think we all should, so the murderer can be found lickety-quick and we can all sleep at night." Lady Margaret affected a shuddering shiver of dread that rattled her jewels anew.

"I cannot imagine how she sleeps at all after eating both Sir Henry's and her own *pastillage* at dinner," Penelope whispered to her sister.

The spots of red on Ann Feathers's round cheeks bloomed hotter.

"That won't do, Margaret," Sir Henry protested. "I cannot allow a man to interrogate you, even a gentleman."

"You will allow it, monsieur," a small man said from the doorway. His ginger moustaches jittered as he perused the assembly. "If you do not, his highness will have you and your family incarcerated in your rooms until we have discovered the murderer's identity. *Sommes-nous bien d'accord?*"

Lord Whitebarrow's face reddened. "Upon my word, who are you?"

"Gaston Sepic," he said with a tight bow. "*Maire de* Chevriot these six years. The closest gendarmerie quarters on the other side of the mountain. The snow will not allow passage. So, in the absence of the police detectives, I will supervise *cette enquête*. This is Monsieur Paul, my deputy." He gestured behind him. Loose-cheeked and red-eyed, the man standing there wore a long canvas coat and worn boots like he had donned them in January and forgotten about them. "He will assist me," Monsieur Sepic said.

Monsieur Paul tugged off his cap, revealing lank hair and a loutish look about the eyes.

"I will not allow it," Lord Whitebarrow stated.

"Come now, my lord." Prince Sebastiao offered the earl a cajoling smile. "Let us follow the mayor's wishes and have this all finished as swiftly as we may and get on with our entertainments. Yes?"

Finally, Lord Whitebarrow nodded reluctantly.

"*Alors*," said the mayor. "I will call the first suspects to interview *cet après-midi*." He snapped about to face the prince and Lord Vitor, turning a shoulder to the room full of lords and ladies.

Conversation rose in murmurs among the guests. Ravenna moved toward Lord Vitor and the mayor. "Monsieur Sepic," he was saying as she approached, "the prince's guards have been instructed to stand watch at all points of exit and entry into the castle and village."

The mayor leaned in to speak quietly, casting his deputy a narrow glance. "Unfortunately, monseigneur, I am hampered by the possession of this single deputy. He is, I regret, *incompétent* for such a weighty task, but we must bear with such limitations." He shook his head. "*Mais bon*, as soon as I possess the facts, I will instruct him to return to the village and interrogate the servants you have sent there." He studied Lord Vitor. "That was wisely done, monseigneur. But now you must leave this investigation to the professionals." He turned to the butler nearby. "*A présent*, Monsieur

Brazil, take me to the body. I will begin my work at once." The butler led him and the deputy away.

"Wretched business," Prince Sebastiao shook his head as though in sorrow. Then his face brightened and he clapped his hands. "Now, who's for cards?"

Several guests followed the prince from the room. Lord Case came forward.

"Saving that boy's skin again, are you, brother?" Lord Case drawled, glancing at Prince Sebastiao's departure. He turned to peruse Ravenna with appreciation, then he bowed to her. "Or perhaps your confidential conversation with Monsieur le Maire just now was intended merely to impress the lady here?"

"That's unlikely," she said. "The other night he tried to kiss me and I attacked him with a pitchfork."

The earl's mouth curled into a grin. "Well done, Miss Caulfield. Shall I call him out on your behalf? It's not the thing, really, shooting one's brother in the heart. But for a lady's sake I could not do otherwise."

"Thank you. I can defend myself. And I intend to help Monsieur Sepic in his investigation."

"Yet he wishes no help," Lord Vitor said, turning his unsettlingly warm, dark eyes upon her. "How do you hope to surmount that obstacle?"

"However you do, I suppose."

He offered her a slight smile.

"What do you imagine Walsh was doing here at Chevriot, brother?" Lord Case said. "At precisely the time we are?"

"I've no idea. Perhaps you do?"

"I don't." The earl's eyes were narrow upon his brother, then they shifted to the remaining guests in the room. "Interesting . . . suspects. Does the prince have any idea?"

"No more than you or I."

A silent communication passed between them.

Ravenna watched it like a tennis game, the surprising anger in Lord Case's eyes and the steady acceptance of it in his brother's.

"Did Sebastiao or his father invite Walsh to this party?" Lord Case finally said.

"He tells me that they did not."

"Ah." A moment's pause. "Did you, Vitor?"

"Why, do you imagine, would I have, Wesley?"

A cry of distress sounded at the doorway. Mademoiselle Dijon stood there, her lovely eyes wide, a pale hand covering her mouth. "*Ma petite* Marie is gone!" she exclaimed through her fingers. "My dog has been stolen!"

MONSIEUR SEPIC AND his deputy studied Mr. Walsh's body and luggage, and declared that nothing had been taken. How they could determine that, Ravenna hadn't any idea. But she had little faith in the mayor's intelligence and less in his deputy's. This mystery needed a wiser head.

She spent the afternoon and evening consoling Arielle Dijon about the loss of her dog and drinking cup after cup of tea while encouraging gossip among the ladies. When evening fell, as Monsieur Sepic enjoyed an aperitif with the gentlemen, Monsieur Paul began interviewing the ladies. Ravenna responded to his monosyllabic questions honestly. Within a quarter hour he dismissed her and reached for a decanter of wine on the table.

The following morning after lighting the fire in her own bedchamber, washing with frigid water, and walking the pugs through the yard, Ravenna returned to the parlor in which the ladies had gathered the previous day. She found only the butler, clearing away teacups and saucers. In his pristine coat and pantaloons and at his age, he looked peculiar performing the task. But with only the cook, scullery maid, and a few footmen still in the castle, and they with their hands full preparing and serving meals, lighting fires, and seeing to all the personal demands of the guests, Monsieur Brazil had to do the work of two dozen servants.

"Lord Vitor has gone, mademoiselle," he said, as though he knew her intent.

Her heart did a little uneven thump. "Gone?"

"*Oui*, mademoiselle."

Ravenna looked out the window at the forecourt below, a stretch of pristine white. Throughout the night, snow had again fallen upon towers and battlements and the hills and treetops around the chateau. Now the sun shone in a brilliant sky. "But where to?"

"He did not indicate, mademoiselle," the butler said stiffly.

"Did he go on horseback?"

"*Non*, mademoiselle."

She went down to the foyer, where she tugged on her cloak, threw the hood around her ears, and went out into the forecourt. Her eyes teared at the bright sparkle. A single set of footprints in the snow made their way toward the main gate. Turning to look at the castle, she caught movement at an upper window, a drapery falling back into place.

A guard stood at one side of the open portcullis. "Good morning," she greeted him. The prince had given orders that no one was to leave the castle grounds. The guard bowed but said nothing. She hurried through the gate.

In the fresh snow, the single track of footprints turned not down to the village but to the right from the gate toward the castle's north flank, following the wend of the river below. Trudging through snow above her ankles, Ravenna followed the footprints along the external lower wall. To one side a line of trees sloped to the river. To her left a cluster of aged cedars bordered a cleared, ascending hill. She had walked this road two days ago before the snowfall. Now unrecognizable beneath the covering of white, it ran above and roughly along the river to a saltworks three-quarters of a mile distant. Hundreds of years ago the masters of this mountain had built the fortress to protect the valuable industry.

The going proved slow as she followed the footprints; her skin grew damp and her breaths hard. She paused on the hill and turned to look back. Rising from the silver river, the castle's towering walls grandly outstripped pines and cypress. Layered with white on roofs and battlements and dark like the river below, it seemed almost at home in this graceful wilderness, a sleeping giant set into the wintry landscape.

At the edge of the bushes across the road, a rabbit, light of flesh from the long winter, poked its nose from the foliage and sniffed the sunshine. Ravenna smiled.

An arm snaked around her waist and a hand clamped over her mouth. She struggled, tried to scream, tears leaping to her eyes again.

"Foolish woman," a hard voice rasped at her ear. But through her own scent of fear she recognized his—clean, masculine, leather. She sagged in his hold.

Lord Vitor released her and with his hands on her shoulders turned her to face him. The sunlight slanted off cheekbones cut as though with a sculptor's blade. "That is how you could come to be the murderer's second victim. Do you have a death wish?"

"I have a clue." She pulled free and stumbled backward. "But if you grab me again without my permission I will do to you what the murderer did to Mr. Walsh."

His midnight eyes glimmered. "Without your permission?"

"Ever."

"A clue?"

"To the murder." Her face felt atrociously hot, her feet frigid. All around, the snow quieted the world, leaving only the twitter of winter birds and her quick breathing. "I know how to do it, you know."

The corner of his perfect mouth tilted upward. "Cattle and sheep?"

"Well, I haven't done it myself. But I have assisted in the procedure a number of times."

"My anxiety on the matter is relieved on account of your professional expertise. Could we now address the clue?"

"You don't object to me attempting to solve this crime?"

"If I did, would it make a difference?"

"Probably not. The murderer was not a man."

"How do you know this?" The sky framed his handsome face in azure. Beyond him, the line of cypresses rose up dark and thick.

"Why are you out here? Hiding behind trees so you can jump out at unsuspecting women?"

"I was at the village observing Monsieur Paul interrogate the servants. The mayor under-exaggerated his deputy's incompetence."

"He is less than helpful?"

"He's a drunken simpleton. Also, the mayor's nephew." His grin reappeared. "Alas, mountain communities."

"You are now here. On the north side of the castle. The village is to the south."

"I must have gotten lost."

She pursed her lips. "You are withholding information from me. This is clear. But Monsieur Sepic is a numbskull. If we hope to discover the identity of the murderer, it will be best if we work in concert. Agreed?"

He seemed to consider this, or rather *her*, then said, "What have you learned?"

She pulled off her gloves and flapped her cloak open to dig in her skirt pocket. She felt watched. It had never before bothered her to be watched by a man; no man ever did unless she worked on his animals. Now her fingers slipped on the packet.

Lord Vitor caught her hand. His were large, without gloves but warm. She jerked back.

"I spoke with Mademoiselle Dijon, and with Lady Margaret and her daughter, Ann," she said too quickly, "then the duchess and Lady Iona. I learned nothing useful, unfortunately. Gossip may not suffice to draw them out."

"You are honest to admit it."

"I haven't any pride to be wounded by admitting my mistakes."

He stepped close to her. "That is refreshing to hear. Pride is one of my worst faults."

"You are admitting to a fault? I am astonished."

"I'm hoping to turn up your good side."

She looked up from the packet in her hands, and her tongue stuck to the roof of her mouth. She loosed it with effort. "Don't look at me like that."

"Like what?"

"Like you intend to kiss me again."

"I am not looking at you like that."

"Are you intending it?"

"Since you have made very clear the consequences of doing so without your permission—"

"Ever."

"—it would not be in my interests, would it?"

"I have never been swayed by a pretty face."

A single dark brow rose. He wore no hat and the sunlight shone in his eyes, lighting them to sapphire like the jewel in his neck cloth the night before. "Pretty?"

"Rather, a handsome face. Beast was the ugliest pup in the litter."

"Who is Beast, I wonder."

"The best—" Her throat closed. "Just don't."

The color was high on his cheekbones and his eyes were abruptly serious, like in the drawing room when he and his brother had spoken. "I do wish to kiss you, Miss Caulfield, however unwise that would certainly be."

Her pulse beat so hard she could nearly hear it. "But you will not."

"Even if I intended to, I have a fondness for the wholeness of my person."

"Are you still limping today?"

"I never limp."

"You did last night."

He held her gaze. "The clue?"

"After I spoke with the ladies, I asked Monsieur Brazil what the mayor thought of Mr. Walsh's wound and clothing. He said Monsieur Sepic seemed uninterested in them. So I studied the clothing again."

"Did you?"

"Don't patronize me."

"I am not patronizing you. I am pondering your keenly curious mind and the pleasure it affords me." The crease had appeared in his cheek again. She ignored it. Still, it proved difficult not to look at his mouth, remarkably well shaped, firm, and nicely contoured, despite the wound. And it had kissed her, which made it unique among men's mouths in that manner, of course.

"I found this caught in a coat button." With cold fingers she withdrew from the paper packet a single strand of hair.

Lord Vitor studied it for a moment on her palm. "Martin Anders's hair is similar."

"Correct. That along with his bruised eye, which he has not apparently explained or justified to anyone, could make him our main suspect."

"My lip and brow are bruised and I have not justified them to anyone. Might that indicate that I am also the killer?"

"You justified them to Ladies Penelope and Grace and Miss Feathers."

"I did, didn't I?"

"The field is narrowed to suspects with long hair."

His gaze came up to her face, then to her hair where the hood of her cloak had fallen back. She had never cared about her hair before, no matter how Arabella and Eleanor tried to teach her how to tame it and no matter how Petti teased. Now she became acutely aware of its tangled mess, damp from her walk through the snow. For an instant she wished she knew how to smooth and bind it like a lady—like fiery Iona McCall or lovely Arielle Dijon or any of the other beautiful girls at the chateau whose shoes and hems were not now soaked with snow and who, she had no doubt, this nobleman had never mistaken for a servant.

But she did not care about her hair. Or her gown. Or her shoes. She never had.

"My mind *is* keen and curious," she said, her jaw unaccountably tight.

"I have said I believe that to be so, haven't I?"

"Yet you think me a fool because I came out here unprotected."

"On the contrary. I know you are not a fool. I only suffered a moment of . . . *concern* over your safety. It rendered my reaction harsh. I beg your pardon. Again." The corner of his mouth ticked up.

She frowned. "Why did the guards at the forecourt allow me to leave the chateau?"

"I told them to allow it."

Ravenna feared she gaped now. He trusted her. He respected her mind. It even seemed that he liked her. She enjoyed the friendship of her elderly employers and of various farmers and grooms throughout the countryside around Shelton Grange. But she had never been friends with a young, handsome nobleman. The idea that she might become friends with such a man sent a twining tingle of pleasure from her throat right into her fingertips.

"You don't know that I did not kill him," she said. "Now you have proof that I might have."

"Proof that you yourself have produced."

"What if this is an attempt at diversion?"

He scanned her hair again, then her mouth for a lingering moment. His hand moved toward her face. Ravenna's blood seemed to all rush to her heart. *He meant to touch her now.* The tingling pleasure in her veins transformed into a surge of swift, hot dread. She pulled back.

"Ow!" She slapped a palm to her smarting scalp.

He brandished the plucked hair. "Let us compare."

"You did that on purpose."

"Did what?" He draped the single black strand over his broad palm as though laying a string of pearls upon a satin pillow.

"You made me think—" Her tongue stumbled. "Oh, bother." She lifted the hair she had found on Mr. Walsh's coat and laid it on his palm. Hers was inky compared to the other, which was brunette with a hint of chestnut.

"My fears are put to rest," he said, and returned both strands to her.

She studied his face. "You were not afraid."

"Not about that." He bent his head. "Guards or not, Miss Caulfield, do not leave the chateau unprotected."

"Rather, I should remain locked inside with the murderer who is also locked in?"

"I have assigned a guard to remain near you in the chateau."

She blinked. "You have? But not out here?"

"He should have followed you outside the walls. I will rectify that. Do you object?"

"My brother-in-law, Duke Lycombe, put a guard on my sister without telling her. She thought it was because he believed she was being unfaithful to him—"

"Which of course is not at issue here."

"—but it was actually because he was concerned for her safety. Would Lord Case serve as protection, if I left the castle with him?" she asked. "Or the prince?"

His brow creased. "The prince, yes."

"Not your brother?"

He looked over her shoulder toward the castle draped in winter's embrace.

A chill shivered along her spine. "In the drawing room yesterday the two of you were like rams pawing the earth. Do you truly suspect him?"

"There was no love lost between my brother and Oliver Walsh."

"What was their connection?"

"Walsh was my father's secretary for several years. My brother at one time intended to marry his sister."

His father's secretary? "At one time?"

"She perished before they were wed."

"Oh. That is tragic! From what did she perish?"

"A broken heart."

Chapter 6

The Quickening

*H*er wide eyes reflected the winter sun. Her lips were arrested in mid-parting, dusky pink and expressive. She had come out with only a cloak as protection from the frost; framed by the wildly black cluster of silken locks, her skin shone rosy from brow to collar. He could place his mouth over her pulse there and feel the life bursting from her as he caressed her. She swelled with it—with pleasure and vitality and an urgent vibrancy that robbed him of sense and made him admit aloud that he wished to kiss her again, despite his promise to himself not to come close to her.

And yet behind her eyes was sorrow. It had glittered forth for an instant when she spoke of the beast, and now again swiftly before she banked it.

"I don't believe in anyone dying of a broken heart." Her words came crisply into the chill air. "What made her ill?"

"A fever."

"Lord Case did not like Mr. Walsh?"

"No."

"You must know your brother better than anybody, and yet I cannot imagine him murdering and castrating a man," she said, a little crease between her brows. "He was kind and gently solicitous to Arielle Dijon about the abduction of her dog."

Another mystery. The animal was gone. A prized breeder, one of only a handful of Barbichons Lyonnaise bitches on the Continent and America, the French girl's pet was worth a fortune, the general had confirmed. It had been with Mademoiselle Dijon when they were all in the drawing room, but moments later it disappeared. The theft benefitted the search for Walsh's murderer: convinced that the dog had merely escaped into a crevice of the vast chateau, the guests had turned all efforts to finding it. Vitor had gone to the village as much to escape the pandemonium of the search as to avoid the woman standing before him now.

"Do you truly think someone stole it?" she asked.

"Perhaps."

Her brow remained knit. "Why are you here?"

"As a favor to Prince Raynaldo, to see Sebastiao suitably wed."

"No. Why are you *here*? Outside here now?"

"To study that." Through her cloak he grasped her arm and turned her toward the chateau. She stiffened but did not draw away. She was a small thing but strong, he already knew, and not easily frightened. He suspected that if threatened she would fight him—or anyone else—before she called for help. But he liked to hold her. He liked to feel her in his hands. "Do you see how that stair descends on the exterior wall behind the trees?"

"I think so. It's covered in snow, isn't it? I don't see its top."

"It begins in the northwest tower and continues around the corner to a platform rock on the bank of the river."

Disquiet settled upon her features. "The murderer might have escaped by boat?"

"It is possible. I have yet to study the platform, but at this distance I see little indication that anyone has used those stairs since it snowed."

"Desperation can make for daring acts. What are the chances that if we go down to the river we will find a person who, two nights ago, tried to leave by that stairway and slipped on the snow and fell to her death?"

"Little."

"Are you saying that because you believe it, or because you don't want me to accompany you to investigate it?"

"The latter."

She whirled about and, like a fawn leaping through snow, headed across the road toward the slope down to the river, her cloak billowing out behind. He followed until she came to the trees where a person might be concealed, then he moved beside her. The sunlight's glare upon the snow made searching the shadows difficult, and he remained close to her, the uncertain footing upon the slope justifying his grasp of her arm when she slipped. She darted him a glance and pulled free of his grasp. He continued close behind her.

Denis's words from the day before played in his mind like Matins chant: The devil liked to take female form to tempt a man. That was balderdash, of course. Vitor knew the truth of it. He wanted this woman because he could not have her, and because she was plainspoken and uniquely enchanting with her black hair tangling about her shoulders and her starlit eyes that retreated when she found him watching her. She made him hungry.

At the base of the castle walls the bank cut sharply into the river, the snow forming a heavy ledge at the edge of the water that reflected the sky like a mirror. Vitor had navigated this deceptively still, broad silver ribbon in the past. It could sweep a man away before he could utter a word of protest. She plowed a path away from its glittering surface directly to the base of the stair that climbed the side of the chateau like a scar to the turret in its uppermost room. Submerged to her knees, she attempted the steps. She tried thrice and three times slipped. The third landed her on her behind.

"Finished now?" he asked from a distance.

"For the time being." She brushed off her cloak and studied the risers. "No one could climb down once the snow began. Do you really believe someone tried to leave via this route?"

"I don't. I do believe that someone made the attempt."

"Why?"

"In the room at the top of the tower, the rug and floorboards near the door are soaked, and footprints lead from the chamber down the stairs. Also, a quantity of rust is scattered about the threshold, suggesting a door opened after long disuse. An attempt may have been made to depart through this door, then abandoned."

"Then why did you wish to come here to study the base of the stairs when the murderer never came down all the way?"

"To encourage my memory." He walked toward the platform from which in warmer seasons a boat could be launched. "To try to imagine what the murderer might have intended by descending."

She moved away, peering at the turret high above as she disappeared around the corner. "Perhaps it was not the murderer who opened that door in the tower room," she called back. "Perhaps it was someone else."

"I found blood on the door handle, and upon the floor a candlestick stained with it as well." Before him, half buried, was a door to a storage shed built into the castle wall. Within he would find a boat and oars. "You might consider searching the ladies' belongings for garments or linens stained unusually with blood."

"I will if I can manage it. It would be fairly easy to disguise such a stain as— *What? No!*"

The splash that followed her exclamation grabbed Vitor's chest and catapulted his legs along the wall to the chateau's corner. A flash of a dark body darted into the trees, but his eyes sought the woman in the river. Her cloak and skirts ballooned with trapped air but in moments they would tug her to the bottom. Not wasting breath to shout, she struggled toward the bank, but the current pulled her away faster than she could paddle.

He stripped off his coat and boots and dove.

Chapter 7

The Hero

 Water burning his skin with cold, Vitor reached her and grabbed her beneath the arms. His legs tangled in her skirts. He kicked them free and pulled her back against the current. She helped him, but her skin was already white.

It seemed an age of frigid pain before he reached the platform. Together they struggled against her sodden garments and dragged her entirely from the water. With shaking hands she fumbled at the fastening of her cloak. Struggling to his feet, he grabbed his coat, pulled forth his knife, and fell to his knees before her.

"Can't—" She plucked at the knot. "Get—" Her words were barely audible, her lips blue.

He pushed her hands aside and cut the cloak fastening, then turned her and at her back sliced a line up the fasteners of the heavy woolen gown and the linen undergarment below. The laces of her stays split beneath the sharp blade, and she struggled out of the garments.

He reached for his coat and she slid her arms into it stiffly as he pulled on his boots. She climbed to her feet in the slushy depression they'd made in the snow. Like a wraith, her black hair was matted about her face and neck and her eyes were sockets of ebony in the stark white oval of her face.

He took her up into his arms and climbed toward the road. As slight as she was icy, she tucked her face and hands against his chest and did not protest, which terrified him.

By the time he strode through the main gate, her body shook in violent tremors. But he felt her hard breaths and knew she was trying to withstand it. A guard followed. No one stirred in the great hall. Vitor carried her to the housekeeper's day chamber, small and easily heated.

"Have a fire laid immediately and bring tea," he commanded the guard. "Then alert Monsieur Brazil and Sir Beverley, but no one else. Be quick."

"*Sim, meu senhor.*" The man disappeared.

He lowered her to the chair before the hearth, drew his coat from her stiff limbs, and wrapped a blanket about her. She allowed it all in trembling silence. But when he tucked the wool around her feet, then took her hands between his to chafe, she tugged them away.

"Go," she whispered between clacking teeth. "Dry."

"You must remove the wet garment. Whom do you wish me to call to assist you?"

She shook her head. "Go."

"When the guard returns."

Damp lashes lifted over the starlit eyes bright with irritation. "*Go.*"

"Damn it—"

"*Meu senhor,*" the guard said, entering with a lamp in one hand and faggot of wood beneath his other arm.

"Monsieur Brazil sees to the tea himself." He moved to the hearth and knelt to make up the fire.

"Go." Her shrunken lips barely moved. "Or I'll tell everyone how you got that wound on your lip."

"I dare you to. And I will leave when Sir Beverley arrives."

She glared weakly, the fight gone out of her. When he took her hands again she did not pull them away.

"What did you see?" he said quietly.

"Nothing." A shiver wracked her. "You must—"

"If you continue to insist that I leave, I will remove that soaked chemise myself."

Her lips made a firm line.

The guard arrived with tea, and the fire warmed the tiny chamber. She sipped from a steaming cup as Sir Beverley and Mr. Pettigrew entered.

"Good God." Sir Beverley came forward, his face grim. "Brazil said she fell in the river."

"She was pushed."

"Dear girl, what a frightful business." Pettigrew sat beside her and patted her hand.

She turned her eyes to Vitor. "Go." Her teeth clicked against the porcelain. "Now."

He took up his sodden coat and went. Monsieur Brazil hovered in the corridor.

"Monseigneur, I have taken the liberty of preparing a bath for mademoiselle in her bedchamber."

"Excellent." His numb lips slurred over the word. His clothing clung. "Inform Sir Beverley." He crossed the great hall. The door to the forecourt—and beyond that, clues to her attacker—beckoned. But he would be of no help to her if he died of fever. He mounted the stairs. In his chamber he hung his clothes to dry, then walked the corridors to her bedchamber. There he stood before her door, nonplussed.

He had dragged her from a river and together they

had examined a dead man's body in the middle of the night. Yet without a servant to assist him now, he was at a loss. He knew nothing more about women's clothing than what he must to remove them. Also, he had every suspicion that if this particular woman learned he had entered her bedchamber even to acquire dry clothes for her, she would do him further bodily harm.

It took him all of three seconds to decide that he could accept that consequence. He reached for the door handle.

"Ah, my lord! There you are. I was looking for you." Sebastiao strolled toward him with exaggerated lethargy. "Why are you staring at that door? Thinking that if you stare long enough it will open by the power of your formidable will alone?"

"I had not considered it."

"Whose bedchamber are you not considering entering?" His half brother's brow waggled.

"Miss Caulfield's."

"Ah, the pretty little Gypsy."

Vitor turned fully to him. "Gypsy?"

"Duskier than a Saracen. If she weren't English she might be an Andalusian. What do you suppose my father had in mind to include her among this party of inestimable maidens?"

Vitor found his hand clenching. "Your good fortune, I suspect."

Sebastiao propped his chin in his palm and his lower lip protruded. "She has a quick tongue. I like that in a woman. But of course there is nothing to like in a woman of virtue *except* conversation." He grinned, then his eyes narrowed with a sly sort of defiance. "I had an Andalusian woman once, you know."

"Sebastiao . . ."

"She rode me like jockey for three days with barely a pause for wine. Seems what they say about the virtue of the women of the south is true." He cut a grin that only a young man who took pleasure in boasting of conquests would affect. "Their blood is especially hot, you know. Down there." He cocked a brow. "Do you think our little Gypsy's blood is hot too?"

Vitor drew in a slow, steadying breath. "Your highness."

Abruptly, Sebastiao's face crumpled. "Oh, don't 'your highness' me. I despise that." His shoulders slumped, the bravado draining away from him in a rush. "I am peevish, only. Whitebarrow stuck his nose in the air at me and I cannot get the odor of his superiority out of mine. I believe he actually thinks he would be doing me a favor to bestow one of his icy daughters upon me," he said glumly. "The mother treats me with deference, though. I imagine she wants grandchildren of royal blood, at whatever the cost." His head snapped up, his face stark now. "My tongue disobeys me, Vitor. You know I did not mean to imply that Miss Caulfield is anything but virtuous. I did, of course, but I did not mean it. You know." It was a question—rather, a plea. For years it had always been thus: outrageous misbehavior, bravado to justify the sin, then abject penitence and pleas for understanding. He was a boy of tender conscience in the skin of a spoiled prince, unstable at worst and too greatly indulged at best.

"You needn't prove yourself to me, Sebastiao."

"On the contrary! You are the one person to whom I must continually prove myself. And Father." Face averted, Sebastiao spoke to the closed door. "He admires you. He trusts you. And he tells me so at every occasion." With a heavy breath of decision he met Vitor's gaze. "You have no idea what a chore it is to try to live up to you."

"We both know that it is foolish of you to believe you must."

"See there? With an economy of words you prove

me the fool. As always." He swung away. "Your life of loyal labor is an example no man should be forced to emulate."

"Your father has never expected you to be anything but who you are."

"My father sent me into exile in this castle with you as my *domini canis* in a last vain hope that I will learn how to be a man through necessity. A wife will cure me of my incontinent ways? Tame my unruly spirit? Ha! If this is not comedy of the highest order, then I have never set foot upon an honest stage."

Vitor said nothing. Swinging so precipitously between elation and abjection, Sebastiao's humors had always controlled his tongue. But, unlike his fits over the past ten years, he was sober now. Suffering distorted his features.

"Ah, brother," Sebastiao cried when he remained silent, "you needn't even speak, for I know what you are thinking. The very breaths you draw put me to shame!"

"Good day, your highness? My lord?" The whisper, uncertain as a mouse peeking its nose from a crevice in a wall, came from several yards away. Ann Feathers stood behind a ray of sunlight slashing through an aperture window. Dressed in layers of scrolling, puffing fabric, with her hair tugged tightly into a knot and rendering the bottom half of her face especially pale and round, she appeared nothing less than a frightened titmouse.

But she was precisely who Vitor needed at the moment. "Good day, madam."

She came forward as though upon tiptoes.

Recovered, Sebastiao swept her an elegant bow. "I found this fellow wandering the corridors and was admonishing him to join me in the drawing room for a game of cards. I beg you, come along and enliven the company."

Her curtsy dipped deep. "I am honored, your highness, though I fear I am neither lively nor particularly entertaining company."

"You mustn't contradict me. I am a prince, you know." Casting Vitor a curious glance mingled with worry, he grasped her hand and lifted her from the curtsy.

"Miss Feathers, may I beg a simple service of you?" Vitor asked.

She nodded.

"Miss Caulfield has suffered an accident—"

She gasped. Sebastiao's eyes went wide.

"She is well." He prayed it was true. "But she requires fresh garments. In the absence of the maids, may I prevail upon you to choose for her suitable raiment?"

"Of course, my lord."

Sebastiao thrust back his shoulders. "I will assist you, madam. A diminutive lady like yourself mustn't be employed in tasks suited to servants."

"Oh, I don't mind it, your highness," she said, staring at her shoes. "I like to be useful."

Sebastiao took her hand upon his arm. "Shall we?" He opened the door to Miss Caulfield's bedchamber and they passed inside. Rubbing the back of his neck, Vitor headed for the great hall and his coat.

"THANK YOU, MISS Feathers. You are kind to lend me these." Ravenna fingered the frothy neckline of the muslin gown that was insanely impractical for a castle in the middle of winter, but she could not have refused it.

"I hoped you would like them. The prince insisted. He said that . . ." Miss Feathers's cheeks colored like round ripe peaches. "That your gowns . . ."

"That my gowns are not as fashionable as everybody else's?" *A vast understatement.* Petti had insisted she pack more than her usual gowns borrowed from the housekeeper. Even so, she had nothing to compare to the potential brides' clothing. "I don't mind it, Miss Feathers. In the usual course of things, you see, I have no need of such finery."

"Miss Caulfield?"

Ravenna took another sip of tea. She couldn't seem to drink enough of it; the chill had only just left her bones. Petti had suggested adding whiskey to the tea, but she didn't fancy having a muddled head the next time the killer tried to dispatch her. Or the next time Lord Vitor Courtenay came within five yards. "Yes?"

"Would you—" Miss Feathers attempted. "That is to say, I wonder if you would not take it amiss if I asked— I mean to say, if you might consider—"

"I would be happy to call you Ann if you will call me Ravenna."

Her face relaxed. "You do not mind that I ask?"

"You haven't asked. I offered."

Ann fingered her ruffled cuff. "I never had a sister. And I have rarely had . . ."

"A friend?" Ravenna reached for Ann's hand and squeezed. "Now you do."

"You don't think I . . . Well, that is . . . that I . . ." Her eyes dropped to her lap in confusion.

"That you are the murderer? I don't. You are far too kind, as evidenced by these gowns and whatnot that you have lent me." She had changed out of her sodden shift into one of Ann's deliciously thin French linen chemises, dry stays of the finest cord and linen, a petticoat embroidered with tiny pink roses at the bosom, and a pale green pin-striped frock. Wrapped in a blanket and curled into the remarkably comfortable chair Mr. Brazil had set by the fire in her bedchamber, she felt like a veritable queen. "You may never have had a friend to call by her Christian name before, but I have never worn such a pretty dress." Albeit with three superfluous flounces at the hem. But those could be removed with the needle she carried in her black bag for emergency surgeries.

Lord Vitor's knife would do the job even quicker, she suspected. He had removed her icy clothing from her as though it was second nature in him to cut women out of their garments. Then he had carried her in his arms, against his chest.

"But, you see, Ravenna . . ." Ann tried the name on her lips as though it were foreign, which it was. Ravenna had no memory of her mother or father and she had no idea why they had named her after an ancient Italian city. Whimsy, perhaps. The same whimsy that had made her mother send three tiny daughters on a boat from the West Indies all the way to England with no protection except an old nurse.

"What do I see?" she prompted.

Ann's eyes darted to the closed door, then back to her, like soft gray flowers now. "I encountered Mr. Walsh the night—" She laid the back of her hand across her mouth and said upon a rush, "I believe I encountered him directly before he died."

Ravenna sat forward with a jerk. Tea spilled on the blanket.

"Oh, no," Ann exclaimed. "Look what I have made you do. I knew I should not have—"

"Ann, I pray you, tell me about it."

The door opened and Prince Sebastiao smiled with every tooth in his mouth, it seemed. Golden epaulets and a sash dotted with medals decorated his vibrant red coat.

"Miss Feathers, you bade me wait, but I could not endure it another moment. I am of an impatient temperament." He swept a flourishing bow to Ravenna.

She and Ann began to stand, but he exclaimed, "No! You shan't rise on my account. Rather, I should be prostrating myself at your feet. Miss Caulfield, I am devastated that you have been harmed in my home." His smile was radiant and teasing at once. He was not a particularly handsome man, but appealing when he wasn't foxed. His eyes crinkled at the edges.

"You mustn't, your highness," she said.

"Ah, that is a relief," he replied with exaggerated relief. "Without my usual bevy of servants, I cannot hope for a new pair of trousers any time soon. I shouldn't sully the knees of these."

"And if you made yourself truly prostrate, your coat would suffer from it as well. Those medals are too pretty to scuff."

He glanced at his chest and fingered the decorations. "They are, aren't they?" The corner of his mouth quirked up anew. "Fakes. Every last one of them. Invented by the royal jeweler for decoration only. I am my father's only heir, and he did not allow me to go to war."

Miss Feathers's eyes widened.

"You are stunned. And well you should be. Ah well," he sighed. "I never claimed to be a noble warrior. Pistols are loud and they stain everything."

"You are too modest, your highness."

"Not at all. Only honest . . . in *this* instance." He bowed. "Dear ladies, you seem to encourage the best in me."

Perhaps he was not dissipated and wicked, after all. Perhaps he was only young and spoiled.

"Enough of me," he said. "Miss Caulfield, say the word and I shall order that wretched river drained and filled in with dirt."

Miss Feathers giggled softly.

"That will not be necessary, your highness," Ravenna said.

His cheeks shone with pleasure. He cast Ann a lazy smile. "She rejects my offer. Ah, Miss Feathers, what is a man to do with an obstinate woman?"

"Allow her the obstinacy," Lord Vitor said at the doorway. "She will learn in time that it is not to her benefit."

"You are a beast, Courtenay," the prince chided, swinging around to him. "No true gentleman could be so cold."

Lord Vitor's gaze came to Ravenna. "Then I mustn't be a true gentleman."

"I know what!" the prince said brightly. "We shall get up a play. Two years ago to celebrate Napoleon's second capture I had a grand masked ball here. Magnificent party. Everybody in spectacular costumes. I'm certain Brazil could find them somewhere about this old place, in the attics or whatnot. It should be precisely the thing to enliven the gloom about here. Miss Caulfield, you shall have the prime seat in the audience."

"But, your highness," Ann whispered. "There has been a—a *murder*."

"All the more reason for entertainment on a grand scale. There is nothing that can be done until the culprit is discovered and the danger is past, and Sepic is working diligently on that of course." He grasped her hand and drew her to her feet. "In the meantime, any one of us might be next! We must live while we are young, Miss Feathers."

She didn't seem to know where to look. The prince laughed and guided her to the door. "Come along, Courtenay," he said with blithe authority. "We will require you to stand about looking grim and reminding us all of our desperation for gaiety. Miss Caulfield, I order you to remain abed four and twenty hours. The bloom in your lovely cheeks must not be made to suffer." He urged Miss Feathers from the chamber.

Lord Vitor did not follow.

Stomach peculiarly tight, Ravenna jumped up. "I will help."

He grasped her wrist to stay her. "You will remain here," he said quietly.

She tugged free and called down the corridor, "Miss Feathers, I hope we can continue our conversation later." Ann cast a swift glance back, in her eyes a confusion of worry and pleasure.

Ravenna turned to her rescuer. "She encountered Mr. Walsh the night of his death. Just now Prince Sebastiao interrupted her confession to me."

"Interesting. Her confession could be a distraction or the truth."

"She seems like an honest person."

"Nevertheless, I would like you to make an attempt at inspecting the ladies' clothing, including hers."

"For blood?"

"For whatever seems amiss. But not until tomorrow. Today you will rest."

"I don't need to—"

"The prince commands it. As do I."

"You have no authority to command me. Neither does he, really. And I will go mad confined to my room when there is so much afoot elsewhere."

"How would you respond, I wonder, if I cajoled with gentle words of encouragement, assuring you that all will be well in your absence from the party and that your health and welfare are of the utmost importance to us all?"

"I would probably doze off in the middle of your speech."

A muscle flexed in his jaw, the crease in his right cheek peeking out.

"Come now," she said. "I am well enough to attend dinner tonight. It was only a—"

"Life-threatening incident."

"I once oversaw a sennight of lambing while carrying a high fever. I can hold my own."

"With you convalescing underfoot, however valiantly, I will be . . . distracted."

"Wear a blindfold."

"Distracted by the danger you might yet face. Someone wished to drown you."

A shiver ran through her, but she said, "I cannot imagine why. No one knows I am investigating the murder. No one except you."

"If I wished you out of my way, I don't quite see how diving into a freezing river to retrieve you would serve my purpose. I might have avoided pushing you in in the first place."

"Perhaps you were hoping I would fall ill with a dreadful fever as a consequence of my swim and be rendered insensible."

"Clearly I was mistaken in that, seeing as now I am wasting precious time attempting to convince you to remain here until tomorrow. Your teeth just clacked together."

"They did not."

"They did."

She glanced with longing at the cup of tea growing cold on the table.

"If I promise to bring you any information I should discover today," he said, "will you remain in this chamber?"

A thread of chill was still working its way through the marrow in her bones. "All right."

He nodded and moved to leave.

"Wait. First, tell me what you saw at the river."

"By the depth and weight of the footprints, the person I glimpsed at the river's edge could have been a light man or a woman."

"The prince is not much over my height and he is slender. Perhaps Mr. Anders. Wait a minute. You went outside again already, to study the footprints, while I lounged in a hot bath drinking tea?"

"If you had invited me into the bath I would have gladly delayed the trip outside."

Her throat clogged. She cleared it awkwardly. "You called me obstinate."

"I do not recall doing so directly."

"You implied it. And yet you say outrageous things to me like you want to kiss me and share my bath."

He crossed his arms over his chest that she had pressed her face into, and leaned a shoulder against the door frame. "What effect, I wonder, do these contrary comments have on the lady?"

"It makes the lady want to box your ears."

"Hm. Then my work here is done." He was smiling slightly.

"How did the person that pushed me into the river escape? How did she reach the river without leaving footprints that might have warned us?"

"A path runs along the cemetery to a break in the wall, then down a steep incline to the trees. I had not known of the break in the wall before."

"I understand better now your wish for me to examine the ladies' garments. But what of the guards at the door? Wouldn't they have seen someone access the cemetery?"

"Only one man guarded the door and he followed you beyond the gate until he saw you meet me."

"During that time my attacker must have left the castle. But what of his return? Her return?"

"The guard knew of only the single exit. He remained with the guards at the gate, waiting for your return."

She sagged against the doorpost. "The size of Chevriot makes this—"

"Difficult," he said. "Not impossible. And now you will be well protected."

"What of you?" she said, not quite able to look at him. "What if the murderer tosses you into a river?"

"I haven't the skirts to hamper me from swimming ashore, of course," he said, and the tenor of his voice made her look up into his handsome face. "Do not even think of attempting to protect me."

She blinked. "I wasn't—"

"You were."

"I was not."

"The prince admires you."

"What? No he does not. I know you've said this to distract me, but I am not an empty-headed female and I will not be distracted."

"He does nothing for others unless devotion precedes it."

"Devotion?" she said thinly.

The smile still played about his lips. She could feel them against hers. A devil inside her wished she had given him the opportunity to truly kiss her in the stable. She had never before wanted to kiss a man. Until he had carried her from the river, she had never before wanted to press her face against a man's chest and disappear into him.

"Impossible," she said. "I haven't spoken with him above three times."

"His passions are often swift. And I have not seen him sober in months."

She didn't believe him. No prince, however young and foolish, would choose her as his bride over all the other ladies in the castle. That a nobleman not actually related to her was even speaking with her now was itself a marvel. "Thank you," she said.

"For giving you hope that you may become a princess?"

"For risking your life to save mine."

His arms unfolded. For a moment she feared he meant to touch her. "This is unexpected. I had anticipated chastisement."

"Chastisement?"

"For rescuing you again. You appreciated the champagne incident with such grace, after all."

"Your wit truly slays me. If you don't like me thanking you, don't rescue me."

"Let us hope I find no occasion to do so again." He stood close but not, in the end, touching her. "The guard assigned to you should ensure that."

"Why did you?"

"For your safety. I told you—"

"Not the guard. Why did you risk your life to retrieve me from the river?"

"I need your help to learn the murderer's identity, of course." Again his smile barely showed.

"I will prove that you need me." Her heart did a peculiar jerk. "That you need me to help you in this," she added swiftly.

He seemed to study her face. "I need you not to be the murderer's second victim due to my carelessness."

"You were not careless. I was."

He turned to depart. "I have instructed Monsieur Brazil to send dinner up to you."

"You knew I would acquiesce."

"Yes. In this."

"And if I had not?"

He gestured. "I would have tied you to that bed."

Nerves spiked in her belly. "Did the pitchfork incident teach you nothing?"

He gave her another half smile, then bowed. "Until tomorrow, Miss Caulfield."

She watched him go. Then she closed her door, tucked the blanket more snugly around her shoulders, and returned to her cold, empty bed.

Chapter 8

The Confusion of Flirtations

Lord Vitor did not return that day or bring news. Petti and the pugs called on her after dinner.

"M'dear, your eyelids are drooping even as I rhapsodize about the bisque. How can that be?"

"I'm sorry, Petti. I am wretchedly weary."

"A dip in a freezing river will do that, I suppose. Not sleeping for two months will too, of course."

She struggled to hold her eyelids open. "What?"

"Beverley and I were on the journey here as well. And at the Grange before that."

"You knew I wasn't sleeping?"

"My dear girl, we are not your nurses or nannies or whatever it is you delight in calling us. Your business is your own," he said with a fond smile. "But we don't like to see you so unhappy."

"I am not unhappy. I miss Beast." Horribly.

He patted her hand. "Of course you do."

The following morning Ann visited to warn her that

the prince had announced that if anyone were to see her face before dinnertime, she must be sent straight back to her sickbed. Ravenna spent the afternoon pacing her bedchamber.

When the dinner gong finally rang, she burst from her cell only to discover the peculiar affair that dinner at Chevriot had become during her imprisonment. Prince Sebastiao presided with regal effervescence at the table's head, relating tales of outrageously opulent parties he'd thrown at the castle since the war. With these stories he drew shy smiles from Ann Feathers at his left and throaty chuckles from Duchess McCall at his right, and subsequently to those two ladies he gave all his attention. The rest of the guests responded to his high spirits in varying degrees of deference while grumbling to their tablemates.

"This incarceration is idiocy and insult," the Earl of Whitebarrow muttered to Sir Henry. "I tell you, an intruder from outside killed the man."

"Who was Walsh, anyway?" Sir Henry replied, his cheek full of fricasseed calf's liver.

"Upstart gentry, I daresay," Lady Whitebarrow said coolly.

"In the absence of my man, I was obliged to carry a pot of hot water from the kitchen to my chamber this morning," Lord Prunesly said with an abstracted blink.

"Good heavens, my lord," Lady Margaret exclaimed. "How horrid!"

"In fact I found it fascinating, madam. As I ascended, water sloshed from the pot in direct proportion to the unevenness of my steps upon the risers."

"I suppose you collected the water from the floor and measured it carefully, Father?" Martin Anders said with a surly brow. "Scientific experimentation above all else, isn't that right?"

"The girl did not arrive in my chamber to make up the fire until nine o'clock," Lady Margaret said to Lord Prunesly with a sympathetic air. "I shivered beneath the covers, entirely unable to rise until ten." Her jewels jingled upon her broad bosom as she demonstrated a shiver.

Ravenna leaned toward Petti and whispered, "Were they like this last night too?"

"And all day today." He bit into goose tart.

"It was an intruder, I tell you," Lord Whitebarrow insisted, lifting his patrician nose and glancing in either direction down the long table. His attention came to rest upon Lady Iona, whose full-throated laughter tripped along the silver and porcelain as though it were a remove to be enjoyed with the wine. Her locks shimmered with candlelight, swept into a scarlet bandeau that matched the web of embroidery across the bodice of her gown. The stark, swirling patterns drew attention to her bosom even more effectively than Lady Margaret's jewels did to hers.

Meeting Lord Whitebarrow's stare, Iona slipped a forkful of brandied cherries into her mouth and allowed the tines to slide out through her lips slowly. Then the pink tip of her tongue stole out to lick a droplet of cherry juice from her lower lip.

Martin Anders gaped and entirely missed his mouth with his spoon.

Watching him, his sister Cecilia's brow pleated with worry. Ravenna couldn't wonder at it. If she had a brother as foolish as Martin Anders, she would probably worry about him as well. Taliesin, the Gypsy boy who had taken lessons from her father, had always been like a brother to her, but he worried about *her*. Eleanor and Arabella too. And Papa—poor, studious Papa who'd been entirely nonplussed not only by the giant black dog he'd brought to his home but also by the black dog's girl.

But in Ravenna's experience churchmen often didn't know how to cope with the world. The prelate now in their midst, Bishop Abraccia, still robed in black and purple clerical garb, couldn't even manage to eat his dinner without his niece's assistance. As she cut his meat, Juliana Abraccia cast Martin Anders swift, coy glances along the table. Mr. Anders's attention, however, remained rapt on the Highland beauty.

Ravenna peered about the room. The prince's guests were not only grumbling to each other. They were looking at each other. All of them. Not simply politely as they conversed. But *looking*. Candlelight illumined faces in amber and shadow, and everyone seemed to be looking at someone else.

Of course they were. One of them had killed Mr. Walsh and might kill again.

But no one was looking at her, and not all stares were wary or suspicious. Perhaps all this *looking* wasn't actually about the murder.

The Countess of Whitebarrow stared coolly at her husband. Lord Whitebarrow continued to watch Lady Iona. General Dijon was watching his daughter, just as the Earl of Case was doing. Arielle returned neither of their stares, instead pushed her food around the plate pretending to eat, which Ravenna understood well enough; she had lost her beloved little Marie only two days earlier. But she wasn't the only lady with a case of the sullens. Lady Grace's dull gaze rested upon her mother.

"In the name of Zeus, is the dog truly gone?" Sir Henry said to the table at large. "That poor girl's face tells me no one's unearthed it yet."

"She is not found," General Dijon said gravely. "She has been taken, but by whom we know not."

"What is the theft of a dog beside a murderer running loose among us?" Lady Margaret shivered—

theatrically this time, though the jewels jingled just as
effectively. "It's enough to give one nightmares." She
stole another glance at Lord Prunesly. The professor
studied his wineglass as he twirled it, presumably
testing his sloshing theory on a smaller scale.

"The dog," General Dijon said stiffly to Lady Margaret, "is one of only four mature bitches of her breed
on this continent or any. She is worth more than all the
jewels in your jewelry box, *je vous assure.*"

Sir Henry set down his fork. "Now see here, sir. I'll
not have you speak to my wife in that manner."

Beside him, his daughter Ann sat with her head
bowed, her round cheeks livid, staring at her lap.

The prince stared at her.

"Dear Miss Feathers," he said. "You appear a bit
flushed. You must drink more wine to revive your
spirits." He gestured to a footman.

"Oh, I could not, your highness, thank you," Ann
peeped. "I don't wish to muddle my head and say
things I mustn't."

His high brow wrinkled. Then he waved the footman away and pushed his own glass from his plate.

"How perfectly dreadful to grow so crimson even
when the climate is frigid," Lady Penelope said to Lord
Vitor beside her, with a glance of sympathy at Ann
which was entirely false. She offered no vulgar shiv-
ers but smoothed her fingertips over her shawl. Snugly
gloved, her slender hands subtly drew attention to her
perfect breasts.

But Lord Vitor didn't seem to notice; he was watching the prince. For an instant he shifted his attention to
Ravenna. His cheek creased.

Dry. Tongue.

Wine.

She grappled for her glass and met Lord Case's gaze
from across the table. But he turned to his brother.

Lord Vitor spoke quietly now with the bishop's niece on his other side. Juliana's eyes twinkled. She giggled, then replied softly. Even at the distance her voice sounded sweet with its Italian accent, like music.

Abruptly, the goose weighed like rocks in Ravenna's stomach, Iona's bright laughter seemed overbright, Sir Henry's chuckles forced, Lady Grace's cheeks gray, and Cecilia Anders's silent worry like a blaring trumpet. Across the table, Sir Beverley turned a sober gaze to Petti. There was something they were not telling her. They had secrets, she knew, that they never shared with her aloud but she understood. This time she did not understand.

Everyone had secrets, it seemed.

Her head spun—from candle fumes or the heavy food or too many humans in one place casting each other glances full of suspicion or worry or . . . *something else*. She had to go. The walls of the dining room seemed to creep closer to the table, the candlelight to grow hazy. She could not breathe properly.

"Miss Caulfield," Sir Henry said. "Sir Beverley tells me you are a medical woman of sorts."

"I have some experience caring for sick animals, yes," she managed. How could the rest of them bear this? The frigid snow outside seemed infinitely preferable.

"I wonder if you wouldn't mind paying a visit to the stable with me tomorrow," Sir Henry said. "One of the beasts I brought along for his highness's inspection has come up lame. My coachman believes it may be an abscess. But he's a Frenchie, of course, and I don't trust him with my cattle like I'd trust an Englishman—or Englishwoman." He gave her a friendly wink.

"I will be glad to examine him."

"Fine, fine." He took a hearty sip of wine. "I don't mind traveling, you see. Neither does Lady Margaret.

But I don't like my animals in foreign hands, and that's the truth of it."

"But don't you intend to do business with Prince Sebastiao's father?"

He cracked a laugh. "In the name of Zeus, I do indeed! But once he's paid for the beasts, they're no longer mine, are they?" He laughed.

She tried to smile.

Now Lord Vitor was smiling at Juliana.

"M'dear," Petti said quietly. "You look as though you might spring up from that chair at any moment."

"I do? I don't." She ducked her head. "I would not embarrass you and Sir Beverley so."

"That Courtenay . . ." Petti drew out the syllables. "He is a fine-looking young man, isn't he?"

Her belly constricted. "Do you think so?"

"Intelligent too, from what Beverley tells me." His fingers played a thoughtful staccato on the edge of the table.

"Fancy him, do you?" she mumbled.

"My heart belongs to another, of course. But I'm not dead. I can appreciate quality from a distance." His cloverleaf eyes danced. "I don't think you should."

"Appreciate quality?"

"From a distance."

"If you continue this," she whispered, "I will stand and leave at this moment, and damn good manners."

He chuckled. "Beverley and I won't be around forever, m'dear. You must find your sanctuary elsewhere while you are still young."

"But—" Panic twisted in her tight stomach. "I—"

He patted her hand. "We haven't let out your room at Shelton Grange yet, dear girl. You needn't fret."

Prince Sebastiao rose and offered his arm to Ann. "Shall we all adjourn to the drawing room? Yes, yes! All of us at once, no gentlemen lingering here. Come,

come, Miss Feathers. Lady Iona." The guard opened the door.

Ravenna escaped, slipping around the wall of the great hall of the medieval keep and to the front door. The guard at the door nodded, but he did not follow when she turned toward the stable. Her personal guard, the man Lord Vitor had assigned to remain with her, was nowhere to be seen. But she carried a knife in her pocket now. Forewarned and armed, she would be fine.

In the stable, scents of comfort filled her nostrils. She tugged her shawl more tightly about her and asked a groom to direct her toward Sir Henry's stallion. A beautiful creature but skittish, it remained at the back of the stall until she encouraged it to her with soft words. It came limping. Its temperament seemed good; still, she would not enter the stall now. In daylight she could examine the hoof more effectively. And she hadn't really come here now for him.

The mother of the puppies now sprawled on her side in the storage stall. Four of the pups nursed, the runt tucked behind its siblings away from the teats, awaiting its turn at the scant leftovers. Wearily the bitch lifted her head and her tail slapped against the straw.

"How you have grown in two days," Ravenna said as she knelt. The runt turned its head at her voice, uncurled from its spot, and stumbled through the straw to her. "This time I have not come empty-handed." From a knot she'd made in her borrowed gown she drew a cutlet of veal encased in a crust of bread. Tearing the food into tiny pieces, she fed it to the runt. Then one by one, she took all five pups onto her lap and examined them. Little bundles of elastic muscle and silky fur, they gnawed at her with sharp teeth as she declared them each healthy. Then she gave the bitch attention, examining her mouth, ears, paws, and abdomen. Someone was feeding her well, which explained why she still allowed the pups to nurse, and the continued existence of the runt.

Finding nothing more to do, she stood. "Until tomorrow." She turned to leave.

Tiny teeth snagged in her hem. The runt tugged on the fabric.

"Good heavens, this is not my gown. You mustn't tear it." She bent and scratched the pup around the ears while she pried its miniature jaws from the flounce of Ann's gown. "Now good night. Again."

In short bounds that rustled the straw it followed her, mewling when she nudged it back with her toes to close the door. It yipped and scratched upon the wood. Ravenna retraced her steps and cracked open the door. The runt wiggled with joy and leaped at her ankles. At their mother's side, his warm, well-fed siblings remained oblivious.

"You want adventure, do you?" She tucked it against her chest. "I once knew a creature like you." She fondled a soft little paw between her fingers. "He was entirely black and grew to be much larger than you ever will. But you have something of his spirit, I think." She rubbed her nose against its silky white brow and breathed in the scent. "I know just what to do with you." Pulling her shawl over it, she enclosed it against her chest.

A groom bid her a good night and she crossed the forecourt into the castle. The last time she'd made this short trip she had run. Thrown to the ground and kissed by a strange man in the dark, she had been frightened and angry and confused.

Now her strides were light and giddy.

Inside the castle she could still hear the guests in the drawing room. Someone played the pianoforte beautifully—Arielle Dijon, probably. Perhaps Lord

Case had cajoled her out of her despair for a moment. Ravenna ducked inside the servants' stairwell and climbed to the bedchamber floor. A guard stood mid-corridor.

"Which bedchamber is Lord Vitor's?" she asked.

He directed her along the passage.

The door opened without resistance. In his bedchamber, she poured water from the pitcher into the washbasin and offered it to the pup. It mewled and yipped again when she shut the door, leaving him behind her. But in the warmth he would soon fall fast asleep right where she had left him. Her smile split her cheeks as she followed the narrow passageways to her bedchamber.

A man stood by her door, leaning against the wall, a candle in one hand illumining his face.

"Mr. Anders?" She did not allow the jump in her nerves to sound in her voice. Her guard had apparently disappeared forever. She was alone with one of their prime suspects in the dark. "This is the ladies' wing. Are you lost?"

"Only lost in admiration." He set the candle on a table and moved toward her.

"Oh." She reached for the door handle. "Well then, I bid you good night—"

He grasped her shoulder and turned her to face him. "Do not abandon me so early in the evening, dearest Miss Caulfield."

She could not reach the knife in her pocket. *Foolish.* "Abandon you?" She spoke lightly. "I've barely ever spoken with you. How on earth could I abandon you?"

He gripped both her arms. "Yet I feel as though the moments that I have admired you across rooms full of bothersome others have been endless—endless torture to be so ardent in my admiration yet so far from the object of it."

He did not smell of alcohol, but he didn't smell of malevolence either.

"Mr. Anders, there is a guard on the other side of that corner," she lied, "who will stick you through with his big Portuguese sword if I call out."

"I would not harm you! I could not harm you! You are a treasure beyond telling."

Fear slipped away from her. This was not an assassination attempt but simply a young man's natural idiocy. She had not really believed him capable of murder anyway. "Sir, do take your hands off me and be done with this nonsense."

Poetically long hair that wasn't quite long enough to match the hair on Mr. Walsh's coat fell over one eye. But the other eye gazed at her ardently. "Now that I have touched you, I cannot release you. You must allow me to remain close. For the farther you are from me the greater my torment."

"Sir, unhand me or you will come to fiercely regret it."

"But I love you!"

"You *do*?"

"Powerfully. Deeply. Truly. My *darling*."

"Not two hours ago you were drooling into your soup over Lady Iona. If this is true love then I don't think I wish to see infatuation."

His brow grew stormy. "She is all beauty and no passion. She has no appreciation for real feeling. But you, Miss Caulfield, are of an emotional race."

"What?" The word came out choked.

"Your dark, exotic blood knows true desire. I can see it in your eyes. They are the eyes of a wild creature. You need a man to tame your heat. I want to be that ma—"

Her knee impacted precisely where she aimed. Mr. Anders doubled over with a groan, and she slipped into her room and locked the door. Without lighting the fire, she stripped off the delicate pin-striped gown meant for a lady, then curled beneath the covers in her bed and waited for morning.

VITOR REMOVED HIS horse's tack, rubbed him down and filled the hay rack, all with a head muddled from his sleepless night. He'd spent more peaceful nights on battlefields. The farther away he'd tied the mongrel from him in his bedchamber, the louder it had whined.

He rubbed his eyes and glanced at the pup rolling about in the straw at Ashdod's hooves.

"Come on, then."

It cocked its head at him.

He opened the stall door. "Your mistress will wish to know how you fare."

In the forecourt his elder brother walked toward him beneath a sky that had turned gray again overnight.

"You are permitted to ride abroad while the rest of us are locked within these walls?" he said, glancing at the puppy stumbling through the snow at Vitor's heels.

"The prince knows that I am not the murderer."

"But the rest of us don't know that." Wesley turned and fell in beside him. "You might have any one of us on your list. I could be next, and then you would be earl and when father is gone all your dreams would come true."

"My dreams have never bent in that direction." Last night his dreams had bent toward a black-eyed woman. Like in that moment by the river when he had removed her sodden clothing, his dream had painted a vision of her body encased in linen rendered translucent by water, the dark points of her breasts poking hard beneath the cloth. In his dream he had peeled that garment off her and warmed her with his hands and mouth. He had never wanted his father's or brother's titles. He'd never wanted much of anything except to make himself useful to both his fathers and kingdoms. Now, however, he wanted Ravenna Caulfield.

"You know that," he added.

"I do," Wesley said easily. "What do you make of the general's daughter?"

"Do I think she is a murderer?"

"Do you think she could be a countess?"

Four years earlier, Vitor had spent an endless fortnight enduring his elder brother's questioning without once speaking a word. Now, despite his surprise at this question, he maintained his even stride. "I suspect so."

"She is of noble blood." Wesley said this as though it were a minor advantage. "Her father is the fifth son of a French count of little land and status, although he enjoyed some notoriety in the early months of Boney's ascendancy. The general first followed in his father's tracks, but when that resulted in a painful venture to Russia, he shifted his interests and went off to the United States. Made a name for himself advising the army and took to breeding world-class hounds, it seems, from which lucrative endeavors he amassed considerable wealth and land. Father could not object to her pedigree, I think."

Vitor remained silent. There was nothing he could say.

"Miss Caulfield is quite taking too." Wesley spoke too casually. "Of course, she has no connection to the nobility, so marriage is out of the question. Did you know that she was a foundling? Her adoptive father would not put up resistance to a temporary arrangement, I suspect, although Sir Beverley might prove troublesome. But I know how to get around these sorts of things. I had an interesting conversation with him last night after dinner while Sebastiao was doling out parts for *Romeo and Juliet*. Peculiar choice of plays given the grim circumstances in which we all find ourselves, wouldn't you say? But his royal highness seems an odd bird in general. I don't know how you bore with him all those years."

Vitor had ceased walking.

Wesley looked back at him. "Brother?"

"Why are you speaking to me about this?"

"Why not?"

"Do not trifle with her in an attempt to hurt me, Wes. If you do, I will make you sorry for it."

His brother's eyes narrowed. "Not denying it, hm? And yet I believe she said that she threw you off already once."

Vitor went to him. They were of a height and he looked him in the eye. "It has been seven years, Wes. When will you set aside your anger?"

"Perhaps it is not anger toward you that inspires my interest in Miss Caulfield but her natural appeal. I would not be the only man here who has given her more than a passing glance."

In the drawing room the night before, Sebastiao had asked after her until Vitor went searching, to be told by the guard he'd posted to her protection that she had retired early.

Wesley seemed to study him. "Ah, he does not know the lady's mind, it seems," he said as though to himself. "Perhaps he thinks she favors another." His eyes narrowed. "Tell me, little brother, how does that feel?" After a moment's pause, he turned and went inside.

Vitor followed. The great hall echoed with the sounds of activity in the drawing room beyond the archway. Ravenna appeared in the opening. Without pause she came to him, crouched to the stone floor, and took the pup into her arms. She caressed its neck and behind its ears with her supple hands.

"Monsieur Sepic is in the drawing room being

thoroughly useless," she said, setting the pup on the ground. It attacked her hem. "He accused Lord White-barrow of stubbornness and arrogance—which of course is accurate—and the duchess of speaking nonsense. He does not understand her when she speaks French and she refuses to speak English with him. It is fabulously entertaining." Her eyes sparkled. Then her brow pinched. "Much more so than dinner last night, at least." She walked across the great hall beside him, the pup trailing. "Have you learned anything useful this morning?"

"Martin Anders's boots and the hem of his coat were soaked through. I discovered them drying by the hearth here when I went out at dawn. He must have been outside for some time to achieve that."

"So was everybody. Guests stroll within the walls under the supervision of the prince's guards. Perhaps he took his walk before dawn to avoid the others. Sir Henry's boots shine despite several trips to the stables."

"Feathers is considerably wealthier than Prunesly. He would have more than one pair. Prunesly's son might not."

"Are you considerably wealthy?"

Vitor couldn't help smiling. "You say the damnedest things."

"My father tried to teach me manners but I didn't listen very often. Petti and Sir Beverley have despaired of me for years. And of course I am not unique between us in saying 'the damnedest things.'"

"I am a second son only."

"Second son of a wealthy peer, they say, which probably makes you at least grandly comfortable if not despicably rich. Why are you here?"

He peered at her.

"What are you doing in the mountains of France

in March at the bride-hunting party of a Portuguese prince?" she clarified.

"How long have you been wondering this?"

"The question only now occurred to me. Rather, it occurred to me when I saw you take out your horse. It is a beautiful animal. Superbly beautiful. He must have cost you a fortune."

Ashdod had cost a fortune, but it had been only a mere fraction of the money he had in London and Lisbon banks.

"Watching from an upper window, were you?" he said.

"I was in the stable examining a sore hoof."

Before dawn? But she had been in the stable after midnight when he first encountered her. This time he had not heard her and she had not revealed her presence to him.

"In that?" He glanced at her gown. The pink frock was youthful and light and damnably tight across her breasts. As though she had only just come inside, her cheeks were bright with cold, and straw and dirt clung to the gown's hem where the dog had not yet chewed it away.

"Recall that you sliced my best gown into shreds." She offered him a too-sweet smile.

He shook his head. "I—"

"Feeling guilty?"

For stripping her to her shift and affording himself a glimpse of her hidden beauty? *No.* He couldn't make his tongue function.

She laughed. "I have other gowns, of course. But thanks to Ann Feathers inviting the prince to peruse my wardrobe while I was in the housekeeper's room, I now know that he prefers that I wear her gowns instead. She lent me this and two others, both with considerably more ruffles and lace. Lady Margaret has astoundingly busy taste."

He bowed and finally managed, "I offer my apologies for ruining your gown."

"Just don't do it again. You may be a wealthy aristocrat but I am a poor vicar's daughter. I cannot afford to repay Miss Feathers should you ruin one of her gowns the next time."

"I do not anticipate a next time."

Her lashes beat twice, rapidly. "Then perhaps you might reconsider the reliability of the guard you assigned to me. He was nowhere to be seen when Mr. Anders cornered me by my bedchamber door last night." ·

Jealousy. Hot and quick. "Anders was still in the drawing room when I retired." Had the guard lied about her retiring early? "When did you see him?"

"I don't believe he is the murderer," she only replied.

"Have you a reason for that?"

"No. Since I am a woman I haven't the ability to reason, as all those medieval theologians my father likes to quote were so fond of insisting. Therefore I draw conclusions based not on evidence but on emotion, of which, according to Mr. Anders, I have a great quantity." A shadow crossed her eyes.

Grasping her elbow, he halted her. "What happened?" *Ravenna.* He wished to speak her name. She had given him leave. But he would be a scoundrel to take it, and a fool. He wanted it too much.

She glanced down at his hand around her arm and her throat moved in a soft constriction. She drew out of his hold. "I had occasion to study the bruise on his eye," she said. "If his health is good and his humors are balanced, which they seem to be, I place the injury within hours of the time we discovered the body. Mr.

Walsh might have struck Mr. Anders in the eye. Rather more to the point, however, is that Mr. Anders is a fool. He had ample opportunity to harm me, even to threaten me, yet he failed to do so."

Vitor tried to steel his voice against the anger. "He could be ingratiating himself to you in order to act later, when you do not expect it."

"Seducing me with ill intent? Not the sort of ill intent you intended, of course." In her eyes were both laughter and uncertainty.

"Ravenna." He allowed himself the pleasure of tasting the word. It intoxicated.

Her gaze dropped, as though for a moment she felt the intoxication too. Then it came up bright to his. "I will not require you to apologize again." She offered him a little grin of impenitence. "But I do like to see you contrite."

"You mistake it. I am only contrite that I did not succeed in making you enjoy that moment in the stable."

Her eyes sparked. "For that admission, I will demand an apology every hour forthwith."

"You won't have it."

"Why not?"

Because absolution for confessing a sin required true penitence. Vitor was neither contrite nor penitent. He wanted her to not only enjoy his touch but to welcome it.

"Why do you believe Anders does not intend ill toward you?" he said.

"I considered that he might be trying to cajole me into trusting him. But I honestly don't believe he's intelligent enough to plan in that manner." She paused. "Are you?"

"I thought you had already decided that I am not the murderer."

"You just sidestepped telling me why you are at

Chevriot. And the guard that you said you had placed upon me is inconstant at best. I am beginning not to trust you."

"I will have words with the guard." He stepped close to her. "You must trust me. You can."

She averted her shoulder, skittish, as though preparing to move away. "Why are you here? Unless you are wearing a truly spectacular disguise, you are not the father of an eligible maiden or an eligible maiden yourself. Are you?"

That she could jest about her wariness gave him hope.

"For ten years I lived at the court of Prince Raynaldo, Sebastiao's father, as an intimate of the family. Matters of state require Raynaldo's presence at home now. He asked me to attend this gathering in his absence."

"To wait upon the prince?"

"To ensure that he chooses a bride."

"Do you have a favorite yet?" Reticence still clung to her voice. She lifted a hand and tucked an errant lock behind her ear, then she drew the corner of her bottom lip between her teeth. "For him?"

Vitor forced his attention to her eyes. "Any one of them that did not murder and castrate a man will do."

"Hm. I see you have high standards. The prince knows you are investigating the murder independent of Monsieur Sepic, doesn't he?"

"He does."

"And he trusts you with this?"

"Yes."

"Why?"

"During the war I did similar work."

She was silent for several moments. "I think we should catalogue the suspects and assess the motivation of each individually. Monsieur Sepic has not yet outlined this obvious course of action, so we may as well suggest it to him. Then we might begin striking from the list those who are unlikely candidates."

Her curiosity seemed infinite, and yet she would not ask him more about himself. "When he returns in the afternoon, then."

She nodded and moved away from him. Then she paused and looked back. "No sign of Mademoiselle Dijon's dog on your ride?"

"None." After a visit to the hermitage to bring Denis a bottle, he had ridden the paths that descended and ascended to the castle, then along the river that had tried to swallow her. Except along the paths that Sepic had traveled from the village to the castle, Ashdod's hooves had broken smooth snow. No stranger had been on the mountain since the last snowfall. "Only the hermit."

"The hermit?"

"The friar that lives in the hermitage beneath the mountain peak."

Her starlit eyes went wide. "A hermit lives on the mountain? Really? Are there any other bits of information that you wish to share with me now? Or does your grace not imagine I deserve to know details that could be relevant to this mystery?"

"I am hiding nothing from you," except that when her eyes took on that distance they held now, it stirred an ache beneath his ribs. "Father Denis has lived there for three decades. He is better known to the prince's family than anyone. And as I am not a duke, 'my lord' will do, if you must. Or Vitor." He wanted to hear her say his name.

"I mustn't." Her eyes remained aloof.

"Why did you put a dog in my bed?"

"I thought you might need company." Offering a quick smile, she turned away again. He watched her go and the ache inside him thickened.

Martin Anders? She thought him an imbecile, but had she accepted his interest? Had she allowed him close? And what of the other men? Which of them in addition to Wesley and Anders saw her as a potential conquest?

With anger simmering beneath his skin like it hadn't in two and a half years, Vitor went to the drawing room. He was not a murderer, but if any other man in the castle touched her, he might very well become one.

Chapter 9

Armor, of a Sort

While Ravenna penned a list of the suspects and the mayor thoughtfully stroked his ginger moustaches, Lord Vitor sat with all evidence of disinterest in a chair across the chamber and watched her. He said very little and only when Monsieur Sepic directly questioned him. But he did not disagree when she set the final list of suspects on the table.

"Martin and Cecilia Anders," she read, "Juliana Abraccia, Arielle Dijon, Prince Sebastiao, and Ann Feathers. All have long dark hair and all are not particularly large. I briefly considered the scullery maid too. But when the cook washed her hair—while she shrieked in terror, never having endured such a thing before—it turned out to be blond beneath all the filth. That is life below stairs, of course." She grinned, but found her lips wobbling. Lord Vitor did not blink a long lash. "So there you have the suspects, Monsieur Sepic. As well as me, of course."

To that Lord Vitor offered her a tolerant stare. The mayor peered at her with a confounded air, which seemed the only manner in which he generally peered, so Ravenna did not credit it with much significance.

"We must ask each of them to write a sample letter and compare their hands to the writing on the note found in his pocket," she suggested when the mayor's silence continued.

"Hm. *Peut-être.*" He stroked his moustache quicker. "*Mais.*" He looked over to the nobleman. "Have you wondered why a man who is not a knight would don a suit of armor at ten o'clock of the night?"

"Or, perhaps, why a murderer might dress a dead man in a suit of armor?" Lord Vitor drawled. The drawl must be pure affectation. The man who had dived into a frozen river, then carried her without faltering through snow all the way back to the house, didn't seem the drawling sort. But he seemed to want Sepic to believe he was. "Will you perhaps study the armor more thoroughly, monsieur?" he said with the same indolent air.

"Ah, *oui.* Excellent suggestion, monseigneur. I will bring the blacksmith from the village to assist me."

"Do you know anything about medieval armor?" she whispered to the nobleman as they left the room.

"Enough."

"An investigation seems in order, but before Sepic and his blacksmith can muddle any evidence we might find."

"Tonight, then, while the others are engaged in entertainments," he said, looking down at her with those midnight eyes that muddled her.

They did not muddle Juliana Abraccia, or Lady Penelope, Ann Feathers, or any other maiden in the house. When he spoke to them they responded with animated pleasure, as though winning his attention was a gift not to be squandered. The gentlemen were not immune to him either. His quiet ease bespoke strength and authority to which even the titled lords among the party and the prince deferred. And his slight smile ensured his sovereignty. When he smiled, ladies fluttered lashes and sighed happily, and gentlemen relaxed their postures. He put everyone at ease.

Except her, apparently.

"Tonight," she agreed, adamantly ignoring the tangles in her belly.

Oblivious to the objections of several of his guests that, given the presence of a murdered man in the castle, dancing was not appropriate, Prince Sebastiao insisted upon it after dinner. Employing Arielle Dijon and Cecilia Anders to play alternately, and assigning Lord Case and Mr. Anders to turn the pages, the castle's young master set about cheering his morose and agitated guests.

"Do bring your right foot over the threshold, m'dear, and enter the room entirely if you will," Petti said over his shoulder. He offered a fond smile as the bright notes of the first set came forth. "None of the gentlemen will bite, you know."

"One of the gentlemen—or ladies—is a murderer," she whispered, and peeked between his shoulder and Sir Beverley's at the men and women lining up. Prince Sebastiao leaped between them with exclamations of pleasure, delightedly pairing ladies with gentlemen. "Biting is the least of my concerns."

"Ah, is that what you were doing closeted with Courtenay for at least an hour after lunch?" Petti's eyes twinkled. "I don't blame you at all."

Sir Beverley lifted a steely brow. "I shouldn't tease her, Francis. She will only dig in her heels more firmly."

"S'truth." Petti sighed and shook his head. "Stubborn girl."

"I do so enjoy it when you two speak about me in my presence as if I weren't here. And Monsieur Sepic was in the room this afternoon, of course. Even if I wished it, biting could not have happened with him present."

"Did you wish it?" Petti asked.

Ravenna's face heated. "Oh, for heaven's sake. Go dance."

With a merry glint in his eyes, he went forward with Sir Beverley. Lady Iona broke from the group and hurried to Ravenna.

"Ye mustn't leave nou, lass. We've finally an opportunity for a wee bit o' fun. Why, just look at those gentlemen eager for entertainment."

"I cannot," Ravenna said, watching Lord Vitor speak with Cecilia Anders. A trickle of nausea wound about her middle. "I've a task I must see to."

"There be no task nou more important than winnin' the hand o' a prince, lass," the Highland beauty admonished. "Whit else are ye here for? An' look! He's no' got a partner yet."

"You don't either. And I don't care for dancing." Ravenna dragged her gaze from the handsomest man in the room. "Go on and enjoy yourself."

Chestnut brows dipped. "Lass, I saw yer foot tappin'."

"Foot tapping is different from dancing."

Iona grasped her hand. "I like ye, Ravenna. An' I'll no' take no for an answer." She tugged.

Ravenna gripped the door frame. "It is not that I do not wish to dance, Iona," she whispered. "I *cannot* dance." Not like these people could. A country dance, perhaps, but even then she made a fabulous wreck of it, always grasping the wrong hands and flying off in the wrong directions. But farmers never cared about that sort of thing as long as the ale and laughter flowed.

This collection of elegant lords and ladies would be different. She could already feel Lady Penelope's scathing sneer. It didn't matter what girls like that thought of her. But she had long since vowed against voluntarily presenting herself for immolation.

"When did ye think to learn to dance, lass?" Iona said.

"Never."

"I'll teach ye."

Over Lady Iona's shoulder she could see Lord Vitor moving toward them. "No." She pulled her hand away. "No, really. I must be going."

Iona's beautiful face lit. "My laird." She grasped his arm because she, a duchess's vivacious daughter, could do such things. Like every other girl in the castle, Iona *wanted* to do such things. Ravenna absolutely *did not* want to, no matter how firm and muscular that arm would certainly be. She felt hot and uncomfortable even considering it.

"Miss Caulfield has just told me a tragic tale," Iona said upon a pretty pout.

No. Oh, no.

"Has she?" His tone was unremarkable but he studied her.

"She doesna ken hou to dance." Iona released him and moved to Ravenna's side to link arms. "There be only one solution: Ye must teach her, my laird."

A smile played about his fine lips. "I should be honored to."

"No. No you shouldn't." Ravenna tripped on her tongue. "And I shouldn't either. I slipped on ice and injured my ankle this afternoon," she invented. "Perhaps tomorrow."

"As you wish, of course. I am devastated to know you have been injured," he said quite sincerely, it seemed. He turned to the beauty. "Would you care to dance, my lady?"

She took his arm. "I would, my laird."

They moved away. Iona cast her a curious glance, then smiled up at him gorgeously.

With a breath of relief, Ravenna slipped out of the drawing room and to the armory.

"How FARES YOUR ankle now?" Lord Vitor's voice came from the armory doorway. The guard stood in sight just beyond him. "Better since you eschewed dancing?"

Ravenna set down the catalogue of arms and armaments she'd discovered on a shelf and stood. "Much better, thank you."

He dismissed the guard with a gesture and moved into the chamber. "A great quantity of ice in Ladies Grace and Penelope's bedchamber this afternoon, was there?"

"Lady Whitebarrow headed me off before I was able to search. I did gain access to Miss Anders's bed chamber, but I found nothing of interest in it, of course." She folded her hands behind her back. "And I did not need to make that excuse. I did so to avoid insulting you."

"Was the prospect of dancing with me so horrifying?"

"Rather, mortifying."

"I am flattered, madam."

"Not you," she said. "Truly, I haven't a jot of coordination. If you think I wield a pitchfork effectively, you would be astounded to learn how deadly a weapon my heels can be when misplaced."

"To thank you for sparing me such a fate would be ungentlemanly and in any case disingenuous. So I shall instead remain silent." He glanced about the small chamber. A storage closet rather than a true room, it was packed with armor in varying states of decay. "Why are you here? The armor Walsh wore remains in the parlor."

"I did intend to go there. Then I asked Monsieur Brazil to unlock this room instead. The other night we found this in his coat pocket." She produced a dagger's scabbard. Embossed with a coat of arms in gold, red, and blue, it was in fair condition, not more than two decades old by the looks of the leather and metal safety clasp, and well used. Also, empty.

He looked over the piece. "You came here to search for the blade before making a search of everyone's belongings?"

"And the refuse heap beyond the kitchen courtyard's wall. And the trees within throwing distance of the south terrace. And the river."

He set the scabbard down by a row of daggers she had collected while she waited for him. She understood why he commanded such admiration from the other guests. He moved with great ease and yet it seemed he had care for each movement, as though everything, even the smallest thing or least important person, merited his full attention.

Now his large, strong hands were deliberate upon the scabbard. Those hands had held her. Had any of the other ladies in the castle experienced that?

It didn't matter. It mustn't matter.

"It seemed the most expedient approach," she said a bit thinly now. "If the dagger were here, it clearly would not be in anybody's room or discarded."

"You ably employ the reason that as a woman you lack, Miss Caulfield."

"You called me Ravenna this afternoon."

"That was before you refused to dance with me." The crease appeared in his cheek. "I must consider my honor."

"Does your honor extend to offering me your opinion on a matter of potentially some delicacy?"

His brows lifted slightly.

She moved to him and held the scabbard up to the light of his candle. "Do you see these fibers? How they seem to be part of the interior fabric of the scabbard?"

"What of them?" He spoke at her brow, his head bent.

"The scabbard is not lined in cloth. The interior is unfinished leather. Those fibers are from rope that had been forced into the scabbard. Or, perhaps, fibers that clung to the dagger after it cut through rope."

"Interesting. And the matter of potential delicacy?"

"Why would Mr. Walsh have been cutting through rope with a decorative dagger? Perhaps more to the point, why would he have been carrying such a weapon to a late-night assignation with a woman, assuming his assignation was with a woman?"

A moment of silence became two. She looked up at him.

"Do you know?" she said.

"No. But I believe you have a hypothesis you wish to share."

"Do you mean the hypothesis having to do with Mr. Walsh's violent proclivities in the bedchamber and the danger such a man might face if his affair were to turn sour before he remembered to hide the tools of his debauchery? Yes, that hypothesis."

"I'm certain I should be shocked that you know of such a thing, and yet somehow I am not."

"The butcher used to visit the cook at the—at the place where I lived when I was a very young child. I'd no idea at the time what went on in the pantry, only that I was obliged to wait an extra quarter hour to collect the headmistress's tea and always got my ears boxed for it. But years later I reconsidered the evidence. Petti told me the rest. He was quite the philanderer in his youth."

"Was he?"

"You are shocked."

"I am not. Though I am a bit curious as to how this slight evidence"—he gestured toward the scabbard—"led you to that conclusion specifically."

"I considered others. None of them were nearly as interesting. More importantly, none led to a crime of passion of the sort Mr. Walsh suffered. His wound does rather speak for itself."

"Perhaps."

"I have searched this room. Now we should search everybody's chambers."

"It must wait until morning. The evening's entertainments were drawing to a close when I left."

He had stayed for all the dancing. Perhaps he had danced with the other ladies. Certainly he had.

"On the other end of the great hall," she said, "there is a display of weapons and armor that we can study now . . . if you haven't danced yourself into such exhaustion that you are unable to help me, of course."

"I believe I can remain awake another few minutes if I try very hard."

She took up her lamp. "As a despicably wealthy second son you must often spend entire nights drinking and playing cards and generally carousing, then sleep all the following day. Mustn't you?"

"Something like that." He extinguished his candle and took her lamp. His fingers brushed hers. She grabbed her hand back and moved swiftly into the great hall.

A magnificent, impressively bellicose array spread before them on the near wall, illumined only by the light of a torch across the hall. Breastplates and other pieces of body armor had been arranged like paper dolls across an iron grille, stretching from one end of the hall to the other. Sprays of lances, broadswords, sabers, and bows had been arranged decoratively. Shields emblazoned with noble crests dotted the whole.

"The lords of this castle knew how to outfit themselves," she murmured.

"That place where the cook met her visitor," he said as the glow of lamplight glimmered off steel. "Where you lived. It was a foundling home, was it not?"

"Yes."

He did not reply, but studied the armor. He was a nobleman and she was an orphan, and she had more in common with a mutton chop than with him. But he trusted in her intelligence and made her laugh. And looking at his profile now made something inside her tighten with both panic and strange pleasure.

"Did you name your dog?" she said.

"He is not my dog."

"But you did name him?"

"Gonçalo."

"Gonçalo? How odd."

"Beatus Gonçalo of Amarante was a priest of the thirteenth century, and worldly despite his vows. He finally turned his life to true holiness. But his nephew, who stood to gain a great deal if Gonçalo remained corrupt, set a dog upon him."

"The nephew did not appreciate his uncle's change of heart, I guess?"

He tilted his attention down to her. "That dog chewed through one of the finest boots I have ever owned."

She smiled. "You still have the other."

"Thank you. That will do me well should I happen to lose the opposite identical boot."

"Do you have an identical pair?"

His brow creased. "What would I do with an identical pair of boots?"

"I don't know. You are the despicably wealthy second son. You tell me."

"I—"

Laughter bubbled from the archway and candle-light danced toward them along the walls. Lord Vitor doused the lamp and drew her behind the iron screen.

"What are you—"

He shook his head and released her.

Light footsteps tripped along stone, and into the great medieval keep flew a delicate lady wearing white froth, followed by a gentleman with shirt points to his ears. Seeming to flee, Juliana Abraccia moved at a pace far too slow to outdistance Martin Anders's determined strides.

"Oh, Signore Anders! You must not!"

"But my darling Miss Abraccia, I *must.*"

Ravenna folded her arms. He had called her his darling only the night before.

Prickling with gooseflesh, she rubbed at her arms. With only aperture slit windows, the great hall was much colder than the tiny south-facing storage room. The muslin gown Ann had lent her was practical for the party in the adjacent chamber, which was well heated by two modern fireplaces and many dancing people, but ridiculously unsuited to hiding elsewhere in the fortress.

The man beside her, however, seemed perfectly comfortable. This must be due to . . . she had no idea. She knew little about Lord Vitor Courtenay, except that he was less equable than he pretended to be among the others, and that the subtle knocking together of her knees beneath her tissue-thin skirts now had more to do with his proximity than with the cold. Absurdly, the recollection of his body atop hers in the stable came to her again, of his weight pressing her into the straw.

He had not come this close to her since he had saved her from the river. Now their arms nearly brushed—his defined by the fabric of his fine coat and hers bared practically to the shoulder. His breathing sounded even and slow. Clearly this closeness did not affect him, despite his teasing on the hillside that he still wished to kiss her. An impromptu swim in frigid water could cool the most insistent ardor, she supposed.

"Why are we hiding?" she said beneath the trill of Juliana's thoroughly insincere protests and Mr. Anders's wine-soaked assurances.

Lord Vitor cut her a Dark Look.

"They cannot hear me," she whispered. "Her giggles drown out all else."

A V appeared between his brows and he seemed to study her face as sometimes he did, as though searching her features for an answer to a question he had not spoken. When he looked at her like this she did not feel the cold. She felt hot and unsteady.

She should have let him teach her how to dance.

The thought came unbidden and unwelcome. She didn't want to learn how to dance and she did not want him to touch her again. Even the caress of his midnight gaze now made her unbearably uncomfortable.

Then, with a hooding of his eyes she had seen only once before, his gaze dipped to her mouth.

"Why am I allowing my toes to grow numb one by one?" she made herself say. Anything to halt the painful pleasure inside her. Anything. For it *was* painful, she understood now. When he looked at her like this, an unendurable sort of misery gathered in her chest and belly that she needed to escape. That was the reason she had fled the drawing room earlier, to avoid his dark regard and to avoid touching him again. "So that I can watch Mr. Anders cajole Miss Abraccia into his arms, since he failed to cajole me?" she forced through her lips. "He believes he is a poet, but in truth he is a boy."

Shifting his attention from her, her companion glanced into the great hall. "Killers may wear masks."

She peeked through the grille, her breaths fogging on the steel breastplate in front of her. Juliana took another dainty step away from Mr. Anders. Then she reversed direction and fell against his chest with all evidence of submission.

Ravenna simply could not watch. It was too foolish. "And you know this because . . . ?"

"Because I have worn such masks. But no longer." His eyes, upon her again, flickered with torchlight. "He failed?"

He was a killer? This man who had risked his life to save her from the river? The only man in the castle who—she was quite certain—was not the murderer they sought? "He who—what? Failed?" Her wits had fled along with her breaths.

Across the hall, Mr. Anders murmured to Miss Abraccia. A muscle in Lord Vitor's jaw flexed.

"You mean he, *him*?" Ravenna whispered. "Martin Anders?"

Lord Vitor said nothing, only watched her.

"Of course he failed," she said. "He is a sorry tease and I don't—"

"He failed." The words seemed to come from deep in his chest. He looked up to the ceiling and then down at his feet and then finally, as though reluctantly, again at her mouth. "Would I fail?" His voice was unmistakably husky.

Ravenna's stomach turned over. Now he did not tease—not as he had at other times. He meant this question and he wanted an answer. She should go. Immediately. Without delay she should slip out of this concealed place and save herself from certain trouble.

"Would you fail?" she heard herself repeat.

He looked very serious. "No."

Heat and confusion tangled beneath her skin now. *Desire*. It suddenly seemed so clear. Too clear. She *wanted* him to touch her yet it terrified her. "No?" she asked, the chill barely stirring between them.

"No," he said. "Unless you bite me again." Laughter sparked in his eyes. Abruptly, Ravenna could breathe again.

Then his hand touched hers.

And breathing became a distant memory.

Chapter 10

The Touch

She had been longing for touch, real touch, not merely the pat of Petti's fingers or the quick clasp of a friend's hand. She had spent nights aching for Beast's warm mass to curl herself around and take comfort in. Then for a few moments when this man had held her in his arms, in her icy stupor she had felt safe.

Now as his hand brushed hers she felt no consolation or comfort, only fear. Everything in her readied to run, but the soles of her feet remained flat upon the stone floor as, gently, his knuckles strafed hers. It was the slightest of touches, but everything inside her seemed to shimmer to life. His fingertips followed the same paths, barely a caress, barely contact at all, yet it filled her. Her breaths would not come. No one had ever touched her like this. No one had touched her as though he wished to feel her—as though he wished to know this small part of her—any part of her.

Without releasing her gaze, he passed his fingertips across the pads of her fingers. She did not expect the tingling shock or the gasp that slipped through her lips.

He stroked softly. Inside her, where she was empty, bloomed longing and heady agitation. His hand was warm. His palm cupped around her knuckles so that she felt his strength. In the torchlight she watched his face, the hard plane of his jaw and the shadows in his eyes. What he did now was intimate and as wrong as the kiss he had forced upon her in the stable. But there was no force now, only need growing inside her and his intoxicating exploration.

Then he stroked his thumb across her palm. *She mustn't allow this.* From her lips issued the barest breath of resistance. He repeated the caress. It was strange, deep pleasure that she knew nothing of, and she was as sensible of her ignorance as she suspected he was of his confidence to make her feel. She could see it in the line of his lips that remained closed while hers had fallen open. With each stroke across her palm her breaths came faster. But she saw that his did too, his chest moving quick and hard.

He turned her hand, laced her fingers through his, and brought their palms together.

Ravenna choked back a sigh. Her eyelids dipped. Skin to skin, she felt him between her fingers and brushing against her palm with tingles that made her a little dizzy. To be connected like this, the heat of a man's life intertwined with hers, seemed miraculous. *Inescapable.* Despite his strength he held her by her will. She had no desire to pull away, only the need to remain with him in this silent meeting of skin and heat. She found her chin tilting up, her gaze dipping to his lips. Their shoulders brushed. She felt it everywhere inside her. He bent his head.

"Ravenna," he whispered so close to her lips.

The crack of a slap echoed through the hall. "*No,* signore!"

Ravenna jerked her hand free. She forced her eyes to focus beyond the grille.

Hands over her mouth, Juliana fled across the hall. Mr. Anders stood still, wobbling slightly, the torchlight revealing his scowl. Juliana disappeared up the stairs. Mr. Anders released a great huffing groan and followed.

Sinking her hands into her skirts, Ravenna forced herself to look at the man beside her. Shoulders stiff, he stood with his hand around the back of his neck. He glanced aside at her. With a deep inhalation his gaze shifted to her mouth, where for a long, silent moment it rested.

"You should go," he said quietly, his voice quite low. "Now."

She took up the lamp and slipped out from behind the screen and went swiftly across the hall. As he followed at a distance he did not mask his footsteps, but she did not look back. She did not know why she had allowed him to touch her. She should not have. Yet she knew that he would silently see her safely to her door.

RAVENNA RUBBED SLEEPLESS hours from her eyes, dressed, and sought out General Dijon's daughter. Arielle sat in the empty drawing room, her fingertips listless upon the keys of the pianoforte. Her pretty eyes lit with hope as she stood and crossed the room.

"Have they found *ma petite*?" she said eagerly. "Have they found Marie?" Her English was soft, her Gallic accent adding music to her voice.

Ravenna shook her head. "Not yet. But I'm certain they shall."

Last night she and Lord Vitor had not spoken of the dog, though she had intended to. They had not searched for the dagger or reviewed any other details of their investigation either. Instead, they had held hands in the dark. And he had nearly kissed her.

Ravenna's cheeks felt warm as she sat with Arielle on the sofa.

"Why are you alone here? The prince ordered that everyone must always be with at least two companions."

"Mademoiselle Anders came here with me, but some minutes ago she became impatient and departed."

"Impatient concerning what? Do you know?"

Arielle shook her head.

"Mademoiselle Dijon, I have not yet had the opportunity to speak with you about the night Mr. Walsh was killed."

The French girl's pretty brow dipped. "Then it is true," she said. "You and Lord Vitor hope to discover the madman who did these crimes?"

"Is that known?"

"Lady Iona said to me she believed this to be. Monsieur Sepic, he is . . ." She made a thoroughly Gallic gesture with her slender shoulders.

Lady Iona was too observant for Ravenna's tastes, and Monsieur Sepic clearly inspired faith in no one at Chevriot.

"Is it true?" the French girl asked.

"May I be frank with you?"

Arielle nodded, black lashes wide against her pale skin. She was loveliness itself, with china smooth skin and black ringlets and perfect lips, like a doll.

"Yesterday Monsieur Sepic suggested to me and Lord Vitor that your dog went missing at precisely the moment that, if you had murdered Mr. Walsh, you would wish to provide a sympathetic distraction to draw attention away from yourself as a suspect."

Arielle's eyes flew wide. "*Mais,* I would not murder a man!"

Ravenna released a tight breath. "I hoped you would say that."

"What else might I have said?"

"That you would never put Marie in danger or part with her, even to disguise your crime."

Distress tweaked her rosebud mouth. "But I would not."

"Of course you would not. I understand your devotion to her. Because of it your immediate insistence that you did not murder a man speaks to your innocence."

"If I did not think murder impossible, I would have spoken first of my Marie?"

Ravenna nodded.

Arielle's slender hand rose to her quivering lips. "But I am devastated that she is gone."

Ravenna grasped her hands. "We will find her. I promise it."

"Ah," came a silken purr from the doorway. "What an affecting scene." Lady Penelope bent her golden head to her sister's silvery locks. "It seems that our friend from the West Country does not know that a lady refrains from mauling her acquaintances." She made a delicate little shrug and moved into the drawing room. "I don't suppose you mind it, do you, mademoiselle? In America you must encounter infinite gaucheries, *n'est-ce pas*?" She dimpled sweetly and lowered her behind, clad in a stunning morning gown, upon a settee. Her sister perched beside her. Despite the absence of servants, both of them appeared each day pristinely elegant. They had each other's assistance, Ravenna supposed.

Arielle wrapped her other delicate hand around Ravenna's. "*Merci*, mademoiselle," she said softly.

Lady Penelope chuckled. "Dear Mademoiselle Dijon, she does not understand French. Miss Caulfield, she said she is grateful."

"Thank you for the translation. I am glad to see

you, in fact. Monsieur Sepic asked me to ask you, your mother, and Lady Grace about the night of Mr. Walsh's murder," she lied without a single prick of conscience. "We can begin now."

"You will speak of my mother as Lady Whitebarrow," Penelope said, "when I allow you to speak of her at all. And I will tell you when I and my sister are prepared to answer impertinent questions from an upstart country pauper."

"Her sister is a duchess, Penny," Lady Grace whispered as though they all couldn't hear her perfectly well.

"Did you enjoy the dancing last night, Miss Caulfield?" Lady Penelope asked sweetly. "Oh, I forgot. You don't know how to dance, do you?"

Heat darted through Ravenna.

"Look, Grace," Lady Penelope said with a curl of her perfect lips. "The blush does show through her skin after all. Remarkable."

"Well, isn't this a pretty gathering of little birds?" Lady Margaret exclaimed upon a labored breath where she stood in the doorway with her hand tucked in Petti's elbow. His eyes twinkled. He preferred the company of loquacious women and handsome men to any other. With Lady Margaret and Duchess McCall in residence, as well as several attractive gentlemen, he'd been in perpetual good humor despite the murder and theft hanging over them all. Ravenna had to smile.

They came forward, and only then mousy Ann appeared in her mother's bustling wake.

"Come, Ann dear." Lady Margaret waved a plump hand. "You must show off the pearls your fond papa gave you this morning."

The mouse peeked from behind the matron.

"Oh, Miss Feathers." Arielle went to draw Ann to a chair away from her mother. "How beloved you must be to your father. It is a fine necklace."

It was large and vulgar and must weigh half a stone. Sir Henry had superb taste in Thoroughbreds but apparently little discernment in ladies' jewelry. Poor Ann's shoulders practically bent over, and two spots of crimson perched upon her cheeks, at odds with her gray and yellow pin-striped gown.

"Dear me," Lady Penelope purred. "What an impressive display." Rather than Ann's necklace, she looked at Lady Margaret's ample bosom that bubbled like slow-boiling soup at the edge of her scooping bodice. Sir Henry's wife had taken to wearing daring gowns and bending over in front of Lord Prunesly. The scholar renowned throughout Europe for his discoveries in natural philosophy seemed to take no notice of the eager biological specimen.

"Agreed, m'dear," Petti said affably, and settled Lady Margaret in a chair beside the twins. "Ladies charm especially well when they are specially adorned."

Penelope nudged her sister.

"But don't you think, sir," Grace blurted, "that given present circumstances it is inappropriate to behave as though we are attending a party every day?"

"But, my dear, we *are* attending a party. And our host wishes us to enjoy ourselves. Therefore, we must. When there is a murderer afoot, it behooves a lady to make herself as pretty as ever. To give us all cheer, don't you know. We must take our cue from that medieval fellow who wrote that clever book. When all the peasants were dropping dead of the plague, the ladies and gentlemen removed themselves to the country and diverted themselves with delightful stories. Ten stories each night for ten days, until the pestilence passed."

"Really?" Ann peeped.

"Certainly, m'dear. Those Italians were vastly clever."

"But, monsieur," Arielle said, "the plague would

remain among us here even as we would seek to escape it. One of *us* is the murderer."

"I plead innocence." Lord Case strolled into the room. "Will you believe it of me, mademoiselle?"

Arielle lowered her eyes modestly. "If you wish it, my lord."

"Speaking of Italians," Petti said, "we lack the company now of only Miss Abraccia, Miss Anders, and Lady Iona to complete the complement of virgin sacrifices in the house. What do you think, my lord? Shall we call the others in and have a portrait painted?"

The room went dead silent. Ravenna stifled a chuckle. Lord Case smiled but his eyes went to the general's daughter. Then his attention shifted to her and lost all hint of pleasure. The laughter died in Ravenna's throat.

"Oh, sir," Lady Margaret chortled with an operatic trill. "You flatter me! It has been nineteen years since I was a bride, though perhaps you would not know it unless my own dear Ann were not seated nearby. How amusing you are." She tapped his hand playfully.

"Mr. Pettigrew." Ann's fingers twisted together in her lap. "I beg your forgiveness, but you do his highness an injustice. He is a fine man. It would not be a sacrifice to marry him. Rather, the opposite."

Lady Margaret beamed proudly from bejeweled ear to bejeweled ear.

"With those words you reveal yourself to be a true lady, Miss Feathers." Petti looked about. "Now, who would like to review her Shakespeare? I've never tread the boards myself, but I knew plenty of actresses in my younger days, so I suppose I am an expert at the theater of sorts."

"Oh, sir." Lady Margaret chuckled. "You are incorrigible!"

"I do like it when a lady calls me that, m'dear. Now,

recite to me your lines and I shall be all that is useful. Miss Feathers, do come assist your mother and me."

Dutifully, Ann moved to sit by Lady Margaret, and the three of them bent their heads together.

"Lord Case," Lady Penelope said, sugar dripping from her lips, "how do you like the part of Romeo's cousin, Benvolio? It seems insufficiently noble for you. Perhaps it should have been assigned to another gentleman."

"With a prince, a belted earl, a baron, and a knight, not to mention my own terrifyingly impressive brother in the house, I should be afraid to demand any role but whichever those inestimable gentlemen delegate to me."

"You are too modest," Lady Penelope purred. "It shows your good taste, which"—she cast a glance at Lady Margaret and, pausing upon Ravenna briefly, returned her attention to the earl—"is sadly lacking among the prince's guests."

He smiled, but hardness settled at the corners of his mouth. "Rather, I speak through begrudging humility. In matters of character I am outclassed in this company."

"I cannot believe it," Lady Penelope demurred, leaning slightly toward him as if Ravenna and Arielle were not present. "But we must give our inferiors their due, I suppose."

Mademoiselle Dijon rose. "Miss Caulfield, I should like your advice on a cap I embroider for my father. Will you assist me?"

Ravenna followed her from the room. Lord Case watched her depart even as the twins demanded his attention.

Once across the threshold, Arielle bent her head, her lips tight. "*Les sœurs* . . . Ladies Penelope and Grace . . . *ce sont des vipères*. Do you say this in England? The vipers?"

Ravenna laughed. "Yes. I suppose women can be horrid in any language."

"But, I must tell you, Ravenna . . . Lady Grace, she does not like all that her sister says."

"What makes you say that?"

"Last night when Lady Penelope danced with the prince, I watched her sister. She stood alone beside their mother. Looking upon Penelope, she wore a face *froide comme la pierre.* Like the stone."

The same as at dinner two nights earlier. At her sister's side, Grace moved and spoke like a shadow, mimicking her sister in everything. But away from her twin she revealed another facade.

"Thank you for telling me this, Mademoiselle Dijon."

"*Je vous en prie,* mademoiselle. *Enfin,* I do not believe you wish to waste your moments at needlework with me, *non*? You must go now. Solve this murder, I pray, and find *ma chère petite.*"

Ravenna hurried across the great hall where the night before she had nearly lost her head at the touch of a man's hand. At the base of the stairs she paused. Men's voices issued forth from a doorway near the dining room, the unmistakable accents of Monsieur Sepic among them. She went toward the open door.

Gentlemen lounged about a beautiful wood-paneled room at the center of which a billiards table reigned. Sir Henry and the prince stood by the table, cue sticks in hand, with General Dijon looking on. Back turned to the game, Lord Prunesly peered through his spectacles at a diagram of hunting dogs framed in glass. Lord Prunesly's son slouched in a corner, his hair falling over his brow in a sullen slant. Sir Beverley reclined with his usual subdued elegance in a wingback chair across from Monsieur Sepic, whose hand clasped a glass of golden-red liquid. Lord Vitor leaned against the wall beside the mantel, watching her, the only man in the room to notice her.

Of all the gentlemen guests, only Lord Whitebarrow, Petti, and Lord Case were absent.

Sir Henry glanced up from the table. "Ah, Miss Caulfield." Billiards cue in hand, he came toward her. "I am delighted to see you. Delighted! You find us gentlemen at our vice early this morning. His highness was teaching my lord here"—he gestured to the distracted Lord Prunesly—"a few tricks of the table, and as there's a new layer of snow on the ground the rest of us are here for the entertainment. But that's all nothing to a clever girl like you, is it? Immensely clever, I say, gentlemen! The poultice she wrapped about my animal's hoof has done the trick. He walked three times about the courtyard this morning without complaint. The lameness persists, of course. That'll need time to heal. But he's mightily improved. In the name of Zeus, mightily improved! I shall have to call you Lady Miracle now." His brow turned thoughtful. "Fine name for a horse, that."

"Ah, mademoiselle." The prince approached, took her hand, and lifted it to his lips. "You brighten this gathering of men with the soft smile in your eyes. For me, it is enough to ensure a morning of joy." He tilted his head. "Churlishly, however, I must command that you give me, your host, a vision of the smile of your lips as well, so that my day will be bright throughout."

She obliged. "Will that do, your highness?"

His fingers tightened on hers. "Sufficient for a lifetime if I weren't vastly greedy." He gestured to the billiards table. "You see we are hard at work."

Not solving the murder. She held herself back from looking at Lord Vitor. "I do. Has Lord Prunesly learned what he must to be a worthy opponent?"

"I fear he has little head for the game," the prince said with pursed lips. He lowered his voice. "You know these bookish sorts. All brain. No bravery." He winked.

"My sister Eleanor is a tremendous scholar and she has the courage of an archangel. But, as this is your house, I will allow you your mistaken opinion."

He grinned and tried to draw her into the room. She tugged her hand away. "I cannot intrude upon your game." Or go any closer to the man she had stood beside in the dark last night. Her pulse was already far too rapid though an entire room separated them. "I hoped to speak with Monsieur Sepic."

"Ah." Abruptly grave, the prince jutted out his lower lip. "Estimable lady, you are dedicated to the task I would pretend did not exist if I could. You shame me."

"I do not intend to."

"See here, Dijon," Sir Henry exclaimed. "I told you she was mighty clever with horses. I'll wager she has a healing way with dogs too. You should allow her to tend to your little bitch when she's found again."

"Thank you, sir," she said, and turned to Mayor Sepic. Legs crossed and hands folded about the glass, he seemed settled in for the day. "Monsieur, might I have a word with you?"

"*Mais bien sûr*, mademoiselle." He popped to his feet.

"In the corridor?" she suggested.

He bowed to the gentlemen all about, several times, and hastened forward. All the men were looking at her now, but she only cared about the man whose dark blue coat stretched across his broad shoulders like it had been made to match his eyes and allow him to devastate any female unfortunate enough to glimpse him. Where last night his gaze had sought hers quite intensely, now only quiet interest lit his eyes.

She went into the corridor. "Monsieur, have you given thought to my suggestion that we should require all the suspects to write out the message found on the note in Mr. Walsh's pocket so that we might compare the hands?"

"Ah, *oui*." He nodded and stroked a moustache. "An excellent idea, *vraiment*. But it would not be useful at this time. My investigation has taken another turn, you see."

A turn right into the billiards room, apparently.

"What other direction?"

"Ah, but I cannot divulge the business of the police to a lady, *naturellement*." He smiled with great conde-scension. "You will see, mademoiselle, all will be well. You needn't—*comment dire?*—fret."

"Monsieur, you have only to instruct the suspects to provide a sample of their writing and I will do the work to compare them to the evidence."

"*Oui, oui.* A very good idea." Again with the mous-tache stroking. "I vow to ponder it." He peered eagerly over her shoulder. "Mademoiselle." He bowed and re-turned to the billiards room.

Ravenna released a frustrated breath. But it was to be expected. Until two days ago he had been merely the mayor of a tiny mountain village. Now men of wealth and status took pains to ingratiate themselves to him in the hope that he would not accuse them of murder. Monsieur Sepic now floated in happy, heady delirium.

She understood. In the great hall last night, when a wealthy nobleman had been caressing her hand, giving her attention as no man had ever given her, she'd gotten a little delirious too.

On the bedchamber level, the door to Lady Penelope and Grace's chamber remained locked. Ravenna re-leased the handle slowly. Sepic would not allow her to assist in the investigation. And Lord Vitor seemed disinterested in the mystery this morning.

But perhaps his diffidence now hadn't anything to do with the murder. Last night he had told her to go and she'd been happy to oblige. Before that unwise handholding, though, they'd gotten along well. That it might now, briefly, be awkward between them she could accept. Another moment alone with him, however, she could not. Perhaps he was of the same mind.

She went to the parlor where they had examined the body. Monsieur Sepic had removed it; only Mr. Walsh's clothing and armor remained. Nothing about his belongings revealed more to her than what they already knew. Trailing her fingers across the last possessions the man had carried before his demise, she stalled on his signet ring. It seemed a grand possession for a mere mister. But so too was a ring of gold and ruby for a woman who had until three months ago been a servant.

She hadn't even looked at her family's ring since Sir Beverley gave it to her. The notion of marrying Prince Sebastiao—or anyone—was laughable. She would tell Arabella that as soon as she returned to England. She would give the ring back into her sister's keeping and return to . . .

Nowhere. She could not remain at Shelton Grange. But to live in Papa's home again, to place herself under his authority after six years of virtual freedom, this time without even Beast for company . . . *Unthinkable.* At Arabella's ducal home the restrictions upon her would be less, but greater than she liked.

She stared at Mr. Walsh's ring. He had once been a marquess's secretary. Perhaps his employer had given it to him. Or perhaps he had stolen it. Perhaps he had come to Chevriot Castle to escape prison too. Like her.

It seemed remarkable that a man would travel to France to a house at which the sons of his former employer were guests solely upon coincidence. Prince Sebastiao had vowed that his father, Raynaldo, had not invited Oliver Walsh to the party, that Walsh was an intruder. But perhaps he didn't know everything. And perhaps Lord Vitor had not told her everything he knew about Mr. Walsh's presence at Chevriot. Perhaps he was not telling her the entire truth.

Heaviness settling in her chest, she peered more closely at the gold ring. A ridge formed the back of a lion's head that jutted outward. Memory stirred. She closed her eyes and ran her fingertip along the ridge, then pressed it into her palm. Two nights ago she had studied the bruise around Martin Anders's eye at close proximity. Buried in that bruise, against the bony eye bed, was a shallow laceration the length of the lion ridge on this ring.

Longing to pocket the ring, and knowing that if anybody searched her belongings she would look like a thief who was especially interested in valuable men's rings, she set it down. But a tiny thread of buoyancy worked its way through her. She had brought together two clues. Neither of them had to do with the Marquess of Airedale or his sons. The tightness in her chest eased. She should share her discovery with Lord Vitor right away.

The image of him watching her in the billiards room, his dark eyes inscrutable, stayed her feet.

Lunch would be soon enough to tell him. Then she would insist that Mr. Anders write a note and they would compare the hands.

She turned to Mr. Walsh's clothing. It offered no new clues. Plucking up the note, she flipped it open, scanned the words again, and ran the pad of her thumb absently over the broken seal as she considered how to force the remaining suspects to give a sample of writing. Perhaps she could trick them, invent some parlor game that required writing and suggest it to the prince. He would do it. Since she'd been thrown in the river he had been overly solicitous and enormously charming. He was bright and somewhat manic, but affectionate and good-humored, not at all the dissipated rogue she'd initially thought him.

How much had Lord Vitor told the prince of their covert investigation? Or, like the kiss in the stable and the moment behind the iron grille last night, was it their secret—except to overly observant Lady Iona and now Arielle Dijon? And Lord Case. He knew about the kiss. She had told him.

Her thumb stalled in the center of the wax disc. The tip of her thumb fit into the smooth indentation perfectly. She held it up to her candle, but not close enough to melt it. The shallowest fingerprint marked it.

The day before, Monsieur Sepic had found the paper and wax upon which the note had been written and sealed in a drawer in the tower parlor. There, however, his curiosity about the note had ended. But someone—a woman—had pressed her small fingertip into a circle of searing hot wax. That must have burned the finger.

Time to start studying fingertips. Ravenna left the frigid little parlor in the castle's farthest corner and headed toward the northwest tower. She'd not yet had time to study the bloodstain that Lord Vitor had told her about on the door handle and she suspected Monsieur Sepic had ignored that evidence too. After she looked it over she would make another attempt at the Whitebarrow twins' bedchamber.

Lord Vitor had suggested that she examine the ladies' garments for blood. How could he imagine she would do that? Perhaps he only wished to busy her with an impossible task. Perhaps he did not in fact wish to pursue the mystery. Perhaps it was not in his interest to discover the murderer's identity. Perhaps . . . perhaps taking her hand behind the rack of armor last night had merely been a diversion to distract her from looking for the dagger.

No guard followed her. Despite Lord Vitor's orders, she had not seen the man assigned to protect her yet. Or had he ever assigned a guard to her?

In the final winding stairwell to the turret room the air was still and cold. Her breaths misted as she reached the top. She turned the door handle and stepped inside.

On the other side of the parlor, a woman was bent forward over a table, her skirts about her waist and her buttocks entirely bared to the winter light streaming through the windows. A man with guinea-gold hair and breeches around his knees stood between her spread legs, clutching her hips and pumping into her like a rutting ram on a ewe.

Lord Whitebarrow was now accounted for.

Ravenna's limbs ceased to function.

The woman groaned. "Harder." Her next groan was a plea. "I beg o' ye, my laird. Harder nou."

"Vixen," he grunted and thrust into her with such force that the table creaked.

Ravenna stumbled backward and knocked her shoulder against the door frame. Her muffled "Oh!" sounded beneath Lord Whitebarrow's grunts.

Lady Iona's shoulders twisted around, her breasts spilling out of her gown, eyes wide as she met Ravenna's stare. They gaped at each other in mutual paralysis. The earl reached forward, shoved his hand into Iona's bodice, and drove into her again. Her stunning features slid into a grimace of pain. Eyes closing, she dropped her head and moaned. "Aye, my laird. *Aye.* Just like that."

Not pain, apparently.

Ravenna fumbled with the door handle, slipped out, and shut the panel as quietly as she could. Pressing her back against the wall, she struggled for air.

Lady Iona and Lord Whitebarrow.

Lady Iona and Lord Whitebarrow?

Miss Abraccia and Mr. Anders, perhaps. Even Lady Margaret and Lord Prunesly would not have surprised her, if he ever turned his attention away from his studies. But Iona? And Lord Whitebarrow? He was married and she was . . . not a maiden after all, it seemed. True, she'd been making outrageous comments about the gentlemen for days to Ravenna. But in company she behaved modestly.

There was nothing modest whatsoever about her behavior in that parlor with Lord Whitebarrow. Ravenna hadn't known a man could take a woman like a stallion mounting a mare. She always imagined people copulated face-to-face. They could, after all. It was anatomically more feasible. Female animals had hooves or paw pads to brace themselves. Women did not. Face-to-face, a woman would not have to worry about scraped knees or, in this instance, splinters in her elbows. But it didn't seem like Iona had been having trouble with the table arrangement. On the contrary. Lord Whitebarrow hadn't seemed particularly inconvenienced either.

Vixen?

Ravenna could not imagine anyone calling her that. *Hoyden*, yes. Frequently. But *vixen*? She wished she could wipe the sounds and images from her mind. Especially Iona's horrified stare. And her moan of rapture. *The entire thing.* Her stays pinched at her ribs and she felt hot all over.

On the other side of the door the grunting and moaning scaled peaks. Breaking away from the wall, she pressed her fingertips into her eyes and hurried down the winding stairway.

VITOR FORCED HIMSELF to endure another several minutes of the gentlemen's fawning over Sepic before he left the billiards room. Sufficient time had elapsed to dissuade any of them from imagining he was following Ravenna.

He *was* following her, of course.

The night before in the hall he hadn't been able to get distance from her quickly enough. But he'd barely closed his bedchamber door when, greeted by the *yip* of the pup she had forced upon him, he cursed his hasty retreat. Encouraging her to flee from him was a temporary measure at best. He had wanted her since the first time he touched her. Until he'd taken her hand in the dark, however, he hadn't known quite how much.

"Monseigneur," General Dijon called after him. "Wait a moment, if you will." He came forward, his posture militarily erect. "My daughter has heard that you and Miss Caulfield are pursuing an investigation of your own into the murder and the theft of her pet."

"She heard the truth, sir."

The general's brow relaxed. "*Bien*. Perhaps the criminal will be found."

"I am afraid we've found more questions than answers."

"Yet I am reassured." The general shook his head. "I intend no insult to Sepic. His service to his community is admirable. But I do not entirely trust in his intelligence."

Vitor thought it best not to respond.

"You see," the general said with an air of urgency, "the dog, it is not only a valuable breeder. My wife gave it to our daughter. For long they were—how do you say?—incompatible, always misunderstanding each other. My wife, she was despondent, sorrowful. You know the way of women, of course."

Precious little. Especially the way of one woman.

"My daughter is dear to me beyond telling," the general said. "But my wife, monseigneur, she is the queen of my heart. She has been that for twenty years. When the gift of the dog brought them into harmony again, I could have asked for nothing else."

"I see."

"I trust you will find it."

"I will."

First he needed to find the woman. He left the general and went searching. A guard had seen her mount the stairs of the northeast tower. Vitor started up the winding stairs and only a breath came between the sound of soft footsteps pattering downward and her body flying around the spiral.

She slammed into him. "Oh!"

He caught her and grasped her shoulders to steady her, and her gaze upon his chest snapped up. Her eyes were distant.

"What is it?" He scanned the curve of the stair and listened for pursuit. But her face showed confusion, not fear. "From what are you running?"

"Nothing. Nothing at all." She ducked her head and tried to shrug out of his hold but he held her. Touching a fingertip beneath her chin, he tilted up her face.

"Tell me."

"I said it is nothing."

"I have never seen you run from anything, not even me. Don't lie."

She was hot to his touch and her gaze darted across his face. "I ran from you in the stable."

"Ravenna—"

"But I am not running now. I am moving with haste away from two people who should not have been doing what they were doing when I accidentally happened upon them."

"Two people?"

She jerked her chin away and he allowed her to shift out of his grip. But color remained in her cheeks.

"What two people?" he said.

"I cannot tell you. I am not Lady Penelope."

"For which I thank heaven daily."

She blinked. "You do?"

"Of course." This morning his contemplation had focused not on the words of the ancient prophets and apostles of scripture, but on her. "How are you not she?"

"I don't spread malicious gossip."

Ah. He leaned his shoulder into the stairwell's central pillar. "Telling me whom you saw is not spreading gossip. I will not share the information with others, as I believe you know."

"I don't know that. How did Lady Penelope learn that I cannot dance?"

"Not from me."

"And how is it that Mr. Walsh once worked for your father but you hadn't any notion that he would be at this castle in France at precisely the time you and Lord Case are guests here?"

"I don't know. My brother might, but if so he hasn't told me."

"Really?"

"Yes. Ravenna, I am telling you the truth."

Her eyes skittered away. "I don't know that the information I just learned is useful to the investigation of the murder." But even as she spoke, he could see that she doubted her own words, and that troubled her. Her nature did not incline toward secrecy, rather honest clarity. She had the hands of a healer and the beauty of a wild creature, and Vitor wanted to take her into his arms and taste her, now, here, until he had his fill.

She worried her lower lip between her teeth.

"I can nearly see the gears grinding," he said to distract himself from what he wished to do to her lips.

Her heel shifted up a step, retreating. "My mind is not a clock. There are no gears."

"Give me your thoughts. Please," he added.

"It was Lord Whitebarrow, but . . . not Lady White-barrow."

Unsurprising. Like most men of his status, White-barrow took what he wanted. More instructive, per-haps, would be the identity of his partner.

A reluctant smile rippled over her lips. "I had the same thought."

"What thought was that?"

"That with an Ice Countess like his, it's no wonder he looks elsewhere."

The general's avowal of devotion to his wife came to Vitor as he looked into the dark star eyes of this woman he wanted. "Whitebarrow was not only looking."

Her gaze retreated into the confusion he'd seen in them when he had touched her the night before. "No," she agreed.

"Who was he with?"

"I cannot tell you."

There were few options. Lady Margaret: unlikely. The duchess: unlikely for different reasons. A maid: possibly.

"Lady Iona," he said.

A breath shot from her. "I cannot confirm that."

She hid her feelings in dissembling as well as she hid her beauty in plain gowns and unkempt coiffures: without success. Watching her with the other guests had left him with few questions as to her loyalties. "In this house among the women, you would only go to the gallows for Lady Iona or Miss Feathers."

Her chin lifted infinitesimally. "Perhaps you do not know me well enough to know whom I would protect if I must."

"I do."

"Really? Then since you have already pronounced upon my loyalty to the women here, tell me, whom among the men would I defend?"

"Sir Beverley and Pettigrew."

"Anybody can see that."

Now he could say what he might have said in the darkness before he had ordered her to go. He could tell her of the desire he had seen in her eyes when he had touched her so simply, the naked longing. He could tell her that he had made her go because he hadn't trusted himself not to take advantage of it.

He said, "And me."

Chapter 11

The Wild Creature

*H*er lashes beat once. "You are astoundingly arrogant. But I suppose handsome men are rarely otherwise."

"I do not speak from arrogance." He spoke from the certainty born of a single meeting of hands that she was as moved by him as he was by her.

A frown marred the bridge of her nose that was not of classical proportions or fashionably pert and as such was infinitely more adorable. Then she pushed by him and hurried down the steps. "I will question her later. After she is . . . finished." She seemed to choke on the last word.

Vitor pivoted and descended behind her and grasped her by the arm. The color drained from her cheeks.

He bent his head, willing her to look at him. "You are as skittish as a filly."

"I have been called many things, but never before a horse. Thank you."

Damn it, he felt all sorts of at a loss. He had never done this—never come close to doing this. He had never needed to say such things aloud. Men simply didn't. He shook his head. "You have nothing to fear. Not from me." He felt her life beneath his hand and he wanted his words to be true. "Look at me, Ravenna. Look at me."

Finally she obeyed, and the black stars glittered with panic.

Now he could not say what had finally come to his tongue, untested as it was, and astonishing, and uncertain as he was of its purport. But he could not bear to distress her either. "What happened last night changes nothing." He would do penance for a month for this lie. "You are a pretty girl and it was a dark place and I am a man and that is all there was to it. We will pursue this mystery and when it is solved the prince's party will commence as planned. Until then let us continue as we were."

For a moment's silence there was only the chill of the medieval tower and his heartbeats battering his ribs.

Then her lips twitched. "As we were when I nearly drowned in a frozen river and you risked your life to save me?" she said. "Or as we were when I attacked you with a farm tool yet you kissed me anyway?"

Her spirit was irrepressible. He smiled. "Perhaps we should establish an entirely new footing."

The softest breath of relief issued through her lips. "That would probably be best."

Now he should release her. But holding her even in this manner felt too good. He sought for words to delay the moment.

"Does their liaison"—he glanced up the stairs—"lead you to believe that she might withhold the truth in other matters?"

"No. Not precisely. But . . . Did you see the faces of

the others at the moment the prince announced Mr. Walsh's death?"

He had not. He had been watching her, as he had not ceased doing since he first saw her. "No."

"She did not think to mask her reaction."

"Which was?"

"Shock, I think. But not generic. She stared as though she were stunned, as though she had not expected him—Mr. Walsh in particular—to die."

"Understandable, perhaps, if she had encountered him earlier in the day."

"But she had not. She told me that she had not made his acquaintance."

"Might she have lied about that?"

"I don't know," she said slowly, her gaze shifting down to his hand still wrapped around her arm. "I shan't tumble down the stairs now, you know."

He released her.

"And by the by," she said, "did you truly assign a guard to me? Because if you didn't, I won't heed another word you say to me." But he could see in her bright eyes that she did not believe this. Her mistrust of him had been momentary, it seemed. "On the other hand," she said, "if you did, he is woefully negligent." She started down the stairs again, this time without haste. "You needn't waste the man on me, you know. I have been going about the castle and stables for two days now without incident. More to the point, before this week I spent three-and-twenty years going about the countryside largely upon my own governance."

"You are not now in the countryside but in a castle in which a murderer still dwells."

She looked over her shoulder at him. "In the normal course of things I can defend myself. Barring the presence of frozen rivers, of course," she added.

He rubbed his lip that was nearly healed. "I believe you."

Delight suffused her face. "What a relief that you don't lecture me. Do you know . . . I like you. You're smarter than most humans."

Vitor's throat was too tight to speak. He bowed.

With a last candid grin, she disappeared below.

SHE HAD FORGOTTEN to tell him about the thumbprint in the wax seal. Her steps faltered in the middle of the great hall. But she continued even quicker. Nothing would be accomplished by sharing her suspicions now. It could wait until later. And she was not at all certain she could maintain the facade of nonchalance that she had forced upon herself the moment he called her pretty and followed that up with the assurance that his interest in her behind the armor screen had been entirely—even predictably—momentary.

She wanted to believe that he was an honest person. No man, however, had ever called her pretty. Not even her father. Petti occasionally called her a "pretty minx" and encouraged her to dress more befitting her station. But *pretty*?

In a distracted haze she shuffled through the icy slush toward the stable and nearly collided with Cecilia Anders.

"Hello, Miss Caulfield. What a surprise to see your head in the clouds. Are you dreaming of a princely husband, perhaps?"

Ravenna blinked. "No."

"He favors you, you know." Miss Anders's hazel eyes were direct, her handsome face without any trace of rancor.

"The prince? I don't think—"

"He does. You must become accustomed to the idea.

You will see. This afternoon when he announces the lady that will play Juliet opposite his Romeo, it will be you."

"But I'm not even in the play."

Miss Anders laughed. "How true. You are the reason for it!"

"And yet you seem entirely unperturbed by this."

"Do not mistake me for those vapid twins, Miss Caulfield. I haven't any intention of throwing myself at the head of a prince."

"Then why are you here?"

"Sir Henry, of course."

Ravenna's imagination instantly conjured an image of Sir Henry and Cecilia Anders disposed as Lord Whitebarrow and Iona had been in the turret. This could only mean her wits were addled by *pretty* more than she liked. "What— That is, what is your interest in him?"

"His stables, of course. Do you know, Miss Caulfield, that Sir Henry's stallion, Titus, is the most sought after Thoroughbred stud in Britain. Not England, Miss Caulfield. Britain."

"Is he?"

"With that stallion, my father and Sir Henry could own the racing industry."

"Your father? Has he an interest in horse racing? I'd thought his scholarship was—"

"Esoteric? Theoretical? It is. He likes a spirited debate over Aristotle's *De Generationum Animalium* as much as the next man. But, Miss Caulfield, he is far too brilliant to confine his studies to the theoretical realm. Last summer upon a lark I set the racing schedule before him and bid him draw a genealogical table of the animals currently active at Ascot, Catterick Bridge, Beverley, and the Newmarket gallop." She bounced on her toes. Ravenna had spent years in the company of men devoted to horses yet she had never seen one bounce on his toes.

"Did your father make the table?"

"Not a table. An entire graph. With every pertinent detail of each horse figured upon the vertical and horizontal axes."

"Oh." Ravenna had never heard of such a thing. It was clearly far more sophisticated than the sort of bets Taliesin used to make on the races at the Gypsy fair each summer, for which her father predictably scolded him. "Interesting."

"I hope to encourage Sir Henry to take on my father as a partner," Cecilia said.

"I see. But you needn't have come all the way to France to meet with Sir Henry."

"I wished to meet Prince Raynaldo too. His son has no interest in horses, but Raynaldo is one of Portugal's most renowned horsemen. Discovering that he was not to attend was a sore disappointment to me, Miss Caulfield."

"Miss Anders, did you engineer your invitation to this gathering?" As Arabella had engineered hers.

"My godmother is the Duchess of Hammershire. She is an old termagant, but in devotion to racing we are well suited. She wrote to Prinny and he wrote to Prince Raynaldo on my behalf."

Lord Prunesly's family had been invited to Chevriot upon a recommendation from the Prince Regent? The layers of privilege and connection and influence among England's elite seemed infinite.

"I must see to Sir Henry's horse now," she mumbled.

"Of course. But first, Miss Caulfield, I wish to congratulate you."

"About what?"

"For telling off my brother."

"Telling him off?"

"I saw you reject him in the corridor before your chamber two nights ago. My compliments."

And yet Ravenna had not known at the time that she was being watched, like Lord Whitebarrow in the tower parlor. "I didn't cause him permanent damage."

Lady Cecilia chuckled, but her eyes were fierce. "I wish you had. However much I adore my brother, he often needs a mighty kick in the pantaloons." Her brow pleated. "I . . ."

"Yes?"

"I worry about his foolishness, Miss Caulfield. I worry that he will hurl himself into danger and I will not be able to help him." She drew a decisive breath. "But that isn't your concern, of course. The prince is. I shall see you indoors."

In the stable, Ravenna changed the hoof dressing on Sir Henry's prized stud. After that, a quarter hour spent with the bitch and her four remaining pups restored her peace of mind. Seeking out Sir Henry's head groom, the only person in the stables with whom she could speak English, she asked after the fifth pup.

"Followed his lordship out riding this morning, miss."

"His lordship?"

"Lord Vitor, miss."

He'd kept the puppy. Or else he'd gone up the mountain to set it loose.

When she entered the castle, luncheon had already been served. All the guests were present except Lady Iona and Lord Vitor. She avoided looking at Lord Whitebarrow and poked at her food. She had never cared before what titled ladies and gentlemen did, the parties they attended, or their scandals. Petti's stories about society had always amused her, but they meant nothing to her. And she had never, ever before cared what a nobleman thought of her.

Why had he not come to luncheon? Where had he gone without telling her? Was she a fool to trust him when no one else in the house was proving trustworthy? Their secrets and schemes seemed infinite.

Monsieur Sepic had departed for the afternoon and Prince Sebastiao announced that in his absence they would rehearse in preparation for staging the play on the morrow. The party adjourned to the drawing room.

At the door to the drawing room, Sir Beverley paused beside her. "Will you keep a hawk's eyes upon the door here too, as you did at luncheon, all the while pretending that you are not?" he asked.

"I am waiting for Lady Iona. I must speak with her about a matter of importance." She dreaded speaking with Iona. What were they to say to each other? All had already been said in a single horrified stare.

"My dear girl," murmured the man who within moments of knowing her had understood her. "You are a remarkably poor liar. I hope you do not attempt it with him."

Miss Feathers stood alone by a window, nearly part of the shadow of the drapery. Ravenna shook her head at Sir Beverley and went to her.

"Oh, Ravenna, how kind you are to come over."

"Of course I came over. You are the nicest person in the room, perhaps alongside Mr. Pettigrew." She refused to include Sir Beverley in that company. "But also, Ann, I am eager to know what you did not finish telling me about your encounter with Mr. Walsh."

Ann's soft face was pale, her eyes rounder than ever. "I fear I have done a great wrong to withhold that information from the mayor while I have shared it with you. His royal highness puts such faith in Monsieur Sepic."

"I beg of you, Ann, tell me the rest of your story."

Ann lowered her voice to the whisper of moth wings. "It was not yet midnight. Perhaps even before eleven o'clock. I had not yet heard the bell chime in the hall. I was walking through the gallery. Papa had bid me braid Mama's hair in the absence of her maid. Mama likes the way I do it. She often asks me to do her hair even when her maid is able."

Ravenna nodded. Eleanor had tried and tried again to bind her hair so it would please the headmistress at the foundling home, and later their father, and to teach her how to bind it herself. For years. Then one afternoon, watching Ravenna struggle over it, Eleanor had snatched away the ribbons and declared that her hands had been made for much greater tasks than primping. "A girl must be what God intended her to be, not what others expect of her," she stated. Then she kissed each of Ravenna's palms, tied a single ribbon around her hair, and sent her out into the summer day with Beast.

"I was returning to my bedchamber later than expected," Ann continued, "and I came upon him in the gallery. He was wearing a suit of armor. I could not speak a word. I thought perhaps that he was— That he was—"

"That he was what?"

Ann whispered, "A ghost."

Ravenna suppressed her smile.

"When I heard that he had died—that he had been *murdered*—I was sorry he was not a ghost from medieval times, instead a poor man who had been living that very day." She looked about with wide eyes and lowered her voice yet further. "Ravenna, do you think that a murdered man might roam about looking for the person who killed him?"

"What? Do you mean in corridors or attics, chains clanging and the like?"

"No. Rather, in bedchambers. Searching. But without chains, I think."

"Have you heard something that suggests to you that Mr. Walsh is haunting this castle?"

"Last night I heard . . . *noises*. In the chamber beside mine."

"What sorts of noises?"

"Creaking," Ann whispered. "And thumping."

Ravenna's mind returned to the turret with Iona and the earl. Whose bedchamber flanked Ann's? *No.* She did *not* wish to know.

Ann's face had paled further. "Do you think it might have been . . . *him*?"

"I suppose a ghost might wish to haunt Chevriot," if it could find a chamber free of amorous couples. "It needn't be Mr. Walsh, though. Please tell me about the armor. Did he wear a full suit?" The hair pressed in ringlets about Ann's face was precisely the color Ravenna had pulled from around the coat button.

"No, I think. Not all of the pieces. There were some pieces over his arms, and perhaps on one leg. A large piece of it flopped away, as though he had forgotten to buckle it."

"Over his chest?"

"Yes. How did you guess?"

"I found him in that suit, Ann."

"Oh, goodness." Ann's hand covered her mouth. "How dreadful. And how frightened you must have been."

She had not been frightened because—it occurred to her now—Lord Vitor had been there too. The boast she had made to him on the turret stairs was not entirely true.

"Did Mr. Walsh speak to you, or you to him?" she said.

"No. He seemed confused. I thought him intoxicated

at first, the way Papa gets after a winning race. He was staggering terribly. Then he began gasping and I feared he was ill. That was when I heard a footstep."

"A footstep?"

"At the other end of the gallery. A light step."

"A woman's step?"

"I believe so. But a small man in slippers could have sounded similar, I guess."

Ravenna nodded. Ann's awkward shyness and frilly gowns hid a mind attuned to details.

"He grabbed my wrist and spoke to me, but I could not understand him. I tried to pull away—we had not been introduced, after all—I had never seen him and though I knew him to be a gentleman from his hair and clothing, he was unknown to me. But before I could escape, he grabbed me against him. I found him to be strangely weak, however, and I was able to break away quite easily. I asked him if he wished me to summon help. That was when I heard the footsteps." Her nose pinched and she pressed her hands together in her lap. "I ran. I am ashamed that I ran, Ravenna! I should have remained to help him, or called out for help. But all I could think was that he was a fiend, and the footsteps were those of his colleague in fiendishness."

A mind for details with a turn toward the supernaturally dramatic, it seemed.

"I shouldn't blame yourself for running, Ann. I might have too."

"I don't believe that." Timidity returned to her round eyes. "I admire you greatly, Ravenna—your free spirit and your courage. I can see that others here admire it too. Especially Prince Sebastiao." Now her eyes went soft and slightly out of focus. "I admire *him* the more for it. You are so delightfully refreshing."

"I asked you about the armor because I found a

hair—a long, dark hair that matches yours—trapped in Mr. Walsh's coat button."

Ann's palm flew to her mouth again. "Do you— But you cannot— Ravenna, I did not kill him!"

She grasped Ann's shaking hand. "I am fairly certain you did not."

"Miss Caulfield." The prince's voice came close behind her. "While I am your servant now and forever, I cannot bear to see this lady distressed. What have you said just now that has turned her cheeks to chalk? You must tell us all at this instant."

Ravenna could say nothing. While her back had been turned to the room, Lady Iona had entered, and now sent her an entreating look.

Ann's lashes fell, but her voice came steadily. "She told me a ghost story, your highness. I am ever so fond of them and begged her for it. I hope you will forgive her, for the truth of it is that I like the sort of distress one feels when hearing a ghost tale."

Ravenna stared at her with new respect.

"Aha, I also enjoy a hair-raising ghost story," the prince said with a smile. "Miss Caulfield, you must repeat it to me this instant."

"Oh, your highness," Ann said, finally drawing her eyes up. "If Miss Caulfield does not mind my intrusion, may I tell it? It would help fix the story in my memory." Briefly she glanced at Ravenna as if in apology. But behind the gray orbs Ravenna now saw a girl who, without the overbearing mother blocking her way, might very well become a force of even greater reckoning than Lady Margaret. She now held the prince's entire attention.

With a reassuring smile, Ravenna excused herself. Before she could escape, Lady Iona came upon her in a swirl of rose perfume, fiery tresses, and pale pink skirts. She had changed her gown and arranged her hair in a braided coronet. She looked stunning and fashionable and every bit the virginal daughter of a duke seeking the hand of a prince.

Ravenna wanted more than anything *not* to discuss what Iona clearly wished to discuss. Instead she wanted to beg Iona to take her to a dressing table and teach her how to make herself into a lady too. She could never actually look like a duchess's daughter; her skin was far too dark and her hair was far too wild and she started throwing out hives after she spent too many minutes in ballrooms or drawing rooms or really indoors at all. But for a moment she wondered if she had looked like Iona—like a *lady*—behind that armor, would he have done more than hold her hand? Would he have kissed her?

"I must speak wi' ye, lass." Iona's brilliant blue eyes entreated. "Will ye? Oh, do say ye will, or I'll go mad wi' it."

The others now combed through boxes of cloth and garments, assisted by Monsieur Brazil and Iona's maid. A few of the gentlemen had disappeared, presumably unenthralled with the prospect of rehearsing the play. Lady Margaret's laughter rose above the conversation as she affixed an enormous wig decorated with a full-sized peacock upon her head.

Lord Vitor had not yet appeared.

Ravenna nodded. Iona grasped her elbow and drew her to a sofa away from the others.

"Dear Ravenna, I dinna ken whit to say to ye nou, in truth. Whit ye must think o' me." Even in agitation she sat erect and graceful. Ravenna tucked in her belly and lowered her shoulders a bit.

"I don't quite know what to say to you either," she said thinly. With her spine so straight, breathing proved difficult. Perhaps if she tied her stays differently it might not pinch so awfully. "I apologize for walking in like that."

"No! 'Tis I that should be apologizin', lass. Ye niver shoulda seen that. In truth, I niver shoulda done it." Her chestnut brows bent. Ravenna marveled at their elegant arch and tried to picture her own eyebrows. She couldn't. It was entirely possible she had never looked at them.

"Why did you do it?"

A light glittered in Iona's eyes. One tapered shoulder lifted in a lovely shrug. "He asked."

"He . . . *asked*?"

"I flirted wi' him, an' he flirted wi' me. But, Ravenna, I niver thought he'd ask. But then he did, an' he's so wonderfully braw, I couldna say no." Iona's hands grasped hers. "Oh, lass, dinna look at me like that, I pray ye."

"I don't know how I am looking at you. I don't really know what to think about it." She lowered her voice. "He is married."

Iona's teeth clenched again. "She's a witch. Ye ken it as well as I, lass."

"Iona . . ." How did one say this, even to a girl like Iona McCall? "Do you think he might have done it to ruin your chances with the prince? That is to say, he is here to marry one of his daughters to Prince Sebastião. You are not only far more beautiful than both Penelope and Grace, but also infinitely more pleasing."

Iona seemed thoughtful a moment. "'Tis possible that was why *he* did it."

"But you?"

Rosebud lips lifted at one side. "I've done it afore."

Ravenna simply stared.

"Wi' any number o' men."

"Any number—that is . . ."

Iona nodded.

"You don't *know* how many men?"

Another lovely shrug. "'Tis nothin' else to do at

home but go to assemblies an' drink whiskey. Wi' the two comes the third, ye see." She leaned forward again. "I canna get enough o' it, Ravenna. I've got the soul o' a penny jo. Why do ye think my mither's brought me all the way here to find a husband? No laird in Scotland'll have me—at least no' for more than a dalliance." She smiled radiantly.

"Have you done—" Ravenna swallowed thickly. Her gaze darted to Sir Henry and Martin Anders sorting costumes with the ladies. "Have you done it with any of the other gentlemen here?"

"Mr. Anders tried, but I'm holding him aff. Young men are potent, but they lack skill, an' they tend to do it too quickly to be o' any use."

Ravenna's throat was dry. "Of use?"

"They're all aboot their own pleasure an' rushin' to the finish."

The *finish*? What was there to it other than the finish?

"I prefer it when a lad makes me come afore he's taken his pleasure in me, when he's still good an' solid," Iona continued. "But if he canna wait, afterward suits me too." Her azure eyes sparkled. "Both afore an' after suits me even better, o' course."

Ravenna shook her head. "Makes you come where?"

Iona's fingertips covered her lips. "Oh, lass. Curse my tongue! I shouldna said a thing. But I thought—" Her gaze swept over Ravenna, then back to her face. "Oh, lass, I dinna ken whit I thought. I beg yer pardon a hundred times."

"No. I'm grateful you wished to apologize. I hope that we can continue as friends."

Iona released a heavy breath and the corner of her rosebud mouth quirked up.

"But . . ." Ravenna said, unable to still her tongue. "Did you . . . That is, was there anyone else here?"

"The professor. But he was all business, an' his prick

is a wee thing. It wasna much fun. Lord Whitebarrow has quite a sizable tool, an' he likes it rough."

Rough? Ravenna had seen "rough" with stallions and bulls. She had never imagined it of titled lords and ladies.

Iona blew out a quick breath. "I've done it again. I've said whit I shouldna. Truly, I should be horsewhipped, Ravenna."

"No, really, I don't mind it. It's just that it's all rather—rather—"

"New to ye?"

"Yes."

"As it should be." Iona took her arm. "I promise to speak more leddylike with ye nou. I flirted wi' Lord Case too, but he's preoccupied wi' Arielle. 'Tis a pity, to be sure." She sighed wistfully. "I think I should've liked it verra much wi' him."

Ravenna swallowed back the nausea gathering at the base of her tongue and detached her arm from Iona's hold. She had to know. "What of his brother?"

The Scotswoman's smile softened. "I couldna do such a thing to ye."

"To me?"

"Why, lass." Iona's voice laughed gently. "Everybody can see he's only got eyes for ye."

Chapter 12

The Trouble with Masks

$\mathcal{H}$e only had eyes for her?

Impossible. "No. He doesn't." And if he did, it was probably when he wanted to speak to her about the murder.

It occurred to her that if Lady Iona had no qualms about pretending to be a maiden while being scandalously intimate with half the men in the house, she might lack the moral fiber sufficient to inhibit her from killing a man after stuffing him into a suit of armor. But despite her lusty nature, her eyes were guileless, her smile open, and her loyalty to Ravenna concerning Lord Vitor—however misplaced—must count for something.

"I think ye'll find yer wrong aboot that, lass. Nou, will ye forgive me?"

"For what, exactly?"

"Why, for leavin' the door to that parlor unlocked, o' course."

Ravenna laughed. At that moment Lord Vitor Courtenay entered the drawing room. He wore a loose coat the same color as his eyes, dark breeches, and he still carried his hat in his hand. As he paused in the doorway, a blur of white and black halted at his feet and yipped. The nobleman looked about the chamber, and his attention came to her.

"Ah, Courtenay," Sir Henry exclaimed. "What is your part in our little production? We older fellows have snatched up Capulet, Montague, and the prince, of course. But Anders here hasn't yet decided if he prefers Paris or Mercutio. If you're quick about it you can claim either. What will it be?"

"Tybalt," he said, and came directly to her and Iona, bringing with him the fresh cold of the day, the pup pouncing upon each of his footsteps. He propped his hat beneath his arm and bowed. "Good afternoon, ladies," he said with great elegance, despite the pup chewing on the costly leather toe of his boot that was speckled with moisture.

"Ye've chosen yer part poorly, my laird," Lady Iona said brightly. "Ye ken ye'll be dead afore the second act, dinna ye?"

"As I am not much of an actor, that should be to everybody's benefit." He smiled, then bent and scooped the dog into one hand and held it against his waistcoat as though it were another hat. "Miss Caulfield, may I beg a moment's conversation with you?"

Iona popped up from her seat. "I'll be aff, then." She cast Ravenna a sparkling glance and went.

Lord Vitor dropped the puppy into Ravenna's lap.

She tucked the cold, soft little bundle against her chest. It nipped at her sleeve. She settled it in her lap, and it laid its muzzle on her knee and promptly fell asleep.

"The groom said you went out with this one, and I

see you have just come in. But he is entirely dry. How did he make do in the snow?"

"I carried it." He sat down beside her, quite close but so that his knee did not brush hers. "You may have it back."

"I cannot. He is yours now."

"He is a pestilence."

"And yet you carried him on your ride, presumably because he could not keep up with your horse's pace? Your coat is ruined with fur."

"Good of you to show concern. My valet will ring a peal over your head when he returns to the castle."

She grinned and stroked the pup's silky fur. "Is he very hard on you?"

"No more than . . . others."

She looked up, surprising the shallow dent in the nobleman's cheek as his attention rested on the pup.

"When you dismissed Lady Iona," she said, "I imagined you wished to speak with me about the murder. But now you are smiling, so that cannot be the case. What are you thinking?"

"That I have never before been quite so jealous of a dog."

Her hand froze.

"I see you have decided," she said.

"What have I decided?"

"The footing to which we are returning."

He smiled. "It seems so." He glanced across the room. "You are still thick as thieves with Lady Iona, then."

"I cannot see any reason not to be. Lord Whitebarrow is either a general philanderer, or he seeks Iona's ruination to the benefit of his daughters. I have no heavy conscience for his sake."

"Ah."

"As for Lady Iona, what a woman chooses to do with

her . . ." She stalled. Though she had assisted with births, including human births, and even had seen any number of animals mate—both domestic and wild— this was no easier to discuss with him now than it had been on the stairs to the tower parlor. "Her . . ."

He lifted a brow. "Virtue?"

"I don't particularly like that word. It suggests that the only virtue a woman can possess is her maiden-hood."

"It does indeed."

"What becomes of kindness, then? Or compassion? What about other virtues women possess? What of charity? Or constancy or—"

"Miss Caulfield." His voice lowered. "If you wish us to remain on any footing of comfort to you, this is not the way to accomplish it."

She could not quite look at him. "I will bear that in mind. What did you wish to tell me about your ride?"

"I discovered a path. I thought I had ridden every trail between the castle and the mountain's peak and base, but it seems I had not until today. This one leads along the river for a quarter mile, then ascends steeply to the mountain's apex."

"You were able to follow it? In the snow and ice?"

"Ashdod was bred in the Pyrenees. These hills are no challenge to him." He spoke without arrogance or even pride.

"You are peculiarly humble."

"Peculiarly, hm?" He rubbed his jaw thoughtfully and something about the flex of his hand and the tightening of the scar between his fingers tugged at her insides. "That doesn't sound flattering."

"For a man of your station you are humble."

"Would you prefer if I boasted of my privilege and spoke harshly to my inferiors, who are, after all, legion? Should I win your respect more securely then?"

He already had her respect, and she had yet to meet another man whose mere entrance into a room had other gentlemen straightening their spines and puffing out their chests, while the ladies batted their lashes and blushed. Even now Miss Abraccia and Lady Penelope both were casting him surreptitious glances.

"You should alienate me eternally by that," she said.

"Then I shall refrain from behaving according to my rightful role in society."

Across the room the poetical young Mr. Anders now sported Shakespearean hose and ballooning sleeves. He looked to Miss Abraccia, who still covertly watched Lord Vitor, and his brow turned stormy.

Ravenna wondered that if she were sitting across the room from Lord Vitor now would she also be staring. But masculine perfection in any species by nature drew females. "Were Mr. Anders's boots soaked through again this morning?" she whispered.

"Monsieur Brazil informs me that they were."

"What reason would he have to walk the path you found each morning, and how is he escaping the guards' notice?"

"I suspect someone is paying the prince's guards to look away when it suits."

Her gaze darted to the guard stationed at the drawing room door. "Are they not loyal to him?"

"Not all. I spoke with the man who should have been near when Anders bothered you by your bedchamber that night. He suggested that you misrepresented the matter to me."

"I did not."

"I know that."

She frowned. "How do you know that?"

"Because the single time you tried to lie to me it was written all over your face."

"How do you know that I haven't lied to you successfully and you simply don't realize it?"

"If we were not in a drawing room filled with people, I would take your hand and show you."

She could not respond and she did not want to understand him. "What of this path? What would take Mr. Anders out before dawn each morning? An assignation with a fellow conspirator, perhaps?"

"Perhaps."

"When will Monsieur Sepic return?"

"Before dinner, I suspect. He plans to gather writing samples from all of us. Upon your advice."

"Which you must have repeated to him. He would not have taken heed of it otherwise."

"More significantly, the mayor enjoyed last night's dinner tremendously. I believe he means to take advantage of this investigation to dine each evening in the castle."

"I am the daughter of a country vicar and until recently a servant. I have no more right to be feasting in this company than he." She looked up from the puppy in her lap to the chamber full of elegant people of rank and fortune, and met Lady Grace's dull stare. In Grace's hands dangled an old-fashioned neck ruff. She seemed to become aware of Ravenna's attention, and she turned away.

"Nor the desire, really," she added.

"Yet I am glad of your presence here," he said. "And since I am a despicably wealthy and vastly privileged man of enormous consequence, my pleasure should be the only consideration in the matter." He stood and swiped a hand across his coat. "With that consequence in mind, I will go dress for dinner."

All vexations were forgotten. The bloom of pleasure in her chest would not be bested by chill distress or sticky inadequacy.

"Wait," she said. "I have news."

Her words drew him back to the seat beside her, this time closer. "Speak, madam. I am rapt."

This flirtation should not make warmth creep into her cheeks. Men like him flirted without thought. "From what Ann tells me, her encounter with Mr. Walsh may have occurred immediately before his death. She said he was staggering and seemed drunken."

"What do you make of it?"

"That he was poisoned, perhaps with a mild poison that required time to take effect. You have had the same thought too."

He nodded. "I have."

"Why didn't you tell me?"

"I assumed you had considered it as well."

"Especially given our conclusions regarding his wound."

"Do you suspect her?"

"No." She hadn't given it one serious thought.

"Why not?"

"She is too . . ."

"Timid?"

"*Good*. Not sweetly good or that sort of foolishness," she tried to explain. "But I think she truly cares about other people. In her way she is solicitous to everybody, and while she most certainly wishes to wed the prince, I don't think she is capable of murder. This said, the hair I found attached to the button is probably hers. She told me he grabbed her, possibly while he was struggling to right his senses. He wore most of the armor at the time, but she said that the breastplate gaped open."

"It was fastened when you discovered him."

"Someone must have buckled the breastplate entirely, then set him on his feet against that wall. Whatever the case, since the hair seems accounted for, our list of suspects has now expanded to include everybody."

He stood up once more. "Then the writing samples may prove especially valuable."

"I hope so." She set the pup upon the floor at his feet. "Don't forget your dog."

He looked Very Dark for a moment. But he took the dog with him.

THE EVENING COMMENCED with dinner, followed by the oddest after-dinner entertainment Ravenna had ever witnessed: Monsieur Sepic required everyone to write on a single sheet of paper, *Come to my chamber at ten o'clock*. The activity commenced in prickly silence and the sheet circled the drawing room slowly. When it had gone halfway round, with a show of exasperation, the prince coaxed Arielle to the pianoforte. She played while the remaining guests signed.

"You will, I presume, require the cook, the two maids, and the footmen to perform this foolishness, as well," Lady Whitebarrow said to the mayor.

"*Naturellement*, my lady. I am nothing if not thorough." He folded the paper, tucked it into his waistcoat, and departed.

Prince Sebastiao announced that the remainder of the evening would be given to final costuming and practicing lines. Bits of costumes were distributed, and guests accepted them, some with enthusiasm, others with reserve. Amidst these distractions, conversation recommenced.

"If that wee silly man puts any blame on my daughter," the duchess said with a glare at the door, the rubies about her throat sparkling in the candlelight, "I'll murder the gadgie myself."

"Mither," Iona remonstrated. "Dinna say such a thing."

"Monsieur Sepic will no doubt discover the identity of the criminal," Lady Whitebarrow said, her thin brows lifting above a white half mask. "I see no reason to imagine he will not." She turned her gaze upon the duchess. "Unless one is the murderer and, fearing detection, seeks to cast mistrust upon him. Monsieur Brazil, you know the mayor. Give us your opinion of him."

The butler's lips tightened. "I am sure it is not my place to say, madam."

Lord Whitebarrow grunted. "Do you see, Olympia? He doesn't trust the man's intelligence any more than the duchess does."

The duchess cast him an approving glance.

"If I valued the opinion of rebels and republicans," Lady Whitebarrow said, "I am certain I should be impressed."

That corner of the room went absolutely quiet.

Lady Margaret burst forth with a chuckle. "Dear me, how diverting fashionable people are. Sir Henry, we must take note. I've never heard such a thing, but I suppose when you are titled as well as rich you can say anything you wish. Rebels and republicans! How positively diverting. Ann dear, do attend to Lady Whitebarrow. She is jesting marvelously well tonight."

Ann stared at her clasped hands.

"If I were a man," the duchess said to Lady Whitebarrow, "I'd call ye out."

"Then 'tis a verra good thing yer no a man, Mither." Iona looked with desperation to Arielle. "Mademoiselle, would ye play for us?"

Arielle played. The prince beckoned the duchess to the overflowing trunks of costumes to dress her for the part of Lady Capulet. Monsieur Sepic returned, said nothing of the writing samples, and immediately fell into fawning over the nobles. A full day in advance of the play, everyone proved themselves marvelous actors, enacting the pretense that he was not investigating them for murder; their modest flatteries encouraged his spirits until he fairly glowed. When Lord Whitebarrow himself filled the mayor's brandy glass a second time, the Frenchman nearly swooned.

Everyone donned bits of costumes: Lady Margaret her peacock wig, the duchess a cloak of royal purple, Cecilia Anders a ruffled cravat, Petti a striped tunic. Even Lord Prunesly set a plumed, broad-brimmed hat atop his sparse pate and pronounced that the Musketeers had been the finest fighting mechanism since the Greek phalanx.

"I have chosen my Juliet," Prince Sebastiao exclaimed, and moved to the center of the room.

"'Tis high time," Iona whispered to Ravenna. In a gown of gossamer white that fit her figure to perfection, she bedazzled. Ravenna could barely look away and wondered that any of the gentlemen could. Lord Vitor had reappeared in the drawing room before dinner, also gorgeously attired in dark coat and snowy cravat, and now sat with them, a glass of brandy suspended from his fingertips. But he seemed to take no special note of the Scotswoman's beauty. Perhaps in company with ladies like Iona as a matter of course, he was simply inured. But the fact of it was that whenever Ravenna looked at him he was already looking at her. *She thought.* The mask of sapphire blue silk that he had accepted from the prince covered only the upper half of his face, leaving visible his mouth at which she had stared in the stable—now nearly healed of the damage she'd done to it—and the hard, smooth line of his jaw.

She was again having trouble not staring.

He's only got eyes for ye.

Earlier, Ann had dressed her hair with modestly successful results, and together they had disconnected two flounces from the least overdone of Ann's extra gowns. Ravenna had left her bedchamber with the heat of nervous anticipation in her cheeks and an ill stomach, only to stand at the drawing room door and curse the foolish waste of time she might have instead spent in the stables before dinner. Among glorious flowers of femininity like Iona, Arielle, Penelope, and Grace—even pretty Juliana and handsome Cecilia—she was a dark little acorn dressed in a borrowed gown. Even the elaborate gold chains Iona pulled from the costume box and draped over her shoulders like a queen's mantle could not make a sow's ear into a silk purse.

"Do tell us which lady you have chosen, your highness," Lady Whitebarrow urged the prince. "We are all eager to know who will stand on the stage beside you."

Prince Sebastiao inclined his head. "There will be no stage per se, my lady. In the great hall we will perform at the top of the steps. The audience shall sit below."

"Why, 'tis the verra opposite o' the theater, yer highness," the duchess said.

"I like to be the tallest person in the place," the prince said with a winning grin. "Don't I, Courtenay?"

"Indeed." The mask hid his eyes.

"Who is Juliet, your highness?" Lady Margaret said. "You mustn't make us wait another moment."

The mothers, it seemed, all thought the prince's choice for Juliet would be his choice for a bride. Ravenna did not have a good grasp of the play's storyline, but she seemed to recall the lovers dying horrible deaths at the end, which didn't bode well for his Juliet.

"My Juliet . . ." the prince drawled, folding his hands behind his back and strolling toward Lady Penelope. Then, abruptly, he turned away and moved toward pretty Juliana. "My Juliet . . ." Again he changed direction, toward Ravenna.

She chanced a glance at Lord Vitor. His jaw looked remarkably tight.

"My Juliet . . ." Prince Sebastiao grinned down at her, then pivoted away. Lord Vitor's sober regard followed him, then it came to Ravenna. It cut swiftly away. But perhaps the candlelight glinting off his mask made her imagine the displeasure there.

The prince halted before Ann and bowed. "Miss Feathers . . ."

Her "Your highness?" was barely audible.

He extended his hand, palm upward. "Would you consent to becoming my Juliet?"

A silence as penetrating as ice filled the air.

"For the play tomorrow," the prince added, and waggled his black brows.

"I should like that excessively, your highness," Ann squeaked. Lady Penelope stood and crossed to her father. Lord Case turned the page of music and Arielle's fingers danced upon the keys.

Lord Vitor lifted the glass of brandy to his lips. "My lady," he said to Iona. "Would you care to join a little game Miss Caulfield and I are playing?"

Iona's gaze darted to Ravenna, then back to him. "Whit game be that, my laird?"

He gestured to Ravenna.

"It's called Find the Murderer," she said.

Iona's eyes sparkled. "I think I should like it verra much."

They spent the remainder of the evening cataloguing clues and motives. While Iona insisted that her maid was above suspicion, she was willing to consider the two footmen, the cook, the scullery maid, Ann Feathers, Cecilia Anders, and Juliana Abraccia. She did not believe Arielle Dijon capable of a violent act. She favored Martin Anders as the killer.

"He's got that tragical, poetical air aboot him," she

said with a smile in Mr. Anders's direction. Recalling what she'd said earlier about the potency of young men, Ravenna didn't chance a glance at him.

"My dear Ann has the perfect gown for the part, your highness," Lady Margaret exclaimed nearby. "She will be the most fetching Juliet ever upon stage." She was gloating and Ann didn't even seem disturbed by it. A quiet glow animated her cheeks.

Lady Whitebarrow sat beside her at the tea table, white-lipped.

Ravenna told Iona about the blood on the turret door handle and the stained candlestick, the path to the mountain's peak and Cecilia's interest in Sir Henry's horses, as well as Mr. Walsh's ring and the cut on Martin Anders's face. She did not mention the scabbard and rope fibers or their aborted search for the dagger because, despite years spent traipsing about the countryside upon her own governance, she'd had only one experience touching a man in the dark—voluntarily—and she was not yet prepared to discuss the circumstances of it while he was sitting right beside her.

That he remained silent about the dagger as well was a curiosity.

"Well then, it seems Mr. Anders is for the gallows," Iona said cheerfully.

"How can you say such a thing so blithely?"

"Dinna take me wrong, lass. I'd feel for him if I thought he'd dislike any part o' it. But I imagine he'd consider it a grand drama."

The duchess called her daughter away and Iona went reluctantly, with a whispered request to be included in any further detective work. "'Tis the most fun I've had all week," she said gaily, then winked at Ravenna and glided away.

Ravenna looked at Lord Vitor. "Why did you invite her to help us?"

He set down his brandy glass and folded his hands. "I thought it would please you."

"Really?"

"No."

She narrowed her eyes. "Really?"

"No. I do wish to please you. But I am also immeasurably vain, and I recognized that it would add to my consequence in the estimation of the other gentlemen if I enjoyed the conversation of two ladies at once. I needed an excuse that would keep you both here."

"I don't believe you."

"No?"

"You might have kept company with Lady Penelope and Miss Abraccia, or any two other ladies in the room."

"Might I have?" He seemed struck with the notion. "Hm. I should consider that the next time."

"You should tell me the truth."

"The truth is that it was high time we collected our intelligence, and I required a third party present because I cannot seem to be alone with you for more than two minutes without saying things I mustn't."

"Things having to do with pitchforks?"

He waved a negligent hand. "And whatnot."

She was warm and somewhat confused, but he seemed at ease. He was, she understood, practiced at ease. That ease was a privilege of his station, a station he jested about but which defined him.

"But what would you say to me that you mustn't if you were alone in my company now?"

"Aha. You seek to trip me up. But I am wise to conniving ways, madam. Recall, I have lived at a royal court."

"Did you miss England very much during that time?"

"If I had known you before I departed, I would have missed England excessively."

Her heart performed an uncomfortable stumble.

"Ah," he said. "There you have done it. And much more swiftly than I anticipated. More the fool, I." He glanced about the room. "Who should I call over now to save me from another verbal misstep? Martin Anders, so we can tease him about guillotines? Or perhaps Lady Margaret? She has not yet shared with you her daughter's success. That might provide a useful brake upon my ungovernable tongue."

Ravenna laughed. "Ann is a kind and gentle person. I shouldn't like to draw her into your sins in any way, even peripherally, and especially not tonight. It is a grand success to win the favor of a prince, even for an evening."

For a moment he did not speak. "She is an unexceptionable lady," he said, but he was looking at her carefully, it seemed.

"You do not believe Martin Anders killed Mr. Walsh," she said.

"How do you reckon that?"

"You would not make light of it if you believed him guilty of murder."

After a pause, he shook his head.

"I don't either," she said. "I haven't since the night he came to my bedchamber door."

"Is this a particular habit of yours, Miss Caulfield?"

"What?"

"Bestowing your admiration upon men who press unwanted attentions upon you. If it is, I should advise you to alter that practice at once. Not all men are as honorable as I or as clumsy as Anders."

"It is not a habit. I have only done it once."

His lips hinted at a smile.

"Mr. Anders, of course," she said.

He looked toward the door. "Monsieur Brazil!"

"*Oui*, my lord?"

"Bring me Romeo's poison now so that I might mix it into my nightcap."

"*Oui*, my lord."

Ravenna laughed. Lord Vitor offered her a one-sided grin and she tried not to notice that he was even handsomer than usual when he smiled.

Monsieur Sepic appeared before them. "*Bonsoir*, monseigneur. Mademoiselle." He affected a charming bow to each of them. His cheeks were rosy with wine and general infatuation. He pointed a single finger upward and ticked it back and forth. "Tsk-tsk, monseigneur *et* mademoiselle," he said with a delighted frown. "I have heard of your *petit enquête* and I do not approve of it. You must cease these detections that you are doing without my approval and leave the murdering to the police."

Ravenna pinned her lips together.

"*Me comprenez-vous?* Do you understand?"

"Perhaps better than yourself, sir," Lord Vitor said with a lazy smile.

"Monsieur Sepic, I am certain the other guests are eager to know your assessment of the handwriting samples," she said. "What did you discover?"

He shook his head with little twitches. "*Rien*. I found no duplicates. But I suspected this. A murderer would seek to disguise his hand, *non*?"

"I suppose," Ravenna said, wishing she could pluck the page from his pocket and study it herself. "But have you all of the evidence? Perhaps you have missed something else."

"*Non*. Impossible."

Frustration bubbled in her. "Perhaps we have collected evidence that you do not have yet. If so, we will gladly share it with you."

"What is this—this evidence?" He scoffed. "You can

know nothing that I and my deputy have not already uncovered."

"Nothing?"

"Nothing."

She glanced at Lord Vitor. He was not smiling, but the crease in his cheek was pronounced.

"What about the ring?" she said.

The mayor's eyes went blank. "The ring?"

"Mr. Walsh's ring. Did you examine it?"

"The ring? Ah, the ring." He nodded. "I examined it thoroughly, mademoiselle."

"Then you must have noted the wound on one of the guests' eyes that corresponds perfectly to the ridge on Mr. Walsh's ring?" She twisted her lips. "But, upon consideration, I don't believe that wound has anything to do with the murder. It is merely a coincidence. Wouldn't you agree?"

The mayor's back stiffened. "But of course, mademoiselle. I have considered all." He frowned at Lord Vitor. "Monseigneur, you must not allow a woman to imagine for herself the notions of rationality which are beyond the nature of her sex. It is unlawful. Furthermore, it is immoral." He pivoted upon his heel and returned to the others at the tea table.

Ravenna bit her lip.

"Miss Caulfield, do you imagine for yourself notions of rationality beyond the nature of your sex?" Lord Vitor said.

"Yes."

He smiled. "Excellent."

RAVENNA AWOKE TO the pale sunlight of early morning. Turning onto her side, she remembered the evening and her pleasure in it, and she ached with the delicious fullness that happiness always gave her, the giddy delight that ran through her from toes to fingertips. She hadn't known such happiness in months. Until last night.

Dragging the bolster to her, she wrapped her arms around it and pressed her face into the linen. For the briefest moment she allowed herself to imagine it was Vitor Courtenay.

The shock of heat that went through her tore a gasp from her mouth.

She thrust away the bolster, sat up, and pushed hair from her face. Her heartbeats pounded, as though she had raced with Beast across the breadth of the south field. Staring at the bolster, she set her fingertips upon her cheeks, then recoiled from the heat there. She could not quite breathe. If she were medically examining herself, she would diagnose a spastic fever.

She climbed from the bed and dressed, but she could not shake off the hot agitation. Still light-headed, she left her bedchamber and from an open door along the corridor heard a banshee's scream.

Chapter 13

The Rationality of Female Nature

What in the hell was the purpose of retiring at midnight when a man was to be awoken at two o'clock, three o'clock, five o'clock, and dawn? Vitor pressed his palms into the mattress, forced his shoulders off the bed, and craned his neck to peer at the mongrel perched on its haunches a foot away from his face.

It whined again.

Vitor scrubbed a palm over his face and stared into its plaintive eyes. "You cannot possibly require another outing."

The whine redoubled.

Vitor dropped his brow to the mattress and groaned. A man had servants for this sort of thing, for God's sake. Damn his valet for agreeing to remain in the village.

A thought jarred him. Men did have servants for this sort of thing. Sir Beverley Clark did, certainly. In an instant, with no effort whatsoever, Vitor imagined Ravenna entering his bedchamber haloed in morning sunlight, removing the dog from his bed and magically placating it, then taking its place beside him.

He buried his face in his hands, and his groan of frustration halted the dog's whine.

Elsewhere in the castle, a woman screamed.

Vitor was out his bedchamber door before he entirely pulled on breeches and shirt. His only need was haste, his only thought Ravenna. Bolting down the gallery, he snatched a sword from the wall and scaled the stairs to the ladies' bedchambers.

Standing in gray light, wearing nightclothes, a cluster of women peered through an open door. Miss Abraccia turned her head toward him and her eyes went wide.

He moved through the women into the chamber. Miss Feathers lay prone upon her bed, her eyes wide and glassy, a tangle of white fabric soaked in red about her. Ravenna sat at the end of the bed, her hand on Miss Feathers's ankle.

"It is wine," she said. "No one is harmed."

Miss Feathers's eyes closed and a great convulsive sob shook her.

Vitor lowered the sword.

"Thank you for coming to our aid," Ravenna said. Her gaze slipped over his open collar, then skittered away. "What an impressive weapon that is." Dusky rose crept into her cheeks.

He set down the rapier and moved forward. "It was the first thing that came to hand."

"A pot of bleach would be more welcome." She avoided looking at him now.

"What has happened?"

Miss Feathers sobbed quietly. "I beg your pardon for screaming." Another sob. "It is nothing."

Nothing had his heartbeats slowing from their frantic pace. The night before, after he'd poured a bottle of brandy down Sepic's throat, the mayor had finally produced the page of writing samples. At least five bore some resemblance to Walsh's note. He'd spent considerable time in the monastery's scriptorium, and he could analyze this evidence well enough; the lightness of stroke and curvature of the letters pointed to a female scribe.

The scream from the ladies' wing of the castle had turned his blood to ice. But she was safe. He could now breathe again.

She took Miss Feathers's hand. "Come now, Ann. Sit up, wipe the tears from your face, and tell us how this gown came to be covered in wine and why it is so tragic an accident."

Miss Feathers pushed to a sitting position and accepted the linen Ravenna pressed into her fingers. She dabbed her nose and eyes. "I designed the gown."

"You designed it?" Ravenna fingered the ruined white fabric. "How clever of you."

"I studied the fashion journals and chose the fabrics and sewed the beads." Miss Feathers sniffled. "It was . . . my princess gown," she whispered.

Ravenna looked up at him and then at the doorway. He went across the room and with a nod to the eager audience, closed the panel.

She stroked Miss Feathers's hair. "Your princess gown?"

The girl's shoulders shook. "I had never had such a gown. Simple. Elegant." *Sniff.* "Lovely." She peeked up at Ravenna. "Mama likes . . ."

"Ruffles."

"And tulle. And quantities of lace. She is ever so fond of flounces and, well, fabric."

Ravenna nodded. "And you wished to have another sort of gown, a simpler gown. So you made it yourself."

"Papa gave me the money, but I sewed it all. Mama and I receive few invitations, so I have a great deal of time to do what I wish."

"You wished to feel like a princess."

"Papa says we are rich enough that I might buy anything I like. But I heard Lady Penelope say that Papa bought his baronetcy from the king and it made me positively wretched. He is so happy to have a title, and he has worked so hard to deserve it." She dabbed at her nose. "But your father is not a trades- man, Ravenna. Lord Vitor himself said the church is a noble profession. You are a real gentleman's daughter, so you will tell me the truth, won't you? Is it wrong? Should I not long for something to which I have not been born?"

Ravenna's hand stilled on the girl's hair. "No. For you, Ann, it is not wrong."

"Yet I think it must be." Miss Feathers grasped a fold of the wine-soaked gown. "Or *this* would not have hap- pened." Fresh tears leaked from her round eyes. "Oh, why did I tell Mama about the gown! I never imag- ined she would speak of it. But then Prince Sebastiao chose me to play Juliet and I saw it in her eyes before she even spoke the words. Then she would have me describe it in detail to everybody, how I made it and how beautiful it was. I was so content and he seemed so interested, I did not think to hide it from them. I did not even object when Mama begged the duchess to borrow Lady Iona's maid to press it in preparation for the play today."

Ravenna's hand had slipped away from Miss Feath- ers's hair. Her shoulders seemed to stiffen. "Ann, how did the gown come to be saturated in wine?"

"I found it in the laundry," she said dully.

"Do you believe that Lady Iona's maid poured wine on it?"

Miss Feathers's lips tightened. She shook her head.

"Who," Ravenna asked, "is 'them'?"

Another tear sped down the girl's cheek. "Ladies Penelope and Grace," she whispered. "I saw them take a carafe of wine from the drawing room when we all went to bed last night. It is my punishment . . . because he chose me for Juliet."

Ravenna's throat worked. Beneath her gown, her breasts rose and fell in sharp breaths. She stood. "Then they must be punished for this in turn." She marched toward him, threw open the door, and strode into the corridor.

He grabbed her arm and pulled her around to face him. "Do not now do whatever it is you are thinking you must do."

"Unhand me." Her brow was a storm of anger yet oddly wounded, as though the prank had hurt her as well. "I will do as I wish."

"Murder has happened in this house." He spoke steadily, wanting only to drag her to him and wipe the distress from her eyes. "You must not court the rancor of any here. Only four days ago your life was threatened by someone that we have not yet identified. Does that not give you pause?"

"It should, I know. But I cannot put my safety before injustice toward another."

"Injustice?" He shook his head. "It is a gown."

"It may be a gown, but it meant everything to her. *Everything.*"

"We do not know what the murderer might do if you displease him. Or her."

She stared uncomprehending at him. "Do you think they murdered Mr. Walsh? Penelope and Grace?"

"I don't know who murdered him. But I will regret it beyond measure should you place yourself in danger by defending a friend from malicious teasing."

"You do not understand." She tried to pull away. He held fast.

"Ravenna, I have only your—"

She wrenched free and whispered, "You do not see. She is the bird." She was shaking now.

"The bird?"

She swallowed jerkily and the movement of her neck was both beautiful and painful to watch. "She cannot defend herself, so I must." She whirled around and disappeared around a corner. Miss Anders and Miss Abraccia stood in the shadow at the other end of the corridor, silent, eyes wide. They flinched as Lady Margaret swept past them.

"My lord? What are you doing by my daughter's bedchamber in such a state? And she weeping? Ann! Ann, my dearest!" She hurtled past him into the room.

"Oh, Mama," came the watery reply.

Vitor took up the rapier and followed Ravenna.

THROWING OPEN THE door, Ravenna found them at their toilette. Lady Penelope sat at a gilded dressing table, Lady Grace standing behind her clasping a pearl necklace about her twin's ivory neck.

"Why did you do it?"

"Ah, Miss Caulfield." Lady Penelope turned her head, her fingertips delicate upon the pearls. "How you do lack every trace of civility. It would be positively diverting to witness if I weren't being obliged to do so in my own bedchamber."

"Why did you ruin her gown? Haven't you sufficient beautiful gowns and delicate noses and perfect lips and pale hair to satisfy you? Must you ruin another girl's single pretension toward beauty?"

"I haven't the slightest idea of what you speak."

"Of course you do. The both of you—you wicked, viperous cats."

"Good day, Lord Vitor," Penelope said to the place behind Ravenna. "Have you come to carry away the madwoman to the attic, I hope?" She stood smoothly and moved forward. "How kind of you."

He did not bow to the viper, for which Ravenna was grateful. She would have preferred him to not appear quite so completely virile while in Lady Penelope's bedchamber, with his darkly shadowed jaw, triangle of hard male chest showing at his open collar, and a sword in his hand. But a hero was a hero regardless of guise, even if he had come to stop her rather than to save her—which, she supposed, could be one in the same in this case.

Lady Grace remained by the dressing table.

"Admit that you did it," Ravenna said to her. "If you do, and then go straight off and apologize to Ann, I will not order him to cut off both your heads with his sword."

His laughter rumbled behind her. She wasn't quite certain she appreciated it.

Lady Penelope's crystal eyes oozed dismay. "Oh, dear. Perhaps you should fetch Sir Beverley or Mr. Pettigrew at once, my lord. I believe she has truly lost her mind."

"I have," Ravenna agreed. She looked over her shoulder at him. "Do make certain to keep the sword away from me so that I don't snatch it from you and do away with everyone in the house before breakfast." She pinned Penelope with her stare. "Starting with you. Apologize to Miss Feathers or you will regret it in a manner you cannot imagine."

"'Tis the right thing to do, lasses." Lady Iona poked her head inside the door frame beside Lord Vitor. "We all ken ye did it. The prince'll ken by luncheon, an' he'll no' be happy wi' ye. Ye may as well make the best o' it while ye've still a chance wi' him." She cut a glance at Lord Vitor, followed his legs clad in tight breeches all the way to his exposed collar and tousled hair, and offered him a saucy grin. "Guid mornin', my laird. Ye ought to come out before ye've dressed properly more often."

"Thank you, my lady."

Ravenna folded her arms. "Well?"

Lady Penelope's eyes narrowed. "All right. We will apologize to the mouse. Won't we, Grace?"

"Yes, Penny."

Ravenna gestured for them to precede her into the corridor and Iona took the lead. Lord Vitor did not follow, the sword point stuck in the carpet and his hands resting upon the pommel as he watched them go. Ravenna returned to him and, edgy with her triumph, had some trouble meeting his eyes. The sight of his chest clad only in fine, thin linen tangled her wits.

"Thank you for allowing me to do that," she said.

"I could not have stopped you had I tried."

"You did try."

"With very little effort."

"You appeared so swiftly. I guess you heard her scream. Were you . . ."

"Was I what?"

Already in the ladies' wing of the castle. In another woman's bedchamber. If Lord Whitebarrow, who was married, practiced such pastimes, why wouldn't a young, unmarried man? Petti had told her enough of the ways of the licentious beau monde that she was not entirely naïve. "Nearby?"

He bent his head and peered at her. "I was damning that canine whelp of yours to perdition and preparing to take him outside for the fifth time since midnight."

Relief slipped through her. "It must be easier to raise a puppy in a kennel than in a vast castle."

"I am not raising a puppy. I am enduring it until you take responsibility for it or return it to the stable where it belongs."

"I cannot. It is too late. He is yours. He will always be yours now."

He looked at her very strangely then, and seemed to be on the verge of speech. But instead he drew an audible breath. "Go, see to your forced apology." He turned away.

"It is a very nice sword. I enjoyed using it as a threat."

He paused. "I have no doubt that you did."

"You could wield it quite dashingly in the play today. Until you perish upon Romeo's blade, of course."

He bowed. "I live to dash, madam."

For a moment he was silent again with that air of waiting. But she found nothing to say, no easy quip in response. She was imagining what it might be like to clasp him to her like she had clasped the bolster, to feel the muscles of his back beneath that fine linen shirt with the palms of her hands. She wanted to hold him like that. She longed for it, but it was not a welcome longing, rather tinted with strange despair.

He walked toward her until they were nearly toe-to-toe and she had to bend her neck to look into his face.

"Will you forgive me for handling you so harshly outside Miss Feathers's door?" he said.

Her mouth was dry. "I took no note of it."

His hand circled her arm where he had held her before, but with gentleness at odds with the roguish figure he now cut. His thumb caressed.

"I fear for you, Ravenna." He said it simply and she wondered how she had ever mistrusted him, even for a moment.

"You needn't. I told you that you needn't."

"Yet I do." The crease appeared in his cheek. "In any case, I am loath to allow a woman to tell me my business. Even a controlling woman like you."

"Are you?" His thumb caressed again and her heartbeats fluttered. "How positively medieval of you."

He bent his head. "Take care, will you? I did not fish you out of that river for naught. I should like you to remain alive for the foreseeable future."

"So that you can order me around and alternately tease me, I suppose."

He smiled. "Yes." Then he did what she did not expect: he kissed her brow. Softly, gently, not a transitory peck but a permanent marking, he took the most innocuous possession of her. When he drew away and looked into her eyes, she could not speak.

"Good," he said. "I am glad we understand each other now." His hand slipped from her and he walked away.

In point of fact she understood little, and now considerably less than before. Only her father had ever kissed her on the brow. Lord Vitor, however, did not stir in her feelings of filial duty or tolerance. Nor did she feel for him the grateful friendship she felt for Petti and Sir Beverley, or even the comfortable affection she bore Taliesin, who had been like a brother to her since childhood. Toward Lord Vitor Courtenay she harbored a tangled confusion of pleasure and fear— tumultuous, gripping feelings that she wished to run both toward and from at great speed.

PRINCE SEBASTIAO PLAYED the parts of both narrator and Romeo in the production. Ravenna and the other women to whom the prince had not assigned roles, with Monsieur Brazil and Monsieur Sepic, sat at the bottom of the shallow flight of stairs in luxurious comfort while the sounds of preparations behind elegant curtains finally quieted.

The prince strode across the top riser, a vital figure in gold silk and black ermine, his hat a masterpiece of ancient haberdashery. He liked fancy dress; that had been clear from the first. But this was unprecedented magnificence.

"Two households, both alike in dignity," he proclaimed, "in fair Verona where we lay our scene, from ancient grudge break to new mutiny, where civil blood makes civil hands unclean. From forth the fatal loins of these two foes a pair of star-cross'd lovers take their life." He recited the verse with fluid comfort.

"He is an actor," Iona whispered in Ravenna's ear. "No wonder he wanted to do the play so ardently."

Sir Henry and Mr. Anders appeared from behind the curtain clad in hose and doublets, swords at their sides and caps covering their heads.

"Gregory!" Sir Henry boomed. "O' my word, we'll not carry coals!"

"No, for then we should be colliers," Mr. Anders replied with feeling.

Lord Case came on and began remonstrating with them. But Ravenna could barely follow. Shakespeare's stories were wonderful, but she never quite understood the poetry, no matter how Eleanor and Sir Beverley had labored to give her an appreciation for it. The trouble now, however, had nothing to do with poetry. Staring at Lord Case and Mr. Anders's legs in hose while anticipating Lord Vitor's entrance onto the stage was causing her the most unpleasant heart palpitations.

As it turned out, the hose suited him to devastating advantage. When he entered, with a mocking air he demanded of Lord Case, "What, art thou drawn among these heartless hinds? Turn thee, Benvolio, look upon thy death." He unsheathed his sword and leveled it at his brother. Stomach in knots, Ravenna wished she could turn away. Even more fervently she wished that he had not kissed her on the brow in that fatherly manner.

Everyone acted splendidly, despite Lord Vitor's earlier humility and Sir Henry's tendency to shout his lines. Juliana's uncle, the bishop, teetered onto the stage to deliver the prince's lines. Lord Whitebarrow made a suitably self-important Lord Montague, while Lady Whitebarrow, playing the part of Lady Montague, glowed in speaking of Romeo as her son. The prince's rhapsodizing over first fair Rosaline then Juliet's beauty won chuckles then sighs from the audience. The true astonishment, however, was Martin Anders. As Mercutio, his monologue on the way to the Capulets' party mesmerized.

"I've niver seen a better Mercutio," Iona whispered.

Full of mad emotion and violent agitation, he seemed not to act but to live the part. Ravenna knew he could not possibly be the murderer. No man who wore his dramatic soul like a brilliant red cloak, openly and with such ardor, could kill without afterward swiftly declaring his guilt to the world.

Her certainty did not, however, swallow the bees battling in her stomach when he shouted, "Tybalt, you rat-catcher, will you walk?" and drew his sword on Lord Vitor.

"They've blunted the blades, lass," Iona whispered. "Dinna fear." But her hands were clenched in her lap too.

"What wouldst thou have with me?" Lord Vitor said to the fool.

"Good king of cats," Mr. Anders scowled and advanced upon him. "Nothing but one of your nine lives."

The audience now included members of the cast not on stage. Drawn into mad Mercutio's furor, they stared, entranced. Apparently alone in being unmoved, Monsieur Brazil stood up with customary formality and walked to the foyer. A man stood just within the castle's front door, cloaked in homespun. A hood concealed his head and his brown skirts scraped the floor.

At the head of the stairs Lord Vitor declared, "I am for you."

Ravenna's attention snapped back to the stage.

"Gentle Mercutio, put thy rapier up," Prince Sebastiao pleaded with Mr. Anders.

Mr. Anders shrugged him off. "Come sir," he urged Lord Vitor. "Your passado."

Metal clashed. Behind Ravenna, Juliana Abraccia gasped. Sir Henry clapped his hands and exclaimed, "Good show, gentlemen!"

But it didn't look like they were mock fighting. Ravenna knew little of gentlemanly sport, but this looked real.

Iona reached over and clasped her hand tight.

"Draw, Benvolio!" the prince called frantically to Lord Case. "Beat down their weapons." Sleeves billowing, he leaped toward Mr. Anders and Lord Vitor. "Gentlemen, for shame, forbear this outrage!"

Mr. Anders cast a swift glance toward the door where Mr. Brazil and the stranger stood. Turning eyes filled with desperation again upon Lord Vitor, he shouted, "He shall not escape my pain!" and thrust his sword forward.

"Shakespeare didna write that line," the duchess muttered with disapproval.

Ravenna's heart stumbled. She pushed up from her chair. Iona followed.

Arielle leaped to her feet. "*Ma petite,*" she exclaimed, and ran toward the door.

Steel clanged upon stone. A sword tumbled down the stairs to come to rest at Ravenna's feet. Amidst velvet and gold on the stage, she made out Mr. Anders's two empty hands and she choked upon a swell of relief.

Mr. Anders dropped to his knees, threw his arm over his face, and cried, "Oh, I am fortune's fool!"

"An' that be Romeo's line, no Mercutio's," the duchess said.

Lord Vitor moved toward Mr. Anders and stood above him. His brother descended the stairs and followed General Dijon to the doorway where Arielle clutched the tiny white dog to her bosom.

"*Merci*, monsieur. *Merci*," she said to the hooded man, her face brilliant. The dog wiggled with joy in its mistress's embrace.

Prince Sebastiao called across the hall, "Father Denis. What brings you down to Chevriot from your mountain peak?"

"Your highness." The hermit bowed. His voice sounded rough and unused. "This morning I smelled smoke in the shed in which I store my gardening tools. When I entered, I discovered a fire that had been doused, and this miserable creature. I guessed that it must belong to the chateau. It seems I was correct."

The general shook the hermit's hand. "*Merci, mon père.*"

"But how did the little dog come to be there?" Juliana Abraccia asked, wide-eyed.

"I did it!" Anguish rang through Mr. Anders's words. "I abducted the dog and put it in the hermit's shed. It was me! I am at fault!" He lifted his face fraught with misery to the general's daughter. "Mademoiselle, will you ever forgive me? Can you?"

"How singular," Lady Whitebarrow said with a pinched nose. "Whatever did you want with the animal?"

He turned a dark glare upon his father. "He made me do it."

Everyone stared at Lord Prunesly.

"What could you have wanted, sir, with my daughter's dog?" General Dijon demanded.

Cecilia Anders stood up. "He wished to study its tongue."

"Study a dog's tongue?" Sir Henry demanded. "In the name of Zeus, that is preposterous, Prunesly."

"You are mistaken," Lord Prunesly stated. "As always, my children understand nothing." He peered through his spectacles as though he were noticing everybody for the first time. "The dog is a rare find. I do not wish to *study* it," he said with a scowl at his daughter. "I have all the information I need about it already. It is the sole living specimen of its breed to bear a black spotted tongue. A breeding bitch, no less. It is a remarkable find. Exceptional."

"If you did not wish to study her, why did you hide her in that shed?" Ravenna asked.

"To freeze." Arielle shivered and hugged her dog close. "*Ma pauvre petite.*"

"She would have been no use to me frozen, mademoiselle," the baron said shortly.

"Papa planned to take her to a scientific meeting of the Linnaeus Society," Cecilia said. "He intended to show her to his colleagues and win renown. Isn't that right, Papa?"

"That dog is the proof I have searched for these past twenty years that recessive traits are carried through the fourth generation of females," Lord Prunesly said. "I would have been awarded the Medal of Linnaeus for proving my theory. My findings would have been celebrated throughout Europe. And you, daughter, would have benefitted from it."

Cecilia laughed, but sadly. "How, Papa? If you mean by marriage to one of your ivory tower acolytes, I am even less interested in that than marriage to a prince." She moved toward Arielle and her father. "Miss Dijon, I cannot tell you how dreadfully sorry I am that my father has done this. I begged him not to steal your dog. I did not entirely believe he would do it until he actually did. And Sir Henry." She turned to the horse breeder. "It was a mistake. Poor judgment on my father's part—exceedingly poor. Can you forgive his vanity? Think only of the successes your stables could see if we joined forces."

"Well, miss," Sir Henry said, his doublet stretching beneath a heavy sigh. "I am an honest man and it seems that your father isn't the sort I like to do business with after all. I should have liked to hear more of your ideas, but we'll have to put that aside now." He shook his head regretfully.

"Your highness," said General Dijon, "will you chastise Lord Prunesly?"

The prince cast Lord Vitor a quick glance, then stepped to the edge of the landing. "My lord," he said to the biologist, "I demand that you apologize to the general and Mademoiselle Dijon, and when the snow begins to melt that you depart my house at once."

"But what of Mr. Anders?" Lady Penelope said. "He is not a child to do everything his father demands. The animal might have died, after all. Should not he be punished for the actual crime?"

"Why didn't it die after all those days in the cold?" Lady Margaret asked. "It's smaller than a capon."

"My brother climbed that wretched mountain every day," Cecilia said, "up to his knees in ice, to care for that dog. He lit a fire every morning to warm the shed, and fed her his own breakfast. For his care of it, and for enduring our father's threats to cut off his allowance if he did not obey, he should not have to suffer further punishment."

"But, he should." Lord Case moved away from Arielle. "Mr. Anders, for the distress you have caused Mademoiselle Dijon and her father, I demand satisfaction." He stripped off his blue and gray Montague gauntlet and tossed it onto the stone floor.

"But—but, my lord!" Mr. Anders climbed to his feet but his shoulders were slumped and his hair fell across one of his eyes entirely. "I cared for that dog like it was my very own—rather, better than that."

"But ye might've told his royal highness instead, lad," the duchess said with a nod. "Ye must pay the consequences o' yer folly."

He dashed his arm across his eyes once more and released a mighty groan. "God, I am undone!"

"Vitor." Lord Case looked to his brother on the landing. "Will you act as my second?"

"No seconds will be *nécessaires*." Monsieur Sepic leaped from his chair like a stiff little martinet. "For you, monsieur"—he pointed to Mr. Anders—"have an appointment with the gallows."

Mr. Anders gaped. "For stealing a dog?"

"That is preposterous." Lord Whitebarrow boomed. "He is no peasant to hang for snatching a loaf of bread, Sepic. He is the sole heir to a peer of the realm."

"No' this realm," Iona whispered at Ravenna's shoulder.

"I will not hear of it," Lord Whitebarrow insisted. "The girl has her dog again, and Anders will face Case on the dueling field tomorrow. That is a gentlemanly end to it."

"There will be an end to it, my lord," the mayor said with a nod. "But not the end you believe. For I, Gaston Sepic, have discovered the answer to the more important mystery that I have pursued these four days in your midst. While I dined and dallied with you as if enamored of you, I, a proud citizen of the nation of La France, collected clues." He lifted his arm and pointed a damning finger at the stage. "Monsieur Anders, you murdered Oliver Walsh."

Chapter 14

The Stable, Despite a Promise

Martin Anders's face went white as lambswool. "I did not!" He seemed to search the chamber for allies. "Tell him. Tell him I did not."

"Monsieur Sepic," Cecilia said, "I don't believe my brother murdered that man. I don't believe he is capable of murder."

"You will of course say anything to protect him," the mayor said with a disdainful sniff.

Ravenna willed Lord Vitor to look at her, but his attention was intent—not upon the mayor but on the others scattered on the landing and floor below. She swung her gaze around, seeking anything amiss in the faces of the prince's guests. All seemed bemused, except Juliana Abraccia, whose pretty pale face crumpled beneath her halo of dark hair. Thrusting a trembling hand against her lips, she burst into tears and dashed from the room.

"*Carina*," Bishop Abraccia rasped at the same moment Mr. Anders shouted, "Juliana!" He started forward but Lord Vitor put a restraining hand on his arm and spoke quietly to him. The young man fell back but stared at the empty doorway with tragic eyes.

"She did love me," he said dully. "Not you, after all. I thought . . . But I must have been mistaken." He turned to Lord Vitor, bowed his head, and placed his hand over his heart. "I offer you an apology, my lord, for my display of unwonted violence during our fighting scene. I am honored to have been disarmed by such a man."

"Apology accepted." Lord Vitor looked down the steps at the mayor. "Monsieur Sepic, what evidence leads you to conclude that Mr. Anders killed Walsh?"

The mayor snapped his fingers. "Evidence that others might have been unwise enough to toss away as mere coincidence. But in an investigation of this sort, no evidence is coincidental. *N'est-ce pas?*"

The bees stirred in Ravenna's stomach again, this time frantically.

Monsieur Sepic reached into his pocket and withdrew Mr. Walsh's ring.

Ravenna's heart fell.

The mayor pinched the ring between forefinger and thumb and raised it so all could see. "This ring, worn by the deceased, possesses a pattern that, when it connected with the flesh of the murderer during the attack, deposited a mark on that flesh." He gestured to Mr. Anders with the ring. "Monsieur Anders bears a wound beside his right eye that perfectly corresponds. He told me that he had received the blow to his eye three days before the murder, but I have determined that this was a lie."

"It was a lie," Mr. Anders admitted. "But I did not kill Walsh." He looked darkly from the eye where the bruise was finally fading, the other eye shrouded by his lanky hair. "The afternoon before he died, I encountered him in the corridor. We fell into a scuffle."

"A scuffle?" the duchess said.

"He'd won a pony from me at a gaming club in London in January and I hadn't yet paid up. He demanded the money like he was some sort of king. I tossed my fives at him, but he got me first, the devil." He glowered. "But I left him after that."

"Where did you go?" Lord Vitor asked.

"To the highest tower to cast myself down in misery," he replied upon a moan. Then he glimpsed Lord Vitor's face and said, "To the chamber at the top of that tower. The one with the turret. I was . . . not myself, and I needed to wash off the blood. But the curtains were drawn and I dropped the candle I had carried up the stairs, so I returned to the hall. Then I went to the village. I was too purpled up to hang about with you all and I didn't want my father to see the eye." He glared at Lord Prunesly. "By dinner the swelling had eased, so I returned here. I didn't even see Walsh again that night," he said to the mayor, and thrust out his jaw.

Ravenna met Lord Vitor's gaze. He believed Mr. Anders too.

"At the village," she said to the dog thief. "Where did you go and with whom did you speak?"

His eyes shifted uneasily. "To the locals' watering hole."

"What did you do there?"

"I don't recall," he grumbled. "My eye smarted like the very devil. I may have had a jug of wine and said a word or two I shouldn't have."

"Such as?"

No one stirred throughout the hall. Finally he answered.

"I declared that I would pay five guineas to the man that gave Walsh what he deserved."

A lady gasped. Gentlemen murmured.

Lord Whitebarrow muttered, "Just as I told you all: it wasn't one of us."

"I never meant for anyone to actually harm him," Mr. Anders exclaimed.

Monsieur Sepic clicked his tongue and shook his head. "*Non, non.* You see for yourselves, *mes amis,* that this man is desperate to escape the noose. He has— how do you say?—invented this confederate to throw suspicion from himself. He hopes that you will believe him, a nobleman's son, rather than the poor peasant that he accuses. *Non.* I do not believe it."

"Mr. Anders," Lord Vitor said, "would you recognize the men from that night if they were brought here?"

Mr. Anders shook his head. "I wouldn't."

"Monsieur Brazil, has anyone from the village come to the chateau seeking audience with Mr. Anders?"

The butler said, "*Non,* monseigneur. No one."

"An assassin would not seek payment in a household under investigation," the mayor said with a snap of his fingers. "It would be imbecilic."

"No more imbecilic than murdering an Englishman for a few coins within a mile from the village in which one has lived one's entire life," Lord Vitor said.

"*Exactement.* This Englishman shall be tried and found guilty," the mayor insisted.

Mr. Anders's shoulders slumped. Ravenna's stomach hurt. She had no doubt that his boast in the village pub had fallen on ears long inured to the foolish arrogance of the gentlemen that visited Chevriot. It meant nothing. To amuse herself and Lord Vitor she had goaded the mayor, and now an innocent man would hang for it.

Lord Vitor was looking at her, his brow drawn.

"But . . ." the mayor said, raising a finger into the air. "To be thorough, I shall investigate his story. I will return when I have determined that it is all lies. *Par conséquent*, your highness, if you will spare two men-at-arms I will take the prisoner into custody."

"Monsieur Sepic," Lord Vitor said. "If it pleases his royal highness, Mr. Anders may remain here in the prince's custody while you investigate the circumstances in the village. In that way, if you do discover an assassin, your jail will be available for the murderer's incarceration."

The mayor stroked his moustaches, then nodded. "*Oui. Peut-être* this will be useful. My deputy will interview the men Monsieur Anders encountered that night. But it will not be long," he said with a confident smile, then pinned Mr. Anders with a hard stare. "Monsieur, prepare to meet your day of reckoning. Father!" he called to the monk. "That man will wish to confess before he hangs." With a neat bow to Prince Sebastiao, he departed.

Everybody started talking. With a gesture, the prince summoned his guards. Head hanging, Mr. Anders left the room between them. The bishop wobbled out in pursuit of his niece.

Ravenna hurried up the steps to Lord Vitor. "You do not believe he is responsible, do you?" she said.

"Not any more than you do."

"The note in Mr. Walsh's pocket remains unexplained."

"My thought, as well."

"It could have been there before he arrived at Chevriot. An old note concerning a former assignation."

"Perhaps." He sheathed his sword. "You mustn't take the blame for Sepic's idiocy."

He knew her worries, like a friend she had known

for years rather than days. "But I am in fact to blame," she said.

"Wise men are never to blame for the mistakes of fools."

"I am not, of course, a man."

"Rather, a woman with notions of rationality." He looked down the stairs. Lord Case stood there, close beside Arielle. The French girl's eyes shone.

"Will you allow him to pursue the duel?" Ravenna said.

"His battles are his own affair. But he has already won the prize he seeks. Perhaps he will relent."

"What Mr. Anders said about Miss Abraccia . . ." she heard tumble from her lips. "He seemed to believe that she had . . ."

Midnight eyes upon her, he waited.

"That she had a *tendre* for you," she finished.

"Mm."

"Did you believe that?"

His brow dipped in pique. "How should I know one way or the other?"

"Then, you did not . . . That is to say, you haven't—"

"I haven't seduced her in all the many hours I've had available when I was not examining a dead body, fishing you from a river, searching for hidden mountain paths, and making certain a damned mongrel doesn't destroy every one of my shoes? No, I haven't. Was that what you were thinking when you asked me where I was before I heard Miss Feathers scream this morning?"

"Oh. I . . ."

He instantly looked contrite. "Forgive me. I should not have spoken to you so."

"I encouraged it."

A crease appeared at the corner of his mouth. "That does seem to be a habit of yours."

"What shall we do now?"

His attention dipped to her lips. "Do?"

She liked it. Him looking at her lips. Despite the hot tangles in her stomach or even because of them. She liked it too much. "What shall we do while Monsieur Sepic searches for the nonexistent assassin?"

Slowly his gaze rose to her eyes. "We wait."

THE WAIT PROVED interminable, but there were costumes to be sorted, a set to be struck, a prince to be consoled over the ruination of his play, and whispering gossip to be enjoyed. Everyone stayed busy. Several of the gentlemen retired to the billiards room, but the prince said he could not bear frivolity at present: one of his guests had murdered a stranger in his house and his play had been halted mid-act. His party was an unmitigated disaster. Instead he sat with Lady Whitebarrow and her daughters, but with dull eyes and such a listless manner that Ravenna suspected he did it as an act of punishment upon himself.

Juliana Abraccia recovered sufficiently to appear for luncheon, though she merely pushed the food around on her plate before transferring it to her uncle's.

For her part, Arielle beamed. Sunshine tripped from beneath her modestly lowered lashes and a sweet smile graced her lips. She had not set down her *petite* since Father Denis returned it, and it sat on her lap throughout luncheon. At her side, Lord Case seemed not to mind it, which Ravenna had to admire.

After lunch she examined Marie and found her hale. Martin Anders had clearly cared well for her. Ravenna's guilt for placing him in danger swelled. She slipped away to the kitchen in search of a bone for the pugs and a crust of bread for the rescued captive.

Ann Feathers found her there in a corner, cutting

ligament to separate a bone from the remnants of a calf's carcass.

"Monsieur Brazil said that he saw you coming down here." She peered in wonderment at the rows of gleaming copper pots, dried herbs and meats hanging from hooks, and the cook, maid, and footmen hurrying about as they prepared dinner. Her gaze alighted upon Ravenna's hands. "Dear me, Ravenna. You are so adventuresome."

"It's true. I am vastly adventuresome." Neither Sir Beverley nor Petti had told anyone that she was perfectly comfortable with kitchens or any other place servants went in large houses. Only Lord Vitor knew, and it seemed he hadn't shared that information either.

"I . . ." Ann's round eyes glittered with moisture. "I *admire* him so greatly, Ravenna."

Ravenna set down the knife. "The prince?"

Ann nodded, tiny little jerks of her head. "He is such a good man," she said softly, fervently. "I have . . . I have heard that in his past he was somewhat . . . wild. But I have not seen it. He never does wrong, always wishes everyone to be happy, and he speaks so highly of others."

"Does he?"

"Oh, yes. Why only yesterday he told me how Lord Vitor's piety astounds and amazes him."

"His *piety*?"

"Why, yes. Why else do you think he has ridden up the mountain every morning?"

To find a hidden path used by a thief or murderer. "Why has he?"

"He visits Father Denis at the hermitage." Ann's pale brow creased. "It is a singular thing to contemplate."

A young, handsome, virile lord paying daily calls on a hermit in a mountain peak retreat? "What is singular to contemplate?"

"Wedding a Catholic." Ann's eyes opened wide and as round as the cut of bone in Ravenna's palm. "Oh, Ravenna, you must believe me horridly presumptuous. The prince is kind to all the ladies, and I know he admires Lady Iona's beauty and Lady Penelope's elegance. And you are quite obviously his favorite. He produced the play to amuse you, after all."

"I think it may have been a case of a suitable excuse," Ravenna said. "He clearly enjoys the theater."

"He is such a fine actor. He says it is the only thing he does better than Lord Vitor. But I cannot understand why that should matter to him as he is a prince and Lord Vitor is only the second son of a marquess." Her delicate brow pleated. "He said that perhaps if he had lived for years in a monastery he might have the presence of mind and noble duty toward others that Lord Vitor does. I assured him that could not be true and that he is as splendid a man as ever I have known." Emotions overcoming her, she threw caution to the wind and grasped Ravenna's sleeve. "Do you think I spoke too forwardly when I said that, Ravenna? I should be ashamed beyond measure if he believed me immodest. But he was so low-spirited. I simply had to say something to cheer him."

Ravenna understood that with Lady Margaret as a mother, Ann Feathers came to her to unburden herself of words as much as concerns. Plenty of farmers' wives did the same when she visited their homes to give care to a child or animal or the woman herself. With no one to speak to all day except their little ones, their conversation often ran like a creek after a spring rain, and she listened. Ann's flowing confidences had not before disturbed her.

Now they did.

Years in a monastery?

She detached her arm from Ann's grip. "I do not believe you have said anything amiss." She wrapped the bone in a cloth. "Prince Sebastiao is still young and uncertain of himself. But so are you young, with, however, the understanding of a woman, which is always greater than a man's understanding. You can truly appreciate him, and for that I am certain he must be very glad."

Ann leaped up and threw her arms about Ravenna's neck.

"Dear, *dear* Ravenna," she whispered. "How grateful I am that Prince Raynaldo invited you to attend this party. When I marry, I wish for you to stand up with me at the altar." She released her. "Will you?"

Ravenna could not decline.

Lady Iona appeared in the doorway, eyes bright with excitement. "Come, lasses. Monsieur Sepic has returned."

They hurried to the drawing room. The Frenchman stood in its center, the focus of all attention. He bowed to the prince, Lord Whitebarrow, Lord Case, and Lord Vitor, then to the duchess and the countess.

"Well, out with it, man," Lord Whitebarrow demanded.

"The assassin," the mayor said gravely, "has been found in the village."

Cecilia's hand flew to her mouth, catching her exclamation of relief. Iona slipped an arm around her waist and squeezed her close. Cecilia leaned into the embrace and tears trickled down her cheeks.

Lord Prunesly turned his face away.

"Who did it, monsieur?" Lady Margaret asked.

Monsieur Sepic became deeply interested in the pattern of the rug beneath his boots. "My deputy, Monsieur Paul," he said in clipped accents. Then he thrust up his chin. "Because he is the son of my sister, the imbecile believed himself to be immune to the law.

The drunkard confessed to me. He is now locked in my jail."

"I've a mind to ask him if Mr. Paul's still got the thither key," Iona whispered to Ravenna, but Ravenna could not laugh. Relief slid through her. Then Lord Vitor's gaze caught hers and the slight crease in his cheek put the last vestiges of her guilt to flight.

MR. ANDERS WAS freed. Wholly contrite, he waited attendance upon the ladies as though he had never been acquainted with angst or drama. Although his poet's hair still fell across one eye, he spoke to the gentlemen without a hint of poor humor.

No one had really known Mr. Walsh. The relief they all felt upon discovering the identity of his murderer—and that it was not one of their own number—was undimmed by grief over his death. Within hours, the members of the prince's party were chatting gaily and laughing, and raising toasts to the mayor's investigative brilliance and the prince's hospitality. Someone suggested making another attempt at staging the play on the following day, and the idea was greeted with enthusiasm all around. Prince Sebastiao soon required Monsieur Brazil to bring additional bottles from the cellar, and the afternoon turned to merry celebration.

The servants returned from the village, weary of sleeping on straw pallets and dining on peasant fare, by all appearances cheerful to be at the beck and call of their masters again. A-bustle with busy maids and footmen and valets, the castle exhibited the sort of industry that only came with a gathering of men and women of consequence and wealth.

Sir Henry suggested that it would be splendid to stretch the horses' legs, and wouldn't the ladies like a ride in a sleigh? Two such conveyances could be found in the carriage house. Horses were harnessed and saddle mounts prepared. As the sun descended everybody had opportunity from sleigh bed to marvel at the white bedecked landscape, the quaint little village in which a murderer now suffered behind bars, and the snow-capped turrets and battlements glowing red in the fading light as they approached the chateau upon their return.

Goblets of mulled wine awaited the chilled hands of the prince's guests in the drawing room. More toasts were raised. The servants had been whipped into a frenzy of activity while the guests disported themselves out of doors. The prince wanted a party, and everybody obliged.

Ravenna had often seen this sort of grand celebration, but always from below stairs. Confronted by it now, she barely knew how to go on. After dinner in the drawing room she watched Lord Whitebarrow approach Iona with a glass of wine, and a sick sensation wiggled through her belly. Lord Case once again stood by Arielle at the pianoforte. The precious dog—a dog for whom a man had encouraged his children to thieve—sat upon her lap sipping from a porcelain cup. For the first time in a sennight Ravenna now noticed the delicate lace on the bodice of Arielle's exquisite gown, the small, glittering tiara set in her dark locks, and the collar fashioned of leather braided with gold filigree about Marie's neck.

Beast had never worn a collar of any sort. Now, surrounded by wealth and comfort, he would have been sitting by the window watching for hare and wishing he were chasing them through knee-deep snow.

Prickles crept along Ravenna's shoulders. As they had done once before in this castle, the walls seemed to creep inward. Toward her. This was a strange world, a world in which amiable young ladies took married men as their lovers, in which rich young men with no occupation goaded poor peasants to commit murder, and in which she had nothing whatsoever in common with the son of a marquess—second son or any. He had not approached her since the mayor's announcement. She could only imagine that he, as she, was now coming to recognize the inequality of their friendship. Mr. Walsh's death had turned the castle upside down and for a moment she had forgotten, as perhaps he had, that this place of ancient towers, glittering crystal, gold and jewels and velvet and satin was not her world.

She escaped. Slipping out of the drawing room, she went to Petti's chamber and collected the pugs for their evening walk about the forecourt. After this, she sought shelter in the single place at Chevriot in which she felt at home.

In the aftermath of the afternoon entertainments, the animal denizens of the stables rested in gentle quiet. Freshly polished harnesses dangled and saddles gleamed in the light of the full moon that peeked through windows. Ravenna walked the length of the building and into the carriage house, her lamp flickering amber light across silvery moonbeams. She found only ancient Bishop Abraccia's equally ancient groom tucked beneath his coat on the floor of a stall, sleeping.

Returning to the other end of the buildings, she drew open the door to the room where the pups and mother lived and stared at empty straw. Setting the lamp on the bench, she bent to press her nose to the straw. No scent of the dogs remained. Mother and litter had been removed, all evidence of them cleaned away, and fresh straw strewn. Civilization had returned even to this tiny corner of Chevriot.

"What can a gentle lady be about in a stable so late at night, I wonder?"

She whirled around.

Lord Case leaned against the doorpost, eyes hooded, his hands behind his back and chestnut hair gleaming in the moonlight. He carried no lamp.

"Waiting for someone, Miss Caulfield?"

"There was a litter of pups in this stall," she said. "I came to see them and have discovered them gone. Home, I suspect, now that the castle gates are once again open and their master could retrieve them." She spoke while her mind sped. The bishop's groom was probably deaf and in any case too far away to hear if she called for help. Martin Anders had not committed the murder but that did not mean that Monsieur Sepic's hurried investigation of his deputy had revealed the truth. Lord Case knew that she and his brother were pursuing their own investigation, and Lord Vitor did not entirely trust him. And someone at the castle, still unknown, had pushed her into the river.

"They were not hunting dogs or lapdogs," she said, "so they did not belong here, I think." Or Lord Case could have pursued her here for less malicious but nevertheless unwanted purposes. Or perhaps had he come to the stable to meet a lover? She could not imagine delicate Arielle Dijon rolling in the hay on a winter night—or any night. Iona's impassioned plea to tell no one of her scandalous behavior rang in Ravenna's ears. How her sister Arabella had lived in this world for so long, and so willingly, she had no idea.

"Ah," Lord Case said. "I recall Vitor mentioning something about keeping a young dog at the house. Was that perhaps one of this litter that has now disappeared?"

"Yes. One of those." Confronted by his keen stare it suddenly seemed outrageously presumptuous that she had forced the pup upon his brother.

"I see." He moved into the room, producing from

behind his back a bottle and two goblets. "I, however, have not come here looking for dogs." He righted one goblet and deftly poured wine. In the moonlight, it shone deep golden. "Have you had opportunity during this tumultuous week to taste the *vin jaune* of the Jura, Miss Caulfield?" he said conversationally.

"I have never been fond of wine." Her tongue had gone dry. He blocked the door, and again a man had trapped her in this room. But she did not believe Lord Case would let her go as easily as his brother finally had. Not until he got what he'd come for.

"This will alter your notions of wine, I think." He held forth a goblet to her. "It is superb, dry and rich. Go ahead. I shan't bite. Not at least if you try the wine." He smiled, and there was something of his brother's smile in the curve of his lips, but without the warmth and humor.

She wrapped her cloak more snugly about her. "I will return to the house now, if you will allow me to pass."

"My dear Miss Caulfield, I haven't any ill intentions toward you." He spread his hands. "I merely wish to talk. Do sit"—he gestured to the bench—"and enjoy some wine, and we will become better acquainted."

"I don't wish to drink wine. Please allow me to pass."

"Yes, Wesley." Lord Vitor filled the doorway. "Allow the lady to pass."

"Ah," the earl said with a lift in his voice. "As always your timing is superb, Vitor. I have just now poured a libation for Miss Caulfield. The next was to be for you." He set down the goblets and bottle on the bench and went to the door. "I wish you"—he looked over his shoulder—"and you, madam, a pleasant night." His footsteps receded into the dark.

"Did he frighten you?" Lord Vitor's voice sounded gravelly.

"Not a bit. The pitchfork is within reach, of course."

He did not smile.

"Failing that," she added, "either the goblets or that bottle would have served."

He came forward and stood close. "Did he frighten you?" he repeated.

This frightened her—the singing of her nerves when he was near, the strange longing to be with him and the contrary urge to run.

"No." She ducked around him and took up the goblet that Lord Case had filled. "But I should actually like to taste this wine. Iona was in alt about it the other day. Even Lady Penelope agreed, and not in the presence of the prince, so it might be considered truth of a sort from her."

He looked at the floor. "The dogs have decamped, it seems."

"I suspect she was not intended to drop her litter here." She sat on the bench beside the bottle and empty glass. "If a bitch cannot find a safe place to deliver her pups close to home, she will look for shelter elsewhere. But the pups were old enough to be weaned. Perhaps their master has finally found her and collected them." For an instant, oddly, she considered her mother, and that neither she nor her father had ever come to collect their three lost daughters.

"What sort of dog is it?" he asked.

"It?"

"Gonçalo and his ilk."

She sipped the wine. The glass was cold and the wine indeed rich, just as Lord Case had said. "A shepherd, perhaps, or a very unusual hound. Perhaps an accidental mix of both. The French no doubt have working dogs that we do not. We might ask Lord Prunesly," she said with a twisted grin.

"Give me a glass of that wine—or five—and I will go ask him myself."

She laughed and poured the wine. He accepted the goblet from her, taking care, it seemed, not to touch her hand, and moved to the window and opened it. Brilliant moonlight cast him in silver.

He leaned back against the wall. "Will I be obliged to pay someone for the creature, then?"

"It's unlikely. As the runt, he probably would have been discarded in the river."

"Ah. But he became my prize instead," he said wryly.

"Don't blame me for it. I only gave him to you. You needn't have kept him."

"What of 'It is too late—he is yours—he will always be yours now'?" He bent and sat down on the clean straw with movements so economical and fluid that she saw how this large, powerfully built man had trained his body to the sort of discipline required of a monk. "Has your philosophy altered since only this morning?" he said.

"Was that only this morning?" she said over the open mouth of the goblet, the golden honey aroma stirring in her nostrils. "What a peculiar day it has been."

"The days that preceded it were so benign in your experience, were they? Clearly you lead an adventuresome life."

She looked at him squarely. "How did Monsieur Paul gain entrance into the chateau past the prince's guards? And after the murder, how did he escape without notice?"

"Perhaps a servant allowed him entrance. I inquired of the kitchen staff. They all denied having seen the deputy in the house. Tomorrow I will interview the other servants."

She might have assumed he would do so. Perhaps he had not avoided speaking with her this afternoon. Perhaps he had merely been otherwise occupied.

She looked into her wine. "Is that the sort of thing

they teach men in Catholic monasteries? To interrogate servants and hunt down murderers?"

He did not reply. Gathering her courage, she looked up at him. A slight smile creased one side of his mouth.

"Another question you have been waiting to ask, hm?"

"No." She rolled her eyes away. "I only learned of your deeply pious past this afternoon." She took some time studying her fingertip as she ran it around the lip of the goblet. "Is it your past?" Butterflies cavorted about her stomach. It should not matter what he answered, but the wine spread warmth in her limbs and she wanted to know. *Needed* to know.

"Why?" His voice was easy. "Do you take some particular interest in it?"

"Only in the event that the deputy turns out not to be the murderer and the mayor should need to reopen the case." Grabbing the decanter, she stood up and went to him. "It would be inconvenient for him to be obliged to hunt you down upon some remote mountaintop."

"You are all consideration for our French friend."

"Aren't I?" She plopped down beside him, tucked her legs beneath her, and extended the bottle to him. "Mostly I wonder if monks are allowed to have dogs."

He topped off his goblet. "I should think it would depend upon the monastery. Some are stricter than others regarding the prohibition of personal property."

"Would you keep him?"

He shook his head and laughed. "Ravenna—"

She grasped his sleeve. "But would you?"

He looked down at her hand and she removed it, but it felt peculiar to release him, as though her hand wanted to remain with him.

"I don't think Gonçalo would allow me to abandon him," he said. "That he is not here now is only due to the deep sleep into which he fell after his run beside the sleighs this afternoon." He paused before adding, "But the issue is moot. That life is behind me."

She fell back in the straw, exhaling panic. It was remarkable, really, how even two sips of wine made one's feelings so *acute* and dramatic. "Do you think Mr. Anders drinks wine?"

"I believe I have seen him do so." His voice smiled.

"I don't mind it when you laugh at me."

"I was not laughing at you."

"Of course you were. Will your brother make Mr. Anders meet him tomorrow at dawn?"

"At the request of Mademoiselle Dijon and the general, he withdrew his challenge. Since the dog was not harmed, the general has also forgiven Lord Prunesly for the theft. It seems it will increase the value of his kennels for a titled lord to have taken an interest in them. They have agreed upon an arrangement by which Lord Prunesly will show the dog at his scientific meeting after all."

"After which all the most fashionable ladies will want one of Marie's pups in their boudoirs. Clever. But I am relieved. Martin Anders is very foolish. I cannot think now how I ever considered him a potential suspect."

"You didn't. Not since your late-night encounter with him."

There was something odd in his voice. She opened her eyes and he was as handsome as she had thought before. Now he was looking into his wine, perhaps also searching for the magic in it that made thoughts tumble and feelings acute.

"I don't believe he meant me harm," she said.

His gaze came sharply to hers. "Anders?"

"Your brother. Just now. And I am terribly grateful for the wine, as it turns out."

He paused. "Are you?"

"Tell me about the woman he nearly wed, Mr. Walsh's sister, the one who died of a broken heart." She should not ask. It was not her place to ask. But he answered.

"Her name was Fannie. In the first years that Walsh worked for my father, she lived with their mother and grandparents in Bath and rarely visited her brother. When she was fourteen her mother and grandfather died of fever, and she and her grandmother went to live at Airedale. I think my brother came to admire her then."

"How old was he?"

"Eighteen."

"Did he court her then?"

"Three years later."

"He was eager."

"Rather, he was certain. He saw no reason to wait longer. And, as she was a very pretty girl of an open nature, he saw great reason for haste."

Ravenna closed her eyes and breathed slowly through her nose, the air cooling her muddled head. "He was heir to a title and she was the sister of his father's employee. What more attractive marriage could she have hoped for?"

In response, he was silent.

Cheeks suddenly hot, she turned her head and studied him in the silvery-gold of lamp and moonlight. His handsome face was set in quiet lines, as so often, and now she understood why; he was trained to it.

"What happened?" she said. "When he offered for her?"

"My father would not allow it. The match was vastly unequal, of course, and I believe he had other reservations as well."

A girl of an open nature. "Her character?"

"Perhaps."

"How did your brother accept that?"

"He fought it, but our father did not relent. When Walsh saw that his sister would not be a countess, however, he accused my brother of having seduced and ruined her. My brother insisted that he had behaved with honor toward her. Infuriated, he called out Walsh. He met Walsh at dawn and shot him in the arm."

"It is remarkable to me how readily gentlemen take up firearms to settle disputes," she murmured. "What happened then?"

"Then?"

"After the duel."

There was another lengthy silence. Then he said, "She transferred her affections to another man." His eyes, usually so warm and direct, shuttered now. "That man did not return her affections. Soon after, she fell ill."

"Her will to live must already have been weak. Animals don't suffer that sort of death if they are loved and well treated. Only humans succumb to illness in such a fashion."

He looked down at her and the lamplight seemed to cut a crease in his cheek. "You said before that you do not believe in dying of a broken heart."

"I don't."

"And yet you have now suggested the opposite."

"Weak people have weak wills. Was this girl—this Fannie—was she weak?"

He rubbed his hand over his eyes. "Might we discuss something else, Ravenna? This wearies me."

"Oh, well, one mustn't weary his excellency."

He smiled. "No."

She turned her face to the window. The moonlight was a winter moon's, aloof and chill, and her breaths clouded upon the air. But wrapped in her heavy cloak, she barely felt the cold.

"On nights like this, Beast and I used to wander the

park at Shelton Grange searching for hare. We could see everything as though it were day. Sometimes better."

"But no longer?"

"He left me. I suppose somewhere up there"—she gestured to the heavens—"is a snowy park in which he hunts for hare in the moonlight."

He did not respond. Then, sleepily: "If he was anything like the monster you deposited upon my pillow, he is probably tearing through pristine angels' boots at this very moment. I believe I can hear the cherubim and seraphim now groaning in chorus."

She laughed. Such pleasure warmed her chest, more than she had felt in months. But unlike the peaceful happiness she had known before, an undercurrent of longing swept through her, as though true joy were just on the other side of a door she daren't open.

Her companion was quiet, his eyes closed, the movement of his chest regular as though he dozed.

"I am sorry Gonçalo has caused you to lose sleep," she said.

Without opening his eyes he made a dismissive gesture with his hand. In repose his face was starkly handsome, and with a day's whisker shadow seemed too rugged for either monk or nobleman. As she had wanted to touch his back earlier, now her fingers tingled with the desire to stroke the plane of his cheek and hard jaw, and to delve into his dark hair and know its silky texture. She wanted to feel him.

"Do you find something amiss with what you see?" he asked without opening his eyes. "Is this the reason for your long study?"

She laughed. "Are your eyelids transparent?"

"At war, a man learns to hone all his senses."

"I am glad you honed them so that you returned home alive," she said.

"Thank you. At this moment, I am as well."

Her head was spinning and her heart beat hard. So much feeling swirled inside that it seemed to fill her entirely. She had never had such a friend. And yet as she enjoyed his laughter and companionship, the longing swelled.

"Today," she began, uncertain of her words, "after Monsieur Sepic announced his conclusions, I wondered if . . ." *What was she saying?* "I want to find the murderer, of course. The actual murderer. But . . . I am afraid of this ending." She whispered, "Please don't let it end."

He turned to her and the lamplight cut across his sober face and shadowed his eyes. He leaned down and slid his hand around her cheek and into her hair. A caress soft as a prayer passed along her jaw, then beneath her lips. It made her shiver with pleasure and fear.

"I thought you were asleep," she whispered. "Before. When I was staring at you."

"How, do you imagine, could I sleep when you are near?" His voice was low.

Butterflies danced in her stomach. "Do you intend to kiss me now?"

"I cannot."

"Why not?"

"You made me promise to never again kiss you in a stable."

She stared at his lips. "I now relieve you of that promise."

Chapter 15

The Wolf and the Hare

He kissed her. Lips barely touching, mostly it seemed that he breathed her, a caress of warmth against the coldness surrounding them.

"You are exquisite, Ravenna." His voice sounded remarkably unsteady. But his words were nonsense.

"I am no—"

Then he truly kissed her. Capturing her lips quite securely beneath his, he scooped his hand around the back of her neck and tilted her face up so that her mouth came against his fully. She had never kissed anyone except him, briefly and against her will. She had not known that a kiss could be like this. Neither harsh upon her mouth nor gentle, his mouth commanded hers to return the kiss, and she did—eagerly. He tasted of golden wine and felt at once like home and danger, delicious and thrilling. Her hands found their way to his shoulders and gripped, and he leaned into her, trapping her beneath him. This time, beset by the most powerful urge to push herself against him, she didn't mind being trapped. When his lips coaxed hers apart, a rushing, insistent heat funneled through her.

She might have made a sound; he lifted his head. His indigo eyes questioned.

She forced words through her quick breaths. "I thought when you kissed me this morning on my brow that you hadn't any more interest in kissing me like this."

"No." He sounded breathless too.

"But—"

"A promise is a promise." He cupped her face in both his hands, and his gaze upon her mouth looked as hazy as her muddled head. The wine was strong, but they hadn't drunk that much.

"If I made you promise to continue kissing me like this now," she said, "until I say otherwise, would you honor that promise too?"

"A man is only as good as his word."

"And deed, I hope," she managed to say before he covered her lips again. This time as he tasted her, his tongue traced the seam of her lips. Ripples of pleasure followed. He did it again and her lips parted. Her mouth wanted him inside her. *She* wanted him inside her. Then he was there, stroking her and making her weak. Pleasure. Longing. Tangled together, hot and wanting. All the feeling inside her needed more than even the thrilling connection of lips, more than these caresses, and much more than the connection of bodies through clothing. Tentatively she allowed the tip of her tongue to stroke his.

"Ravenna." Her name came upon a groan that seemed to come from his chest. She felt it rumble against her breasts. "You mustn't tease me."

"I'm not teasing. I want to touch you."

He gave her what she wished, and the confident caress of his tongue against hers shot spikes of yearning straight down her body. She ached profoundly, and she knew it was the mating urge. She wanted to be closer. As close as possible. *Intimately* close. The need surged everywhere—upon her tongue that he caressed and between her legs where the ache was fiercest, and in her breasts too.

"And to be touched by you," she said. She wanted him to touch her. Needed him to.

His palm smoothed from her face to her shoulder, then to the neckline of her gown above her breasts. He bent his head, and where his fingers played at the edge of her bodice he put his mouth.

Shocking pleasure. Soft heat with the rasp of his whiskers against her skin. His lips caressed. She sank into ecstasy.

"Beautiful," he murmured, his voice muffled against her skin, his mouth hot upon her. "This. You." His hand curved beneath her breast and cupped it. His groan mingled with her gasp.

He lifted his head. His eyes looked fevered, almost hazy, and as full of desperation as she felt. Her throat made a whimpering sound of protest, and she reached up and clamped his hand to her firmly. Fingers laced over his, she made him hold her. Her nipple was tight beneath the fabric. His dark eyes held hers as he stroked over the peak. Another whimper escaped her, then another. Now nothing mattered but the need to feel him more, to have him where she ached hardest. She separated her thighs and pressed up to him. But the narrow gown made it impossible.

She broke her lips free and tugged at her skirts. "Help me. Help me." Desperation drove her.

With strong, remarkably capable hands, he pushed her skirts to her thighs, then higher. She spread her knees and let him bear up against her. *Yes*. Yes. A thousand times yes. A sound came from her throat, a sound she'd never heard, of pure pleasure, echoed by rumbling pleasure in his chest.

"*Ravenna*."

Bending his cheek to hers, he pressed her into the straw, and there was only feeling and pleasure and the aching that grew yet more desperate now as she clutched at him and urged him against her.

"Oh," she sighed. "I want this."

His mouth covered hers and he kissed her, deeply, hungrily, possessing her mouth like she wanted him to possess her entirely. He touched her face, his skin against hers hot, perfect, making her wild, making her clasp his hips with her thighs and groan. She shuddered, wanting him even closer. Wanting *more*. His hand slipped along her throat and he followed it with his mouth, each caress new pleasure. He encompassed her breast again and she pushed into it. Her nipples strained against her clothing, swollen and sore with need. She wanted him to touch them. She wanted him to remove her clothing and touch *all of her*. Wild for his hands on her, she needed to be connected with him.

He spoke against her throat. "I did not come here with this intention."

She grabbed his shoulders. "I think I may have."

"I needed only to find you. I need . . . I have the most powerful need to be near you."

"I think I want you nearer now." Wild birds had ejected the butterflies and taken up residence in her belly. Her legs felt weak, every part of her quivering. "As near as possible."

"Ravenna—"

"*Please*."

There was little to do. He was already where she wanted him and she felt his male readiness. Only the fall of his trousers and perhaps a shirttail stood between her and the satisfaction of her ache.

"Please," she whispered.

She did not expect him to delay and he did not. There was the most extraordinary shock of being touched by flesh that was not her own, then probed, then *broken*, like she was soft pine wood and he was an awl. She gulped in air and for a moment she regretted. But the moan that came from his chest, so powerful and satisfied, rolled through her and made her weak with yearning. Without further cajoling her body simply opened to him and he entered her completely. His instrument was large and she felt stretched and filled and *extraordinary*.

His chest heaved. He dropped his brow to hers.

Panic slipped through her, and she abruptly felt the cold air on her stockinged legs and the weight of the man atop her. Rams and stallions never paused like this. They did their business before the female escaped. "What's wrong?" she whispered.

"A moment," he said in a strained voice.

She tried to swallow. Could not. Her throat was closed. Completely dry. He had been a monk. Had she made him break a vow? Oh. *No.* "You have done this before. Haven't you?"

"Not with you." His voice was so deep.

"Well, it's good that one of us has because—*unh!*"

He thrust into her and her world exploded. He filled her and it was *perfect*, as though her body had been made to be filled by him. She clutched his shoulders tighter. *This*—this was what she wanted.

"One of us?" he said roughly, thrusting again, jarring her into the straw, delectably hard and deep inside her.

He thrust again. *Yes.* This friction. This delicious meeting. This deep caress. "*Ohh.*"

"One of us?" he growled.

"Now both of us." How hadn't she known of this? How would she ever have enough of it now? "Oh, *yes.*"

"Ravenna—"

She never wanted it to end. Having him inside her was pleasure and desperation and satisfaction all at once. "Yes. Please—"

"*Ravenna.*" His body went perfectly still. "Are you a virgin?"

"Not now."

Breaking her grip, he pulled out and off of her. She had barely time to register the shock of her empty body and the cold air on her inner thighs when he yanked down her skirt and swiftly set to buttoning his breeches.

"How can you be a virgin?" His voice shook. He scraped his hand through his hair and his eyes looked confused. "How is that possible?"

She couldn't quite breathe. "I thought you said you had done it before. Am I wrong in supposing that means you should know how a person can be a virgin, then subsequently not?"

He stared at her uncomprehending. "You said 'please.'"

"A virgin cannot be polite?"

"What was all that talk of a woman's virtue not residing in her maidenhood? And your unstinting loyalty to Lady Iona?"

"That was me speaking my mind and being a nonjudgmental friend." She sat up, the chill curling around her. "Would my family really have sent me to woo a prince if I weren't a virgin?"

He gestured toward the door. "Half the girls in that house aren't virgins."

"How do you know that?" Oh. No. He could not have done this with other potential brides. Could he?

But he was so handsome. He could have any woman he wanted. "Have you . . . ? That is . . . With . . . ? Oh." She pushed herself up, her stomach ill.

He grabbed her wrist. "No. I have not. That is not how I know. It has been my project this sennight to learn these things, if you recall." He released her.

She snatched her hand back and sank it into a fold of her cloak. "You didn't know it about me."

"I haven't been investigating you." His voice sounded peculiarly slurred. But he'd only drunk two glasses of wine . . . here. Perhaps he'd had more earlier. Perhaps he had been foxed when he came to the stable. Perhaps he had come to find her only because he had been foxed.

"Well maybe you should have been," she said, entirely uncertain now, and starting to hurt in a way she had not anticipated. She hadn't wanted their friendship to end but she had ended it quite effectively herself. "Anyway if that is the case, then it should have been your project to make my first time being ravished a good one."

"Your first time being ravished?" His eyes looked fuzzy, like he was trying to recall. He looked up, and it seemed that he struggled to focus. "I was not ravishing you. You were willing. I thought."

"And ready."

"And drunk. And I'm drunk." He put a hand over his eyes. "My God, what am I doing? I am going to regret this in the morning,"

Ravenna's stomach cramped. She backed up. "There is nothing to regret. Nothing happened."

His brow grew dark. "Nothing happened?"

"I may not be a woman of great experience—or, rather, any at all—but I have seen enough animals mating to know that nothing just happened here. Even birds mate for longer than that."

"Birds mating?" He was not laughing. But she had not meant it in jest. The indignation in her chest had become a burrowing core of hurt.

"You know, I don't think I will thank Lord Case for supplying the wine, after all." She pulled her cloak about her and ran.

FOR A MOMENT Vitor could do nothing. Shock, lust, and confusion all battered at his cotton-wadding head. Legs leaden, he lurched to his feet and set off after her. He reached the stable door in time to see her enter the castle, but his vision was blurred, spotty, and his head was astoundingly heavy. He shook it, but the fog remained.

It needed but seconds to return to the stable room, take up his empty glass, and curse himself for a fool. He slewed his gaze around. Nestled upright in the straw, her goblet was nearly full. But he had drunk two glasses.

Poisoned wine.

He could not believe it of his brother. *He could not.* Despite the past. But . . .

He smelled no scent other than fermented grape, but in truth he knew little of poisons, only that some left small trace. Taking up the bottle and goblets, he strode as well as his bandy legs would carry him, staggering and spilling the wine from her cup into the snow. His feet sank in the slush.

Melting?

No wonder the stables had not been unbearably cold. That, drugged wine, and her body beneath him had warmed him.

Her virginal body.

In his right mind he wouldn't have done it. In his right mind he would have halted it, no matter how she pleaded.

Balderdash. In his right mind he'd been wanting her beneath him again for a sennight.

A guard waited inside the door. Vitor bypassed him—none of the guards could be trusted—but he'd no time to stash the wine. He carried it to the ladies' wing, set it down on a table, and knocked on her door.

She opened it only a crack. *She was well.* He tried to focus on her eyes. They'd shone with desire in the stable . . . *he thought.* But he trusted none of his senses now. Now he saw only blurred shadow. "Are you all right?" His tongue was thick. "No one— No one followed you?"

"Except you?"

Was she angry? Irritated? Hurt? He couldn't see her face or read her tone. His head spun.

He clutched the door frame. "Are you all right?" he repeated. Or did he?

"Yes. But I don't see how—"

"Drugged." Had he spoken? "Poison." He couldn't feel his legs. "The wine."

"Oh, no." She opened the door entirely and touched him, perhaps. "Your eyes are peculiar. Oh, God." Now he felt her hands gripping his arms. "What should I do? Tell me."

He could not keep his eyes open. "Sebastiao," he managed.

"The prince poisoned you? But Lord Case—"

"*Help.*"

Only a pinpoint of candlelight pierced the darkness. No moon like in the stable. No warm woman beneath him, giving him her body. Only exhaustion. Bone-deep and cold. The pinpoint spun.

He was walking, his legs heavy. But the bindings were like hands, the ropes like fingers this time. He would say nothing. He had nothing to say. He'd done no wrong. He had been loyal to king and country. He would not allow them to force untruths from his lips.

They were trying to drown him. The water flooded his mouth and he choked, but he made himself swallow, again and again. He would not let them win.

Voices came in muddled whispers. Occasionally shouts. Familiar voices. Before, the voice had been familiar. Beloved. This time too. But different voices. A man's and a woman's. There had been no shouts before. Only quiet, constant sound. This was a new tactic. But . . . *Sebastiao?* He could not believe it. Would not. And not Ravenna. Never Ravenna.

He clamped his teeth together and did not speak. Not even the truth. If he allowed himself to speak even once, as soon as the pain came he would say anything they wished.

The pinpoint of light ticked back and forth like the pendulum of a clock. Then it stilled, holding in one place.

He was lying on his back in a bed, the bindings gone. Above, the canopy glowed golden.

He closed his eyes.

VITOR AWOKE TO pain slicing beneath his brow. Amidst the pain he knew only that his tongue was dry and his arm peculiarly warm.

He cracked his eyes open.

Dawn. Early morning. His bedchamber. His bed. A dog curled in a ball against his arm.

He pulled in breaths, dragged himself up, and rubbed his hands over his face. The pup stretched and greeted him with enthusiasm. He scratched it behind the ears, but his hands were stiff, his limbs weak. Gonçalo pushed forward, demanding more.

"No."

The dog dropped its ears and flattened himself to the mattress.

He should have said no to the woman in the straw the night before. The moment he'd felt the wine go to his head, he should have taken himself off. But her hands on him, her soft skin, her gasps of pleasure and intoxicating mouth . . . He hadn't needed wine. The woman stretched out in the straw wanting him had been more than enough.

A folded paper rested on the bed not far from Gonçalo's wagging tail. Astounding that the pup hadn't eaten it. No doubt he'd had enough finely cured leather to satisfy his hunger. Vitor took up the missive. The wax seal and hand were Sebastiao's.

> *The wine is safely stored in my bedchamber. The woman is likewise safely stored in hers.*

His younger brother had always fancied himself clever. This morning Vitor was not amused.

> *She knew to keep you awake until the poison had worked its worst. She insisted upon water, though I argued her choice of treatment and recommended wine or at the very least tonic. But she held fast. I was obliged to melt snow—snow!—upon the fire. She would have it no other way, nor allow a servant to do the task. I carried the snow inside like a maid. I have never been more humiliated but it was night and no one else stirred, and of course it was your life and I could not argue it. I allowed her to be present during the dosing with water, but not the subsequent results*

*of that. You may feel free to thank me for that consid-
eration at your earliest convenience. I admit, I thought
you were bested, and as you seemed unable to speak
we could not know. She did not relent in her conviction that you would survive. She is remarkably clever.
I've no idea what you did to rouse her ire, but if she
had not been so hell-bent upon making you live I think
she might have taken a fireplace poker to your head.
Perhaps I will marry her and prove myself the better
man after all.*

Vitor summoned his valet and dressed. Though he
would have preferred to shave himself, his hands were
not entirely steady, and he did not wish to alert anyone
to anything out of the ordinary.

Two notes were swiftly written and sent with footmen to each of his brothers' rooms. Then he searched
out Sir Beverley Clark.

The baronet sat alone at the dining table, sipping
coffee. He nodded when Vitor entered the room. "My
lord."

Vitor went to him. "I would like a word with you,
sir."

"Concerning Mr. Pettigrew's ward, I presume," he
said as though men sought audience with him every
day about Ravenna.

"Ward?"

"Three years ago he made Miss Caulfield his ward
and heir, though she does not know of it." Serious eyes
studied him. "So you see, she is not the penniless servant you believe her to be. Quite the contrary."

"I understood her to have a family. Sisters. A father."

Sir Beverley lifted his coffee to his lips. "A poor
country vicar who allowed her to seek employment
in an unknown gentleman's distant household at the

tender age of seventeen with nothing but a great black dog to defend her. When Pettigrew applied to him for the transfer of guardianship, the Reverend Mr. Caulfield allowed it without trouble." He sipped. "So you see, Pettigrew and I have long considered her our responsibility." He set down the cup. "She lost the dog not long ago. This loss has been difficult for her. I have no doubt that she would be wearing black now if she went in for such displays."

This was a warning. Vitor nodded. "I understand," he said. "Now tell me about the bird."

RAVENNA DID NOT quite imagine that Lord Vitor Courtenay would appear at her door this morning with a bouquet of flowers and a profuse apology upon his perfect lips. But she did not imagine either that when she tried to leave her bedchamber to go to breakfast, the prince's own personal servant would bar her way.

"By order of Lord Vitor, mademoiselle."

"Lord Vitor has no say over whether I come or go. Let me by."

"I cannot, mademoiselle. His highness commanded."

For ten minutes she endeavored to convince him otherwise. Then she shut and locked her door, and climbed out her window. Vines snaked up the castle on the southern side and it wasn't so far to the ground if one didn't mind tearing one's skirt a bit. She would ask her sister Arabella for a loan and pay back Ann in full for all the ruined gowns. Her stockings had not come out of last night's sojourn in the stables very well either.

Her stockings and her pride.

She understood that he meant to protect her from Lord Case. But upon entering the castle by the front door she learned from a footman that the earl's valet had not yet been summoned to his rooms to dress his master. Lord Case had not yet arisen. She could go about without fear for her life, especially if she didn't drink any wine.

Hours of walking the floor of Lord Vitor's chambers had her stomach gnawing and now she headed for the dining room. Relief made up the other part of her hunger.

He had not died. Of all her healings, the relief she had felt when his delirium had turned to regular exhaustion had no equal. Tears had pressed at the backs of her eyes and she had nearly exposed herself disastrously before the prince. But he seemed as moved as she.

"He is inestimably dear to me," he had uttered, his shoulder beneath Vitor's as they lowered him to the bed. "I should not know how to go along without him."

"Needn't," he had mumbled, surprising them. "Either of you." But his eyes were closed and he seemed to sleep as he spoke. The prince himself had pulled the coverlet over him and told Ravenna he would remain with him while she went to sleep.

She poured tea and drank it in a gulp, knowing she should not be aching with both relief and confusion. But every time she allowed herself to dwell on the feeling of him inside her, hot, delicious agitation washed over her. Perhaps he would not remember what had passed between them—her words, or his, and their brief, astounding mating. It would be better if he didn't, really. Then they could go on as they'd been before, until the party ended and he returned to his world of entitlement and wealth and she returned to her life outside that world not even bothering to look in.

"Ah, mademoiselle," the general said from the doorway. "Good morning. I hoped to speak with you in private. May I?"

"Sir?"

"Miss Caulfield, I keep substantial kennels at my home in Philadelphia. Both hounds and nonsporting dogs like my daughter's Marie. Recently my kennel master returned to Ireland and I was obliged to hire a new man. Unfortunately, he has proven incompetent. I feared to leave him in the care of my dogs during my journey here."

"How worrisome."

"My wife remained to oversee the keepers, so I have no worry now. She is infinitely capable." He lowered his voice. "I do not wish to overstep, mademoiselle, but I must speak to you of a matter that interests me. In the strictest confidence, Sir Beverley shared with me your expertise in caring for his animals. He said that you wish now to perhaps take on a greater role, one more suitable to your talents."

"He did?"

"He told me that you are a woman of science and medicine."

"I have cared for his animals, and Mr. Pettigrew's, for six years, both house pets and oftentimes horses. I have some experience with farm animals as well."

"And dogs?"

"Especially dogs. Sir Beverley is not a hunter, but he has many house dogs. His close neighbor, however, keeps a pack of spaniels that I often treat."

"Sir Beverley has recommended that I offer to you the position of kennel master. He suggested that I write to his neighbor to gain an independent recommendation. My daughter and I are impressed with your good sense. Moreover, Sir Henry Feathers continues to praise your care of his Titus. Would you be interested in the position I have to offer?"

She could only imagine one reason Beverley would have done this: now that she could no longer live with him and Petti, he wished to provide her with an alternative to marrying.

"But I am a woman."

"My wife was master of five hundred acres of farmland before I married her. Since then she has been much more than a hostess in my house. She has been steward of my property and kennels during my many absences. I have never heard a man sing such praises as Sir Beverley has sung of you, nor I suspect will I hear the end of Sir Henry's encomiums until I depart from this house. If you wish, we could arrange for a year's contract. At the end of that time we can both assess the success of the venture."

"I don't know what to say. In truth, sir, I have never imagined such a thing." She had dreamed it. But across an ocean? It would be years before she saw her sisters again.

"You will like time to consider it," the general said. "In a month we will sail for America. If I have your answer within the fortnight I will be able to arrange for your passage on our ship."

"Thank you, sir. I am honored." She set down her teacup, and walked in something of a haze to the hall. She almost didn't hear the whimpers coming from the armory room. Reversing direction, she went toward the door that stood partially ajar, and pulled it open.

Her first thought was that from this moment onward she would *always* knock before entering a room. Her second was that, unlike Iona with Lord Whitebarrow, Lady Grace did not seem to be enjoying herself with the guard who had her trapped in a corner.

"What are you doing?" she demanded.

The guard lifted his head from Grace's neck. His eyes went wide and his hands dropped from Grace's breast, but anger crossed his face. She recognized him as one of the guards usually stationed at the castle's gate. He backed up and Grace's skirt slithered down her legs.

Palms over her face, Grace turned toward the corner and a sob shook her slender body.

"Get out." Ravenna's voice trembled. She stepped away from the door.

He came toward her, for a moment bristling in silence. But he stood not much taller than she, though much thicker, and she looked him firmly in the eye. He brushed past her and out the door.

She hurried to Grace.

"My lady." She touched her on the shoulder. Grace flinched. "Grace, did he harm you?"

Grace shook her head. Her flaxen hair was falling from its pins and the top buttons of her gown below the nape were torn.

"Grace, you must tell me. How did this happen?"

Grace whispered into her hands. "I . . . invited it."

"You invited that man to maul you in the corner of this room?"

Grace turned a face to her patchy and stained with tears. She nodded.

"That is not the truth," Ravenna said. "But you needn't tell me. You must, however, tell the prince and your father."

Grace grasped her arm. "You mustn't tell them."

"I am obliged to. You were not screaming for him to stop, but I don't believe that you wished him to . . . to do that. Your father must be told."

"Tell Papa, if you must. But not the prince. I beg of you, Miss Caulfield. Do not tell his highness. Mama would—" Her voice broke and she released Ravenna and pressed her hand against her mouth.

"What will your mother do?"

Grace shook her head. Her eyes seemed oddly glassy as they welled with tears anew. "I beg of you."

She nodded. She would tell Lord Vitor and he would undoubtedly tell the prince. In this case the partial lie was justified.

"Ladies?" Petti's bright voice came from behind Ravenna. "What an interesting spot for two delightful girls to find amusement. All about us thrusting swords and spears, yet not a man in the place to employ them." His eyes twinkled.

"Petti, Lady Grace is overset. She has just had an unpleasant encounter with a—a wild animal."

"In the castle! What an adventuresome place this has turned out to be. And everybody said the Franche-Comté was the most civilized place in the world. Ah, well. What does everybody know anyway?" He came forward and took Grace's hand between his palms. He patted her fondly. "Dear girl, allow me to see you to your room to rest. After that I will share with you my secret recipe for cucumber and rose tonic." He drew her gently toward the door. "Oh, no, you never drink it, m'dear. You soak a warm cotton square in it and lay it over both eyes, and the nose, should that be required. Within a quarter hour you will be as lovely as you were before this unfortunate incident. But it must be cotton. Linen won't do and wool will have the very opposite effect desired. Cotton is absolutely required."

He was still offering her beauty advice when they moved out of Ravenna's hearing. He must have done the same for her any number of times, though not about her *toilette*, which he knew she didn't care about. But in the past months he had drawn her from a brown study with stories about the pugs or invented complaints about the birds. An alarmed report of a stray colt had become a long, strolling search across a frost-covered field during which he had regaled her with outrageous stories from his scandalous days on the town. Returning home she found the colt in its own stall.

Petti was a treasure, and she could not imagine life without him.

But if she moved to America, he would be lost to her. Sir Beverley would write her long letters; he did so when he and Petti were only in London or visiting with friends elsewhere in England. But Petti was a creature of the moment, a light soul with a wise, kind, and pleasure-loving heart. He would not write, at least not at length, and she would miss him beyond telling. She could not bear to lose another piece of her heart so soon. But when again would she receive such an opportunity for employment like this? It was unheard of, though perhaps not in America. She'd heard that in America the rules of society were much less strict. Perhaps in America women served as stewards and groundsmen just like in England they could be shopkeepers.

She left the armory as the prince's butler crossed the hall. Lord Whitebarrow could wait. Grace was in safe hands now, and while Ravenna wished it could be otherwise, she must share her news with Lord Vitor before she did anything else.

Would he sleep all day? Would he recall anything of the night's events?

Arabella had once told her that men were wolves. Lord Whitebarrow, Martin Anders, the rapacious guard . . . they proved her sister's words true. But if men were wolves, that did not necessarily make women hare. She had encouraged his kiss and begged for him to take her in the stable. Delicate ladies like Grace might be prey, but she was not. She would not be left broken and bleeding in the snow.

She waylaid Monsieur Brazil.

He bowed.

"Has—"

"*Oui*, mademoiselle." Again he anticipated her question. "Lord Viton departed an hour ago with Père Denis."

She stared. "Departed?" With the priest? "He couldn't have." What sort of man was close to death by poisoning yet six hours later rode up a snowy mountainside?

A man with extraordinary reserves of strength and discipline, it seemed.

"Claude saddled his horse, mademoiselle, and I watched him depart through the gates myself. Would you like your cloak?"

"Yes," she said, perplexed.

The forecourt had melted to sloshing snow and puddles, but the going beyond the gates proved treacherous with packed ice. Ravenna trudged and slipped until she reached the trees and moved into the mottled shadows where the snow had not penetrated as deeply.

Grabbing onto the bared trunk of a young beech to propel herself up an incline, she saw him leaning back against a spruce that soared to the sky. The sky shone silvery-gold through branches bared of leaves or prickly with conifer spikes. Two reddish-black birds perched on leafless branches, speaking to each other in the silence of the morning. White and dark, there was solitude and a kind of stark peace in the scene. Farther up the path, a tall gray Andalusian stood tied to a tree branch, its head turned toward her, ears pricked high.

Lord Vitor also watched her approach. "You should not be here."

So this was how it would be: unvarnished rejection.

Ravenna squared her shoulders. "As I came here to tell you news, I will not remain more than a minute. I don't want to see you any more than you want to see me."

He pushed away from the tree. "Ravenna—"

"No." She thrust up a hand. "Don't say anything, I beg of you. I hope only that you remember very little of it." She added, "Preferably nothing at all."

"Sebastiao told me what you did. I am grateful."

She nodded, unable to ask what she wished. "I discovered a guard—one of those that watch the castle gate—with Lady Grace in the armor room not an hour ago. When I came upon them she was protesting, but afterward she vowed to me that she had invited his attentions. I don't believe her. He did no real harm to her, I think, but she was distressed and her gown was torn. If she did invite him, it was not because she wished it."

He stepped closer to her. "Did you tell any other of this? The prince?"

"Not yet. Mr. Pettigrew took her in hand and I looked for you, to be told that you had already left the castle. You are remarkably quick to recover."

"I don't believe the poison was meant to kill, only to incapacitate."

He hadn't been in the least bit incapacitated in the stable. Rather, the opposite. Her body remembered it now with delicious little thrills. She pressed down upon the sensations.

"Did anyone see you leave the castle?" he said.

"The guards at the gate, of course, and my progress up the road to the path may have been noticed by villagers if their attention was pointed in that direction. Likewise someone at a north-facing window in the castle. Do you suspect that the same person who put the drug in the wine is watching me today?"

"I have no reason to suspect otherwise."

His brother's name hung between them unspoken.

"What if the drug had been intended for someone else?" she said.

"Do you believe it was?"

"I don't know. But I don't see any reason why someone would wish me incapacitated. Except the most obvious reason." She looked away and to the ground. "He is enamored of Miss Dijon. He challenged Martin Anders for the sake of her honor. He was turning pages for her at the piano only half an hour before I encountered him in the stable." She looked up at him. "Do you truly believe your brother would have left her to come seduce me?"

His face seemed severe in the pale light. "I do not wish to. But I would not have you harmed. I will consider all possible threats to you and take whatever action necessary to protect you."

Her heart turned over.

"Do you—" Her throat caught.

He touched her chin and another half step brought him to her. Slowly, his gaze traveled her features. "Do I?"

"Do you remember what happened between us in the stable?" she forced out. "What the drug caused you to do?"

His palm curved around her jaw and his thumb stroked across her cheek. "I remember. And I can assure you that I would have done the same if I had not been drugged."

"The same—as in, recoiling in horror when you discovered I was a virgin?"

The crease ticked in his cheek. He bent his head and whispered across her lips, "Guess again."

Chapter 16

The New Promise

He touched his lips to hers so gently that for a moment she ceased to breathe.

Then he kissed her. She tasted no wine or other spirit, only warmth and his desire. He held her face between his hands and made of their mouths a tender, passionate coupling, with every caress a deeper meeting of lips and tongues until her knees grew weak and she reached for him. He drew her against him. Then Ravenna discovered what it was to be touched on her shoulders and back, to be held with broad, strong hands as though she were delicate crystal that at any moment might shatter. Thrilling. Intoxicating. Humbling. It was as though he wished to show her that he believed her to be a lady.

Then, with a deep rumble in his chest, he turned her back to the tree trunk and all evidence of gentlemanly restraint vanished. With his mouth and hands he demanded. She submitted—enthusiastically. Their bodies came together taut and needy, the parting of greatcoat and cloak allowing for a fleeting satisfaction that left only frustration for greater contact. He kissed her deeply, breathlessly, his hands tangling in her hair and the slow, powerful rhythm of their bodies pressing together driving the ache inside her. She had only known his kiss a day, yet the flavor of his lips and the perfect cadence with which their mouths met and bodies hungered felt deliriously familiar. Her thighs parted to his urging and the meeting of her need to his forced a moan from her throat.

"Ravenna." He whispered her name with urgency. "I wish to make love to you. I must make love to you. Properly."

She clung to him, her breasts tender against his chest. "Properly?"

He kissed the joining of her lips, her jaw, the sensitive curve of her throat. She shivered upon the pleasure of his touch and ran her fingers into his hair, stretching her neck to allow him to continue kissing her and making her ache for him.

"Tonight," he said.

She couldn't get enough of his mouth on her skin, his hands on her waist, his hard, powerful body pressed to hers. "Why not now?"

"Because now," he said, muffled behind her ear where his kisses made her tremble, "for all that I would have you here in an instant, you deserve better. And I must meet someone shortly. He will be at our meeting place in moments, damn him to Hades." He kissed her lips and cupped her face in his palms. "I wish it were otherwise." The certainty in his eyes rocked her.

"A moment ago you told me I should not be here."

"A moment ago you were not in my arms and I still possessed a breath of self-restraint. But, good Lord, however much your lips entrance me"—he kissed her again—"I prefer them pink to blue. You are frozen and I am expected elsewhere. You must go. Immediately." But he did not release her. Instead he tilted her head back and his gaze now traced her face as though searching. The severity she had seen before returned to his eyes. "Ravenna . . ."

"I don't want your money or estates or whatever else despicably wealthy second sons have," she said hastily.

A moment's pause, then his voice came quietly: "What?"

"I wish to be clear." She was trembling. "So there is no misunderstanding between us. I am not trying to entrap you into marriage."

Anger flashed in his midnight eyes. "Aren't you?"

"No! I hadn't a thought of it."

For a moment he seemed to seek something in her features again. Then abruptly he released her and swung away, his boots crunching in the snow as he started up the path. "Go, Ravenna. Rouse Father Denis from his prayer and with his escort return to the castle," he threw over his shoulder. "Return to your tower," he said in a lower voice.

"My bedchamber is not in the tower," she called after him.

He only shook his head.

"Will you come to it?" she made herself say, the tangles of heat and longing never more confused. "To my bedchamber—my bed—tonight?"

He slowed, then, and turned partially to her, but his backward footsteps continued to move him away. "I will."

Her heart beat hard enough to bruise her ribs. As though he knew it, a smile crossed his lips, full of confident dash. "Neither wild dogs nor tame would keep me from it."

He reached his horse, climbed into the saddle with

grace that made her peculiarly breathless, and disappeared between the trees. Feet sunk in snow and insides aching and unsteady, Ravenna felt like the hare left by the wolf with the promise that he would return later to finish his meal.

As instructed, she headed toward the hermit's hut and an afternoon of waiting to prove that she could be a wolf too.

COLLAR HOT AND fists tight, Vitor was entirely prepared to pummel his elder brother's face the moment Wesley appeared on the path before him. He knew Wesley would come in response to his note, and he knew what he would say. He only wished to hear it from his mouth before he made him suffer for it.

Now he had not only justification and motivation, he had frustrated anger that required an outlet. Wesley's face would do. For beginners.

She was willing—indeed eager—to give him her body, but she neither anticipated nor apparently wished for anything from him beyond that. He had breached her virtue but not her faith. That she wanted him he did not doubt. That she was prepared to avail herself of his services then continue along her merry way seemed likewise clear. Unprecedented and astonishing, but clear.

He considered for a brief moment holding her off until she gave him what he wanted most, with as much fervor as she gave him her kisses. But that moment proved exceedingly brief. He couldn't wait another night to have her. That he must wait even hours was a noxious burden whose blame he would gladly place at his brother's feet.

The sooner he got to it, the better. Pressing his heels into Ashdod's flanks, he urged him up the icy path.

"Vitor!" His brother's shout came upon the snap of gunshot.

The walloping crack to the back of his head came an instant later.

EVENING FELL TO the sparkling glory of hundreds of candles throughout the castle. Monsieur Brazil had enjoined the footmen to illuminate the chandelier in the great hall. The cook, again with his retinue of assistants, prepared a feast for his master and guests. Everybody dressed in their finest: the younger gentlemen arrayed in starched cravats and coats of gorgeous colors; the older men garbed in elegant black satin knee breeches; and the ladies resplendent in gowns that showed off their arms, long gloves, superbly styled coiffures, and jewels glittering upon wrists, earlobes, necks, and in their hair. Ann came to Ravenna's room an hour before dinner and presented her with a ball gown. Cut from watery blue silk and embroidered with delicate white lace and tiny mother-of-pearl beads, it was fit for a true lady.

"I spent the day removing ruffles and lace and I think it came out well, don't you?" Ann said shyly. "I hope you will wear it tonight, even if you do not keep it afterward. Lord Vitor will enjoy seeing you in it, I think."

Ravenna could think of nothing to say that would not send heat to her betraying cheeks. She accepted the gown with thanks, then accepted Ann's assistance in dressing her hair as well.

A knock sounded upon her door. While her heart jumped, she knew that he would not come to her bedchamber door at this hour, no matter what promises he had made for later.

Ann opened the door. Garbed with sublime elegance, Sir Beverley and Petti bowed to her. Ann smiled and slipped away.

"You are both remarkably handsome," Ravenna said. "I never knew you could clean up so well."

"I might say the same to you," Sir Beverley said, gesturing for Petti to take the chair before the fireplace. "But I am not a hoydenish girl who resisted learning manners since the day I was born, so I shan't."

She smiled, the joy of celebration and wicked anticipation for the night to come filling her up despite her certainty that the murderer had not been found. But one night could be enjoyed—one night in which she might be wanted.

Petti settled himself into the chair and perused her thoroughly. "Splendid, m'dear. You are a princess indeed."

"I don't wish to be a princess, of course." Only *pretty*.

"That is a shame," Sir Beverley said, coming to her side and producing a small leather case from behind his back. He flipped open the lid and Ravenna gasped. "I suppose we will have to give this to some other young lady, Francis."

Upon a bed of sapphire velvet the color of Lord Vitor's eyes rested a circlet of gleaming silver decorated with diamonds.

"That is not for me," she stated. Her hand crept to her mouth. "That is for *me*?" she whispered.

"Our princess," Petti said fondly.

She kissed them both, first Sir Beverley on the cheek, then Petti upon the brow. Then she threw her arms about Petti and squeezed him. "Thank you. Thank you. I never wanted such a thing in my life. But thank you for thinking I should have it."

"Now, now, m'dear, my valet will disapprove of this wanton destruction of my neck cloth."

"Oh!" She released him and tweaked the starched

cloth with her fingertips. "Oh, no. I'm sorry, Petti dear."

He caught her hands and kissed her knuckles gallantly. "For you, princess, I would suffer a crushed cravat. At least until I can return to my room and require Archer to fold a new one."

"That was the most inelegant thanks I have ever heard," Sir Beverley said. "You are an impertinent girl."

She curtsied, grabbed the box from him, and went to the mirror. Drawing the glittering circlet from its bed, she set it atop the curls that Ann's efforts had partially tamed. It sparkled brilliantly. "Oh, my," she sighed.

"She is happy with our little gift, Bev."

"Mm. I daresay."

On Petti's arm, she floated to the drawing room. Nearly everybody was there, gorgeous and giddy to begin the prince's party in earnest. Except Lord Vitor. Ravenna tried to enjoy Iona's whispered commentary on the gentlemen's finery. But each time the door opened to admit another of the prince's guests, her stomach climbed to her throat, then fell to her toes when the newcomer was not the only man she wanted to see. Finally the prince arrived wearing a military-styled coat sparkling with the medals he claimed were merely decorative nonsense but nevertheless rendered him elegantly regal. Moving directly to Ann, he lifted her hand and kissed her gloved knuckles, then teased her for the blush that rose to her round cheeks.

"Shall we go in to dinner?" he said to everyone.

"Whit o' Lord Case, yer highness," the duchess said, looking about. "An' Lord Vitor?"

A footman was sent to fetch them. But the Courtenay men were not to be found in their bedchambers. The prince dispersed more footmen to search the battlements and below stairs. Everybody chatted gaily as they waited and Ravenna's heart beat quicker.

The towers and servants' realm did not produce the missing gentlemen. Brow puckered, the prince greeted Monsieur Brazil's appearance at the drawing room door with evident relief.

The butler bowed. "Your highness, the dinner is served."

"Excellent. Come, everybody. Our friends are no doubt occupied with some important task and will find their way to dinner when they are able. Monsieur Brazil, enquire of their manservants when the earl and Lord Vitor are expected back, then send one of my guards to the village to hasten their return," he said in a quiet aside as the guests moved toward the door. "Ten to one they're drunk as emperors in that wretched wine shop, relieved that the murderer is found at last." He winked and took the duchess's hand upon his arm.

Dread sped through Ravenna's belly. The murderer was not found and Lord Vitor was not drunk on wine or anything else, not after last night, and not with the promise he had made to her today. She could not believe it.

Mr. Anders approached her and extended his arm. "Miss Caulfield, I am delighted to learn that you are to be my dinner companion tonight. May I walk you in?"

"I— Yes." She took his arm, but before they reached the corridor she released him. He turned to her, the swatch of hair swinging across one eye.

"I beg your forgiveness, Miss Caulfield," he said swiftly and quietly. "Will you ever forgive me for the insult I offered you the other night at your door—"

"No. Yes," she said. "I don't care about that."

"But—"

"Yes. Yes, I forgive you."

His face fell into relief. "I am grateful beyond—"

"Oh, *hush*." She gripped his arm. "Mr. Anders, I must beg a favor of you."

"Anything," he said fervently. "I am yours to command. Yours, that is," he added with light chagrin, "until after dinner when my dearest Miss Abraccia must claim all my attention."

"Yes, yes, fine. Please go now to the stables and ask the grooms if Lord Vitor returned with his horse this afternoon."

"The stables? Across the drive? Now?"

"Yes. Now. As quickly as you can."

"But I am wearing evening slippers." He pointed his toe upward to illustrate.

Her patience snapped. "Mr. Anders, the man that protected you from Monsieur Sepic's ridiculous accusations not to mention his fetid jail could be in great danger at this moment. The least you can do is dampen your slippers to help him."

"Danger? But the murderer is apprehended and incarcerated in that very jail."

"Monsieur Paul is not the murderer. You inspired no one to murder. We don't yet know who did kill Mr. Walsh, but it was not the mayor's nephew. Now, I beg of you, *go*."

He went. When she reached the dining room she made an excuse for him and endured a moment of Juliana Abraccia's hotly jealous stare. Conversation remained general while the removes were served, but Ravenna could do nothing but watch the door and wait for Martin Anders's return. When he finally came, his brow was drawn and cheeks flushed from the cold.

"I fear I have no good tidings," he said quietly as he slipped into his seat beside her. "Earlier today Lord Vitor's horse returned riderless."

Panic sped through her. "What of Lord Case?"

"He had not taken out his horse, and none of the grooms reported seeing him today."

"Why did they not report the peculiar return of Lord Vitor's horse to his highness?"

"The groom I spoke with gave the news to one of the prince's guards, who assured him that he would inform his master." He shook his head. "He must not have."

"I must know which guard," she said, pushing back from her seat.

"Miss Caulfield, you cannot leave the table before the prince does."

"Make my excuses. I am ill," she uttered, and hurried from the room. She went straight to the stable. The groom Mr. Anders had spoken with described the guard to her, explaining that he was one of the newer men among the prince's guard that had not before visited the castle. He matched the description of the guard she had seen with Lady Grace.

She went to Ashdod's stall and ran her hands over the horse's withers and powerful neck, the panic beating at her like waves. "Tell me." She pressed her lips to the gray's coat and whispered. "Tell me what has befallen him and where he is." The horse hung its head for a moment, then tossed it back.

As she crossed the drive toward the house beneath a sky heavy with clouds, Iona and Sir Beverley met her.

"Ye've come out withoot yer cloak, lass. Yer cold as death." Iona stripped off her cloak and slung it around Ravenna's shoulders.

"Mr. Anders told us of your discovery," Sir Beverley said. "The prince sent for the guard that the groom spoke with. He is missing."

Iona grasped her fingers. "We'll find them," she said. "We'll find them an' it'll be well, lass. Ye'll see."

TORCHES WERE LIT and servants and gentlemen bundled into woolens and tromped into the night to search. The clouds that blocked the moon now released their heavy contents, washing the snow into deep puddles and soaking Ravenna as she stood at the gate with Iona and Cecilia and waited.

"I should have gone." She could not bear being useless.

"The prince forbade it," Cecilia said. "The searchers mustn't feel they need to protect ladies while they are searching."

"I'm not a lady," she whispered.

"There are thirty men looking for them, Miss Caulfield. They will find them."

"But I was the last to see him."

"They'll search where ye've said. They'll find them." Iona wrapped her arm around Ravenna's waist and hugged her close.

The torches returned in pairs and trios, faces visible in the circle of their glow, shimmery with rain and grim. When the final pair of guards returned with Sir Beverley, who had climbed to the hermit's refuge, his lips were purple and his eyes grave.

"We will find them tomorrow, my dear," he said.

But later, as icy rain clattered against the windowpane in her bedchamber, Ravenna huddled against the glass wishing she had the eyes of a wolf to see through the dark and a wolf's strength to hunt through the night. Tomorrow would not be soon enough.

Chapter 17

Lo, What Light

Consciousness returned to Vitor with the awareness that he preferred to wake to a mongrel's whine than to bone-chilling cold and throbbing pain in his head. Body not quite prone, his face was pressed against a hard surface, his arm pinned at an angle beneath him. He shifted, and agony exploded across his shoulders. His groan sounded like a wounded animal's.

"Awake finally, brother?" came a murmur beside him. "Featherweight."

"Damn you." He lifted his free arm and touched the back of his head. He remembered the blow that had knocked him off Ashdod, yet felt only fiery tenderness.

"Are you broken or bleeding?" Wesley asked diffidently.

Vitor cracked open his eyes to make out his brother beside him in murky shadow. "Only bruised," he replied.

"Then damn *you*," Wesley said.

The chamber was tiny and round, less than three yards in diameter, void of windows and door, and tapering outward as the walls climbed. There was no visible ceiling, only hazy gray.

"Where are we?"

"An empty ice cellar, I believe. But that may be the loss of blood speaking."

"Were you shot?"

"In the arm. I have managed to stanch the bleeding, and the cold assists in slowing the flow. But I have lost the use of it."

Testing the strength of the arm beneath him, Vitor pushed up and smothered another groan. The cold burrowed into the pain and drove it deeper. But none of his bones was broken.

"The shot was meant for you," Wesley mumbled.

"How do you know?"

"He was pointing the pistol at you."

Wesley had stepped between him and the shooter?

Vitor climbed to his feet and ran his hands over the wall. The earth was packed hard and smooth, without even notches where a ladder might fit. Perhaps the cellar was yet unfinished. If it belonged to the chateau it would be within Chevriot's walls. If it belonged to the village it could be farther away.

"How deep is the—"

"Twenty feet. Perhaps more. Even if I were able to stand we could not climb out."

"How did he carry us down here?"

"There was no carrying. Rather, tossing. Rolling, really, as the walls are slanted. And he was not he, but they. Two of them."

The lying guard he had assigned to Ravenna's protection and perhaps the man she had found with Whitebarrow's daughter.

"How long have you been conscious?"

"I never lost consciousness entirely. Huzzah for my hearty constitution," Wesley said dryly. "Of course, I was not bashed in the skull with a branch rigged like a catapult. And you broke my fall into this hellhole. Thank heaven for small blessings. See, little brother? I told you a life of monastic discipline would be to no avail. All that tedious prayer yet you cannot even summon a saint to rescue you from assassins."

"How long?" he repeated.

"It wanted but a quarter hour to carry us here on the back of your horse. Since then it has been perhaps six, seven hours. The light has been fading swiftly this hour. Soon we will be in darkness."

Seven hours. The guests at the castle would be gathering for dinner.

"Did they take my horse?"

"They argued about it for some time. In the end they decided he was too fine to pass off as their rightful property and would only bring them trouble on the road. They sent him off. It sits right with me that the knaves know their worth is less than a gentleman's mount."

Ashdod would have returned to the castle stable hours ago, his arrival alerting the grooms. Vitor breathed deeply through bruised ribs, rubbed his hands over his face, and discovered the knuckles of one hand battered and sticky. He could not bandage it. The cellar was too cold for him to use his neck cloth for anything but warmth. He leaned back against the wall, taking care to keep his head bent.

She would wonder at his absence. She would look for him in the drawing room and be piqued when he did not appear. Would she mention his absence to another guest, Lady Iona, or Sebastiao? Would her skittish heart lead her to the wrong conclusion or would she trust in him and sound the alarm?

Hours earlier on the mountainside, as the sun had shone through bare branches, he had stood amidst the quiet and seen her in every silvery ray and glittering drop of ice. She was astoundingly confident, brazen even, and strong-willed. But at moments she became that creature he had seen on the turret stairs: wary and uncertain and ready to flee.

"Why did you follow her to the stable?" he said into the cold silence.

"I did not follow her. I came upon her entirely by chance and decided to take advantage of the opportunity."

No monastic training had prepared Vitor for the rage that seized him now. "With a bottle of wine and two glasses?"

"I never drink alone."

"A sprained ankle and shot in the arm will be as nothing when I am through with you, Wesley. I will break your legs. Both of them. You know I will do it. I will break every bone in them and you will never walk again."

His brother was silent for a long moment.

"I did follow her. I sought an opportunity to question her about her intentions toward you."

Vitor snapped his head around to stare at his brother in the gathering dark.

"I have only your best interests at heart, Vitor. She is nobody, the orphaned daughter of God knows whom. Her sister is a duchess, true. But only months ago rumor in town had it that their mother was a plantation whore in the West Indies and that Lycombe's new duchess had not fallen far from that tree." He said it plainly, as though reporting on a horse race.

"Only fools listen to rumor."

"Perhaps. But the hue of Miss Caulfield's cheeks and hair suggest that in this case rumor is not far from truth. Has it not occurred to you that she could be the daughter of a less-than-pure union between master and slave?"

It had occurred to him. But he had seen more of the world than his brother. Her features bespoke not mestizo or mulatto, but Andalusian, from the southern lands of Spain, where centuries ago Christians and Moors had intermingled.

"Even if her blood is free of taint," Wesley added, "she is a servant and entirely unconnected in society except for her sister's extraordinary marriage to Lycombe."

"And I am the bastard son of a Catholic profligate. How do you suppose I am enjoying the insult you are dealing her with this patronizing show of false concern for me, brother?"

"I have said none of this to her, of course."

The darkness had become complete, and with the gathering blackness the cold seeped more mercilessly into Vitor's blood, making him sluggish.

"What did you wish to say to me when you summoned me up the mountain, Vitor?"

"I did not wish to say anything. I wished to beat you to a pulp and leave you for the vultures."

"Ah. Violence from my monastic brother." He sounded thoughtful. "But I suppose there is a first time for everything. Remarkable that a girl should inspire it."

"A lady."

For a moment his brother said nothing, then: "A lady."

"Did you drug the wine you brought her?"

"Drug? Why, no." Wesley's surprise sounded sincere. "Was she ill?"

"Where did you find the bottle?"

"In the butler's pantry."

Vitor had not believed his brother put the poison in the wine. His methods of chastisement had never been trickery, and only once had they resorted to secrecy.

The muffled sound of rain came down the cellar shaft now, at first in patters, then faster, angrier, as though it sought to wash away the snow in a flood. Vitor's head was heavy, the bruise throbbing, every one of his muscles sore. He closed his eyes upon the darkness and listened to the rain.

"It was I."

Sleep snatched at Vitor. "Huh?" he mumbled.

"I was the man in the belly of that ship off Nantes. The man on the other end of the knife."

Vitor drew a long breath and rubbed his hand across the back of his neck. "For God's sake. I know that."

His brother's sharp inhale sounded through the stillness.

"Enlightened men do not employ the tactics of medieval inquisitors, Wesley. Have the lessons of the great men of our age entirely passed you by?"

"It was not by my design that I did what I did to you." His voice was tight.

Vitor turned his head as though he might see his brother through the blackness. "How could you have believed treason of me?"

"I didn't. They did. You had not lived in England for a decade. Your loyalties were for a foreign king."

"An ally."

"In France they lost sight of you."

"And because of that they believed me a traitor? How simple the minds of Englishmen are. How foolishly black and white. He is a son of the kingdom or he is a treasonous spy." *She is a servant or she is a lady.*

"My superiors would not listen to me. They believed that because of our bond you would confess to me without . . . unnecessary force. I told them they were fools to believe you would ever say a word, force or not. To no avail." He paused for a long moment. "But when you said nothing, spoke not a word in that horrid cabin of that wretched ship, despite how they—I— threatened you, I began to mistrust you. It was again like . . ."

"When she lied to you."

"Your proud, stubborn silence allowed me to believe in her lies." Wesley's voice had stiffened.

"Blame me all you wish, brother. It will not change the truth that on that ship you broke both the law and my faith in you."

"I regretted it even as I obeyed their orders, Vitor. I did it for England but I suffered. It was as painful for me as for you."

Vitor rubbed the scar between his thumb and fore-finger. "I doubt it."

"Is that why you wished to meet with me this morn-ing? To repay me?" His voice shook.

"You know me so little."

There was another stretched silence during which the damp cold of rainy mist settled on Vitor's hair and skin.

"I blamed you because she did not love me," Wesley said. "I was furious. She did not want me, so I blamed you for it."

Vitor understood. Even two years at the top of a mountain in Portugal had not cured his anger en-tirely. But perhaps he had always been angry. Perhaps he had been running since he was fifteen and left the only home he knew. Not seeking adventure. Running from shame into dangers again and again not because his fathers asked but because nothing else drove the anger away.

Then there came a moment during the war when, weary of running, he had finally returned to Airedale, to the family he had abandoned. He might have stopped running then.

"I did nothing to encourage her." Fannie Walsh had needed no encouragement. He had put her off firmly, informed the marquess of the matter, and left for Portugal, where Raynaldo had again sent him into war. "I did what you would have done in my place."

"I know. Father told me."

"And yet you still hated me for it."

"I was blind to reason." Wesley's voice muffled. "Until now. Until this week . . ."

Until Arielle Dijon.

Vitor understood that well enough.

Neither of them spoke for some time.

"Do you wish to fight me now?" Wesley finally said. "With my useless arm and gimp ankle it will be a brief scuffle. But if it will satisfy you, I shall make my best effort at defending myself."

"Thank you, no. I don't fight injured men. Even if I did, the tilt of this floor would make it an uncomfortable endeavor."

"Mm. I daresay."

"Wes, we are going to die here."

"We are."

Vitor drew a slow breath. "You first."

"No, you. I insist."

"As the eldest, you deserve the honor."

"Vitor." Wesley's voice was sober again. "If I die now and you are rescued, and you succeed to our father's titles, there is something you should know."

He waited.

"I am no more Airedale's son than you."

Vitor lifted his head.

"Father could not give her a child," Wesley said. "They wanted children, desperately, he no less than she. He asked her to do it. He begged for years before she agreed to it. Together she and he chose our fathers, men both of them respected, and of noble blood so that if it should ever become known and we lost all, at least we would not feel the full shame of it. She was never unfaithful to him. Not as you have believed."

Vitor sat stunned. It did not undo the years of knowing that he was not a true Courtenay and of imagining his mother's inconstancy. But there was some measure of peace to be had in knowing.

"Who was he?" he finally asked. "The first?"

"It hardly matters now. He is long since gone. A naval hero. Died in sea battle. Enormously wealthy but not even a lord in his own right. A second son. How do you like that for irony, young demi-princeling?"

"Well enough, bastard."

Astoundingly, Wesley chuckled.

For a long while there was nothing but the muted driving rain above and the trickle of chill water somewhere closer by and solid darkness wrapping about them like a pall. Vitor no longer felt pain in his knuckles or his shoulders, and where the bruise rose on his skull was only a numb throbbing. He dozed and listened for voices, hooves, cart wheels—for anything that might announce a person nearby. The rain drowned out all.

Into the frigid stillness, Wesley eventually spoke again. "I wished to save you . . . from the pain I suffered." His voice was shallow. "No punishment . . . worse than a woman's . . . faithless heart."

"I am disappointed . . ." The heat in Vitor's body was nearly gone. His words did not even warm his lips.

"Hm?"

"Disappointed that . . ." A weight pressed upon his chest, the cold sucking at his lungs. "I shan't have the chance . . . to prove you wrong . . . in this."

After that there was only silence and cold and waiting for the end.

LORD VITOR AND his brother did not return during the night. The villagers had been alerted and, when dawn arose, those who were able assisted in the search. Ravenna tied on her boots and went out with the men, with Cecilia and Iona at her side. Crisp cold gripped the mountain again and puddles froze underfoot, every step treacherous.

On the bridge that stretched across the river that gave a view of the entire chateau through the trees, Ravenna clutched the wall and stared into the water below. Iona slipped an arm about her waist. Everyone thought the same, Ravenna suspected. But she had felt his strength and did not believe the river had taken him.

They searched for hours, the parties of three—for safety—returning to the chateau or ducking into the village wine shop to warm fingers and toes. On the path from the village, Martin Anders and Sir Henry met them with furrowed brows.

"The mayor's nephew has confessed to lying," Mr. Anders said grimly.

"Lyin'?" Iona exclaimed. "Aboot murderin' a man?"

"Seems the fool's roof collapsed under the snow," Sir Henry said. "He only wanted a spot to sleep."

"He thought that since his uncle was the mayor and there could be no proof to convict him, he would be set free before a trial," Martin Anders said. "It doesn't mean another drunken villager did not take me up on my boast."

Cecilia grasped her brother's hand.

"The prince's two guards—the guard at the gate

and the other," Ravenna said, "were not to be found in the castle this morning. I do not believe a villager murdered Mr. Walsh." She walked away from them, down the center of the icy bridge, not looking to the banks below. She had already searched by the river. They would not find him there. He was still alive. She could feel him alive.

As the sun slid into the western sky everyone straggled back to the castle. She resisted, but Iona and Cecilia took her arms and forced her inside with them.

She went to his bedchamber and found it empty of his valet. With an ecstatic yip, Gonçalo leaped off the bed and hurled himself at her. She fell to her knees and gathered his warm, wagging body into her arms and pressed her face into his fur.

"Where has your master gone?" she whispered, biting back tears gathering in her throat. "He said wild dogs would not keep him from coming to me. He is too honest to lie, so whatever spirited him away must be stronger than wild dogs, for you and I both know there is nothing more clever." The pup smelled of the lord's cologne and faintly of cheroot smoke.

He wiggled free of her hold and flew across the room to set upon a ruined boot as though it were a villain.

Wild dogs.

Wild dogs . . .

Nor tame.

Ravenna watched the pup tear at the leather and her breaths halted.

A dog of no more than ten weeks knew nothing of scent hunting. And who knew if Gonçalo was even a scent-hunting breed? But he had spent a sennight in the nobleman's chambers, destroying his clothing and apparently sleeping in his bed.

No. It was impossible. But so was the ache in her

chest, impossible yet more real than anything she had ever felt.

She sprang to her feet, and scooped up the puppy and a scrap of the boot.

Iona saw her. "Where be ye goin', lass?"

"To hunt."

She slipped across the ice of the forecourt to the gate and set Gonçalo on the ground. She allowed the pup to nuzzle the piece of boot, then withdrew it. "Now let's go find him."

She started off and the pup stumbled after her, his big paws clumsy on the slippery road at first but taking to it swiftly. He bounded about as she walked away from both village and river, biting at crusty ice and yipping. But also sniffing. His attention would stray to a bird or branch blown by the wind, then his nostrils would quiver and he would press his big nose to the ice and yip again.

Centuries ago an outer fortress wall had offered additional protection to the inhabitants of Chevriot from invasion from above, and protection for the stores of salt that had made the region rich. Remnants of the wall crept low along the slope of the hill that rose into the tree cover climbing the mountain. Ahead of her Gonçalo disappeared over a mound of earth flanking the ruined wall. Ravenna called to him. He did not reappear. She hurried, struggling to ascend the slick rise, her stomach tight. There were holes and drains aplenty around the castle walls. If he had fallen into one—

She rounded the mound and her breaths stalled. The pup stood at the mouth of a cave set into the far side of the mount, his forepaws against a waist-high earthen wall blocking the cave's entrance. He yipped. Only the whisper of frozen branches above answered. Then a voice sounded from the shadows of the cave. *His* voice. Relief broke from her throat in a sob.

Gonçalo barked frantically as she stumbled forward to grab the wall. She jerked back. Not a cave. An ice cellar. She bent to peer into the dark below.

She did not collapse or weep or shout in joy. She whispered, "You are alive," and her legs nearly gave out.

He did not reply. He sat back against the wall directly below her. Lord Case lay on his side nearby. Both were still.

It was not far down, no more than six yards, still, impossible to manage without a ladder or rope. But if they'd been in the cellar for all this time, no time could be wasted returning to the village or chateau to seek help.

Hands shaking, she tore the lowest flounce from Ann's gown, then the middle flounce, then the top. Blessing Lady Margaret's poor taste, she tied the fabric together. But the rope was not sufficiently long to wrap around her chest and still to reach the bottom of the hole.

The skirt went next in broad strips that she secured to the flounces. In petticoat and shift, she hefted the rope over the wall.

"You must grab this and pull yourself up," she said. He did not move. "You must," she said louder. Below, both men remained still as death. "Wake up!" she shouted. "You must take up the rope and save yourself. You must, for I cannot do it without your help." She tossed the rope about until it landed against the back of his hand. "Please," she said. "I beg of you."

His hand flexed and he grasped the fabric.

When he moved to bind the rope about his brother, she shouted and remonstrated with him until he obeyed her. Pushing first to his knees then his feet with labored movements, he took the rope in both hands. She crouched with her back against the wall and braced herself. Gonçalo danced about, barking. Then with perked ears he darted off.

"Now!" she called. "Climb now."

The rope pulled at her chest until she couldn't breathe. Eventually, after what seemed far too long, his hand, white to the bone, the knuckles bloodied, grabbed the edge of the wall. Footsteps crunched in the ice nearby and Gonçalo appeared leaping in circles around Martin Anders and Sir Henry.

"In the name of Zeus! They're found!"

They grabbed Vitor and pulled him over the ledge. His eyes were closed and she put her hands on his face and withheld her sobs as men—more men—seemed to fill the tiny opening of the ice cellar. They carried him back to the castle, others remaining to pull Lord Case from the hole. She ran ahead, calling for warm baths to be prepared, specifying the exact temperature of the water and the oils to be added, and demanding bandages and dressing. Everyone did as she bid until they carried him into the room with the filled copper tub.

Ann appeared and took her arm.

"Come, dear friend," Ann whispered. "You may not remain, and you must see to your own comfort now."

Ravenna went, frustrated to be ejected when she was the most suitable person in the castle to see to a man's injuries, and weak with joy.

Chapter 18

A Lord in the Kitchen Yard

She was not permitted to see either man that night.
The prince himself and a bevy of servants waited upon
them. She was unneeded.

Unlike Arielle Dijon, she could not bear to sit in the
drawing room with the others before dinner, remaining modest and demure while the gentlemen, Lady
Margaret, and the duchess speculated on the purpose
the betraying guards had in harming Lord Case and
his brother. Unable to eat, she took out the pugs and
then asked after Gonçalo. She was told that the hero of
the day was sleeping soundly in his lordship's room.

She retired to her bedchamber, unnoticed.

Late, after she finally ceased pacing and climbed
into bed, a scratch at her door roused her. By the light
of a candle, Lord Case's valet was white with agitation.

"He has taken fever, miss." He wrung his hands. "I
haven't any notion of how to care for him. His lordship
has a physician to see to such things."

"I can help." She changed clothes and took up her medical bag to follow him to his master's quarters through dark, silent corridors.

The earl's brow was hot, his face and nightshirt damp with perspiration. "You must change the bed linens and his nightshirt as often as necessary to keep him dry," she instructed the valet as she poured an inch of water into a tumbler and emptied into it a packet of the fever powder she carried for Sir Beverley and Petti in case of emergency. "If the fever should break and he remains for long in a damp state, his lungs could take an inflammation."

The valet lifted his master and she propped pillows behind his back.

"My lord," the valet whispered. "Miss Caulfield wishes to dose you with medicine."

The earl's eyelids fluttered but did not open. "Ah, an angel of mercy," he mumbled. "She may do as she wishes if she smells this devilishly good while she's about it."

She set the glass to his lips. "Drink, my lord, and don't dribble or I will scold you for wasting my powder."

"Lucky devil, m'brother," he said against the rim of the glass, and swallowed.

They lowered him to the mattress.

"While I examine the wound you must remain very still."

He mumbled unintelligibly, but when she unwrapped the poorly tied bandage and began probing at the wound, he squeezed his eyes closed. "Bloody hell. Call off the witch, Franklin."

"I cannot, my lord. Excepting the cook, who is asleep and refuses to be roused, she is the only individual in the castle with medical knowledge. If you should like, I will summon the village midwife—"

"I am not giving birth, you idiot." He clamped his jaw.

"Quite right, my lord."

"Mr. Franklin," Ravenna said, "I require clean linen to bind this wound."

"Yes, miss." He hurried away. She bathed the wound with wine, then set her needle and thread to the torn flesh while the earl's chest rose upon hard gasps. The bullet had passed cleanly through the fleshy part of his muscle, and the wound was easily mended. Still, he would have lost considerable blood, yet he did not swoon.

"Did you mix a drug into the wine that you invited me to drink the other night, my lord?" she said quietly as she worked. "Do tell me the truth, or I will poke this wound with my sharpest fingernail before I bandage it."

"Hippocrates spins in his grave," he said upon a rasping breath.

She tied off the thread and dabbed the wound with salve oil. "I should like to hear from you the truth. My finger is poised."

"I did not."

"Why did you follow me to the stable?"

His eyes opened, dull with fever but aware. "To offer you gold in exchange for your promise to leave my brother alone."

She swallowed over the catch in her throat.

Mr. Franklin returned and she bound the earl's wound, gave instructions that the poultice should be changed every three hours, and left. Candlelight skittered along the walls as she trod on quiet feet to the ladies' wing of the castle, wishing that now that the danger was over she still possessed the courage of a wolf, enough to cast away fear and go to Vitor's room and demand entrance. But Lord Case had reminded her that in their world she was merely a hare and would never be otherwise.

WHEN SHE AWOKE, she found a message delivered from Mr. Franklin informing her that while Lord Case's fever had not yet broken, he continued to sleep comfortably.

She rose, dressed in one of her own woolen gowns, and left her bedchamber.

All eyes followed her about the house, to the dining room and then to the parlor where Lady Margaret and Ann sat with the duchess, Iona, and the Whitebarrow ladies. Each held a frame of embroidery, which they plied with needles much tinier than anything Ravenna had ever used to tie a wound shut. They all stared at her as though she wore horns atop her head.

Iona came to life first. "Miss Caulfield!" She hurried over to her. "Have ye broken yer fast?"

"I—"

Iona pulled her into the corridor and whispered, "Everybody's heard whit ye did for Lord Case in the wee hours. His valet told Lord Prunesly's man, an' the news spread like fire. Well done, lass!"

"I see." She could not return to the parlor now, and wanted to see only one person, to assure herself that he was well. She hadn't a care for her own reputation, only how it might reflect upon Sir Beverley and Petti. But if the whole household knew she had been in a gentleman's bedchamber in the middle of the night with only his valet as chaperone, how could it hurt for her to now demand an audience with Lord Vitor?

She squeezed Iona's hand and went to his bedchamber. Her heartbeats pounded in her throat as the door opened.

"My lord is not in, miss," his exceedingly proper valet said.

"Not in? Is—is he well enough to be not in?" She sounded like a fool.

"His lordship has a remarkably strong constitution," the valet said stiffly.

"Do you know where he has gone?"

"I should think to breakfast, miss." He tilted up his nose. "But as his lordship did not share with me his itinerary, I cannot say with certainty."

Her fingers itched to pinch him for that. Instead, she went to the hall. Monsieur Brazil spoke with the guard in the foyer.

"His lordship is in the chapel, mademoiselle."

"Father Denis's hermitage?" she asked in disbelief. A quick healer he might be, but this seemed miraculous.

"*Non*, mademoiselle. The chapel here at the chateau."

"At the chateau?"

"*Bien sûr*." He motioned for the guard to open the front door, then pointed across the forecourt. Flanked by the cemetery, a substantial church structure rose between the keep and curtain wall between two towers. She had not noticed it before. In all her perambulations of the cemetery with Petti's dogs, she had not once lifted her attention to the huge building beside it.

"If you wish, mademoiselle," he said, noting her slippers, "one may access the chapel beyond the dining room."

She went, but slowly now, her pulse hard and uneven.

Across the hall, Arielle descended the stairs upon her father's arm, her tiny dog trotting beside them. She hurried to Ravenna, but her steps glided. "Dear Miss Caulfield, how brave and wise you are, and how blessedly competent. I should not have known how tend to a wound."

"I shouldn't think you would ever need to know how to do so."

"Lord Case owes his life to you."

Twice over, in fact. Yet still he had insulted her. "You

mustn't worry about his fever. It will pass as soon as the wound begins to knit."

"Oh." She dipped her delicate lashes. "I should not presume to burden him with my anxiety." Her cheeks pinkened with pretty modesty, a color Ravenna had never seen in her own face. It was impossible. Her skin was not fair like this delicate girl's, this girl whose father had offered Ravenna employment while her noble beau bribed her to stay clear of his brother.

"Will you join us for breakfast, mademoiselle?" the general asked.

"Thank you, no. I must see . . . see to a matter." She continued toward the dining room, skirting the billiards parlor from which male voices emanated. Palms damp and throat thick, she went through the door into the chapel.

Inside the chapel the air hung still and peculiarly warm, like a stable but not with life, instead with some ephemeral quality of age, candle wax, and sacred stuff that her papa's small church only hinted at. Sunbeams angling through tall windows of pale blue, red, and gold painted brilliant colors upon stone arches and pillars. A modest number of chairs were clustered close to the far end, before each a kneeler fashioned of carved wood and brocaded satin. To either side stood massive tombs, sentinels of power topped by effigies of men and women with coronets upon their regal heads.

He stood below the steps that rose to the altar, facing it, his stance easy and his shoulders square.

Ravenna's breaths failed. Hopeless thoughts crowded her. This was *not* her world, even less so than the rest of the castle. This was a place of ancient holiness, of sculpted stone and exotic incense and all the civilization of men. Her lungs fought for air. What could she say to a man from this world that he would wish to hear? *She did not belong here.*

He turned and saw her.

She whirled back through the door. Hurrying from the dining room, she ran into Sir Henry and Lord Prunesly leaving the billiards parlor.

"Ah, Miss Caulfield, the hero of the hour!" Sir Henry chuckled. "Rather, heroine. Isn't that right, Prunesly? Miss Caulfield, you've done great deeds, I hear. Good show, miss. Good show, I say."

The door to the dining room opened and Lord Vitor came into the corridor.

"Forgive me," she muttered to Sir Henry. "I must . . . that is . . ." She broke away. A servants' door opened off the corridor. She darted through it and tripped down a narrow stair in the dark. Exiting by the kitchen, she turned from the scents of fresh bread and roasting meat toward the door that led to the courtyard where the fowl and cow and goats were kept and refuse was dumped through a hole at the base of the castle wall. The crisp air snapped against her cheeks as she burst outside.

She pressed her back against the cold stone wall. Inside its stall across the small yard, the milking cow turned its head to her and swished its tail. Chickens cackled in the henhouse against the far wall that was bathed in morning sunlight.

The breath shuddered out of Ravenna. He would not find her. If he followed her into the servants' stairwell, Sir Henry and Lord Prunesly would remark upon it. Even if he did, he would never look for her here. No nobleman dressed in starched linen and pristine boots would think to go into a kitchen courtyard. In her six years at Shelton Grange she had never once seen Sir Beverley or Petti anywhere near either kitchen or livestock. A marquess's son would not come here.

But he did. The door from the kitchen opened and he

came through it, strong and handsome and perfectly well, it seemed.

He might have died.

"Now I have rescued you," she blurted out. "To accomplish it, I used my skirts that can, as you previously pointed out, prove so inconvenient in a water rescue, but were wonderfully convenient in this instance." She fought to make her voice light. "A fitting counterpoint to your fishing venture in the river on my behalf, wouldn't you say?"

He came directly to her, seized her face between his hands, and captured her mouth beneath his. He kissed her powerfully, deeply, as though he would have all of her through this kiss, and she held on to his waist and gave herself up to him.

He lifted his lips. "In that cellar—"

"Do not speak of it."

"All I thought of was this. Touching you. I wanted only to touch you once more." His thumb stroked across her lips and he followed it with his mouth. It was not a gentle kiss, but demanding. His hands covered her shoulders, then moved to her waist. She wrapped her arms around his neck and let him pull her against him. She melted into him, into his kiss and his hands spread on her back. She had barely known a man's touch, and she felt as she had on the occasion when lightning struck the old tree in a field where she had been dancing in the rain, as though the lightning was sizzling through her marrow.

"Why did you run from me just now?" he said against her lips.

"I thought perhaps—that perhaps I had been mistaken in seeking you out—that you had not come looking for me this morning because you did not—did not want to see me. That you did not want me."

He pressed his brow to hers, his hands tight around her ribs. "I have wanted you since the moment I first saw you and every moment after that."

"Since the moment . . . ? But I thought we were f—" She stumbled upon the word. "Friends."

"Friends with advantages." He took possession of her mouth again, completely, until there was nothing on the earth but his kiss making her need him, his strong arms holding her to him, and the weightlessness of her body that wanted to fly and join with him all at once. She felt the thrilling hardness of his chest and thighs and needed to be closer. Sinking her hands into his hair, she met his tongue with hers, and pleasure so intense came over her that she gasped. She struggled to get closer, to satisfy the urgency, to feel him *more*. Her heels left the ground as he pulled her up and tighter to him, lifting her as though she weighed nothing. But even that did not suffice.

Her knee stole upward along his leg. Then she jumped. He caught her up easily and she clamped her thighs about his hips and halted his laughter with her mouth. She felt him with her hands and mouth and body, and he met her kiss with hunger like hers, hunger that made her seek the bulge in his breeches with her hand, then press to him. She rocked against him and his hands aided her, holding her fast.

"Ravenna, you drive me mad," he uttered against her lips.

She bore down on his arousal, needing him, needing to be closer still, needing to be joined in the manner of all creatures. She felt like a clock wound too tightly, like steam pressing at the lid of a pot on the fire. She wanted him desperately. He gripped her to him and she ground against his hardened cock and she *wanted*.

Her pot exploded upon a crashing, unexpected rush, bursting inside her and tumbling, and seizing her throat for a moan of pure ecstasy as she shuddered against him. She gasped. He kissed her neck and she shivered in pleasure. She accepted his lips on hers. Breathless and boneless and warm, all she wanted was for him to kiss her. *Forever.* "What was that?" she whispered.

"That was a dream I have been having lately," he said deeply, his arms still holding her hard to him, his mouth upon her neck making her wild with tenderness in every hidden crevice. "Rather, part of the dream."

"What is the other part?"

"We must remove to a more private location for the other part."

Ravenna lifted heavy eyelids. They still stood in the kitchen yard, entirely visible to a dozen internal windows in the castle.

"I should get down."

"Are you certain you wish to?"

No. "Yes."

He lowered her feet to the ground, then took her hand.

The door opened and she tugged away. His grip tightened, but she pulled and he allowed her liberty.

"Ravenna?" Iona poked her fiery head into the sunlight. "Oh! Guid day, my laird." Bright blue eyes scanned him then Ravenna, traveling from her cheeks to her skirts tangled about her calves. A grin twitched the corner of her rosebud lips, then her face sobered. "Ravenna, I've got to speak wi' ye. Wi' the both o' ye."

They went inside and to the servants' stairway and up, all the while Ravenna feeling him close behind her. Her limbs trembled peculiarly now, as though she had run up a hill. But when they entered the empty dining room and he closed the door behind them, he seemed at ease, still elegant despite the somewhat disordered state of his hair from her fingers raking through it.

She could not find her tongue.

Iona filled the silence. "I was with Mr. Walsh the nicht he died."

SHE INCHED AWAY from him, subtly yet steadily putting the dining table between them as Lady Iona spoke. But Vitor knew the signs of her retreat well enough now: averted profile, skittish eyes, balancing upon the balls of her feet in preparation for flight.

When she had gone to her toes and wrapped her arms about him, he'd nearly lost all control of himself. Soft and lush and naturally brazen as only a woman who did not heed society's restrictions could be, she had shocked herself with her own pleasure. With Herculean effort he had yet again forced himself to retreat. The daylight had not stopped him, only his need to show her that the advantages he offered were not to be discarded lightly. Her first real experience making love would not be a hasty outdoor coupling.

Now her eyes lit with confusion. "Why did you not tell me before?"

"I couldna afore! Ye must understand." Hands extended, Lady Iona moved toward her with the impetuous grace that marked her as a girl of breeding and privilege.

Vitor stepped between them. "My lady, do explain yourself."

Her lips parted upon surprise, then chagrin. "Aye." She nodded and looked past his shoulder to Ravenna. "'Twas no' long after dinner, perhaps ten-thirty or eleven o'clock. I grew weary o' that young—" Her gaze darted to him. "O' conversation in the drawin' room, an' thought to do a bit o' explorin'." Her eyes spoke meaning to Ravenna that she did not know he understood; she had been heading to an assignation with a lover.

"Where did you meet him?" Ravenna asked.

"Oh! I didna meet him by design. I'd niver seen the man till that moment. But he was clearly a gentleman, so . . ." Her manner turned diffident and she glanced at him again. "I bid him guid eve."

"I told him about Lord Whitebarrow in the tower," Ravenna said. "You must speak candidly now or we will have to consider you a suspect."

Lady Iona faced him. "Imagine o' me whit ye will, my laird. 'Tis nothin' I've no' borne afore."

"Where did you encounter Walsh?"

"In the long gallery where there be all the knights on display." Her nose wrinkled. "Rusty old things. I dinna ken why a man would want them in his house. But yer peculiar beasts, aren't ye, my laird?"

Ravenna moved to his side. "Was he wearing armor when you spoke with him?"

Her eyes widened again. "No."

For the first time since the kitchen yard, Ravenna looked directly at him. "Then she encountered him before Ann did."

"Ann?" Lady Iona exclaimed. "But what could a little thing like Ann want wi' a fine man like that?"

"Not, presumably, what you did. I believe she came upon him by chance, just as you, but later. Did you and he speak?"

"Aye, but no' for long. He'd been drinkin' spirits an' though he pawed me a bit, he couldna hold my eye. I've no need o' a man that deep in his cups." She offered Vitor a defiant stare.

Ravenna's cheeks were aflame, spreading dark along her neck and beneath her gown.

"But it was the oddest thing," Lady Iona said thoughtfully. "He called me his gracious leddy—three times he did—an' though he could barely hold up his head, he went to his knee afore me, as though he were playin' at bein' a knight, like the suits all aboot him."

"His gracious lady?"

"Aye."

"And he seemed out of his senses with drink but amorous?"

"Aye."

Ravenna's throat constricted jerkily. "Could he have drunk the drugged wine?" She meant the wine that Vitor had drunk. Still she did not believe he wanted her, despite all.

"He might have," he said. "Yes."

"Drugged wine?" Lady Iona said. "I'd thought the poor man was stabbed."

"Why?" Ravenna said before he could. She was quick and clever and attentive to detail even as she blushed in embarrassment, and he wanted her. "We told no one about how he was killed." She turned her dark eyes up to him. "Did you?"

He ought to be concerned with Walsh's death, if only to ensure her safety and the safety of the other innocent people in the castle. But all he could think was that she was his and he would not allow her to run from him again.

"I told no one." He forced his attention to Lady Iona. "How do you know he was stabbed?"

Her brow wrinkled. "Leddy Grace spoke o' a knife, I think. Or perhaps a dagger. I dinna recall. She was lookin' for the thing earlier this week, thinkin' she could aid in the mayor's investigation. I told her it would do no guid, that if the murderer were worth his salt, he'd thrown it in the river days ago. But the lass seemed determined to find it."

"Grace. The dagger. The river . . ." she murmured. "The wax . . ."

"The wax?" he said.

"The wax seal on the note Mr. Walsh received. The impression in it was that of a small finger. A woman's finger most likely."

"When did you determine this?"

"The morning before— That is to say . . ." Her gaze shot to the Scotswoman, and roses bloomed in her cheeks again. "I forgot to tell you. In fact I forgot about it entirely. But I should not have. Ladies Penelope and Grace have worn gloves at nearly every moment since the murder. Lady Penelope made such a complaint of the drafts in all the rooms that I didn't think a thing of it. And Grace does everything her sister does."

"Leddies wi' cold bluid wear gloves because they be afeard to touch a man's skin, lass. Poor things, missin' out on the best o' life."

"I did not think to consider either of them before because of the dark hair. Then after we determined the hair was Ann's, I never seriously reconsidered. What if one of them is hiding the burn mark that hot wax left on her fingertip? What if through my lack of thought the true murderer has gone free all these days?"

"You imagine that the incident with the guard in the armory had something to do with his assistance in killing Walsh, perhaps?" he said.

"Or in seeking to harm you. And Lord Case was brought into it by accident simply because he was present when the guard attacked you." She spoke with outward calm but her eyes glittered with distress. "One of the guards might have killed Mr. Walsh, or both of them that have now disappeared. But why would they have? His traveling bag seemed intact."

"Seemed."

"But if they had stolen something of his, why wouldn't they have run away then?"

"A foot o' snow upon the ground might o' stayed them," Lady Iona said.

"I don't believe it," Ravenna insisted. "The guards had no reason to imagine we would consider them suspects until after I found the man with Lady Grace in the armory. Everybody has known all along that you and I were investigating the murder. Monsieur Sepic himself said he'd heard it from the others, and I haven't made a secret of it that I dislike the Whitebarrow twins." She twisted her hands in her skirts. "Perhaps whichever of them did it—or both—imagined I disliked them because I suspected them of the murder."

"It seems unlikely," Lady Iona said.

"Yet not impossible." He wanted to wrap his arms around Ravenna and assure her that she had not caused any of the violence, that she was blameless. "Why do you imagine either Lady Grace or Lady Penelope would wish to murder Oliver Walsh?"

"I don't know. But I don't know why anybody else would wish to either, other than the most obvious person," she added, "and we know it was not him."

Lady Iona's eyes went wide. "Who?"

"He might have done it to divert our attention from him," Vitor said.

"You don't believe that. I don't believe that. He was shot. You were both—" Her voice broke. "And he told me why he came to the stable that night."

"Ye met Lord Case in the stable, lass? But—"

"What did he say to you?"

Ravenna shook her head. "It doesn't matter. He didn't do it. I don't believe he likes me but I also don't believe he wished to harm either of us."

"I showed the bottle to Monsieur Brazil. He himself had placed it in Lord and Lady Whitebarrow's chambers before guests began to arrive last week."

"He did? Lord and Lady Whitebarrow's chambers? Why didn't you tell me that?"

"I learned of it only this morning." Then he'd taken a moment in the chapel to prepare to see her. But she had fled into the sunshine, throwing into disarray his carefully rehearsed speech.

"Then the murderer must be Grace, for a reason as yet hidden to us. Or . . ." A new spark lit her eyes. "Penelope. Yes! Have you observed her? Grace, that is? The day everyone arrived here, and the next in the drawing room that evening and at dinner, she was the shadow to her sister's practiced nastiness. You saw it with Ann. There was cool disdain in her face then. But that changed the next morning after the prince announced the murder. After that, she grew entirely silent, almost grim."

"But, lass, all o' us were stunned by the news o' the poor man's murder, an' frightened that we might be next."

"Of course. But Grace's shock has seemed to me so . . . so . . . personal. As though she were . . . *grieving*," she uttered as if she were only at this moment understanding, and understanding too well.

Vitor moved a step closer to her. "You believe that when she realized that her sister murdered Walsh, her fear for what might happen to Lady Penelope if her crime was discovered—"

"Or the horror o' it."

"—might have shocked her beyond her ability to dissemble?"

"Twins have a particular bond. Everybody knows that. Grace is clearly the weaker of the two, the follower to her sister's lead."

"But why would Penelope wish a man dead?" Lady Iona said.

Ravenna chewed her lip. "And if she did do it, how could we prove it?"

"Gather ev'rybody together an' accuse Penelope. Mebbe ithers have evidence o' her guilt but havena yet thought o' it as evidence. Then make her remove those silly gloves an' inspect her fingertips."

Ravenna looked to him. He nodded. She started for the door, Lady Iona following.

Vitor caught Ravenna's arm. "You will not speak," he said quietly, firmly. "I will."

"I don't understand. I must."

"You will not place yourself in further danger by revealing that you know every detail of the murder."

"But—"

"You will not." He could not bear it.

Without assenting, she drew out of his grasp and followed Iona.

THE PRINCE SUMMONED his guests to the chamber in which he had announced Mr. Walsh's death. Only Lord Case remained absent.

Standing at the door and flanked by two of his largest and most loyal guards, Prince Sebastiao cleared his throat. "As yesterday's harrowing events proved to us, Monsieur Sepic was mistaken in assigning the murder of Mr. Walsh to his nephew. We celebrated too precipitously. Monsieur Paul did not do the deed. My good friend Courtenay, however, has discovered the truth and will now reveal the murderer's identity."

As theatrical announcements went, it served its purpose. Guests gasped. Cheeks went pale. Lady Grace's gloved fingers clenched in her maidenly white skirt. But Ravenna's mind still sped. Why would Penelope have killed Oliver Walsh? What had she hoped to gain from it? Or had it been an accident? An accidental *castration*? Impossible.

"This is preposterous," Lord Whitebarrow protested. "How can Courtenay know any more than the rest of us about Walsh's death?"

"Because," came a weak voice from the doorway, "my brother spent years in France during the war as an agent of the crown, unearthing secrets of Napoleon's tactics which would no doubt turn all our hair white if we knew them but which benefitted England enormously." Lord Case leaned against the doorpost, his clothing immaculate but his breathing labored and his face ruddy with fever.

Ravenna went to him. "You must return to bed at once."

"Ah, the lovely nurse. Will you threaten me now too, or am I never to be so fortunate again?"

"Do as she says, Wes," his brother said.

"I've no doubt she would make me suffer for it if I did not. And Franklin too, though he of course would deserve it." His fevered gaze sought across the room for Arielle. He put a hand to his waistcoat, offered her a bow, and then clapped his brother on the arm. "Trust me, my lords and ladies, if this man speaks, it is because he has excellent information. Good day."

Mr. Franklin assisted the earl away.

"Who was it, then, Courtenay?" Sir Henry said. "In the name of Zeus, it's about time we got to the bottom of this mystery."

"The note found in Walsh's pocket bears a wax seal that was effected with a fingertip rather than a stamp," Lord Vitor said. "The author of that note may bear a scar on her finger from the wax."

"Her finger?"

"The seal is small. Though this does not rule out a man entirely, other evidence suggests it was a woman.

Lady Penelope, would you be so good as to remove your gloves?"

Her pale eyes blinked. "I will not, my lord."

Lady Whitebarrow stood. "This is insupportable. My daughter did not murder a man."

Grace's palms covered her face and her narrow shoulders crumpled.

"Grace?" her father said. "Did your sister commit this horrible act? Did she?"

"Of course she did not," his wife said.

"That ye must ask her if she done it, my laird," the duchess said, "tells a sorry tale."

He stared blankly at her for a moment while the room hung with tension, then he looked again at his younger daughter. "Grace? You must tell us."

"Courtenay," Sir Henry said, "what is the other evidence that led you to believe this young lady did it?"

"A missing dagger, and certain evidence surrounding the circumstances of the death."

"But what of the handwriting comparison?" Cecilia asked. "Monsieur Sepic determined that none of us were guilty because none of the hands matched the note found in Mr. Walsh's pocket."

Lord Prunesly scowled. "You foolish girl. Any of us could have disguised our hand to throw off suspicion."

"Lady Penelope's hand, however, was the closest to the script on the note found in Mr. Walsh's coat." The voice that spoke from the corner of the room was light and sweet with rounded Italian tones. All eyes turned to Juliana Abraccia.

"How would you know such a thing?" Lady Whitebarrow demanded. "Are you an expert in deciphering script?"

"*Si,*" Juliana said with a taking little smile. "I have spent ever so many hours and days in my uncle's chancery sorting documents and studying the scripts. For six years my tutor was the renowned Jesuit paleographer Padre Georgio di Silvestro. He was ever so entertaining." Her mouth fell into a pretty pout. "Of course he was terribly strict with me when I failed to study." She gave a dainty shrug that fluttered the sleeves of her muslin gown like little butterflies circling her shoulders. "Wasn't he, Uncle?"

The bishop patted her on the head as though she were a child. "*Sì, cara mia.* My bright little sun."

"After Signore Sepic studied the hands and found no similarities," Juliana said, "I could not resist checking his work. He mistook it. Lady Penelope wrote that note."

Ravenna could not remain silent. "But why didn't you tell us this when you discovered it?"

Juliana's lashes batted over innocent eyes. "I did not think anybody would believe me. We are all here to win the prince's favor. To accuse a competitor of murder would have seemed poor sportswomanship."

"Vulgar chit," Lady Whitebarrow said. "You will retract this accusation at once."

"If you withheld the accusation before, Miss Abraccia," Lord Vitor said, "why have you made it now?"

Juliana directed a sweet smile at Martin Anders. "Because I no longer wish to marry a prince." She fluttered her lashes again, this time at Prince Sebastiao. "*Perdonate me*, your highness? I am ever so grateful that you invited me to this *festa.*"

He bowed.

"*Mama.*" Penelope's face had turned white as her gown.

"That girl's claim proves nothing." Lady Whitebarrow offered a contemptuous sniff.

"But!" The prince jutted a finger into the air. "I may have further proof." He snapped his fingers. "Alfonso, bring me the scripts." A guard bowed and disappeared.

"The scripts, yer highness?" Iona asked.

"The scripts of *Romeo and Juliet* with which I tested the thespian capabilities of the ladies before I chose my Juliet." He peered at Penelope. "You wrote notes on your script."

"I did not," she said between clenched teeth, adding, "your highness."

"You did," Mr. Anders interjected. "I recall it. You asked me how you might deliver the lark and nightingale lines, and as I advised you, you noted it on the page."

Her nostrils flared in swift breaths, but she did not respond.

The guard brought the scripts to the prince. He flipped through them then announced, "Aha!" and pulled one forth. The remainder fell to the floor. " 'It is the lark,' " he read, "and in the margin, 'with gentle resistance, *doucement*.' " He looked up. "Who has Walsh's missive?"

The butler proffered a silver tray that bore a single sheet of folded paper. "When you began to speak of this matter, your highness, I took the liberty of retrieving this from the parlor in which Monsieur Sepic stored the evidence."

"Excellent." Prince Sebastiao snatched it up and studied the pages side by side. The silence of strained breathing gripped the chamber. "The hands are identical," he declared. "Lady Penelope, you wrote the note that enticed Mr. Walsh to his death."

"I will not hear of this," Lady Whitebarrow said. "My lord." She turned to her husband. "You must put a stop to this slanderous accusation. Our daughter is innocent."

"What reason did you have to write that note, Penelope?" Lord Whitebarrow said.

"Perhaps she's no' so innocent as ye would have us believe, nou?" the duchess said to Lady Whitebarrow.

Lady Whitebarrow's lips were as white as Penelope's face. "You would like to believe that my girls are as besmirched as yours, wouldn't you?"

"Enough, Olympia," Lord Whitebarrow commanded. "Tell me, Penelope, why you wrote that note."

Penelope rose to her feet, her chin high. "I did not murder Mr. Walsh," she stated in a softly trembling voice. "My sister did."

Grace's head shot up, her eyes awash in betrayal. "*Penny.*"

"Look." Penelope stripped off her gloves. "I do have a burn on my finger, but not because I killed him." She pointed to her sister. "Grace told me to write the note. She loved him but he scorned her, and she used me to bring him to her so she could kill him."

"Penny! How could you?" Tears streamed down her twin's cheeks.

Lord Whitebarrow's face was stricken. "Gracie, is this true?"

"Oh, *Papa.*" She covered her face with her hands again and she wept. Ravenna's heart did churning turns in her chest. Grace's misery was so powerful. And suddenly she understood. Grace was grieving over Mr. Walsh's death. Now it seemed so utterly clear—her dull, glassy stare, her lack of animation for everything, her sadness. Her pain reached out to the grief in Ravenna's heart, and to the new fear she had felt the day before, the fear of losing someone she had never thought to cherish, and she was breathless with it.

"The mystery is solved," the prince said flatly. His mood of triumph had disintegrated. "The murderer is discovered."

Lord and Lady Whitebarrow stood as though stunned, Penelope beside her mother with bright cheeks. Grace's quiet sobs filled the silence.

Ravenna went to Grace, knelt beside her, and reached for her hand. Grace gave it without resistance, as though she had lost the will to do anything at all.

"You truly loved him, didn't you?" Ravenna whispered.

Her sobs came like her very soul jolting forth from inside her.

She is not the murderer. The truth battered at Ravenna.

"Lady Grace," Lord Vitor said. "What weapon did you employ to kill Oliver Walsh?"

"Good God, man," Sir Henry choked. "Can't you see the poor girl is all broken up about it?"

"My lady?" Lord Vitor said.

Ravenna squeezed her hand. "Tell him, Grace.

Grace shook her head and mumbled, "Poison. In the wine." Then she choked and the tears began anew.

She did not do it. Ravenna looked across the room and saw in his eyes that his thoughts matched hers.

Penelope took her mother's arm. "She made me give him the wine, Mama. She told me it was to relax him so that he would accept her when she offered herself to— I am too ashamed to say it." She pressed her palm to her mouth and shut her eyes as though horrified by her sister's wanton indiscretion.

"He was a handsome man, Grace," Iona said quietly. "Ye coulda done much worse." She understood too. Grace had not killed the man she loved.

Penelope was lying.

"Grace." Ravenna leaned forward and said beside the girl's bent head, "If you do not tell the truth now, they will hang you for the murder of the man you loved."

"I don't care." Her words were barely a breath. "I don't wish to live now."

"If you do not do this for yourself"—Ravenna's throat caught—"do it for he who loved you and would wish your happiness now above all."

Grace's shoulders stiffened. Then she lifted her head and looked straight at her mother. Her face was blotched red and white, and damp, but her eyes glittered.

"I did not ask Pen to offer him wine to make him accept me. I had given myself to him before and he wanted to marry me. He begged to marry me and I wanted to be his wife more than anything in this world." She looked to her father. "But Mama would not allow it. I offered him the wine because Mama said I must. He came here to beg you for my hand, though Mama had warned that she would ruin him if he came between our family and marriage to a prince. When I refused to endanger him, she told Pen to write the note and then she poured a drug in the wine to make him sick." Her face crumpled. "But instead she poisoned him. She gave him too much and she killed him." She dissolved into sobbing again and Ravenna drew her against her shoulder and stroked her smooth locks.

"I did not," Lady Whitebarrow said coldly.

"What did you not do?" Lord Whitebarrow's face was hard with fury. "Indulge in overweening pride sufficient to break our daughter's heart, or kill a man in cold blood? For, let us make no mistake, I believe you capable of both."

"He was unsuitable," Lady Whitebarrow said through pinched lips. "Their liaison was unseemly."

"So speaks the coldest woman I have ever known," her husband said.

"His situation was vastly inferior to that which I intended for my daughters."

"So you killed him?"

"Of course I did not." Scorn coated her words. "I intended to make him ill so he would not be able to press his suit upon Grace here. I only dosed him with the smallest amount, enough to sicken him but certainly insufficient to cause permanent harm." She turned to Grace. "It was for your good and your sister's. Do you see how you have ruined us now, bringing scandal upon our family? What prince will have your sister now?"

"Not I, that's for certain," Prince Sebastiao said with a shrug.

"Lady Grace," Lord Vitor said, "why in his drugged state did Mr. Walsh don a suit of armor? Do you know?"

Her lips made a quavering smile. "He always called me his gracious lady. He pretended to be my knight and he said he would build me a castle and make my dreams come true. Perhaps the drug made him imagine that . . . Perhaps . . ." She looked to her father. "He wanted to make me his queen."

"How was he killed?" Lord Whitebarrow demanded of Lord Vitor. "With poison?"

"He bled to death," Grace said quietly, as though all her grief had been spent and now she knew only numbness. "After Penny and Mama went to bed, I went searching for him. I f-found him." Her voice broke again and her chin trembled. "There was nothing I could do. It was too late. I closed his eyes and kissed him and bid him adieu." She looked at her twin and her eyes hardened. "Did you do it, Penelope? Did you cut him there because you had never known a man's touch and you were jealous of me? Of Oliver and me together? Do you fear that your heart is so cold that even if a man does touch you, you will never enjoy it?"

Penelope's eyes shot wide. "I don't know what you are accusing me of, sister, except that your mind is disordered. I did nothing to him. I wrote the note and watched you offer him the wine, but I did nothing else." Her gaze shot between Lord Vitor and the prince. "I swear it."

"Guid heavens," the duchess exclaimed, "was the poor man unmanned?"

Prince Sebastiao dropped back a step and looked to Vitor. "Unmanned?"

Lady Margaret fluttered her kerchief over her bosom. "Ann, dearest, cover your ears. My lords, this conversation is unsuitable in present company."

"Was it you, Olympia?" Lord Whitebarrow said to his wife. "Did you castrate Walsh?"

Lady Margaret gasped. Ann's eyes went round as carriage wheels.

"If I wished to do such a thing to a man, Frederick," Lady Whitebarrow said icily to her husband, "don't you imagine I would have begun closer to home?"

Cecilia grinned. Martin Anders turned green. Iona bit her pretty lip.

"Grace," Ravenna said, "who forced you to meet that guard in the armory? His disappearance since yesterday suggests that he was connected in some manner to the murder. It was clear to me that you did not meet him voluntarily."

"My sister. As soon as everyone started whispering that you and Lord Vitor were pursuing the murderer, she feared you would discover my family's blame, and her chances of being a princess would be ruined. She paid those guards every penny she had to frighten you and Lord Vitor from investigating further. But they demanded more."

"They demanded you?"

"They demanded her." Her eyes narrowed upon her twin. "So she sold me to them instead. She said that while she was still pure and fit to wed, I was already— already defiled, so I would not be harmed by it. I told her I could not, that I would swoon." Her voice tightened. "So she made me drink the drugged wine before I met him. She said it would make it bearable."

Ravenna's stomach sickened. She leaned in to Grace. "There is no defilement in what you did with Mr. Walsh." Animals mated whenever the urge to breed came upon them and that was considered acceptable. "The joining of two people in love cannot be wrong."

"Well, then," Sir Henry exclaimed, "who did the dirty deed in the end? Who in the name of Zeus *is* the murderer?"

From beside the prince came the clipped Gallic accents of the butler of Chevriot.

"*C'est moi,*" said Monsieur Brazil. "I killed Monsieur Walsh."

Chapter 19

Naturally

"The *butler* did it?" Sir Henry gaped.

Everyone stared. Wide-eyed. Astonished.

Vitor watched Ravenna release Lady Grace's hand and rise to her feet.

"That night, Monsieur Brazil, after you assisted in carrying the body to the parlor in which we examined it," Ravenna said, "you left for a time. When you returned I noticed that you wore a fresh coat and trousers. It seemed odd to me that you would change your clothing only in order to lock that parlor door and bid us good night. You had not touched the body while it was moved, and you must have belatedly noticed that a piece of your clothing was stained with his blood. You did not wish us to see that."

"*Oui*, mademoiselle," he replied. He stood perfectly erect and formal and immaculate, but Vitor had attention only for her. Intelligent, lovely, brave, forthright—she commanded the drawing room.

"You had the keys to the entire house," she said. "You gave me entrance into the armory when I was searching for the dagger."

"*Oui*, mademoiselle."

"I suspect you locked away the dagger in a safe hiding place? The butler's pantry, perhaps?"

"*Oui*, mademoiselle. I washed it then stored it in my cupboard. I will be glad to show it to you now, if you wish."

"Why did you kill him?" Vitor said.

"I meant no harm to *le gentilhomme anglais*, monseigneur. I mistook him for his royal highness."

Sebastiao backed a step away from his butler now, horror slipping over his face. "You mistook him for *me*?"

"*Oui*, your highness." Monsieur Brazil bowed. "Monsieur Walsh wore upon his breast several medals of superior quality and garish display. I believed them to be your highness's. He was of a size and weight with your highness, as well, and he was insensible from drink and dressed in a ridiculous costume."

"You *killed* him because you thought he was *me*?"

"I took the dagger to him only to remove the offending organs. It was an unfortunately hurried affair." He shook his head regretfully. "I felt I must act quickly, lest your highness awake and find me at my task. You might have cried for assistance."

"I would have indeed!"

"You did considerably more damage than what you say you intended, Brazil," Vitor said.

"Monsieur Walsh did not remain asleep. It seems that he was not unconscious but merely resting. He struggled. The dagger . . . slipped." A furrow dug its way between his brows. "I did not open the visor of the helmet until he grew still. I regretted the mistake *énormément*."

"Well, one doesn't like to kill a man," Sir Henry said, eyes round as his daughter's.

Monsieur Brazil turned his attention upon Sir Henry. "I regretted it, monsieur, because it was not his highness whom my blade had dismembered."

A horrified hush rippled through the party, a shocked recoil from the brutality he so calmly recounted.

"Why did you wish to harm me, Brazil?" the prince asked, his cheeks stark. "After all these years? And in such a manner?"

"Two years ago," the butler said stiffly, "your highness celebrated here at Chevriot the recapture of *l'Empereur* and the finale of the war with a cadre of your *amis peu honorables.*"

Sebastiao's brow knit. "I don't recall . . . Vitor . . . ? Ah. Yes. You were at San Antonio at that time. I came here alone on that occasion."

"Oui," Monsieur Brazil confirmed. "Monseigneur would not have borne with those men your highness brought to this house." His chin rose. "He is a man of honor."

"What did I do, Brazil?" Sebastiao's voice quavered. "What could I have done to make you despise me so?"

"It was not your highness but one of your disreputable friends. He enjoined my daughter, my young Clarice, to serve him in a manner she did not like. When she protested, he forced himself upon her. The following spring she gave birth to a son."

Gasps again sounded throughout the drawing room, but Vitor cared only for Ravenna's response. She had accused him of trying to use her because he believed her to be a servant. Now her starlit gaze came to him, but unreadable.

"Why didn't you tell me?" Sebastiao said to Brazil. "I would have had him horsewhipped."

"I informed you of the wrongdoing. Your highness, however, was too intoxicated to understand me."

"For the entire *month*?"

"*Oui.* Then your highness departed."

Sebastiao's mouth opened without sound.

"You chose to punish the prince because of the dishonor he had brought to your family," Vitor said.

"His highness dishonored Chevriot." Brazil's chest puffed out. "I did not wish to murder anyone."

A murmur of disbelief arose from the guests all about the room. Disbelief with good cause. The artery had been severed.

"Didn't you intend it, Brazil?" Vitor said.

The butler's chin jerked around. "I only wished to make his highness suffer for the villainy he had allowed his friend to commit. I regret, however, that my act of justice harmed an innocent man." He turned to Lady Grace and placed his fist over his heart. He bowed. "Mademoiselle, *je suis navré.*"

She turned her face away.

"Monsieur Brazil," Ravenna said. "What became of your daughter and the babe?"

"Clarice wed," he said stonily.

"Who?" Lady Iona asked.

"*Cet imbécile*, Sepic. She is"—his lips pursed— "*amoureuse.* And he with her, as well as the child he believes to be his son. It is *dégoûtant.*"

Sir Henry said, "Well, in the name of Zeus, that seems to settle it!" He looked at the disoriented faces all around, then at Vitor. "Doesn't it?"

Vitor turned to Sebastiao's guard. "Go to the village. Bring Monsieur Sepic but do not tell him the reason he has been summoned. We will leave that for his wife's father to impart." The guard nodded and went. "Monsieur Brazil, take me to the place you hid the dagger."

"I have your back, Courtenay," Lord Whitebarrow said.

"The mistake of the aristocracy," Monsieur Brazil said with an arch sniff, "is to believe that the common man has no honor." He turned his back on Lord Whitebarrow and spoke to Vitor. "Monseigneur, you are safe with me."

Vitor nodded. Brazil's mind was clearly damaged. He would be hanged for the murder of Oliver Walsh, at best deported to a penal colony. Only a man possessed by an ungovernable passion would pursue a dangerous course without first considering all potential pitfalls.

He accepted Whitebarrow's offer. For years he had put himself in harm's way without concern for the future. Now he had a powerful wish to remain alive.

THE DAGGER WAS retrieved, and the butler sent off with Sepic and two of the palace guards to the village jail. The party dispersed, to muse upon the bitter and the absurd, and to rest in the relief that the murderer no longer dwelled among them.

Lord Whitebarrow took Vitor aside. "Penelope assures me that the guards acted against you and Lord Case independent of her instructions. She paid them only to frighten you away from investigating the murder, but not to harm you. She suspects they intended to blackmail her and Grace into theft of the others' jewels and such, but when they accidentally shot Case, they panicked and fled."

"Do you believe her?"

Lord Whitebarrow's face remained grave. "I believe that she is as cold as her—" His nostrils pinched. "She would say anything if she believed it to be to her advantage. I do not, however, believe she has the courage to intentionally cause a man's death, Walsh's or anyone else's. But you have my word, as a man of honor, that she will be punished. I've a remote property in Cumbria near Workington that will suit the purpose."

"Mining country, isn't that?"

Whitebarrow's eyes narrowed. "Precisely."

Vitor went searching for Ravenna, but she had disappeared. In neither house nor stables could he find her.

As though in apology for the atrocity committed by their leader, the staff of the chateau prepared a sumptuous evening repast. Sebastiao took up his position at the head of the table, with Ann Feathers at his right, and behaved for all the world like he intended to keep her there. As his guests moved into the dining room, Lady Whitebarrow and Penelope remained absent. Lord Whitebarrow and Lady Grace entered, and she came to Vitor.

"Thank you for what you did, my lord." Her eyes were rimmed with red, but dry.

"Miss Caulfield deserves your thanks. It was she who solved the mystery." He lowered his voice. "I am sorry for your loss."

"She said that Oliver would not wish me to grieve too greatly. She said he would wish me to be happy."

The woman he'd searched for all afternoon appeared then in the doorway, arrayed in a gown of deep rose that caressed her curves and revealed her arms—unadorned by sleeves, bracelets, gloves, or other decorations—as shapely and beautiful. She tilted her head, and her hair glittered like a night sky studded with stars.

Lady Iona took her hands. "The gown be perfect, lass."

"Thank you for the loan of it." Without casting him a glance, she walked to the other end of the table and sat between Pettigrew and the general.

After dinner she settled in the drawing room at the tea table with Lady Margaret, the duchess, and several other guests as though she meant to remain there for the duration of the winter. But Vitor had had enough. He went to the cluster of ladies and bowed.

"Miss Caulfield, might I have a word with you?"

She lifted wide black eyes to him. "Now?"

Lady Iona chuckled.

Vitor's collar had shrunk two sizes. "If you will."

"Go on, dear," Lady Margaret said. "Mustn't keep a man as handsome as that waiting. His eye is likely to stray, don't you know."

Ravenna rose to her feet stiffly and walked beside him to the door. Her steps dragged.

"What do you wish to say to me that you could not say over there?" She looked back at the group around the tea table.

"Have you injured your ankle again, Miss Caulfield?"

Her eyes snapped up to his. "No. What— Why do you—"

"I was obliged to halve my already-halved strides just now to maintain your snail's pace across the drawing room," he said, and gestured her out the door and along the corridor.

"Oh. Well. The conversation I was enjoying with Lady Margaret was so—so—"

"Enjoyable?"

"Yes. Of course." Her gaze darted about. "Where are we going?"

"And what subject were you conversing upon that enthralled you so, I wonder?" He touched her elbow, guiding her across the hall toward the armory rack.

"It was wildly diverting," she mumbled, and cast another glance back at the corridor to the drawing room. "What was that we were discussing? I did so enjoy it. Perhaps it was . . . Hm . . ."

"The day's remarkable revelations?"

"That was it." She looked up at the display of armaments as he urged her into the crevice behind them. "I don't understand. There are no more clues to be studied. What are we doing here?"

He pulled her into the alcove and against his chest. "What we should have done here five nights ago."

She resisted for a fleeting moment. Then she went soft and willing against him. With a little sigh of pure surrender, she lifted her face to be kissed.

He had already memorized her features, yet he could look upon them every day and never tire of the sight. In the flickering torchlight, he drank in the vision: lush lips, lashes black as coal shading sparkling stars, perfectly imperfect nose, tumbling hair, delicate lines radiating from the corners of her eyes that bespoke a lifetime of laughing in the sunshine.

"Are you going to kiss me?" Her breath stole across his lips, sweet and warm. He felt drunk—drunker than drugged—intoxicated upon her and the prospect of having her entirely to himself tonight and every night—drunk upon holding in his arms the woman he'd had to cajole and command in order to be with her alone now.

He backed up a step and held her off. "I don't believe I will, after all." He released her. She seemed to sway. Then her eyes popped wide.

"You won't?"

"Not at this time." He stepped out from behind the screen of armor and started across the hall.

"But." She came fully into the light. "Why not?"

"I have changed my mind." He reached the stairway and ascended.

Her footsteps pattered swiftly to the base of the stairs. "You have changed your *mind*?"

He paused on the top step where eight nights earlier he had looked into her starlit eyes and had, without will or effort and against all that was wise, become her servant. "I've realized I have several other pressing matters to attend to."

"Other pressing matters?" She stared up at him bemusedly. He moved into the corridor. She hurried to follow. "What sorts of matters?"

"You know how it can be." He strode along the gallery where she had discovered a dead man and from which, later, he had swiped a sixteenth-century rapier to protect her. "Hours of this. Hours of that. Before you know it, the day has passed and yet"—he rounded a corner, halted, turned, and she came flying into him—"you haven't managed to do the one thing you ought to be doing." He grabbed her up. "Where were you all afternoon?"

"Here and there." Her breaths came quickly. She stared at his mouth. "Kiss me." Her lips were perfect, full and dark.

"Where here and there?"

"Lady Margaret's chamber. She asked me to examine a joint that has been causing her pain. Then the duchess required my advice for a feminine matter of some delicacy that I cannot, of course, detail to you. Then General Dijon wanted my opinion on the use of arrow root to cure distemper, which he read about in a journal. And Sir Henry wished me to look in on Titus again, though he is perfectly—"

He halted her speech in the most effective manner. She sank into his kiss, parting her lips and sighing deep in her throat. When she offered her supple tongue to caress, he entwined it with his and drew her fully against him. Lush and sweet and wild and good, she captivated him and made him furious, frustrated, and hard as mountain stone.

He lifted his mouth. Her eyes remained closed and she released a delirious little sigh.

"I also looked in on your brother," she murmured. "The fever persists. But he will recover soon. Kiss me again."

"Why do you continue running from me?"

"I am not running now."

It was some effort to speak now, he found. "Wesley Courtenay is not my only brother."

Her lashes fluttered up, eyes questioning in shadow.

"Sebastiao and I share the same father," he said.

"Sebastiao, the prince?"

"Yes. The prince that your sister sent you here to wed."

She blinked several times. "You remember that I told you that?"

"How could I forget it?"

Her breasts rose against his chest. "Hold me," she said.

He laughed. He had not known what response to expect from her, but this would do. "I am holding you."

She ran her fingers through his hair and drew his head down. Pressing up onto her toes, she whispered against his ear. "Hold me . . . down."

She allowed him to kiss her, and to circle his hands around her bared arms and caress the lithe beauty of them, the softness of her skin all the way to the tender veins in her wrists where she was not a maddeningly tempting fury on the verge of flight, but a woman of sighs and quivering desire. He took her hand and guided her the remainder of the distance to his bedchamber.

Gonçalo greeted them with frantic joy. She went to her knees on the floor.

"No," Vitor said firmly. "He must wait his turn." He snapped his fingers and the dog scampered into the dressing chamber. Vitor shut the door and turned to the woman on her knees, her vibrant skirts spread about her and eyes wary now.

"Is your valet in there too?" she asked.

"I dismissed him for the night."

"For the entire night?"

He crouched before her and she gave no resistance when he drew her up between his knees. "I have often been without him. I find I like my privacy. And I hoped I would have company tonight. Finally." He lowered his mouth to hers and she wrapped her arms about his neck and met his kiss eagerly. He stroked back her hair with his fingertips, her skin and scent and willingness an intoxication, and it seemed as though heaven hovered precipitously close. "Ravenna." His voice came forth unsteadily. "I must know that this is what you wish."

Her fingers worked at his neck cloth, untying the knot and discarding the linen, then unfastening the shirt button. "It is what I wish." She set her soft lips to his neck, and the pressure of her hands upon his chest sent his pulse spinning. She brought her mouth to his as her hand slid down his waist and she stroked his arousal—a light touch, tentative. Upon his groan she whispered, "Tonight."

Not the word he wished to hear. But it was far too late. He ignored the constriction beneath his ribs and answered only the need to have her beneath him. She pushed his coat and waistcoat off his shoulders. When he drew his shirt over his head and took her into his arms, she spread her hands across his chest. Her breaths deepened. She watched herself touch him, exploring, her hands supple and strong but uncertain. He fought for control.

"*Ravenna.*" He grasped her hands.

"Your wounds," she said huskily, running her fingertips around the abrasions on his knuckles.

"It is nothing."

"I should have tended to this."

He tried to grin. "You did not tend my bruised leg or broken lip."

"I wished to, despite myself." Her hand escaped his grip and stole again to his chest. She smoothed her palm along his skin, curving her fingers over his muscle, stalling his breaths.

"I . . ." she said in a wondering hush. "This is not what I imagined."

He found the fasteners of her gown. She let him draw the fabric away from her breasts, and untie the laces of her petticoat, then tug down the ribbons that served as chemise straps and release her breasts from the stays. She was beauty. Such beauty.

"What did you imagine?" He stroked his thumb across one perfect peaked nipple. She shuddered, her lashes dipping.

"I never imagined anything," she whispered. "I never thought this would happen to me."

He could wait no longer.

He took her there, before the fire. Stripping away her garments and his, he brought them skin to skin, and as she trembled he made of them one flesh. Without words, but with caresses and kisses and the earnest rhythm of her body, she told him that she needed him, urging him to enjoy her and then begging until he gave her release. He took his own, and the world ended and began at once.

When it was over and their skin was slick and hot and she lay beneath him panting, he could not leave her. If he released her she might be gone in an instant. It could be days before he captured her again, only to be obliged to release her once more when she sought to flee. He kissed the tender arc of her throat, tasting the salt on her skin and drinking in her scent of passion. Contentedly she stroked her fingertips down his back, her hands bolder now upon him.

"What do we do now?" she whispered without opening her eyes, her lips parted upon pleasure and perhaps uncertainty.

He stroked the valley between her breasts, over the bony ribs that protected her fortressed heart, and down her belly, the softness of feminine beauty, then through dark curls to the heat and moisture below. "We do that again."

Her breaths deepened. He found the center of her pleasure and stroked. She spread her thighs, inviting more.

"And again," he said.

"Again," she repeated upon a sigh.

His hand stilled. "But not until you say my name."

Her eyes opened and glittered with candlelight as she stared at the ceiling. "I beg your pardon?"

He withdrew from her, stood, and reached for his dressing gown. "Your fee for my services, madam. My name upon your lips or nothing more from me." He shrugged into the garment, the caress of fine satin against his skin little pleasure now that he knew the caress of her hands. He took up the decanter and crystal goblet from his nightstand. "Wine? I don't believe it is drugged, but we managed that hurdle well enough once already. If it should happen again, your clever physicking will put us to rights."

She sat up and wrapped her arms around her knees. Black tresses tumbled gloriously about her shoulders and down her back, wild like her heart and free like her spirit. Deep in the ebony waves, a circlet of diamonds glittered. "Your name?"

He took a swallow of wine, as much for courage as to appear nonchalant. "Seems a fair price, does it not? I am, after all, a despicably wealthy second son of a marquess, however ill-begotten." He gestured with the glass. "I suspect third and fourth sons of dukes and

princes—both the legitimate and illegitimate sorts—
require the same fee. But I shall have to confirm it
with the boys the next time I visit my club." He turned
from the astonishment registering upon her face and
the vision of her intimate femininity that she seemed
entirely unaware she displayed to him now, and set
down his glass. "Are you certain you don't wish some
wine?"

"Fairly." She reached for her clothing and stood up,
her glorious naked beauty in the middle of his bedchamber nearly sending him to his knees. "I prefer not
to drink with madmen," she muttered.

"You don't say?" He leaned a shoulder into the
bedpost and watched her struggle with the chemise.
Finally she managed to pull it over her head, but the
ribbons caught in her hair.

"I am not accustomed to these sorts of undergar-
ments," she grumbled, and tugged.

He went to her. "Allow me to assist."

"I can do it myself."

"I am certain you can." He removed her hands and
worked the satiny strands free of the ribbon. "But I am
a gentleman. My sort are bred to assist a lady when she
is in need." He smoothed the ribbon into place over her
shoulder, stroked back the thick mass of her hair, and
set his mouth to the supple juncture of her neck and
shoulder. A puff of air escaped her lips, then like a cat
she stretched her neck to allow him greater freedom to
caress her. He circled her waist with one hand and slid
the other over her hip and between her thighs. Stroking inward, through the thin fabric, he felt her. "Are
you in need, Miss Caulfield?"

She tilted her face, bringing her lips near his. "Yes,"
she whispered. She leaned into his touch.

Slowly he gathered the skirt of her undergarment,

baring her thighs and lifting the linen to find her damp heat. But he did not touch her. He allowed the moment to lengthen, her breaths to quicken.

"My payment?" he repeated.

"Mad," she whispered, "man."

He bent his head and brushed his lips over hers. "Not yet, but you are driving me there." Her scent of beauty filled him—sweet, rich, wild. "Say it."

Her eyes closed and her body trembled. "Vitor."

He stroked her flesh, and as she shuddered he dipped his finger into her shallowly. *Perfect*. Perfect beauty. Perfect woman.

Her back arched, her hand fumbling for the bedpost. "What—what are you—"

"You did not know of this," he said, knowing it from her staggered breaths, the surprise in her eyes. He dipped in again.

"I did not," she whispered, and moved her hips to seek him. He felt her, learning her beauty here with his hand, the hot, soft core of her womanhood. "But I am glad to know of it now."

"And this?" He penetrated her deeply.

She gasped. "This too." She bent her head back against the bedpost, shining locks cascading over shoulders and breasts, nipples making hard points beneath the linen. She was exquisite. He wanted to take her naked again, her breasts in his hands and her belly flat against his. He wanted all of her.

She made soft whimpering sounds, her hips in motion as she pleasured herself on his finger. He drew out and she rasped, "Don't *stop*," then moaned when he thrust two fingers together into her. He kissed the swell of her breast, then covered the peak with his mouth and sucked on her through the fabric. Her body shuddered and he felt her convulse around his fingers.

"That's it," he murmured. "Come for me."

She dropped her brow to his shoulder and whispered, "Now, my lord. I beg of you."

He hitched her knee over his hip. Wrapping her arms about his shoulders, she lifted her other leg and let him take her as he wished. He had her with her back to the post, and she reached up and clung to the carved wood, accepting his thrusts with moans of pleasure. Moisture from his tongue accentuated the dark peak of her breast, her nipples pressing through the thin chemise as her back arched, straining against confinement. She was wild beauty and she was his. He dragged her to him, bone against bone, and she sought him in urgency, the tempest of her need serving him, gripping and stroking his cock. Eyes closed, she cried out as she climaxed.

Taking her down onto her back on the mattress, he spread her thighs and sank into her again, harder and deeper with each thrust, to feel her fully, to know her as completely as she would allow. He would never tire of this, of her body beneath his, of touching her and taking her, of her hands clutching him in need.

"In the name of Zeus," she said breathlessly, "if this is the result of calling you 'my lord' then I will have to make a habit of it."

A crack of delight shot from his chest. He could not, for a moment, continue.

"No! *Don't* stop, I beg of you. My accursed mouth."

"Your beautiful mouth." He surrounded her face with his hands. "Your gorgeous mouth which, however, just quoted Sir Henry Feathers while I am inside you." It was too much for him. He fell into laughter. She kissed him and twined her ankle about his and the sound that came from her lips was of pure joy.

"Now, my lord," she said, reining in her mirth and smoothing her hands over his shoulders. "You must continue, for I have rendered payment and expect full service."

He brushed a damp lock of hair from her brow. "Do you?"

"I do indeed." She drew up her knees and pressed to him. "Lord Vitor Courtenay, stop making me laugh, and instead . . ." With a hand on the back of his neck she drew him down and set her lips softly to his, then fully for a long, decadent moment. "Make me sing."

HE MADE HER sing. At least, her sighs certainly sounded musical to *her*.

He made her dance—after all—patiently, in truth generously, teaching her the moves to an intricate pattern that rendered her breathless in his embrace. It was a dance that did not require standing up.

Later, after she dozed then awakened to the heat of his body shielding her from the cold night and the caress of his hands, he made her want him inside her with such wicked intensity that she sobbed and pleaded, which seemed to her at once despicable and divine.

Finally giving her what she needed, he made her cry out his name again. Rather, she cried it voluntarily, helplessly. Quivering, she pressed her mouth to his skin to stifle the sound of her ecstasy. But she heard it and she suspected he did too.

Afterward, she wrapped her arms around him and held him close.

Then he made her laugh. Summoning Gonçalo from the dressing chamber, he offered her a tour of all the objects from his wardrobe and other personal items that the pup had destroyed, beginning with his shaving brush and—after a lengthy list—culminating in two pairs of what had once been very fine boots.

"You cannot give him up now," she said upon a sleepy smile. She ached all over with glowing warmth. Curling into the bed linens, she sighed quite foolishly but probably predictably for a woman who had been made love to four times in four hours. "He has eaten so many of your belongings that his tastes are trained to you," she murmured. "He is ruined for anyone else."

The nobleman sitting on the bed beside her, wearing only a dressing gown of the same midnight blue color of his eyes, gave her a sidelong perusal. "Ruined, you say?"

"Oh, yes," she mumbled. "Entirely ruined."

He stroked a lock of hair from before her eyes.

Her eyelids drooped. "I must go."

"No," he said quietly.

A yawn shuddered through her. "I must return to my bedchamber before I—"

"You will remain here."

She felt his hands upon her as though in a dream. But he did not touch her now where he had given her such pleasure already. Softly, he traced the curve of her shoulder and the length of her arm, then each finger in turn. Fighting against thickening shadows, she felt his hands on her waist, his arms around her, his shoulder beneath her cheek, her palm upon the hard, warm plane of his chest.

"Sleep," she heard. Or felt.

Then sleep claimed her.

Chapter 20

The Good-bye

No beautiful black-eyed woman ornamented his bed when Vitor awoke to the gray light of dawn. Nor was she to be found in the chair by the fire or the dressing room, which was empty. He scratched his fingertips across his jaw that was rough with whiskers and wondered how and when she had returned to her bedchamber in the gown she had worn to dinner, and how she would explain to anyone she now encountered how she happened to be in the company of his dog before the sun had fully risen.

His dog.

His woman.

The next thought stalled his hand upon his jaw: *Her man.*

He lay very still as his heartbeats stumbled and he considered the implausibility of it.

Upon his fifteenth birthday he had learned the truth of his paternity, and within a fortnight had boarded a frigate bound for Lisbon. Three years later when the Portuguese court fled Lisbon, he took up the project both his fathers approved: serve Portugal and England in Spain or France or wherever else their need took him. Swiftly wearying of the tedium of intelligence gathering broken by days, sometimes weeks, of horrifying peril, he journeyed to England and unwittingly stepped into the disaster that was Wesley's courtship of Fannie Walsh. Returning to Portugal, again he crossed the Pyrenees into France, where he came into the hands of mercenaries who turned him over to the British for a hefty sum, who in turn used his vengeful brother to torture him.

Honor and loyalty and all the lessons he had learned at school and war and from his fathers . . . betrayed in a fortnight. After that, the monastery hidden in a remote crevice of the Serra dal Estrela seemed the ideal place to burn away his anger in hard labor and silent contemplation of higher things. Even as he accepted the cowl he'd known that he was unsuited to monastic life, and he had been quite certain he would miss women. But solitude and an end to rushing headlong into danger had appealed to him at the time.

The respite had been brief. Two years. Then he'd been ready to set off again.

Now, for the first time in his life of chasing adventure and courting danger, Vitor was terrified. Denis often chided him for his vagabond ways. But this was no laughing matter. After fourteen years could he cease running, finally? For a woman?

But Ravenna Caulfield was no ordinary woman.

He bent his head and closed his eyes.

A furtive scratching sounded at the door; the lady returning with his pet before she was discovered, no doubt. Vitor drew on his dressing gown and went to the door.

His elder brother's valet stood there in shadow, his face taut.

"My lord." The words quivered. "His lordship is terribly ill. You must come."

IN LONG, RUSHING slides and dripping as loud as rainfall, the snow on the mountain melted. Trees, roofs, and walls gradually reappeared from beneath their icy mantle, spring valiantly attempting to show its face.

Ravenna's shoes splashed across the forecourt as the sun poked its golden nose over the mountain, and she thought it especially fitting that the roads should begin to thaw today. Lord Whitebarrow and his family would be departing. Along the route their carriage would certainly become mired in mud. Pity.

She grinned.

Grace did not deserve it, though. A weak character had led her to follow her sister's example. But she had loved truly, despite the censure society would have heaped upon her for the unequal union. Oliver Walsh's death had broken her heart. Ravenna understood that pain. For the unkindnesses of her past, Grace's grief was punishment enough.

As she neared the front door, nerves danced in her belly. She'd slept little and awoken to the heat of a man's body beside hers, his big hand loosely clasped around her arm in sleep. Through the night he had done things to her that she'd never before imagined and that now, at the mere thought, made her face and the excessively tender place between her legs hot. Then he had ordered her to remain, as though it were perfectly reasonable to demand that she sleep in his bed and to awaken there too. Clearly he'd had no thought of how she would depart or when, only that he must have what he wished, by his command and upon his terms.

Standing in the halo of dawn by his bed, watching him sleep, she had wanted to touch him, to trace with her hands the sculpted contours of his chest and arms that the bed linens revealed, and to wake him with her lips upon his skin. Her body had warmed and she wanted to wrap her arms around him and breathe him in, then to caress him as he had taught her to caress him during the night, as she had done willingly, eagerly.

Some commands were not so difficult to obey.

With a secret smile and Gonçalo at her heels, she entered the house and tracked the scents of coffee and freshly baked bread to the dining room. Ann met her in the corridor.

"Oh, thank heaven, you are found!"

Ravenna's nerves spiked. After dinner the night before, she'd left the drawing room quite obviously with him. Iona would think nothing of it. But Ann was truly modest. She might not understand.

"We have searched for you everywhere," Ann said. "I've just sent the footman to the tower thinking you might have gone there. But Mr. Franklin—"

"Mr. Franklin? Is Lord Case unwell?"

"Terribly unwell. Mr. Franklin despairs of him. You must help him, Ravenna. It could not be borne if such a fine man were to be lost like this. And poor, dear Arielle . . . She must not suffer Grace's—" Her voice broke off and her hands spasmed around Ravenna's.

Ravenna pulled away. "I will gather my medical bag and go there directly."

At Lord Case's door, Mr. Franklin admitted her. The bed curtains were parted and Vitor sat in his shirtsleeves in a chair by the head of the bed, elbows bent to his knees and hands over his face. He lifted his head and his handsome face was stark. Swiftly he came to his feet. She crossed the chamber. Lord Case was utterly still, his face waxen. She drew back the coverlet from his injured arm, and the scent that arose curled her nostrils.

"Remove his nightshirt." She set her medical bag on the nightstand and opened it.

"But, madam—" the valet said.

"Remove it this instant. Cut it off if you must. The bandage too."

Vitor reached for his coat, withdrew the knife he had used at the river to cut her free of her gown, and sliced through the earl's nightshirt from neck to wrist.

"My God," he uttered.

The arm was swollen twice its size to the elbow, and crimson. A yellowed bandage dug into the flesh.

"Cut off the bandage," she said. "Even if he feels it, it will only be a relief."

Vitor did as she said, and the wound was revealed, a raw, running sore. Mr. Franklin choked and backed away, pressing a kerchief to his mouth. Lord Case did not stir.

"I need red wine," she said. "The wound must be bathed and drained. When did you last dose him with the fever powders, Mr. Franklin?"

He did not answer.

Vitor said sharply, "Tell her."

"Yesterday morning, my lord."

She snapped her gaze to him. "Why haven't you dosed him as I instructed?"

He pressed the cloth to his mouth. "Mr. Pierre said that I was not to give him any further medicines that would thicken his blood, but that today he would bleed him—"

"Mr. Pierre?" She pressed the wine-soaked cloth to the wound, allowing it to pool, her pulse speeding. "Is there a physician in the village, after all?"

"Monsieur Pierre is the cook here in the castle," Vitor

said. "Franklin, did you consult with the cook on his lordship's care?"

"Yes, my lord. He treats the ailments of the staff and the villagers when—"

"Did you dress the wound with the salve I left with you, Mr. Franklin?" The festering flesh was slick, the wine sliding off in beads.

"No, miss. Mr. Pierre recommended fat cured from a swine—"

"Pig fat?" She swallowed over panic. "Good Lord, you have poisoned his blood. Flaxseed. Charcoal. Even dung, if you must. Not animal fat. But I will fix it." She willed her hands not to shake. "I will fix it. There is nothing to fear." *Nothing to fear.* No more death in this house. No more loss. Her hands would save him. She *must* save him.

"Why did you follow the cook's counsel when I had made it clear to you that Miss Caulfield was to be consulted on Lord Case's injury?"

"My *lord*," she barely heard the valet say. As her hands worked, her pulse washed in her ears like the ocean crashing upon shores of hard hewn rock, a sound from her earliest childhood, years almost beyond memory but not quite. Never quite far enough away.

"She is a *woman*," the valet said.

"Get out," Vitor said. "Send my valet and inform his highness that I require his presence here at once. Now." He came to her side. "I trust you. I do not fear."

But she did. She feared that she could not endure one more loss. She would lose him—this man beside her whose world had nothing to do with hers. She knew it as surely as she knew how to heal his brother. And deep in her heart she wished for the hundredth time that on that day so long ago she had flown away with the little bird and, like it, had never returned.

SHE WOULD NOT be alone with him except by his brother's bedside. Vitor bade her sleep but she would not admit him to her bedchamber, nor would she welcome her friends. At luncheon the prince's guests lingered morosely over their plates. They could imagine no entertainments while the earl's life was in danger. When Ravenna appeared it was to eat only what Lady Iona set before her, then to allow Vitor to join her while she examined Wesley. She spoke only of the wound, the fever, and her treatment of both.

"The ice must be changed frequently. Cold is essential to keep the heat of the wound from encouraging it to fester further." She bathed Wesley's arm and dressed it again, settled new packets of ice around it, then closed her medical kit and went to the door.

"Ravenna—"

"I will return in an hour. You should remain with him. Do not trust his care to another."

"I will not."

"You did when you were in the dining room."

"I went there looking for you."

"Don't do that again. Send a servant for me. If there is any change, send for me instantly."

"Ravenna, allow me—"

She turned away. Lady Iona and Miss Feathers hovered at the door.

"He is unchanged." She brushed off their solicitude and strode away alone.

THE SWELLING IN the earl's arm decreased throughout the night. His fever broke after dawn the following day. A footman brought Ravenna the news. She ran to his bedchamber and entered without knocking.

Lord Case was sitting up in bed, his brother in the chair at his side.

Vitor stood.

"You see, Vitor," the earl said weakly. "She saunters in here as if I wished her to witness me in this state, which it is true I might under other circumstances but not now, for God's sake." He spoke slowly but clearly, and the knot around her heart began to unwind. He studied her beneath hooded lids. "She has no respect for a man's vanity or pride."

Steadying her nerves, she moved to his side. "I am happy to see you improved." She reached for his wrist and pinched it between her thumb and forefingers and counted silently.

"Was I a wretched monster while I was insensible?" His voice had lost some of its hauteur.

"Perfectly dreadful," she said. "Wasn't he?"

"Yes," Vitor said. "Nothing out of the ordinary for you, Wes."

"You wound me. The both of you. I would throw you out but that imbecile Franklin would probably kill me within the hour. I am stuck with you, I suppose." He looked up at her face. "Am I dead?"

"Not today." Ravenna tamped down her giddy smile and released him. "I have sent to the kitchen for broth and tea." She turned to Vitor. "Make him drink them both. No wine or spirits, or I shall be very cross."

"I shouldn't like to see that," the earl murmured, but Vitor smiled. It went to her belly and toes, curling deliciously and making her want to laugh, to run across a field of wildflowers and feel the warmth of sunshine on her skin and make love to him again.

She took up her bag and moved to the door, training her face to sobriety. "I will call upon you again after breakfast."

"Miss Caulfield," the earl said. "Wait a moment, if you will. Vitor, go away now, do."

"Not even on your life am I leaving her alone with you."

The earl's eyes were serious.

"You may go," she said to Vitor. "I am impervious to ravishment and in any case I am probably ten times stronger than he is right now. If he can stand, I would be amazed."

"It isn't standing that concerns me," Vitor said, but he came forward. As he passed her, he touched her hand, and a rush of warm pleasure went through her. "I will wait just without."

She closed the door and faced the bed.

"Miss Caulfield," Lord Case said, "I beg your pardon and I hope quite fervently that you will someday bestow upon me the mercy of forgiveness."

"That was a very pretty speech. I think the prince miscast his play. You ought to have had more lines."

"I was a beast."

"No. I have loved a beast," she said, "and you are far inferior to him, in fact. But I am not a fool—"

"Quite the opposite, if my brother is to be believed."

"—and I recognize that you spoke and acted according to your kind. I will forgive you for insulting me if you promise to not be such a sorry specimen of a man if the occasion should again arise."

He shook his head. "You have no sense of the superiority of my station, do you?"

"A sense of the superiority of your station and everybody else's in this house is my constant companion. But I am fully aware of my place and, what's more, happy with that place. Your insult did not offend or hurt me, but I think more highly of you for offering the apology."

"When do you imagine the occasion would again arise?"

"I beg your pardon?"

"When do you imagine I will again feel the need to protect my brother from a woman who might intend him ill?"

Her heartbeats stumbled. "I—I—"

"I should think, madam, that particular task would be yours in the future."

She had nothing to say to that and turned away, her cheeks hot. In the corridor, Vitor stood against the opposite wall. She closed the door and he came to her and without a word took her hand, only her hand, when he might expect to take all of her if he wished.

"I must go, to wash and change my clothes," she said somewhat unsteadily.

"You were magnificent, capable and focused throughout. Thank you for what you have done."

"I—"

Then he did take her, but only her face gently between his hands, and he kissed her. It was not a long or particularly passionate kiss, but when he released her she longed to go fully into his arms and press her cheek against his chest and breathe in his solid strength and life.

"Now, go," he said and, with visible effort, stepped back from her. "Wash. Change clothes. Eat, if you must. You look skin and bones. As I like a bit flesh on a woman, you must remedy that immediately."

"To please you?"

"To please me, of course." He gestured her away. "Off with you, now. When you are finished, I am easily found." He offered her a smile that went not to her stomach, but traveled beneath her ribs with a sweet, deep ache that gave her pain, a good, joyful sort of pain.

She went, her steps quick and her bag swinging in her hand. Her bedchamber door was open. She crossed the threshold and recognized the straight, elegant back of the man in whose house she had lived for six years. He stood by the window.

"Good morning!" Happiness pressed at her, seeking to have its scandalous way. "Have you heard the news? Lord Case is on the mend. His fever broke and his wound is again healing well. There are no murderers about the place and even that horrid Penelope and her mother have departed. That last, I tell you, is true cause for celebration. All is well with the w—"

Sir Beverley turned from the window, his face ashen. Tears stood upon his cheeks. In the six years in which she had known him, she had never once seen him weep.

"Francis is gone," he said simply.

It was as though the world went stark, blazing white and just as cold. She shook her head. "Take me to him. I will help. I—"

"It happened hours ago, my dear," he said. "He went in his sleep. Peacefully, it seems, without sign of distress. I found him thirty minutes ago when I called upon him for breakfast."

"No." She could not seem to stop shaking her head. "No. He cannot have left us."

"No," Sir Beverley only said, and the early spring sunshine glimmered off the tears on his face in mockery.

SHE DID NOT call for him or come to find him. The morning waned into afternoon and when Vitor finally left his brother in the care of his own competent valet in order to seek her out, he learned the reason for it.

"We are all stunned. Stunned, I tell you, my lord." In the drawing room where Lady Margaret sat with her daughter, Sir Henry, and Sebastiao, she swiped her eyes with a kerchief. "Such a charming man. Such an amusing man. Far too young to be swept off at night like that. He could not have been above five-and-sixty. But Sir Beverley said his heart was weak, and that dear Mr. Pettigrew had anticipated this. Yet they told none of us, not even that poor girl. I am stunned. And devastated. Devastated, I tell you."

"A damned shame." Sir Henry shook his head. "In the name of Zeus, I've never met another man who knew his horses as well as his cravats."

Vitor bowed and went to the door.

Sebastiao followed. "Vitor, wait."

He paused, but he wanted to be gone, to find her and . . . He didn't know what, but whatever she needed he would give it to her.

"It is dreadful timing," Sebastiao said, "but I must share news with you before the others discover it. I have asked Sir Henry for his daughter's hand. He gave his approval and Ann—Miss Feathers—despite all that she knows of my past, has accepted me." Sober for nearly a fortnight now and once more resembling the boy he had been, eager to please and bright, he looked at Vitor with hopeful eyes.

"Congratulations, Sebastiao. I wish you and Miss Feathers happiness."

"Father will be satisfied, don't you think? Sir Henry's stables are superb and the portion he intends to settle upon her is substantial."

"I suspect he will be glad for this marriage."

"I suppose it shouldn't matter that I like her," he said more airily now, flirting with his accustomed insouciance. "Quite a lot, in fact."

"I should think that matters above all else."

"Thank you for accompanying me here, Vitor. You needn't have, and it's been a horrid disaster of a party, of course. But I am grateful for what you have done. For what you have always done."

Vitor nodded and moved away.

"Returning to Case's chamber?" Sebastiao smiled. "You are a devoted brother, in truth. How fortunate he and I both are."

"I am searching for Miss Caulfield. Have you seen her?"

"Not a quarter hour ago in the forecourt, supervising the preparation of Sir Beverley's carriage for those ridiculous little dogs— Ah." His grin slipped away and he scowled. "One should not speak ill of the dead. I believe the dogs were Pettigrew's. What an idiot I continue to be."

"Carriage? Is Sir Beverley departing?"

"They hope to take advantage of the cold weather to remove the body to England. The team is being hitched to Sir Beverley's rig as we speak."

"Today? They are leaving today?"

"You did not know?"

As Vitor strode outside, the shock pressing at his chest became a ball of anger in his gut. Footmen loaded luggage onto a traveling carriage. At a distance, a cloaked, hooded woman walked between the gravestones in the cemetery. By her shape and the movement of her body he knew her.

She moved from behind a mausoleum, about her heels clustered three squat brown dogs, three woven lines dangling from her bare hand. As though she felt his attention she looked up.

She waited motionless until he reached her. But when he would have taken her hands she withdrew them inside the cloak and stepped back. Her face was pale and her eyes shadowed.

"Ravenna, I am sorry."

"You have done nothing for which you should apologize," she said without animation. "But I take your meaning. Thank you."

"They tell me you are leaving, and I see it with my own eyes, but I cannot believe it."

"Yes. The quicker we travel north, the less ice we will be required to purchase along the—"

"Sebastiao explained." He stepped toward her but she backed away again. He could not manage to draw a full breath. "I will of course accompany y—"

"No." She averted her body, hiding her face behind the hood. "Sir Beverley is an experienced traveler. We shan't want for anything on the journey. You needn't worry."

"I have no concern on that account. I will accompany you because I wish to be with you."

She turned fully to him, her brow pleated. "I cannot be with you as we were the other night."

"For God's sake, I don't want that from you now. What sort of a man do you imagine me to be?"

"A man of privilege accustomed to having what he wants. As you have made it clear that at this time you want me in that manner, it would be foolish of me to imagine—"

"*Stop.*" He moved to her, but as much as he longed to take her into his arms he could not. Touching her without permission would only prove her right. He gripped his fists at his sides. "I wish only to give you comfort, to make this tragedy easier for you to bear."

"Then I thank you for your kind offer. But I am already well prepared with Petti's dogs as distraction, and another distraction as well, one that should occupy my thoughts and plans for some time to come: General Dijon has offered me a post in Philadelphia. I am ideally qualified for it—"

"No."

"Of course I am qualified."

"I have no doubt you are qualified, for that post and many others. But this is ridiculous, Ravenna."

"Ridiculous?"

He shook his head. "Do you truly intend to travel to America now?"

"It is not ridiculous. I have wished for a position like this. I have dreamed of it. Now it has fallen into my hands. Women are not offered such posts regularly. Ever, really. It is the opportunity of a lifetime."

The anger in Vitor was disintegrating, leaving only confusion. Could he have understood her so wrongly? Could he have seen skittishness where in fact there had been honest indifference? Her calm conviction now suggested it. Her passion when she touched him said otherwise, but he'd made love to women without deep attachment. Why couldn't a woman as well? This woman was wholly unique. To have imagined she would behave predictably had been his mistake.

"After you return with Sir Beverley to his home," he said, struggling to reorder all he had been imagining since that moment on the tower steps, to remember her words and see them in a different light. *Please don't let it end.* Perhaps that had been the wine speaking for her. She'd told him directly that she had no wish to entrap him in marriage. Yet he had never imagined he would not win her. He was, perhaps, as unaware of his own expectations of privilege as she had said, and he was most certainly the greatest fool alive. "You will travel to America alone?"

The corner of her lips lifted slightly. "I am well accustomed to being alone, of course." Again she turned her face away and urged the dogs forward.

"Ravenna," he said to her back, prickling panic rising in him, the sort he always experienced before he decided to move on, to seek a new adventure, a new danger. "You must allow me to accompany you to England."

"No. It will be best to say good-bye now." She looked over her shoulder. "I have enjoyed knowing you, Lord Vitor Courtenay. I have never had a friend quite like you. A friend with advantages." The partial smile peeked forth again briefly. "But now our ways will part."

He did not believe her. He could not.

Only a man possessed by an ungovernable passion would pursue a dangerous course without first considering all potential pitfalls.

She blinked swiftly, then turned and moved away. But again she paused.

"How do they say farewell in this country? Is it *au revoir* or *adieu*?"

"*À bientôt,*" he said. "They say *à bientôt.*"

She nodded, and he stood amidst the gravestones and watched her disappear.

So long. He would not say good-bye or farewell to her, no matter what the French said. *So long.* Because even a moment without her now seemed forever.

Chapter 21

The Gift

*T*hey buried Petti at sea. In his adventurous youth he had briefly served as an officer in his His Majesty's Royal Navy and had always wished to be put to rest in the briny deep wearing naval blue and white. Never mind that he'd only been a sub-lieutenant or some such thing. Ravenna was certain he'd been as charming standing on the deck of a ship as he had always been on land. Sir Beverley did not again shed tears, but as the sailors tilted the plank and the sea swallowed his life's companion, she took his hand and found it trembling.

Before continuing on to Shelton Grange they stopped in London, where Sir Beverley placed a death notice in the *Times* and met with Petti's solicitor.

"Sixty-eight calling cards," she exclaimed, dropping the pile onto the tiny gilded table in the foyer of Sir Beverley's house. "The notice only ran in the paper this morning and we were only gone three hours. I always knew he was popular, but I never quite understood how very popular." Removing the leashes from around the pugs' chubby necks and sending them up the stairs to their favorite parlor, she paused on the middle riser. "By the by, Beverley," she said over her shoulder, "what will you do with his house?"

"Why, my dear?" He stood at the table, an elegant portrait in black, filing through the stack of correspondence. "Do you wish to abandon me and live there in solitary splendor?" He jested, she knew, but there was a note of anguish beneath his urbane drawl.

"Of course not. I only wonder what will happen to it. I adore that old rose trellis and the gardens and fishpond. They are so spectacularly unkempt."

"Francis preferred to spend his money on wine rather than gardeners, of course." He discarded several pieces of the post, then came to the bottom of the stairs. "As to the house, impertinent girl, he left it and all his other worldly goods to you."

Ravenna was obliged, then, to sit for many minutes on the step in order to find her breath. Sir Beverley brought her a beverage in a crystal glass that made her cough and sputter. When a knock on the door echoed through the foyer, he said, "More callers, I suspect." She leaped to her feet and hurried up to the parlor.

The pugs were not in the parlor. Instead, a tall man with black hair nearly to his shoulders and a crooked smile across his darkly handsome face sat in the window box. Arms crossed and eyes on the door, clearly he awaited her entrance.

"Tali!" She flew to him.

Taliesin accepted her embrace with manly tolerance, then extracted himself.

"Hello, mite."

"What are you doing here?" She went to close the door, and when Sir Beverley's excessively correct

London footman gave her a disapproving frown, she bit her tongue between her teeth.

"I see you've grown into a real lady," Taliesin said with a chuckle. Often his laughter had been a balm when the church ladies had scolded and she escaped to the Gypsy caravan to forget about it. Now that laughter came from a deep, broad chest. "Which of your sisters taught you that showing your tongue to a grown man was a wise idea? Arabella, I suspect."

"Neither. I learned it on my own. I am very clever like that."

"I hear you're very clever in general."

"Do you? How? Have you been to visit Papa?"

"No."

Not in years, Ravenna suspected. At one time Taliesin had been nearly a son to the Reverend. But now when he traveled to Cornwall for the summer fair, he did not visit the vicarage where Eleanor still lived with Papa.

"A man named Henry Feathers was speaking to me of you only yesterday," he said.

"Sir Henry! Is he here in London?"

"He has a breeding mare I might purchase. We were doing business and he mentioned that he'd recently met a girl, a young slip of a thing, he said, who knew everything any horse doctor he'd ever met knew about healing an animal's hoof."

"I do," she said. "You taught me most of it, of course."

"He also said you saved a man's life. A titled lord."

"I did that too." *With help.* Her stomach tightened, and the door inside her chest that she was obliged to close every hour because its lock was broken burst open anew and filled her with aching.

"A titled lord?" Taliesin said again.

She shook her head. "Don't look at me that way."

"I am not looking at you in any particular way." Then he repeated. "A titled lord?" He folded his arms across his chest again. "Arabella, certainly. But you pursuing a titled lord, mite? I sense a hidden motive."

"I was not trying to encourage him to hire me. He was actually ill."

"His property must be hundreds of acres larger than Clark's," he said with a spark in his eyes that were as black as hers. "Acres and acres of land." He knew her nearly as well as her sisters did. He had fetched her home from the far edges of the parish as often as Arabella or Eleanor had. He knew of her escapes. She suspected that he, raised among wandering souls, understood how no land was ever big enough.

"I have been offered an enviable post in Philadelphia," she said. "I still haven't decided whether I will accept it."

His response was as unlike Vitor Courtenay's as possible. Vitor's perfect, handsome face had shown perfect shock. Now Taliesin's single raised brow spoke everything.

"What are you running from this time?"

"Arabella still—" she began, but had to draw an extra breath to continue. "Arabella still has that foolish notion the fortune-teller put in her head that one of us must marry a prince."

"I thought she married a duke. Lycombe, isn't it?"

"She did. Now she wants me to marry the prince, but I don't wish to."

"And you think you need to sail all the way to America to avoid this fate?" He laughed. "Ravenna Caulfield, you may be gifted with animals, but in all other ways you are as shake-brained as a—"

"My brains do not shake, and I think if I found someone else who would marry me, Bella would stop pestering me about a prince." Beneath her ribs, her heart was so tangled she could barely think. "Would you?"

Both brows rose now. Then his eyes changed. Slowly

he shook his head and smiled at her with some pity but mostly sympathy. "You know I cannot, mite."

"I know it, of course." Then to pique him she said, "And I suppose all that *being* married business would be awkward."

His mouth curved into a wicked smile. "I don't know about that."

She lobbed a book across the room. He dodged it and chuckled again.

"You are a beautiful girl, Ravenna, with a good heart. You deserve a man who can give you his heart in return."

"Like you gave yours away long ago?"

He did not respond, but a muscle in his jaw flexed.

Finally he said, "Go on," and jerked his chin toward the door.

"Go on, what?"

"Go find him."

"Who?"

"The man you're running to America to escape. A prince, is he?"

"No." *Better than a prince.*

"Do it, mite." His brow darkened. "Or would you rather I break his arms?"

She twisted her lips. "He would give you a good fight."

"He wouldn't win."

"With swords, you wouldn't have a chance."

He pushed away from the window and walked to the door, a tall, lean Gypsy horse trader incongruously in a gentleman's London house. "Go find him, Ravenna. Quit running for a change."

"Tali," she said quickly, "have you ever thought that we might be related? Brother and sister?"

"Ravenna . . ."

"I don't mean—" She halted her words. They never

said Eleanor's name at these moments. "I mean that we look alike, still, after all these years, as though we could have the same . . . the same father." For years she had not allowed herself to consider it. Then Vitor told her of his father.

"I don't know who my father is," Taliesin said.

"Arabella's fortune-teller said that if one of us married a prince we would learn who our parents are."

For a moment he did not speak. Then: "Does she believe this prophecy?"

She. Not Arabella. *Eleanor.*

"Perhaps." She looked into his eyes so like hers—black and long-lashed, *yet not Gypsy.* Despite what the girls at the foundling home had called her, she—and he—looked nothing like the people with whom he had lived his entire life and who had reared him as one of their own. Instead, he and she looked *foreign.*

She wondered why he did nothing to find his real parents. As the man he'd always been, he traveled to Cornwall each summer, to the Gypsy fairgrounds near the vicarage, hoping that upon some chance he might catch a glimpse of the girl he had once loved. Did he believe that if he found his real parents that would change? Or did he simply care nothing for that distant past, as she hadn't for so long.

"Taliesin, should I tell Arabella that I cannot wed a prince? That she must pass our destiny on to Eleanor to fulfill?"

Hand upon the door handle, he paused. "If you should need my help . . . any of you . . . you know where to find me." Opening the door, he left.

WHEN THE LAST of Sebastiao's guests had departed, descending down the mountain through groves of spruce and fir, Vitor went to his bedchamber and packed his traveling case. He had already dismissed his valet. Where he intended to travel now, he would not need a personal servant.

Perhaps he had simply chosen the wrong monastery before. Or the wrong religious order. Denis was a friar. Perhaps he would take that direction. Friars did all sorts of good in the world, feeding the poor and . . . doing other things. He thought.

He would learn well enough. His English family would think he'd gone mad again. Wesley would tease for the remainder of their lives. But Raynaldo would understand. And the marquess.

Gonçalo sat at his feet, chewing the edge of the rug and watching him. Vitor tucked his starched cravats and stiff collars in the bottom of the case. He would not need these either. Nor his sapphire pin or gold watch or pureblooded horse.

"I will not give up Ashdod," he said aloud. "I will simply take myself to another monastery and then another until I find one that will allow me to keep him."

The mongrel lowered his chin to his forepaws and his tail thumped the floor.

"All right. I will keep you too."

He would avoid preaching orders, of course. He'd no advice to give to people looking for salvation, except of course that they shouldn't be blind asses. He knew plenty about that.

Nothing else kept him from adopting the cowl now. The thought of being with any woman other than one inspired no interest in him whatsoever. In time he supposed that might change.

No. It would not change.

"Do you depart, *mon fils*, without bidding an old man good-bye?"

Vitor swiveled to the friar standing in the doorway. "I intended to call upon you, of course. Have you come to bless Sebastiao's journey?"

"I have come to give you this." He drew from his wide sleeve an envelope. "Young Grace gave it to me the morning she departed with her family. She said she did not hold with 'the ignorant superstitions of Papists,' as I believe she phrased it, but that in leaving this with me she would unburden herself of the guilt of having lied."

"Lied? About the murder?"

"Read it. She did not, after all, give it to me under the seal of confession."

"She must have meant for you to keep her confidence, Denis."

He shrugged. "I am only bound by my vows, *mon fils*, not the unsteady consciences of young girls."

My Gracious Lady,

Though it pains me to write this before I have again set eyes upon your lovely face, I must now bid you adieu. The objections your family raises to our union are too powerful to fight. Your mother has made it clear that, should we wed, your family will cut you from its heart and home. I shudder, dear lady, at the inevitable outcome of this alienation. My income is small; our home would be poor. The image of you forced to live in a wretched flat, your beauty waning under cares as I work day and night to maintain you in even the most meager comforts—it is too painful to contemplate.

I wish for you, gracious lady, not ignominy and poverty, but contentment and a place among those with whom you rightfully belong. If only your parents would relent and consent to our marriage, all could be well! But they will not, and my hopes for happiness are dashed. By the love I bear you, I must release you now. Go and wed a man of your equal rank who can stand beside your father with pride. Dear lady, forget about me.

> *Your most loyal knight, OW*

"*Eh.*" the friar said. "How do you find our deceased Lothario's withdrawal?"

"Either he ceased wanting her when he became certain her parents would not pay him a penny . . ."

"Or?"

Vitor's hand closed around the letter, crumpling it. "Or he was a coward."

"A coward? You are harsh, *mon fils.*"

"Not harsh." He should not have allowed Ravenna to go. "I am a fool." Lady Grace had lied to them all because she had not believed that in the end her lover would desert her. She had believed in his constancy. And, despite the letter that was meant to be a goodbye, when she summoned him, he had gone to her.

I am well accustomed to being alone.

Ravenna had never said she did not want him.

He should not have doubted.

Please don't let it end.

The hermit folded his hands into his sleeves. "Have you, *mon fils*, finally discovered an adventure worthy of your pursuit?"

"I have." It remained to be seen if in his pursuit he would ever catch her.

As a MEMORIAL for his friend, Sir Beverley threw a grand party with champagne fountains, French culinary delicacies, an Italian puppeteer who did caricatures of all the guests, and Turkish dancing girls. According to the gossip columns, London society was scandalized. But they all came. It was a fantastic success, and in the carriage the next day on the way to Shelton Grange, as Sir Beverley slept sitting upright against the squabs, Ravenna finally wept.

The following afternoon when they drove up the drive and halted before the house, she stumbled out of the carriage, walked to the mound of earth beneath the old oak tree, and lay down upon it.

"I miss him, Beast," she said into the grass. "I knew him only a fortnight and yet I miss him like I miss you and Petti. I love you," she whispered. "I love you."

A sennight later a letter arrived from General Dijon with news of the betrothal of his daughter to the Earl of Case. Since he would be remaining in England until after the wedding, he did not require Ravenna's response to his offer of employment quite yet. Extending an invitation to the wedding, he indicated that a formal invitation would arrive shortly from Airedale.

"Will you accept?" Sir Beverley said.

Ravenna dropped the letter onto the grate and watched the flames eat it. "I haven't yet decided. With Petti's house now, and all the work I already have in this county, it seems absurd to take a post in America. I am thinking of setting up my own practice from the other house."

"But will you accept the invitation to the wedding?"

The door beneath her ribs cracked open again and the ache sprang out.

She affected a shrug. "Why wouldn't I? Arielle is a sweet girl. I like her very much. And Iona will probably attend. I would be glad to see her again."

Sir Beverley peered at her through half-lidded eyes. "Why wouldn't you, indeed?"

Because he allowed me to walk away.

She had not bluffed. She had anticipated his disenchantment and had been wise to put him off swiftly.

Another letter arrived, this one posted from London.

The wedding will be in Lisbon. Papa is thrilled at the prospect of joining Prince Raynaldo's stables with his. Oh, dearest friend, how is it possible that I could be so fortunate, so blessed to be marrying the man I admire above all others and making my father and mother happy at once? It seems a dream, but I never wake from it! You must come stand beside me. Sebastiao has sisters and cousins that will attend me for the ceremony, but I will not be happy unless you are with me on that day. You vowed to me you would. I expect you in June.

Ravenna set that letter on the grate too.

"It is possible . . ." Through the drawing room window she watched the setting sun bathe the park in dusk. "Is it possible to love a man after knowing him only a fortnight?"

Paper rustled, a page of Sir Beverley's journal turning. "It is possible, my dear, after only an hour."

She stared at Petti's empty chair, now in shadow. "And yet, given . . ."—grief, loneliness, pain—"given all, you do not regret it?"

Sir Beverley lowered his paper. "Given all, how could I?"

When she received word that the first of the tenants' ewes had dropped a lamb, she walked to the farm to assist. As always, the lambs all came within days of each other, tiny and confused, then hungry, then sleeping. She wanted to sleep too, to fall into a field of wildflowers beneath the spring sunshine and disappear.

The long days and nights of lambing came to an end

on a morning dark with clouds that stretched across the sky. Dragging her weary legs and arms from the barn, she declined a ride home in the farmer's cart and set off, cutting through the wood carpeted with bluebells.

The rain began in thick droplets spaced far apart. As the trees thinned, it grew heavy, splashing off her nose and cheeks in giant splotches, washing away the dirt and straw, soaking through her hair and filling the woods with its soft, steady rhythm.

At the edge of the woods Ravenna's footsteps faltered, the exhaustion of every limb, every thought, every feeling that she had held at bay now overcoming her. She halted and for a moment swayed, and the rain slid down her cheeks, tasting of salt as it mingled with tears. The scents of spring and birth stirred by the downpour rose around her, urging her to lift her face and spread her arms and run as she had always done. But her legs would not obey.

Her knees buckled and she dropped to them in the bed of flowers. She sought the ground with her palms, then laid her head upon the sodden carpet, curled up on her side, and closed her eyes. She thought perhaps that if she were Arabella she would imagine this was fate: to be soaked to the bone, then fall ill with a fever and perish just when she had finally understood the truth of her heart. If she were Eleanor she would ponder something profound, then write about it.

But Ravenna did not believe in destiny and she was not an adept writer. And the grief was too powerful to bear. Tucked into a ball, she lay aching until, eventually, she fell asleep.

The lathe of a dog's tongue on her cheek woke her. Not even in dreaming could she mistake the modest size of this animal's greeting for Beast's giant lick. Still, her heart constricted. Then it constricted again, harder, for another loss altogether, because it did that lately, collided one hole in her heart with another to make one gaping wound.

She opened her eyes to discern which of the farmer's sheep dogs was cleaning the salted raindrops from her face. Her breaths stuttered. She lifted her hands and held the soft white and black head far enough away to study him. His muzzle was a bit longer, his ears floppier and his nose a shade broader, all in the manner of young animals that grow at astounding speed. But his face was entirely familiar.

"Gonçalo," she whispered, her heartbeats quick.

He yipped and sprang away.

Shoving hair from her eyes and swiping a damp sleeve across her cheeks, she pushed up to sit and peered into the thinning rainfall. Toward her across the field cantered a handsome dappled Andalusian, the man astride the mighty animal handsomer yet. She could not stand up or indeed move at all; her trembling limbs rebelled.

Vitor drew the horse to a halt, dismounted with agile elegance, and walked toward her.

"What—" She coughed upon rainwater and stumbled to her feet. He was real, here, in the rain before her, his dark eyes taking in her bedraggled hair and gown covered with sheep muck. "What are you doing here?" she finally managed.

"Are you all right?" His gaze swept the impression that her body had made in the bluebells, then her body.

"I—I was— The lambing, you see— That is to say, I haven't slept since—" *Since she had left him.* She drew a tight breath. "On my way home, I paused to rest. I suppose I fell asleep."

"In the rain," he said. "In a patch of wildflowers."

"Oh, you know," she said airily, waving a damp, unsteady hand. "It's a remarkable challenge to keep goose feather pillows dry out of doors. Substitutions are occasionally necessary."

"I daresay." His dark eyes quietly smiled.

"Why are you here?"

"I came to give you this." He opened his greatcoat and from it produced a lump of shaggy white fur barely bigger than his hand. The rain pattered upon the pup's silky head. It lifted its nose, cracked opened it eyes, and sniffed the air. "He is not Beast, of course. But I don't like the thought of you being alone. And this one"—he glanced at the long-legged pup dancing around his knees—"likes him, so I supposed he would suit."

She was afraid to reach out and touch it—*touch him*—lest he should disappear and prove a dream. "How do you know about Beast?"

"You told my brother. After I decided through careful consideration that the beast you spoke to him of was not a man, I recalled that you had mentioned him to me before. Sir Beverley has just now taken me to visit the old oak. I am sorry, Ravenna."

"You have come all the way here to give me a puppy? To replace my dog?"

He seemed unhappy with her question. "Not to replace. I don't suppose that's possible."

It wasn't. Just as it would not be possible to replace him.

"Will you accept it?" He extended his arm.

She moved forward and took care to lift the pup from his hand without touching him. But through the rain she smelled him, familiar cologne and horse and leather and *him*, and longing clogged her throat. She backed away.

"Thank you." She could say nothing else. He was giving her a puppy because he cared about her and did not wish her to be alone. They truly were friends.

"Are you en route somewhere . . . else?" Kent wasn't so far from everywhere. He must have stopped at Shelton Grange as he passed through the country. "Airedale?"

He removed his hat, ran his hand over his jaw, and looked away across the field. "Yes. I—" He frowned and returned his attention to her, raindrops settling upon his hair and cheeks. "My brother's wedding will be in several weeks and our mother is already in a state of high agitation over preparations."

"I see." If he did not leave now she would burst into tears. It would startle the pup. Awful way to become acquainted, that. "I suppose you should be on your way, then," she said through the prickles in her throat that signaled the hated tears.

He looked grim. "I should."

"Thank you. Again. For him." She drew the pup against her neck.

"Well, then. Good day." He bowed and it was so beautiful and lordly that she didn't even care that it was positively silly for him to be bowing to her in the middle of a patch of bluebells in the rain. He took several steps away and she felt like someone was squeezing her heart with a fist.

"No. I cannot," she heard him utter quite firmly. He pivoted to her. "Ravenna, I love you. These past weeks have been hell. I did my damnedest to believe that I could walk away from you, that we could be friends, or rather some idiotic fond memory of a passing acquaintance. But we cannot, not on my part, and I don't wish to be without you. I want you and I need you with me. If you go to America now and abandon me you will be doing to me just what Beast and Pettigrew and that damned bird did to you. I don't know if you want this, but I cannot let you go. I will follow you across the Atlantic if I must."

For a long moment she could say nothing; the tide of

joy overwhelmed. "I did not think you could love me. I thought your world was so distant from mine that you could not possibly find in me what I found in you."

He walked right to her, very close. "Tell me that means you love me."

"When I thought you were— That night at the castle, when you did not return, and the next morning, it was as though my life had ended. I could not bear it. I thought that if I pretended that my heart was not bound to you already, I could— I could . . . escape."

"Escape?"

"Escape the pain of losing you."

He stood perfectly still, tension in his arms at his sides, the emotion in his eyes beautiful. "If you will allow me to hold you, I will never let you go."

Delirious happiness filled her and tumbled across her tongue. "I will allow it. I—"

He caught her mouth with his, sank his hands into her hair, and united her to him in abandonment to their love. She flattened her palm over his heart. The strong, steady beat of his life thrummed through her.

He kissed her cheek, her brow. "Why did you run away from me?"

"I knew you would leave me."

"You knew a falsehood."

"I did not wish to be taken by surprise."

His smile was both tender and amused. "You are a controlling female." He brushed his lips to hers. "Ravenna Caulfield?"

"Yes, Vitor Courtenay?" She smiled fully now, because the holes inside of her were sealing up, all of them, as though this love was swallowing the grief of loss and making her whole again. "Lord Vitor Courtenay, that is. I am using the title, you see, in hopes of inspiring your ardor."

"You inspire my ardor by simply existing, so really the title isn't necessary after all. Now, could you put the dog on the ground?"

"Yes." She suited action to word, nestling the pup in the grass. "Why?"

Vitor drew her into his arms, fitting her snugly against him. "Because I am going to make an offer of marriage to you now, and I would like to receive your enthusiastic assent without any impediments to my enjoyment of it." Rain ran down his nose and over his sculpted lips. She pressed onto her toes and kissed those lips that were hers now to kiss forever.

"Vitor?"

He nuzzled the corner of her mouth. "Mm?"

"After we are married, will you allow me to continue working with animals?"

He drew back and his smile was gorgeous, the crease in his cheek pronounced. "Have you just consented to becoming my bride?"

"That depends on your answer."

"I love you, Ravenna." His voice was beautifully rough. "I love who you are and what you do and how you do it. You must continue to go on in that manner, and I will rejoice that you are mine. Given that I am a man prone to sin, I will also boast about you to everybody I encounter. Pride, you know. One of the Seven Deadlies."

There was another kiss then, this one quite lengthy, in which she expressed her appreciation of his position on the matter.

"However," he said over her lips, "if you put another wild creature in my bed, I will annul you instantly. The paper will be signed in Parliament by the end of that very day."

She laughed. "What if the wild creature is me?"

He pulled her tightly to him. "She will always be welcome in my bed, as she is always in my heart. Now, say you will marry me."

"I will marry you. Is it my turn now?"

"Your turn?"

"To order you about like you have just ordered me about?"

"I suppose." He nodded. "Having just been accepted by the woman who commands my heart, I am currently of a magnanimous mind."

"Make love to me now."

"With pleasure." He looked about them curiously. "Here?"

She twined her fingers into his hair and kissed his jaw. "It has been a dream of mine for some weeks now to make love to a handsome lord in a field of wildflowers. You are a handsome lord. This is a field of wildflowers. Also, we are both very wet and that reminds me of when you pulled me from a river and held me in your arms and I thought that despite the cold and damp I could remain there forever."

His smile lit her heart. "As long as there are no pitchforks about, I am at your service, madam. But when did you leave off referring to it as mating?"

"When you made me say your name and I wanted to run away. The trouble of it was, I wanted you to come with me." She pressed her brow to his chest and held him tight. "Vitor, I love you."

He served her then, in the field of wildflowers as spring rain gave way to golden sunshine, proving himself both her lord and servant at once. And in return, as before, willingly, truly, she adored him.

Author's Note

*I*n 1807, threatened by Napoleon's imperial ambitions, the Prince Regent of Portugal fled Lisbon, sailing across the Atlantic to establish his court in the lucrative colony of Brazil. Upon mainland Portugal's political landscape bereft of its leaders, I placed my fictional lesser branch of the royal family in hiding in the mountains. An era of tumult, the early nineteenth century in Europe and Britain provides a rich and thrilling context within which to tell a tale, even if that tale technically takes place in a remote, snowbound castle. I had great fun stocking my murder mystery with an international cast of characters and flavoring it with little bits of information about the wider world from which each of the actors had come.

Like Raynaldo's branch of the Portuguese royal family, a few other historical details in this book are my inventions as well. Barbichons Lyonnaise, with their rare black spotted tongues, are a breed of bichons frise born entirely of my imagination. So too is the Linnaeus Society. Although Carl Linnaeus, a Swedish zoologist, botanist, and physician who lived from 1707 to 1778, was indeed a pioneer in genetics, and farthinking scientists of the early nineteenth century followed his cutting edge theories, my Lord Prunesly is a member of a fictional scientific club. For its part, Chateau Chevriot, while resembling magnificent Cléron on the exterior as well as in its landscape and location in the Jura, is wholly fictional on the interior, renovated by my fictional Sebastiao's fictional grandfather in the modern style (that is, the style current in the late eighteenth and early nineteenth centuries), and thus much more agreeable for my characters in terms of creature comforts than a medieval castle would be.

My imagination, however, embellished only some of the historical details in this story. Other details arrived the old-fashioned way: via the actual historical record. The *Treatise on Veterinary Medicine* that Sir Beverley reads aloud to Ravenna was written by a man named James White and published in 1807. This and John Hinds's *The Veterinary Surgeon or Farriery*, which was published in Philadelphia in 1836, afforded me hours of fascinating reading in the David M. Rubenstein Rare Book & Manuscript Library at Duke University— hours I'm sure Ravenna would have dreaded but which I enjoyed thoroughly. (The full title of Hinds's book, by the way, is *The Veterinary Surgeon, or, Farriery Taught on a New and Easy Plan: Being a Treatise on All the Diseases and Accidents to Which the Horse Is Liable, the Causes and Symptoms of Each, and the Most Approved Remedies Employed for the Cure in Every Case.* Aren't old print titles marvelous?)

On another note, it was not unheard of for Catholic royalty to wed non-Catholics, but it wasn't particularly run-of-the-mill either. Neither was it typical of royals to wed commoners. But since the Anglican Prince George, Regent of England at the time of this story, contracted such an alliance (albeit secretly, scandalously, and without lasting success of the union), I decided Ann and Sebastiao's match could happen.

For the sake of the Courtenay brothers I must say a word here about bastardy in Regency-era England. In short, if no one cared, it could remain under the rug forever. On the other hand, if anyone cared, it could matter a whole lot. Usually the truth of paternity rested in the word of the child's mother. Especially if she was a noblesse—unless her husband accused her of adultery (in which case she was entirely out of luck), or unless her word could otherwise be proven false with incontrovertible evidence—her child belonged to the father she claimed for it. Since both Vitor and Wesley's fathers were willing secret accomplices in the Marquess and Marchioness of Airedale's pursuit of children, neither of them had any wish to stand in the way of their illegitimate sons' legitimacy in the eyes of the world. In reality, from the medieval to the modern eras in England and Europe there was quite a lot of adulterous and illegitimate begetting of children upon both high- and lowborn women, married or unmarried, both with and without their consent. The Marchioness of Airedale and poor Clarice Sepic née Brazil are two sides of the same historical coin, as it were.

On a literary note, if there is one work of fiction in all of history that I wish I had written, it is William Shakespeare's *Romeo and Juliet*. It is such a brilliantly told tale, with romance and adventure and intrigue and profound emotion, that every time I watch or read it I am stunned—indeed grief stricken—when the young lovers perish. Their love is so powerful, so impetuous and passionate, and the writing so sublime, the story told so gloriously, that I simply cannot believe the whole thing ends in a funeral procession. I suppose this reveals the eternal optimist in me (which is of course why I write romances and not tragedies). But for this book I enjoyed putting Shakespeare's immortal verse into my characters' mouths more than I can express.

Fulsome thank-yous for assistance in writing this book go to Helen Lively for help in inspiring my vision of Vitor, Dr. Diane Leipzig for the book's fabulous title, Noah Redstone Brophy for his counsel on animals and various things medical, Brian Conaghan for his wisdom concerning former monks, Laura Berendsen Hughes for her beautiful painting "Dawn" that inspired an entire scene, Heather McCollum for counsel on ladies of the Highlands, Beth Williamson for sharing with me her research about poisons, and Sandie Blaise and Dr. Teresa Moore for their invaluable assistance with French. Heartfelt thanks go to the wonderful people of Triangle Veterinary Hospital, especially Dr. Robin Scott, Dr. Chuck Miller, and Dr. Mari Juergenson, whose devotion to healing and endless compassion are my inspiration for Ravenna's character. Thanks especially to Georgie Brophy and Mary Brophy Marcus for reading and commenting on the manuscript, to its great benefit. I hope it will be understood that any mistakes in this book, historical or otherwise, are to be attributed to the little elves who live beneath my front porch and like to make trouble.

I am ever grateful to my agent Kimberly Whalen, my editor Lucia Macro, and all the other fabulous people at Avon who invest so much brilliance into my books, especially Nicole Fischer, Gail Dubov, Eleanor Mikucki, Pam Jaffee, and Katie Steinberg.

Thank you to my mother, husband, and son for their love and support, and for giving me the space and time I need to write.

To my readers, whose love of love stories is only eclipsed in my reckoning by your kindness and joy of spirit, I send you blessings and gratitude for sharing this adventure with me.

Finally, to my "Beast" who is no longer with me, and to my "Gonçalo" who is: Atlas and Idaho, you cannot read the pages of this book, but you are both on every one of them as well as in every corner of my heart forever.

If you enjoyed *I Adored a Lord*, please consider posting a review of it online. You can find links to do that here: www.KatharineAshe.com/I-Adored-A-Lord.

Thank you!

Next month, don't miss these exciting new love stories only from Avon Books

Once More, My Darling Rogue by Lorraine Heath
After rescuing Lady Ophelia Lyttleton from a mysterious drowning, Drake Darling realizes she doesn't remember who she is and plans to bring her to heel by insisting she's his housekeeper. Ophelia does not recall her life before Drake, but her desire for her dark and brooding employer can't be denied. But when her memory returns, she is devastated by the truth, and Drake must prove she can trust him with her heart once more.

What a Lady Most Desires by Lecia Cornwall
As the call to arms sounds, Lady Delphine St. James bids farewell to Major Lord Stephen Ives with a kiss that stirs them both. After the battle, Stephen is wounded, blind, and falsely accused of cowardice and theft. The only light in his dark world is Delphine, a woman he never imagined he could desire. As their feelings deepen and enemies conspire to force them apart, can their love survive?

The Princess and the Pea by Victoria Alexander
A true American princess, Cecily White stands to inherit her father's business empire, and the independent beauty has no intention of marrying some foreign nobleman seeking her money. Then, on a trip to England, Cece meets a dashing peer. But Cece won't surrender her heart to the virile Earl of Graystone until he proves that the only treasure he truly wants is her love.

The Casebook of Barnaby Adair novels from
#1 *New York Times* bestselling author

Stephanie LAURENS

WHERE THE HEART LEADS
978-0-06-124338-7

Handsome, enigmatic, and deliciously dangerous, Barnaby
Adair has made his name by solving crimes within the
ton. When Penelope Ashford appeals for his aid in solving
the mystery of the disappearing orphans in her care, he is
moved by her plight—and captivated by her beauty.

THE MASTERFUL MR. MONTAGUE
978-0-06-206866-8

When Lady Halstead is murdered, Barnaby Adair helps her
devoted lady-companion, Miss Violet Matcham, and her
financial adviser, Montague, expose a cunning killer. But will
Montague and Violet learn the shocking truth too late to
seize their chance at enduring love?

LOVING ROSE
978-0-06-206867-5

Rose has a plausible explanation for why she and her children are residing in Thomas Glendower's secluded manor.
Revealing the truth would be impossibly dangerous, yet day
by day he wins her trust, and then her heart. But when her
enemy closes in, Rose must turn to Thomas to protect her
and her children.

LAU6 0814

At Avon Books, we know your passion for romance—once you finish one of our novels, you find yourself wanting more.

May we tempt you with . . .

- **Excerpts** from our upcoming releases.

- Entertaining **extras,** including authors' personal photo albums and book lists.

- Behind-the-scenes **scoop** on your favorite characters and series.

- **Sweepstakes** for the chance to win free books, romantic getaways, and other fun prizes.

- Writing **tips** from our authors and editors.

- **Blog** with our authors and find out why they love to write romance.

- **Exclusive content** that's not contained within the pages of our novels.

Join us at
www.avonbooks.com

AVON *An Imprint of* HarperCollins*Publishers*
www.avonromance.com

Available wherever books are sold or please call 1-800-331-3761 to order.

FTH 1013

*G*ive in to your Impulses!

These unforgettable stories only take a second to buy and give you hours of reading pleasure!

Go to *www.AvonImpulse.com* and see what we have to offer.

Available wherever e-books are sold.

AVONIMPULSE

IMP 0811